A Matter of Justice

A Matter of Justice

Charles Todd

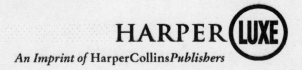

HARPER LUXE

An Imprint of HarperCollinsPublishers

A MATTER OF JUSTICE. Copyright © 2009 by Charles Todd. All rights reserved. Printed in the United States of America. No part of this book may be used or reproduced in any manner whatsoever without written permission except in the case of brief quotations embodied in critical articles and reviews. For information address HarperCollins Publishers, 10 East 53rd Street, New York, NY 10022.

HarperCollins books may be purchased for educational, business, or sales promotional use. For information please write: Special Markets Department, HarperCollins Publishers, 10 East 53rd Street, New York, NY 10022.

FIRST HARPERLUXE EDITION

HarperLuxe™ is a trademark of HarperCollins Publishers

Library of Congress Cataloging-in-Publication Data is available upon request.

ISBN: 978-0-06-171976-9

09 10 11 12 ID/RRD 10 9 8 7 6 5 4 3 2 1

In remembrance . . .

Samantha
June 1995 to September 2007
&
Crystal
November 1995 to March 2008

Who gave so much to those who loved them.

A Matter of Justice

1

Ronald Evering was in his study, watching a mechanical toy bank go through its motions, when the idea first came to him.

The bank had been a gift from a friend who knew he collected such things. It had been sent over from America, and with it in a small pouch were American pennies with which to feed the new acquisition, because they fit the coin slot better than the English penny.

A painted cast-iron figure of a fat man sat in a chair, his belly spreading his brown coat so that his yellow waistcoat showed, and one hand was stretched out to receive his bribe from political figures and ordinary citizens seeking his favor. His name was "Boss" Tweed, and he had controlled political patronage in New

York City in the aftermath of the American Civil War. Through an alliance between Tammany Hall and the Democratic Party, graft had been his stock-in-trade. Now his image was encouraging children to be thrifty. A penny saved . . .

The note accompanying the gift had ended, *"Look on this as a swindler of sorts for the swindled, my dear Ronald, and take your revenge by filling his belly full of pennies, in time to recoup your pounds. . . ."*

He hadn't particularly cared for the tone of the note, and had burned it.

Still, the bank was a clever addition to his collection.

It had been a mistake to confide in anyone, and the only reason he'd done it was to vent his rage at his own impotence. Even then he hadn't told his friend the whole truth: that he'd invested those pounds in order to look murderers in the face, to see, if such a thing existed, what it was that made a man a killer. In the end all he'd achieved was to make himself known to two people who had no qualms about deliberately cheating him. The explanation was simple—they wanted no part of him, and losing his money was the simplest way to get rid of him without any fuss. He hadn't foreseen it, and it had become a personal affront.

He had sensed the subtle change in the air when he'd first given his name, and cursed himself for not using his mother's maiden name instead. But the damage was done, and he'd been afraid to let them see what he suspected.

Yet it had shown him—even though he couldn't prove it—that he'd been right about them. What he didn't know was what to do with that knowledge.

Vengeance is mine, saith the Lord . . . But the Lord had been remarkably slow exacting it. If anything, these two men had prospered.

And he had had no experience of vengeance.

There was only his mother, crying in his father's arms, this quiet, unassuming woman fiercely demanding that whoever had killed her dear boy be punished. A ten-year-old, listening from the shadows of the stairs, shocked and heartbroken, had endured nightmares about that moment for years afterward. And it was his mother's prodding after his father's death that had sent him to Cape Town in 1911, to bring her dear boy home from his South African grave.

"Your father couldn't do it. But *you* must," she'd urged him time and again. "It's your duty to Timothy, to me, to the family. Bring him home, let him lie beside your father in the churchyard, where he belongs. Find a way, if you love me, and let me see him resting there before I die!"

Trying to shake off the memory, Evering took another penny from the pouch and placed it in Boss Tweed's outstretched hand.

Almost quicker than the eye could follow, the hand slid the penny into the waistcoat pocket as Boss Tweed's head moved to nod his thanks.

The man smiled. It was no wonder he preferred these toys to people. He had come home from Cape Town with his brother's body, after two years of forms and long hours in hot, dusty offices in search of the proper signatures. What he hadn't bargained for was the information he'd collected along the way. Information he had never told his mother, but which had been a burden on his soul ever since. Almost ten years now. Because, like Hamlet, he couldn't make up his mind what to do about what he knew.

Well, to be fair, not ten years of single-minded effort.

The Great War had begun the year after his return from South Africa, while he was still trying to discover what had become of those two men after they left the army. It wasn't his fault that he'd been stationed in India, far from home. But that had turned out to be a lucky break, for he discovered quite by accident where they were and what they were doing. In early 1918 he'd been shipped back to London suffering from the bloody flux, almost grateful for that because he was able at last to look into the information he'd come by in Poona.

Only he'd misjudged his quarries and made a fool of himself.

It wouldn't do to brood on events again. That way lay madness.

On the shelves behind him was an array of mechanical and clockwork toys, many of them for adults, like the golden bird that rose from an enameled snuffbox to sing like a nightingale.

Banks were a particularly fine subject for such mechanical marvels. A penny tip to the owner sent a performing dog through a hoop. In another example, a grinning bear disappeared down a tree stump as the hunter lifted his rifle to fire. Humor and clever design had gone into the creation of each toy. The shifting weight of the penny set the device concealed in the base into motion, making the action appear to be magical.

He had always found such devices fascinating, even after he'd worked out the mechanism that propelled them. His mind grasped the designer's plan very quickly, and sometimes he had bettered it in devices of his own. Skill calling to skill. He took quiet pride in that.

He reached for another penny to put into Boss Tweed's hand, thinking to himself that it would be equally as fascinating to trick human beings into doing whatever one wished, by placing not a coin in a slot but an idea in their minds.

He sat back, stunned at the thought.

Hadn't he gone to South Africa to please his mother? To earn the love she'd always lavished on his elder brother, hoping in some fashion that when he had accomplished what she asked of him, he'd be loved as much too? She had used him, as surely as if she had slipped a penny in the proper slot.

His mother had died six weeks after they had buried his brother in the churchyard, and it wasn't *his* name on her lips as she breathed her last—her final thoughts had been turned toward that glorious reunion in heaven with her dear boy.

It was over her corpse, lying in her coffin in the hall of this very house, that he'd poured out all he'd been told in South Africa. Wanting to hurt her as much as she had hurt him, but well aware that nothing he said could touch her now. Knowing himself for a coward, even as the words drained him.

And in the silence of the empty house, he could almost hear her voice, as clearly as if she spoke from the closed coffin, telling him to do his duty once more.

"Kill them, Ronald. See that they pay. Send them to hell, my boy, and I'll love you then."

Easy enough for her to say, but how did one go about finding one murderer, let alone a pair of them? And once found, how did one go about punishing them? Does one conceal a revolver in one's pocket and shoot the bastards there and then?

Both men were equally guilty—he had no reservations about that. One for the act itself, the other for never reporting it and seeing that justice was done.

He didn't want to hang for them or his mother or her dear boy. He had tried to persuade the Army to look into the matter, and they had turned a blind eye. They hadn't even initiated an inquiry, hadn't so much as taken down names. His only evidence was the word of an aging, drunken Boer who hated the English ten years later as much as he'd hated them during the fighting. And what was that worth, I ask you, the Army had said, against the word of two Englishmen?

And yet the Afrikaner, who had been left for dead by his comrades, had lain there wounded within sight and hearing of the train until he'd stopped bleeding and could crawl away. He had *watched* the horror unfold. And it must be true—in God's name, how could he have made up such a monstrous tale? What he couldn't tell Evering was *why* it had been done, except that he had heard two men arguing over money. And Evering hadn't cared about that, only about the death of his brother.

In the hall, staring down at the coffin, Ronald Evering hadn't been able to shut out the voice of his mother even after swearing he would see that the devils paid.

For months afterward, it was as if she could see his ambivalence and cursed him for it. *Hadn't he loved his brother? Didn't he want revenge for what had been done to him?* Yes, but how? Dear God, *how?*

It was a vicious circle, and he'd gone round and round it, looking for a solution until he had learned to shut her out. Even when he'd tried to take a first step, it had been disastrous. He'd crept home with his tail between his legs, like a whipped dog.

Too bad he couldn't set into motion a little scene of his own, paying one figure a penny to scurry across the cast-iron stage to bury his woodsman's ax into another figure's skull while the wolf—himself—leered from behind painted cast-iron bushes.

It could be done in iron, he knew, given the right counterweights and the right penny. It would take less than a day to create a drawing.

Would it work with flesh-and-blood people as well as these mechanical devices?

No reason why it shouldn't. His mother was proof of that.

He sat back and reviewed everything he'd learned about the two men. Where was the penny, the chink in the armor they had built for themselves? What was the instinct or desire or fear that would send a human being headlong into action, without thinking about consequences? Like the mechanical hunter or the mechanical dog—once set in motion, the outcome was inevitable. Inescapable.

Surely he could work out a revenge that would in no way make *him* vulnerable, either to the police if he succeeded, or to retribution from those two men, if he failed. A cowardly wish, he was willing to admit that, but hadn't he already suffered enough on his brother's behalf? Perhaps afterward he could get on with his own life. . . .

Engrossed by the idea, he sat there for some time, staring into the painted features of the New York man who had run Tammany Hall for years and grown fat on trickery and power, now reduced to a Victorian concept of thrift and good humor.

No one took *this* Boss Tweed seriously. A figure of fun, not a figure of fear. And perhaps that was the best trick of all. Those murderers had dismissed *him*, Ronald Evering, as no danger to them, hadn't they?

They'd even taken his money, as proof that he was harmless, no doubt laughing behind his back at how clever they'd been, making certain that whatever he might tell the world about them, *they* could claim he was no more than a disgruntled client.

He reached for pen and paper.

After half an hour spent putting together his design, weighing the balances and counterbalances, he rather thought it could be done.

Amazing how simple it was, really. He hadn't known he was capable of such a scheme.

His mother would have been horrified.

2

SOUTH AFRICA

Twenty Years Earlier: The Boer War

The military train pulled out just after dawn, three carriages guarded by a company under Lieutenant Timothy Evering. It was carrying weapons and ammunition forward, and bringing wounded back. The Boers were masters at ambush, and three trains had been stopped on this line in the past month alone. Spread out through the carriages, his men were silent for the most part, their nerves on edge as they watched for the danger that was invisible somewhere out there in the bush.

Evering, hunkered by the window in the last carriage, was all too aware that he had been given green men, men who hadn't faced a baptism of fire. He didn't want to think about how they would respond if the Dutchmen attacked. If they didn't shoot themselves in the foot in their nervousness, it would be a miracle. And he'd already thanked God for Sergeant Bellman, an old hand at war and steady as a rock.

He turned to say something to the private nearest him when the engine brakes caught with a screech of metal that deafened him. The train lurched and fought against the brakes, and for an instant he thought the engine or the cars would jump the tracks. Then they came to an abrupt stop that nearly threw him across the carriage floor.

The Boers had blocked the bloody right of way.

He could hear Sergeant Bellman yelling orders somewhere ahead and the thud of his boots as he ran back through the train, encouraging his men to hold their fire until he gave the order.

Evering, scrambling to his feet, called to the men in the next carriages to keep a sharp lookout, and then, before the words were out of his mouth, the Orangemen were on them, dead shots all of them, and fearless.

It was a short fight. The British soldiers were out-numbered and outgunned.

Private Quarles, cringing behind a large crate, swore, a steady stream of profanity that was in effect a prayer. His rifle, on the floor beside him, hadn't been fired.

What ran through his mind at that instant was purely self-centered. He'd taken the Queen's shilling to get himself out of the mines his father and his brothers had worked as long as he could remember. The army was better than breathing in the black dust until he coughed his lungs out, better than hearing the timbers over his head creak and snap as they gave way, better than living without his legs because the coal face collapsed on them before he could get clear.

And now he was going to die anyway. Those bloody men out there would kill them all, and leave their bodies in the harsh southern sun to rot or be picked apart by those bloody great vultures he'd seen digging into carcasses—

Someone was screaming just behind him, jabbing at his back with the butt of a rifle, and Quarles wheeled, ready to lash out from sheer self-preservation. Boer or British soldier, he didn't care, nothing was going to make him come out and fight.

But it was only Penrith, trying to squeeze his thin body into the space that could hardly conceal one man, much less two. Quarles swung at him, forcing him back, and in that few seconds silence fell across the veldt.

They stayed where they were, two privates so frightened that the sweat soaked their uniforms and ran down their pale faces like rainwater.

Quarles could hear horses now, riding fast. He thought for an instant that they were coming to search the train and shoot the survivors. Someone was groaning in the carriage up ahead, and he could see the sergeant crumpled by a window, his breath bubbling in his throat. *If only the damned fools would be quiet, the commando might believe they'd already finished the killing.*

The lieutenant was lying in a pool of blood, and after a few seconds, Quarles reached out, dipped his hand in it, and wiped it across his face and through his hair. Another handful went down the front of his tunic. He could pretend to be dead, if he could stop shaking. But it wasn't him shaking, it was Penrith behind him.

"They've gone. Is it a trap to lure us out? For God's sake, what are we to do?" he was whispering frantically.

Quarles ignored the man, trying to hear.

Nearly a quarter of an hour passed, and nothing happened. Flies were already buzzing loudly in the stillness. Whoever had been groaning up ahead had stopped. But now someone was calling for water. It was a London voice, Cockney.

Quarles shoved the shivering man beside him out of his way and, keeping his head down, crawled to the nearest window, unable to stand the uncertainty.

There was nothing as far as the horizon. Neither man nor animal. The Boers had vanished as swiftly as they'd appeared. Evering had put up a good fight, but the commando sharpshooters were used to hitting their mark.

He crawled into the next carriage, to be sure, shoving the sergeant aside. The man was dead, his body unwieldy. Quarles carefully lifted his eyes to another window. Nothing to be seen on that side, either.

The Boers had gone.

He stood up, his legs shaky from crouching so long, and wiped his forehead with his hand. He was close to laughing at the sight he must make, bloody enough to be a hero.

It was his first fight, and by God, if he had anything to say to it, it would be his last. Looking around, he grimaced at the amount of blood covering the carriage floors. He hadn't realized that a man had so much in him. Or that it could sicken the stomach with its stench.

Penrith, peering out from behind the crate in the last carriage, pleaded, "Is it over? *Say something.*" His frantic appeal carried in the silence.

Quarles ignored him. He went through the rest of the carriages, to see how many of Evering's men had survived. Then he came back to the last one, where Evering lay badly wounded. The man's eyes blazed up at him, and his voice, only a husky whisper, demanded, "*Where were you?*"

As if one more man might have mattered. As if another rifle could have held them off.

Quarles dragged the lieutenant out of the sun and propped him against a box of shells.

It was only then that he saw what the lieutenant was lying on—two leather bags, one of them torn open, with the edges of pound notes just visible in the white African light spilling through the window.

He knelt over the bags and reached in, unable to believe his eyes. There was more money in them than he'd seen in his lifetime, more money than God himself had. He wasn't sure where it was being taken, or why. It was *there*, and he couldn't stop looking at it.

Evering was saying something, but Quarles didn't listen. His mind was enthralled by the sight, and he knew he wanted that money more than he'd ever wanted anything. Ever.

Penrith came stumbling toward him. He said, "Most of them must be dead—"

"I counted four wounded," Quarles answered, quickly shoving pound notes under the edge of Evering's tunic, out of sight. "Not including *him*." He jerked his head at the lieutenant.

But Penrith had seen the money. "Good God!"

Falling on his knees, he reached out to touch the bag just as Quarles snatched it away. Evering, behind them, said quite clearly, "Put it back!"

But Quarles had no intention of obeying. He picked up the two bags. "Four wounded," he repeated. "Five counting him." He got to his feet and reached for his rifle, starting toward the engine. "Wait here."

"I'm coming."

"Stay with him, I say!"

Quarles went forward to find three men bleeding profusely but still alive. The fourth was already unconscious, his face gray.

"Water?" one of the men begged, reaching out, his hand shaking like a palsy.

Quarles shot him, and before the others could move, he shot them as well. Then he moved on to the locomotive. Both the engineer and the fireman were dead. Looking out, he could see the Boers had pulled out the tracks and piled the ties in plain view, to force the engineer to stop. There would be no going forward now. And no returning to the depot unless Penrith knew how to manage the damned controls. He went back to the last carriage and knelt beside Evering.

"Is there any more of this?" He held up the bags for the lieutenant to see them.

Evering shook his head.

"What's it for, then?"

Evering, fighting to stay alert, didn't answer.

Penrith, crouched in a corner, said, "I heard gun-fire! They're back—"

Quarles was on the point of shooting him as well. And then he thought better of it. "I was afraid there was something out there. Never mind, it was nothing. Nerves. Penrith—can you run the locomotive? The way ahead is blocked, we have to go back."

"Me? No. What are we to do, then? We've got to get the wounded to cover, and one of us ought to go for help." Even as he said the words, he read the decision in Quarles's face, and began shaking his head. "Why does it have to be *me*?"

Quarles was in no frame of mind to argue. "I'll see to the men. Go on, then, walk as far as you can before dark, then find somewhere to dig in. I'll stay here until you come back."

"I don't want to go. And what about this money? What are you going to do with it?"

"I'll see to that as well. Mind you don't mention it to anyone! Otherwise they'll take it from us."

"I'm not leaving it behind. I don't trust you."

"You've done nothing to earn it, my lad. Not yet. Go for help. Leave me to clear away here. And when you find that help, mind you act dazed, confused. Just tell them the Boers attacked, and the lieutenant here sent you for help. The less you say to them, the better."

Without warning, he set aside his rifle and swung his fist as hard as he could, catching Penrith on the cheekbone, and then hit him again. Blood ran from a torn lip, dripping onto his uniform.

Penrith, angrier than he could ever remember being, lunged at Quarles, but the man had already retrieved his rifle and kept him at bay.

"Don't be a fool, Penrith! If you arrive after a fight with the Boer looking fresh as a bleeding daisy, they'll be suspicious."

Something in his face made Penrith look sharply at him. "I counted four shots. You killed them, didn't you? The wounded."

"Yes, and I'll kill you too, if you don't listen. You want a share of that money? How are we going to do that, hmmm? Tell the Army we've taken a fancy to it? Tell them no one else is alive, so we thought we'd help ourselves? They'll hunt us like animals. First we must deal with this lot. Go back to the camp. And think about it as you walk. If we're smart, we'll let the Army blame the Boers for the money going missing. We know nothing about it, eh? It was the lieutenant's little secret, and we never laid eyes on it."

"But he's alive—"

"Look at him. Do you think he'll last the day? I'm no doctor, I can't save him. He's the only one can talk, if we keep our heads. What's it to be, then? Do your part or die with the others. It's all the same to me."

Penrith, staring at the rifle in the other man's hands, said with as much bravado as he could muster, "I'll go. But play any tricks on me, and I'll see you hang."

He backed out of the carriage, his gaze on Quarles, and nearly stumbled over a railroad tie as he stepped down. Then he stopped. Fool that he was, he'd left his own rifle in the train.

As if he'd read Penrith's mind, Quarles reached down, picked up a rifle, and tossed it to him. "Take the sergeant's. You won't get far without it."

Penrith caught it, retreating, watching those cold eyes watching him and expecting to be shot in the back when he turned. When he was safely out of range, Quarles was still standing there in the carriage door, his face a mask of blood and determination. Penrith turned on his heel and began to walk the tracks back to the depot. He didn't trust Quarles. On the other hand, he told himself, the man was right. If he didn't share the money, Penrith could turn him in. And he thought, on the whole, the Army was more likely to believe him, a curate's son, than Quarles, a less than exemplary soldier. Time would tell what would come of this day's work.

He could still see those pound notes, thick wads of them.

It was all he could think of as he walked steadily toward the depot.

On the train, Quarles waited until Penrith was out of sight and no threat to him. Then he did three things. He went through the carriages again to be certain there were no more wounded, he scanned the veldt for miles to be certain the Boers had gone away, and then he searched every inch of the last carriage for other bags of money. As he did, he could feel Evering's eyes on him, baleful and full of pain.

There was no more. He'd found it all.

Quarles took the two bags, ignoring the weak protests of the severely wounded man, and stacked the notes to one side. He remembered an oiled cloth he'd seen near the dead fireman and trotted forward to fetch it. It was thick with coal dust and torn, but it was still large enough for his purpose. Wrapping the money carefully in the cloth, he took it outside and searched for a place to dig. He found that some thirty yards from the tracks, and with his bare hands he worked furiously at creating a hole deep enough to conceal the bundle.

It took him over an hour. But when he was finished, there was nothing to show that he'd been there. A small branch, swept across where he'd worked, erased any signs of digging. He stepped back, considering his handiwork. The question was, how to mark the spot? Looking around, he saw a flat rock, shaped like a turtle. It was heavy, but he carried it across to where the money was hidden and set it on top. It was the best he could do.

When he got back to the carriage, he was surprised to find Evering still alive. The man was holding on tenaciously, determination in the set of his jaw. His eyes watched Quarles, bright against the flushed skin of his face, as if recording everything he saw for the court-martial to come.

Quarles ignored him, going about his next task with cold efficiency. He placed the empty money bags at Evering's feet, and then went searching for lanterns.

After pouring all their oil over the last carriage, he took the lanterns back to where he'd found them. Evering was still watching him, but with alarm in his eyes now.

"What are you doing, man?" he managed to say with sufficient force to be heard.

"You're the only one who knew about the money. And when they come, they'll want to know where it is.

They're not going to believe that the Boers took it, are they? So I don't have any choice."

He had found matches in the sergeant's kit, and he struck them now and lit the spreading puddles of oil. The old carriages were tender dry. They'd burn in a hurry, they wouldn't need the oil after a few minutes.

Evering cried, "You can't do this! It's inhuman—"

"Watch me," Quarles said and jumped out of the carriage. He tried to walk far enough away to shut out the cries of the burning man, but he could hear them in his mind if not his ears. They would haunt him for a long time.

But it was so much money. It would set him up for life. Even if he shared it with Penrith. Or not. It would depend on how useful the man was.

He waited until the flames had nearly died down, then went back to the blackened carriages and thrust his hands into the remnants of the fire. He hadn't known it would hurt that badly, but he forced himself to put his face close enough to singe his hair and his skin.

And then, fighting the pain as best he could, he crawled under what was left of the first carriage, out of the sun.

He hadn't looked at what was left of Lieutenant Timothy Barton Evering.

When help arrived many hours later, Quarles was half out of his mind with pain and thirst. They dealt with him gently, and the doctor did what he could. He didn't see Penrith and didn't ask for him. He lay on the stretcher, calling Evering's name until someone bent over him and said, "He's dead. There was nothing you could do." After that he shut his eyes and was quiet.

The inquiry into the ambush was not lengthy. Penrith supported the account that a shot could have broken a lantern and set the last carriage on fire. "But I didn't see it burning when I left. All I could think of was the wounded, and getting help for them as fast as possible." His face was pale, and his voice tended to shake.

Penrith was the son of a curate. They believed him. Quarles, when interviewed, remembered only beating at the flames to reach the lieutenant. His burns were serious, and his bandages spoke to his courage.

He was sent to Cape Town, where doctors worked on his hands, and Penrith, whose feet had been badly blistered by his walk, was sent to a hospital in Port Elizabeth. They didn't meet again until the end of the war, in 1902.

It was Penrith who came to find Quarles, and he asked him outright for his share of the money. "I've earned it now. And I'll have it before we're sent home."

Quarles smiled. "Oh, yes, and you on a spending spree a private's pay couldn't explain? No, we split the money and take it home with us. We wait a year, and then decide how to hide it in plain sight. Do you think we've fooled them? Stupidity will get us hanged yet."

"As long as we split it now," Penrith said. "I want it in my hand, where you can't trick me or hide from me. Once we've split it, we're finished with each other."

"Did you hear they found the Boers that attacked our train and hanged the leader? I wouldn't press my luck if I were you. A misstep now, and we'll be decorating the gibbet he kept warm for us."

But Penrith was not to be put off.

Quarles took five days of leave and found a carriage and horse that he could borrow, though his hands were still stiff and almost useless. He located the site of the attack after some difficulty, found the flat stone after walking in circles for three hours, and dug up the packet in the oiled cloth. Most of it he split into two black valises he'd brought with him. For the rest, he found a black woman in an isolated hut and asked her to sew the money into pockets in the lining of his tunic. She thought him a mad Englishman, but he promised to pay her well. When the tunic was ready, he drowned her in the stream where she washed her clothes, for fear she would gossip. If he'd been a superstitious man, he'd have believed she put a curse on him as she died. As it was, she fought hard, and he was glad he hadn't put his tunic on before dealing with her.

Penrith was waiting for him at the livery stable when he brought the carriage back, and demanded that he take his pick of the two valises. "To be sure the split was fair and square."

"As God is my witness," Quarles answered him, "you'll find both hold the same sum. Look for yourself. It's more than either of us can ever expect to earn. Don't be greedy."

Penrith said, his curiosity getting the better of him as he examined both valises, "Does it ever bother you, how we came by this?"

"Does it bother *you*?" Quarles retorted, picking up the nearest case. He walked off and didn't look back.

As luck would have it, the two men arrived in London on the same troop ship and were mustered out of the army in the same week. Quarles took Penrith to the nearest pub and made a suggestion: "We've got to find work. Until the Army's forgot us. It wouldn't look right, would it, for either of us to be rich as a nob, when we joined up with no more than a shilling to our names."

Penrith was stubborn. "You've put me off long enough. I have my share, I'll spend it as I please."

"You do that, and I'll tell them you stole the money while I was trying to save the lieutenant."

In the end, Quarles put the wind up Penrith, who was afraid of Quarles and would be for years to come. They each took up positions at a merchant bank, Penrith as the doorman because of his fair looks and his air of breeding, and general work for Quarles, with the ugly scars on his hands. His eyebrows had never grown out again properly, giving him a quizzical expression. But he was a big man with pale red hair and a charm that he practiced diligently, turning it on at need. The account he gave of his burns elicited laughter and sympathy, for he kept the story of rushing into a burning house to save a child droll rather than dramatic. There was no mention of the army or South Africa. And as far as anyone knew, neither Penrith nor Quarles had ever left the country.

Quarles had been good at numbers in school, and that training, together with a clever mind, was put to work. It wasn't long before he caught the eye of one of the junior partners, and six months later, he was promoted to Mr. James's clerk.

On that same day Quarles said to Penrith, "I can see that there's a way to be rich without suspicion," and outlined his plan.

Penrith, ever slow to see what might be to his own advantage, said, "But we've got money, we don't need to work. You promised—"

Quarles looked at him. "Have you counted what you've got? It's nothing compared to what comes in and out these doors every day. It looked like a king's ransom, there on the veldt, but I know better now. I've asked Mr. James if he'd be kind enough to invest what an old aunt left me. I told him I'd run through it in six months, else. And he's agreed. You'd be smart to do the same. Soon we'll be twice as rich, and then there's no stopping us." He smiled. "Mr. James sees a coal miner's brat with brains in his head. He's a snob, he thinks I'm a clever monkey doing tricks to amuse him. But in the end, it's Mr. James who's jumping through hoops of *my* making. I'm a clerk now, and mark my words, I'll go higher, as high as I please. And if you're a wise one, you'll hang on to my coattails. I didn't do you a bad turn in the Transvaal, did I? We haven't hanged yet, have we?"

Penrith said, "You're a clever monkey, all right. The question is, do I trust you? And how far?"

Quarles laughed harshly. "Suit yourself. But don't come whining to me when your pittance runs out and there's no way to replace it. And don't think you can blackmail me into saving your arse. You'll hang beside me."

3

SOMERSET, NEAR EXMOOR

May 1920

There was a stone terrace on the northern side of the house, with a dramatic view down to the sea. The town of Minehead was invisible around the next headland to the east, and to the west, Exmoor rolled to the horizon, empty as far as the eye could see.

Not even a gull's cry broke the stillness, though they sailed on the wind above the water, wings bright in the morning sun. Rutledge sat in a comfortable chair by the terrace wall, more relaxed than he'd been in some time.

Half an hour later a faint line of gray was making itself known in the far distance, storm clouds building somewhere over Cornwall. A pity, he thought, watching them. The weather had held fair so far. All that was needed was barely another twenty-four hours, for tomorrow's wedding. After that the rain could fall.

He had taken a few days of leave. Edgar Maitland, a friend from before the war, had asked Rutledge to come to Somerset to meet his bride and to stand up with him at the wedding.

This had been Maitland's grandfather's house, and Rutledge could understand why his friend preferred to live here most of the year now, keeping his flat for the occasional visit to London. Edgar had also inherited his grandfather's law firm in nearby Dunster and appeared to be well on his way to becoming a country solicitor.

Rutledge and Maitland had lost touch after 1917, but when Maitland had come to town in April to buy a ring for his bride, he'd tracked Rutledge down at Scotland Yard. France had changed both men, but they understood that these differences were safest left unspoken. What had drawn them together at university had been an enthusiasm for tennis and cricket; what had made them friends was a feeling for the law, and this each of them, in their own way, had held on to through the nightmare of war, seeing their salvation in returning to it.

Maitland had often good-naturedly berated Rutledge for choosing to join the police. "A waste, old man, you must see that."

And Rutledge always answered, "I have no ambition to be a K.C. I've left that to you."

When Rutledge had met Elise on his arrival in Dunster, he'd had reservations about the match. She was young, pretty, and in love. The question was whether she was up to the task of caring for a man who'd lost his leg in France, and with it, for many months, his self-worth. Unlike the steady, happy man Rutledge had seen in London, now Edgar was by turns moody and excited as the wedding day approached. And that boded ill for the future.

Indeed, last night when they were alone on the terrace, darkness obscuring their faces and only their voices betraying their feelings, Edgar had said morosely, "I can't dance. She says she doesn't care for dancing. Or play tennis. She doesn't care for tennis. She says. But that's now. What about next year, or the year after, if she's bored and some other bloke asks her to dance, or to be his partner in a match? What then? Will she smile at me, and ask permission, and be relieved when I give it?"

Rutledge had grinned. "Cold feet, Lieutenant? Where's the bane of the sappers, the man who never backed out of anything, even a burning tunnel?"

"Yes, well, I was brave once too often. And it's cold foot, now. Do you know, I can still feel pain in my missing leg? Phantom pain, they call it, the nerve endings looking for something that isn't there and worrying themselves into knots."

"That's common, I think?"

"Apparently. But it's damned odd when it's *your* foot itching, and there's nothing there to scratch."

They had laughed. But Edgar had drunk a little too much last night and was sleeping it off this morning.

Rutledge watched that thin line of gray cloud for a time, decided that it was not growing any larger, and turned his attention to the sea below, tranquil before the turn of the tide. Behind him, the terrace door opened, and he looked up, expecting to see Edgar.

Elise came out to join him. He hadn't heard her motorcar arriving in the forecourt, but she must have driven over from Dunster, looking for Edgar.

He wished her a good morning as he rose to bring a chair forward for her. She sat down, sighed, and watched the gulls in her turn.

"A penny for your thoughts?" he asked after a time.

"I wish I knew what was worrying Edgar. It's frustrating, he won't talk to me. That makes me feel young, useless. And the wedding's tomorrow."

He realized that she had come to find him, not Maitland. "You're several years younger in age," Rutledge pointed out gently. "And a hundred years younger in experience."

She shrugged irritably. "I know. The war. I've been told that until I'm sick of it. It doesn't explain *everything!*"

"In a way it does," Rutledge replied carefully. "It marked most of us. I expect that it will stay with us until we're dead."

"Yes, but that's looking back, isn't it? You survived— and so there's life *ahead,* marriage, a family, a future. You and Edgar were the lucky ones. You lived. Now get on with it."

He laughed. "Would that we could."

"Oh, don't be silly, Ian, you know what I mean. If you stay bogged down in the trenches, then they've won. *You* went on with your profession. Edgar can go on with his. He's not the only man in England with one leg. He's not a freak. He's not unique. A solicitor can *manage* with one leg, for heaven's sake."

He couldn't tell her why he'd returned to the Yard last year. At what cost and for what reasons. He answered only, "Have you ever had a terrifying nightmare, Elise?"

"Of course. Everyone has." She was impatient.

"Think about the worst one you can recall, then try to imagine waking up to find that it was real and would go on for years, not minutes, without respite."

"That's not possible—" She stopped. "Oh. I see what you mean. Trying to shake off a nightmare is harder than having it." She turned her head, watching the gulls. After a moment she went on. "When I was five, I was frightened by a friend's little dog. I was creeping up on her to surprise her, and the dog heard me first and attacked me. After that, I was always afraid of dogs. Any dog."

Rutledge nodded. "Are you still afraid of dogs?"

"Not afraid. Wary, perhaps?"

"Yes. That's what war does to you. It leaves you wary because you can't erase what you saw or felt or did. It can't be safely tucked away in the attic until you're fifty and decide to bring it out and look it squarely in the face. And Edgar is reminded of his missing leg every time he puts on a shoe or tries to walk across the room or step into a motorcar. It's a fact he can't escape, however hard he tries. And in turn, this is a constant reminder of a day he doesn't want to remember."

She turned to look at him. "Where are your scars?"

"They are there. Just a little less visible than missing a leg." He found it hard to keep the irony out of his voice. Thank God no one could see Hamish. Or hear him. He couldn't even be explained away logically. A haunting that was no ghost, a memory that was filled with guilt, a presence where there was none. *Except to him.*

Elise said, "You're telling me that patience is my cue."

"I'm telling you that getting on with it will always be easier for you. And so you must teach Edgar to forget, not only with patience but with the understanding that some memories may never fade. If you can't accept him as he is, then you must walk away. Now."

She smiled, a pretty girl barely twenty. He felt like a grandfather in her presence, though he was the same age as her older brother. How on earth would Edgar cope? Or had he deliberately chosen someone so young, someone who had no experience of war, in the hope that it would help him forget?

It was not his business to ask. He was here to support the groom, and that was that.

Elise was saying, "I appreciate your candor. I'll try to understand. And when I can't, I won't judge."

"Then you'll make Edgar an admirable wife."

Her laughter rang out, fresh and untroubled.

Inside the house, silver rattled against silver.

"Aha. I hear sounds from the dining room. By the way, my matron of honor has arrived. I'll bring her along to meet you this afternoon." She got up and went inside, leaving Rutledge with his thoughts.

4

Ronald Evering stood by his bedroom window that same morning, watching the small mail boat make for the harbor at St. Anne's. There was only one passenger on board; he could pick out the blue jacket and white trousers of Davis Penrith, who was standing amidships, his face turned toward the landing, his fair hair blowing in the wind.

The launch came in, tied up, and Davis stepped ashore, looking up the winding hill that led to the only large house on the island.

Evering wondered what he was thinking.

No doubt gauging how many pounds this venture might bring him. Was he so foolish that he thought he would be trusted again with a small fortune? Did he feel no twinge over cheating a man twice—of his brother and of his money? Apparently not, or he wouldn't have come.

Evering turned away from the window and went down to await his guest in the hall, but the memory of his mother's corpse lying there at the foot of the stairs prodded him to move on to the stone steps of the house.

St. Anne's was one of the smaller of the inhabited Scilly Isles. The Romans had come here, and then the Church, and finally Cornishmen looking to make money any way they could. Cut flowers had become the latest source of wealth, for they bloomed here earlier than anywhere else in England, and so they had been very much in demand for country houses and London weddings. The war had put an end to that, of course. Getting perishable flowers across to the mainland and to their hungry markets had been impossible, what with workmen gone to fight or to factories, the government taking over the trains for troops and the wounded, and the German menace out there waiting to sink whatever vessel sailed into their sights.

He doubted that the market for fresh flowers would be as profitable again, not the way it was before 1914. It would be too costly now, workmen's wages too high, and no one was entertaining on the scale they once had done. Great vases of flowers in every room, profligate and beautiful, were a luxury now, even for the wealthy.

He was glad his father hadn't lived to see this day. He had mourned his elder son, then given his only remaining child all that he had dreamed of for Timothy—a fine education, this house, and a love for the Scilly Isles that in the end had come to be the strongest bond between them.

If this day bore fruit, the senior Evering would have lost both sons—one to murder and the other to an unconscionable act that would damn him.

For an instant he was torn. Penrith hadn't seen him yet. Let him knock at the door, and when no one answered his summons, go back to Cornwall and thence to London, cursing a wild goose chase. Or tell him to his face that it had been a mistake, there was no money left to invest after all.

Evering turned and went back inside.

It would seem too—eager—to be seen waiting by the steps.

Invisible in the quiet parlor, he soon heard shoes crunching in the shell walk that led through the trellis gate up to the door. At the sound of the bell, he counted to ten, then he himself opened the door to Penrith. Welcoming him as his father would have done, with an old-fashioned courtesy Evering was far from feeling.

It's not too late . . .

Penrith stepped into the cool hall and said plaintively, "I thought perhaps you'd have sent a cart to meet me. The boatman said it was usual."

"Alas, the horse is lame. But the exercise will have whipped up your appetite. Breakfast is waiting in the dining room."

"I could do with a cup of tea." Penrith followed him down the passage to the dining room, its windows looking out to sea, where nothing stood between the stone walls of this house and the great expanse of the Atlantic.

Penrith took his tea standing up, looking out at the cloudless sky. "Is that a bank of sea mist out there on the horizon? I didn't notice it from the boat, but of course we're higher here. I can tell you I wouldn't care to be caught in one of those. I've heard tales of what it would be like—dank and damp, like cotton wool. Worse than a London fog. No wonder the Cornish coast is famous for its shipwrecks. I see the boat has continued on its rounds—I thought it might stay on for a bit. How long before it returns to St. Anne?"

Evering smiled, deliberately misunderstanding him. "I promise you we'll have more than enough time to discuss our business."

"It must be quite lonely here. I should think you'd open your London house for the summer," Penrith went on as he set his cup down on the table and accepted the plate Evering was holding out to him.

"Not in summer. That's the best season for us. Next winter perhaps." Evering shrugged. "That is to say, if I am luckier in my investments than I was the last time and can afford to open the London house again. Surprisingly enough, I've never found it lonely here. Perhaps because I was born in this house."

He searched Penrith's face for signs of—what? Something, anything—a conscience, a reason to put a stop to what he was about to do.

But all he read there was impatience and greed.

"I brought the papers you asked for. I think, given the state of business these days, that we've got something to offer. Something that might well recoup that earlier loss. Something with long-term potential, and an excellent rate of return."

"That would certainly be desirable. Frankly, I could use the income. But you told me much the same story the last time, and look where it led."

"Yes, well, we apologized for the Cumberline stocks. No one was more surprised than I when they went down with a crash. I lost money myself."

Evering raised his eyebrows but said nothing. He had heard rumors that Penrith and his partner had had a miraculous escape. A word of warning in the right ear at the right time . . . But not passed on to clients. Not this client, at least.

Penrith took his filled plate to the foot of the table and sat down, picking up his serviette. "I say, this is a wonderful spread. We're still trying to get decent food in London. You have a fine cook, as well. My compliments."

They ate their meal in a drift of light, stilted conversation, touching on events in London, the state of the economy, the worsening situation in Russia.

"No money to be made there," Penrith said with a sigh. "You'd think, given their way of looking at land reform, that they'd put it to good use. In my view, they're going to be hard-pressed to feed their own people. And their factories, such as they are, produce only shoddy goods. Europe isn't going to be back on its feet for another dozen years, if I'm any judge. But there are opportunities in South America. Cattle. Coffee. Mines. That sort of thing. It's what I intend to talk to you about."

Thus far Penrith had made no mention of his business partner, and the omission was glaring. Evering brought him up instead.

"And what is Quarles doing, to keep himself out of trouble?"

Penrith grimaced. "I daresay he manages. We no longer handle joint ventures. Which is why you contacted me, I think? You never liked Quarles."

Nor you, Evering thought, but was silent.

They finished their meal and adjourned to the study. It too looked out across the sea, but there were other islands in this direction, scattered blue smudges. Penrith glanced toward the long bank of mist one more time before sitting down. There was some anxiety in his face, as if he was trying to judge how far it had advanced since last he had measured it.

"Let's get down to business, shall we?" Evering asked.

"By all means."

The next two hours were spent in intense exposition of the properties that Penrith had brought for discussion.

Evering listened carefully to everything he was told, then sat back with a frown.

"I don't know—" He pulled at his lower lip, a study in uncertainty.

Penrith said persuasively, "It's the best opportunity I can see to improve your position. I like what's here, and I have a feeling that we're moving into a decade of handsome rewards for the farsighted investor."

Evering said, "Yes, yes. You've done your work well. Still—would you mind leaving these papers here for a week? I'm to travel to Kent shortly, and I can bring them to you with my decision." He smiled wryly. "I've learned to be careful, you see."

"Caution is important. There are no guarantees that what I tell you will be right in five or seven years' time. However, time is something we must consider as well. I suggest you make your decision within the fortnight. Or we stand to lose as the shares go up. They aren't going to be overlooked for long, I can assure you."

Evering studied the earnest, handsome face. Penrith, fair and tall and very presentable, gave the impression of coming from old money, and it stood him in good stead, this impression. More than one woman and many a man had fallen for this quality and trusted the advice tripping so lightly from his tongue. In their partnership, Penrith had been the velvet glove, Quarles the iron hand, though Quarles could be very pleasant when it served his purposes. And very coldblooded when it didn't.

The contrast between the two men was something Evering hadn't been prepared for when first he met them. One obviously a gentleman, the other a blunt Yorkshire man with unreadable eyes and a tight mouth. In God's name, what had drawn them together in South Africa, much less kept them together all these years? He couldn't fathom what it was, unless it was the strength of Quarles's personality. Weaker men were often drawn to that. If Quarles had manipulated Penrith, surely he himself could manage it as well. And yet the weak could be as cruel as the strong, he'd had cause to know in his own mother. It was the main reason why Evering had chosen Penrith as his penny. Quarles would not be as easily influenced.

"I assure you, I'm as eager as you to see this under way. But—well, I'd feel better if I had a little time to consider."

Penrith nodded. "Suit yourself." Though it was clear that he was not pleased about being put off. He got up and stretched, walking to the window, staring worriedly at the fog bank. Evering swore silently at the distraction, cursing the weather.

Penrith turned to his host. "When did you say the mail boat comes back this way?"

Evering glanced at his watch. "It should be here within a quarter of an hour. It makes the rounds of the inhabited islands before going back to the mainland. Naturally it depends on how much mail and how many passengers there are on a given run, but for the most part, it keeps to its schedule."

"That's a small vessel to take on storms in some twenty-eight miles of open water. It's a wonder anyone has the courage to live this far out."

"Think of it as our moat. At any rate, the master is a good man. He can read the weather the way you'd read a book. Many of us have made the crossing on our own in heavy seas, when there's no other way."

"All the same, I'll take my chance on dry land, thank you."

Evering laughed and got to his feet. Joining Penrith at the window, he said, "Yes, in fact, there the boat is now, pulling around the headland. You've got about twenty minutes before you need to be at the harbor. I'll walk you down. Good exercise. I've become quite fond of taking my constitutional earlier this time of year. Before the heat builds. Come along, then. Have everything there, do you?"

Penrith had shoved the remaining papers back into his case, his eagerness to be away getting ahead of his professional manner. "Yes, all here." He cast a last glance at the spread of unsigned documents on the table and added, "You will let me know, won't you? What you decide to do?"

"I give you my word," Evering assured him.

They walked out together, taking the shell path through the flower beds to the ornate garden gate where the island's only road crossed the track down to the harbor. But as they passed through the gate, Evering paused in the middle of the road. Penrith, a little ahead, turned and said, "Aren't you coming the rest of the way?"

"Yes. I've just been debating with myself." He had—whether to go on or not. To keep his hands steady, he reached out and caressed the white wooden necks of the swans that curved gracefully to form the top of the gate. "Old man, there's something else I wish to say to you, and I'm afraid I don't know quite how to find the words."

Penrith frowned. "I don't follow you. I thought I'd answered all your questions." He was annoyed, standing there with the sunlight glinting on his hair, an eye on the mail boat. "I really must get back to London tonight—"

"You did answer my questions, and admirably. This is—to be truthful, it's a personal matter. In point of fact, a little gossip that came to my ears recently. I found it rather shocking and brushed it aside as nonsense. But now that I'm face-to-face with you—"

Penrith bristled. "I've done nothing to be gossiped about. I assure you. That business with Cumberline—"

"No, no, your reputation is sound. Or you wouldn't be here. No, this is a personal matter. I told you."

Penrith gestured toward the harbor. "Can you tell me as we walk? The boat is coming in."

"Yes, of course. It's just that—look, to be honest, I'm uncomfortable mentioning this at all, but you've been kind enough to come here and advise me. I can only say that it's very likely the purest gossip. Still, I owe you something—"

"What are you trying to say? I don't follow you at all." Penrith's eyes were hostile now, as if expecting accusations he wasn't prepared to answer. His defensiveness clearly centered on his business, and Evering found that interesting.

"All right, I'll be blunt, if you'll forgive me. It's the stories going round about Quarles. And your—damn it man, about your wife."

"My wife?" Caught off guard, Penrith stared at his companion. "I don't—you must be mad! What is this about? Is it your way of—" He broke off, unwilling to say more.

"No. Just rather embarrassed to bring the matter up at all. Forget that I said anything. It was a mistake. A mistake born of friendship. Nothing more."

He walked on, but Penrith didn't move. "No, you brought this matter up, Evering. I demand that you tell me what it is you're hinting at."

Evering took a deep breath. "It was at the Middleton house party. I wasn't there, of course. But someone—I shan't say whom—saw Quarles coming out of your wife's bedroom at some ungodly hour of the morning. Shoes in hand. There was a little talk among the guests, when that got about. But for your sake, nothing was said. Then, two weeks later at the Garrisons' house—"

"Damn you, you're a liar!" Penrith's face was flushed with anger, his fists clinched at his side. "Take it back, Evering! Now, on this spot! Or we shall do no business together."

"All right. I apologize. I'm sorry. I thought—I don't know what I thought. I was wrong to bring it up at all—"

"You're paying me back for Cumberline by telling me this, aren't you?"

Evering said, "No, Penrith, on my honor. I—it's the *gossip,* man, I didn't make it up. And I thought you should know, if you didn't already. It's vicious and meant to hurt, I'm sure. I was wrong to tell you. I'm sorry."

Penrith turned to walk on and then stopped. "I shan't need your company the rest of the way, Evering. I'm rather disgusted, if you want the truth."

"I understand. I'm sorry."

Penrith stalked off, shoulders tightly squared.

Evering watched him go, an angry man with time on his hands to dwell on his anger. And the wife he doted on was in Scotland, visiting her sister, where Penrith couldn't question her easily. Yes, that journey had been a stroke of unexpected luck, worth the effort he'd expended on perfecting the details of his plan.

When Penrith reached the mail boat and stepped in without looking back, Evering returned to his house, shut the door against the incoming fog, and in the parlor poured himself a large whiskey. Too early in the morning for it, he scolded himself, but it was what he needed.

His hands were shaking. *What would come of this day's work?*

Then he went up to his room and was sick in the basin on the table by the window.

5

Elise came back for drinks in the afternoon, bringing with her the rest of her wedding party. Rutledge had gone up to change after walking down to the water's edge, and the laughter announcing their arrival drifted up the stairs to him.

On his way down to join them, he heard Hamish's voice in his ear. " 'Ware!"

A young woman with dark red hair and freckles was standing in the doorway at the foot of the stairs, listening to the ominous rumble of thunder in the distance. She turned and said, "Hallo, I'm Mary," as she offered her hand.

Assuming she was the newly arrived matron of honor, Rutledge introduced himself and added that he'd been looking forward to meeting her.

She gestured toward the clouds. "I don't relish the drive back to Dunster if it storms. Edgar may have to put us up. I've never cared for lightning."

The unmade road from Dunster to Maitland's house ended in a pair of nasty turns, and driving them in the dark and heavy rain would be tempting fate.

Rutledge said, "I'm sure there's more than enough room here."

Mary resolutely turned her back to the storm, and Rutledge kept her busy with questions about her journey until a little of her anxiety had faded. Then they joined the rest of the guests in the dining room, where the wedding party had gathered.

Watching them, Rutledge thought that Edgar and Elise made a striking pair. And she was carrying out her duties as hostess with smiling grace. Edgar's eyes followed her, and his happiness was reflected in his own smile.

Rutledge had already met Elise's parents, and he was standing with them at the edge of the crush of people when someone, he thought it was Mary, said, "And Ian, I believe you know Mrs. Channing?"

He spun on his heel, trying to keep the shock out of his face.

Meredith Channing smiled up at him and gave him her hand. "Yes, we've met before. Hallo, Ian, how are you?"

She was giving him time to recover.

Managing it somehow, he said, "I'm well. And you?"

"I'm well, thank you. It appears we've just made it before the storm."

"Yes—you were fortunate."

And then Elise's cousin was greeting him, and Meredith Channing moved on, her voice drifting back to him as she said something to Edgar about the setting of his house.

When he had a moment to himself, Rutledge turned to watch her crossing the room and helping herself to the refreshments on the drinks table.

He had met her first on New Year's Eve, at Maryanne Browning's house, where Meredith had come to conduct a séance for the amusement of Maryanne's guests. Something about her had struck him then, a certainty that she knew more about his war years than he was willing to tell anyone—he'd even been absurdly afraid that she would find Hamish in his mind. A fear that had been reinforced when he learned that she'd served as a nurse at a forward aid station and remembered seeing him there.

They had been thrown together a number of times since that night, and he'd come to an uneasy truce with her. Meredith Channing had never spoken of his past or her own, keeping their friendship, such as it was, firmly anchored in the present. And yet, an undercurrent was always there, her warm charm and that quiet poise so unusual in a woman only a few years his junior, a snare that drew him and repelled him at the same time.

She came across the room later and stood before him, looking out the windows as the rain pelted down and the thunder echoed wildly across the moor.

Before she could say anything, Mary, the red-haired bridesmaid he'd met earlier, came up to claim his attention. He'd been standing a little apart from the others in the room, his claustrophobia getting the better of him. His back was to the windows that looked out on the terrace, and he suddenly felt cornered.

Glancing uneasily at the swirling rain as a sheet of lightning lit up the sky, Mary said, "Doesn't it bother you?" She shivered, her hands cupping her elbows, as if to hold warmth in.

"Shall I find a wrap for you?" he asked, dodging the question.

Mary shook her head. "It's the thunder. It reminds me of the guns in France. We could hear them in Kent, where I lived then. And sometimes even see the flashes."

Her words were suddenly loud in a brief lull in the conversation, and people stood still, as if not knowing how to break the spell they cast. Then Elise's father said, "Thank God that's behind us," and changed the subject.

Mary turned away from the dark glass. "I think I'll make some tea, if Elise hasn't. Sorry."

"Don't apologize. I understand."

She gave him a grateful smile and left him there.

Meredith Channing said, for Rutledge's ears alone, "You needn't worry. The storm will pass soon, and then we'll be gone."

He said, "I'm not sure it will be safe, even then. The road is tricky."

"There's a moon. When it breaks through the clouds, there will be enough light to see our way." Against his will, her calm assurance enveloped him.

He said, "Everyone seems quite content to stay until then."

"Most of us have known one another for some time. It's like a family gathering, everyone catching up on news. The war years were hard, and we've all paid a high price for this peace."

He wanted to ask her what her price had been but couldn't bring himself to introduce such a personal note.

Yet he found himself comparing Meredith Channing to Elise. They were only a few years apart in age, but Elise had been sent to live in the comparative comfort and isolation of Dunster, with no troop trains arriving in the night with the wounded, no outbound trains filled with cheering soldiers marching away to war, shielding her from the cauldron of anguish and suffering Mrs. Channing had seen at the Front. And so age was not a measure of the differences between them. Only experience could be.

That thought reminded him of an earlier one, that perhaps Edgar had deliberately chosen someone like Elise. As perhaps he himself had held to the memory of his former fiancée, Jean, long after any hope of reconciliation. Were they both so desperate to wipe away the bitterness and fear and nightmares they'd brought home with them?

Mrs. Channing smiled, as if she'd read his mind, and he swore to himself as she said, "I believe they'll be happy, those two. Elise is steadier than she appears. Right now, she's giddy with happiness, and has a right to be. Edgar wouldn't propose until he was sure he was well enough. He didn't want to be a burden, I imagine, but Elise was afraid he'd never work up the courage. He needs her brightness. In a few months he'll forget he's lost a limb and agree to one of those artificial ones that are available now."

Edgar had said nothing to him about replacing his leg with an artificial one.

And again, Meredith said, apropos of that, "He was afraid he'd make a fool of himself tomorrow, falling. He feels safer just now with his crutches."

"Did Elise tell you that?" he said. *Or had you read it in Edgar's tea leaves?*

A twinkle appeared in Meredith's dark eyes. "Ian. I've seen Edgar any number of times when he has come up to London. If he brings Elise, she stays with me. For propriety's sake. And we've talked a time or two."

He felt himself flush with embarrassment. Managing a laugh, he said, "Sorry. I met you first as a necromancer, remember."

"Yes. I remember. It was not the best of footings for friendship, was it? I can sometimes guess what someone is thinking—anyone can, if he knows human nature. A policeman employs the same skills, surely. It isn't so strange a gift."

"A policeman," he responded dryly, "doesn't care to have those skills used against him."

She laughed. It was low and husky and somehow intimate. "Touché."

As the storm descended on them in earnest, the party moved down to the kitchen and made a spur-of-the-moment tea out of what they found there, carrying it triumphantly to the room overlooking the terrace and sitting on the rugs or in the chairs, conversation flowing smoothly. Rutledge found he was enjoying himself.

Meredith Channing was talking with Neal Hammond, and Rutledge could hear her voice but not what she was saying, though it was clear from the expression on Hammond's face that he found her attractive. From the way he touched her arm at one point, it was also clear that they had known each other for some time.

Hamish spoke, startling Rutledge. He had been silent since that first sharp "'Ware!" as Rutledge had come down the stairs earlier in the evening to join the gathering. "Ye canna' let your guard down. It would be foolish."

But the evening had unexpectedly turned into a very pleasant few hours, and when the storm had passed and it was too late to adjourn to The Luttrell Arms for dinner, no one made a move to leave.

Edgar, coming to sit beside Rutledge, was in the best of spirits, all qualms apparently quashed for now, and he smiled at his friend with wry warmth.

"Thank you for coming, Ian. I thought I needed support through this. Now I'm glad I have a friend beside me."

"A thunderstorm can work wonders," Rutledge said, grinning at Edgar. "Did you order it up yourself?"

"If I'd thought about it, I'd have tried. I think Elise's parents are satisfied now that she's not marrying a cripple with no prospects. They knew my grandfather, and I've heard they told their daughter in the beginning that I wasn't half the man he was. That, thank God, was on my last leave, before I'd lost my leg. I was greener then. They seem to be enjoying themselves tonight." He stretched out his leg and said, "I hadn't realized that you knew Meredith."

It was a fishing expedition, transparently so.

"I met her at Maryanne Browning's," Rutledge replied.

"She's been a widow for several years now. I'm glad to see her out and about again." Edgar Maitland was matchmaking.

Rutledge smothered a smile. "I'll keep that in mind," he said dryly.

"You could do worse. I'm not one to speak ill of the dead, but Jean wasn't right for you. I could have told you that in 1914, but you wouldn't have listened."

"Probably not."

Edgar laughed. "You have no idea what happiness is until you've found someone to love. Just look at me!"

Elise came over to join them, saving Rutledge from finding an answer to that. He stood up to offer her his chair, but she said, "It's near the witching hour. And the storm seems to have dwindled to broken clouds. We must leave. I have it on good authority—my mother— that it's bad luck to see one's bride on the day of the wedding, until she walks down the aisle."

"We don't want to risk that." Edgar got to his feet with some difficulty, then shoved his crutches under his arms with the ease of habit. "Let's start rounding up the guests."

In a flurry of farewells, Elise collected her family and friends and set out for Dunster. Edgar watched them go, the headlamps of the convoy of cars twisting and turning down the road.

"You didn't wish Mrs. Channing a good night. Not that I saw."

"I'll see her tomorrow and apologize profusely."

"You're incorrigible, my friend. Hammond will snap her up if you don't."

Laughing, they went up to bed.

The wedding was held in St. George's, a small gem that had once been part of a long-vanished priory before becoming a parish church. It boasted a magnif- icent wagon roof and what was said to be the longest rood screen in England, but all eyes were on the bride as she walked down the aisle. Photographs of the wed- ding party were taken in what had once been the

Prior's Garden, and there was a breakfast, and music, but not for dancing, in The Luttrell Arms, across from the Yarn Market. A quartet played softly in the background, and the cake was a masterpiece of culinary art. On the top sat an elegant sugar swan, wings spread wide and a ribbon in its beak bearing the names of the bride and groom in gold lettering. Rutledge, seated next to Edgar, led the toasts, and then as the conversation grew more general, discovered that Elise's father was a longtime friend of his godfather, David Trevor, who lived now in Scotland.

"Wonderful architect," Caldwell said. "It's a pity that he retired so early. But then I understand—I also lost a son in the war. Elise's middle brother. Not something you get over, is it?"

"No, sir, it isn't. Have you also retired?"

"To my sorrow, no. I advise people on how to invest their money. And they won't hear of my giving it up." Caldwell smiled. "The day will come, inevitably. I expect I shall have to ease them into accepting it. My wife is eager for me to grow roses and spend more time with her." He made a face. "I'd much rather fish, you know. I'm an angler by nature, not a gardener."

In the early afternoon, the bridal pair set off on their wedding trip. Edgar drove, waving gaily to guests as he and Elise bounced over the cobbles and turned beyond the castle. The motorcar had been modified so that he could manage. It was, he'd told Rutledge, a matter of pride. Once out of sight, Elise would take the wheel for the rest of their journey.

The remaining guests left the inn in the next hour, many of them on their way back to London, and Rutledge found himself face-to-face with Meredith Channing as she came to say good-bye. They had been thrown together often during the morning, and Rutledge had to admit that he'd enjoyed her company.

"Safe journey," he said, and she nodded.

"Same to you. I'm driving with friends. We ought to make good time. That was a lovely toast you proposed to the bride and groom. You have a way with words."

"Thank you. It was heartfelt."

"Yes, Edgar was touched. It was good to see you again, Ian." She offered her hand, and he took it. They shook briefly, and then she was gone, leaving an unexpected emptiness behind her.

Rutledge told himself it was because everyone else had left, and the day that had begun with such glorious sunshine for the wedding was now changing.

He turned to say good-bye to Elise's parents as they followed the last of the guests out the door. Caldwell clapped him on the shoulder and said, "If you're in the City, stop in."

"I will, sir. Thank you."

And then he was back at the house on the hill, where the view was magnificent and his footsteps echoed through the rooms. The ghosts of laughter and excitement and happy voices made the silence seem almost ominous, and he shrugged off the sudden upsweep of melancholy.

He spent the next hour clearing away, as Edgar had asked him to do, preparing to close up the house before he left in the morning. And then he sat on the terrace to watch the sun set behind a bank of clouds. Restless, he was in no mood to sleep, but finally he took himself off to bed, with a small whiskey and the voice of Hamish MacLeod for company.

When someone knocked at Maitland's door shortly after midnight, Rutledge came awake with a start. He fumbled for his dressing gown and slippers, then went to answer the summons.

At first sight of the grim-faced uniformed constable standing on the doorstep, he thought, *Oh, dear God, Edgar insisted on driving all the way—and there's been a crash.* And then the next thought, *Pray God they aren't hurt badly!*

He could feel the presence of Hamish, stark and loud in his ears as he said, "Good evening, Constable. Not bad news, I hope!"

And waited to hear the worst.

But the middle-aged man standing there in the quiet night air asked, "Mr. Rutledge, sir?"

"Yes, I'm Rutledge. What is it, man?"

"There's been a telephone call from London. Chief Superintendent Bowles, sir. He says you're the nearest man to the scene and would you return his call at the Yard straightaway."

Relief washed over him.

"Let me find my shoes and a coat."

He went back up the stairs to the guest room, leaving the constable standing in the hall, waiting for him.

When Chief Superintendent Bowles wanted a man, it paid to be prompt. Throwing his coat on over his pajamas and thrusting his bare feet into the shoes he'd worn for the wedding, he wasted no time wondering about the summons. Closest to the scene generally meant that Bowles had little choice in the matter of which man to send and was putting speed before preference.

He helped the constable lash his bicycle to the boot of the motorcar rather than the rear seat, unwilling in the dark to risk finding Hamish in what always seemed to be his accustomed place, just behind Rutledge's shoulder. It was a silent drive down to Dunster; the air was warm and heavy, the stars vanished. The only sign of life they saw was a hare bounding off into the high grass by the road.

The constable commented as they reached the town's outskirts, "Easier coming down by motorcar than peddling up as I did on that confounded bicycle."

Dunster's streets were quiet, the police station's lights almost blinding as Rutledge stepped through the door. It was five minutes after the connection was made before Bowles's voice came booming down the line. "In Somerset, are you?"

"Yes, sir. I took several days' leave," he reminded the chief superintendent. "For a friend's wedding. I'll be back in London on Monday."

"Indeed. Well, there's a change in plan. You're to go at once to Cambury. It's just south of Glastonbury, I'm told. The local man is on the scene already, and he's handing the case over to us. You're the closest inspector I've got to Cambury. By my reckoning you can be there in three hours or less."

"Why is he asking for our help at this early stage?"

"A man's been killed. Name of Quarles. His place of business is in Leadenhall Street here in London. His country house is in Somerset, and apparently he'd come down for the weekend. Ghastly business, I can't think why anyone would wish to do such a thing, but there you are. They're expecting you, see that you don't dally!"

"No, sir—"

But Bowles had cut the connection and the line was dead.

6

Rutledge closed up Maitland's house, left a note for Edgar regarding the sheets the laundress wouldn't be able to collect with the door locked, then took his luggage out to his motorcar. He thought ruefully that evening dress and casual attire would hardly be what Cambury was expecting, but it was all he had with him.

A low-lying mist had crept in on the heels of the warm air, wreathing the night in a soft veil that threw the light from his headlamps back in his face and from time to time made the road seem to vanish into a white void.

He was given directions to Cambury by the police in Dunster and found that the road was fairly good most of the distance. "It's a village that's outgrown itself," the constable had said, "and much like Dunster in its own way. Though we have the castle, don't we, and there's none such in Cambury. Still, there are those who claim King Arthur knew it, and might be buried thereabouts. My wife's sister plumps for Glastonbury, of course. That's where she lives."

When he could relax his concentration on the road, Rutledge considered what Bowles had told him. The chief superintendent took a perverse pleasure in giving out as little information as possible to any subordinate he didn't like. But everyone at the Yard knew that it was one of the methods Bowles used to weed out men he didn't wish to see climb the ladder of promotion.

The victim, Quarles, had a place of business in Leadenhall Street and thus lived in London. Who then was taking over that part of the inquiry while Rutledge was busy in Somerset? It would be revealing to have the answer to that.

Rutledge drove on through the mist with only Hamish for company, the voice from the rear seat, just behind his ear, keeping up a running commentary. Hamish had been—for him—unusually silent during the weekend, his comments brief enough to be ignored. It was never clear why Hamish sometimes had nothing to say. Like an army that had lost contact with the main body of the enemy, Rutledge was always on his guard at such times, distrustful of the silence, prepared for an attack from any quarter when he least expected it.

Dr. Fleming, who had saved Rutledge's sanity and his life in the clinic barely twelve months ago, forcing him against his will to acknowledge what was in his head, had promised that his patient would learn to manage his heavy burden of guilt. Instead, Rutledge had become a master at hiding it.

All the same, he answered that voice aloud more often than he liked, both out of habit and because of the compelling presence he could feel and not see. He stood in constant danger of disgracing himself in front of friends or colleagues, drawing comment or questions about the thin edge of self-control that kept him whole. Shell shock was a humiliation, proof of cowardice and a lack of moral fiber, never mind the medals pinned on his breast. And so the tension within himself built sometimes to intolerable levels.

It was the only scar he could show from his four years in the trenches. Unlike Edgar Maitland. His men had commented on his luck, watched him with misgivings at first, and then with something more like fear. Many an inexperienced officer gained a reputation for reckless daring and wild courage, believing himself invulnerable. More often than not, he died with most of his men, not so much as an inch of ground gained.

But the young Scots under Rutledge soon realized that their officer put the care of his men above all else, and so they had followed him into whatever hell was out there, across the barbed wire. Knowing he would spare them where he could, and bring them back when he couldn't.

And that had finally broken him. Aware of the faith put in him, trying to live up to it, and watching men die when it was impossible to save them—even while he himself lived—had taken an incalculable toll of mind and spirit. Hamish's unnecessary death had been the last straw. Finding a way back had somehow seemed to be a final betrayal of the dead.

In that last dark hour before the spring dawn, the road Rutledge had been following rounded a bend and swept down a low hill into a knot of thatched cottages. Then, like a magician's trick, the road became Cambury's High Street, leading him into the sleeping village. The mist that had kept pace with him most of the way was in tatters now, a patch here and there still lying in wait, and sometimes rising to embrace the trees on the far side of the duck pond. The Perpendicular church tower, to his left, loomed above the clouds like a beacon.

The village's modest prosperity was visible in the shop fronts and in the houses that lined the street.

Typical of Somerset, there was an air of contentment here, as if the inhabitants neither needed nor expected anything from the outside world.

He noted several lanes that crossed the High Street, vanishing into the darkness on either side. Like Dunster, whatever Cambury had been at the height of the wool trade, when it had had the money to build such a church, it was now a quiet byway.

What, he wondered, had brought Quarles here? It wasn't the sort of village that had much to offer a wealthy Londoner. Unless there were family ties to Somerset . . .

Hamish said, "Ye ken, it's a long way to London."

In miles and in pace and outlook.

An interesting point. What reputation did Quarles have here, and was it different from that of the man of business in the City? And could that have led to murder?

He saw the police station just ahead and pulled over.

Inside a constable was waiting for him, yawning in spite of himself as he got up from his chair to greet Rutledge.

"You made good time, sir," he said. "I'm to take you along to the house straightaway. My name is Daniels, sir. Constable Daniels."

For the second time that night, Rutledge helped a constable lash his bicycle to the boot, and then the man cranked the motor for him, before getting in and shutting the door.

"Where are we going?" Rutledge asked as Daniels directed him out of the village.

"The house is called Hallowfields. This was mainly monastery land once, and there's a tithe barn built to hold whatever goods the local tenants owed the monks as rent."

The High Street had turned back into the main road again, and as they crested a slight rise, walled parkland on their right marked the beginning of an estate.

"The tithe barn is on his property, and so Mr. Quarles set himself up as squire, taking over from the monks, you might say."

"Was this popular in the village? Surely not?"

"He wasn't the first owner to claim squire's rights, but as he was mostly in London, it wasn't hard to ignore him. Though some of the farmers came to him for help when their crops were bad or their plows broke or their roofs leaked." Daniels grinned at Rutledge, his face bright in the reflected glow of the headlamps. "A costly business, being squire. There, you can just see the gates coming up ahead. We'll pass them and turn instead at the entrance to the Home Farm."

Hamish said, "He doesna' grieve o'er much for the dead man."

A pair of handsome iron gates, disembodied in the mist, closed off what could be seen of the drive before it vanished into the night, a gray ribbon that appeared to go nowhere.

They came to a break in the wall, where a small, whitewashed gatehouse marked the way into the working part of the estate. The cottage was very pretty, with roses climbing up the front, framing the windows and the single door.

"Here we are, sir."

"Does anyone live there?" Rutledge asked, nodding at the gatehouse.

"No, sir. It's been empty for some time."

Rutledge turned into the lane that led to the farm, and almost immediately his headlamps picked out a track bearing to the left.

"That way, sir, if you please. We don't go as far as the farm."

Rutledge bumped into the rutted track that curled through a copse of trees. Ahead, his lights picked out the rising bulk of a gray stone building that appeared to block his way. The mist lingered here in the trees, as if caught among the branches, and then without warning he drove into a thicker patch, like cotton wool. It swallowed the motorcar, and he felt the sudden shock of claustrophobia as the track seemed to vanish as if by magic, leaving him in an opaque world. Just as suddenly he came out into a small clearing, where a bicycle and two other vehicles were clustered together, as if for comfort.

At the edge of the clearing stood the tithe barn, vast, dark, and hunched, as if it had lurked there for hundreds of years, waiting patiently for the return of its builders.

Judging from the size of it—a good 200 feet long and possibly closer to 250—this part of Somerset had been prosperous under the monks' rule. The roof soared high above their heads as they got out of the motorcar, and something about the way it loomed in the darkness and shreds of mist was almost evil.

He laughed at himself. A night without sleep played odd games with the imagination.

Where once there had been a roofed entrance on the side of the barn facing him, there was a single door now, dwarfed by the heavy stone walls rising into the night sky.

He turned to ask Daniels a question as the constable gestured toward the door. "That way, sir. They're expecting you. I'm to fetch the doctor, now that you're here." He went around to the back of the motorcar and took down his bicycle, nodding to Rutledge as he mounted the machine and peddled into the mist.

Rutledge walked toward the entrance. The heavy door creaked under his hand as he shoved it open and stepped inside.

It was like stepping into the truncated, unfinished nave of an enormous church. There was no great west front, no transepts or choir or altar or apse, only a forest of huge squared wooden timbers rising like columns into the darkness overhead, where they supported a handsome array of beams. The silence was almost that of a church as well, where a whisper would carry round the bare stone walls.

The only light came not from wax sanctuary candles but from three lanterns that rested on the flagstone floor, picking out three startled men standing staring at him, as if he were an apparition walking through the door.

The taller of them, the one with a square face, cleared his throat.

"Inspector Rutledge, I take it?"

"Yes, I'm Rutledge."

"We weren't expecting you for another two hours." The speaker walked forward, hand outstretched. "Inspector Padgett. And two of my men, Constable Horton and Constable Jenkins. I expect you've met Constable Daniels. He was waiting to bring you here."

Rutledge acknowledged the introductions, and just as he shook hands with Padgett, something in the rafters caught his eye.

He stopped, his head raised, his gaze fixed.

Above them, like an avenging angel high among the beams that held up the roof, was a man with out-flung arms and immense feathered wings springing from his back.

"Gentle God," Rutledge murmured before he could stop himself.

"Quite," Padgett replied.

"Is that Quarles? Is he dead?"

"Yes, on both counts. We didn't touch him. I sent Constable Daniels to call Scotland Yard and then wait for whoever was coming. Of course we recognized him straightaway. It's Harold Quarles, beyond any doubt. This is his land—his barn."

"What killed him?"

"We don't know yet."

"How in the name of God did anyone get him up there?"

"It's easy, if you know the trick. Quarles puts on a Christmas pageant here, complete with live sheep and a donkey and even an inflatable camel he brought down from London. The figures are local people, and it's considered an honor to take part. Wise men, shepherds, and so on. There's an angel as well, with a rig to hold him or her up there. Quite comfortably, I'm told, if a little hair-raising. I wouldn't want to try it myself, I can tell you." He gestured toward the shadows along the walls. "Trestle tables and benches over there, and on this side the manger and the bits that create the stable and its roof. And along there as well, the apparatus for the angel. It's kept in a chest, out of sight, along with the wings. It's very well known, our Christmas pageant. Even the London papers have written it up. And a gazette featured it one year. My son was the babe in the manger that Christmas."

"Which tells me a good many people knew the apparatus was here, and that it works."

"I would say so, yes."

"Is the door kept locked?"

"It hasn't been for some years. The hasp rusted through, and no one has replaced it. Where's the need? We've never had any trouble before."

"Who found him? How long has he been up there?"

"We don't know how long. We're hoping the doctor can answer that. I came past here on my way home. It's a little out of my way, but I'd told Constable Horton here that I'd do his last patrol for him before he went off duty at eleven. We'd had a busy night of it with a pair of quarrelsome drunks, and we were tired. Just by the turning for the Home Farm, I heard a dog barking in an alarmed sort of way, and I stopped to investigate. The noise was coming from the trees here, and I walked in toward the barn. I saw that the door was ajar, and I thought perhaps the dog had cornered a badger inside. I went back to my motorcar for my torch, and by that time the dog had given up and gone away. I was on the point of leaving myself but decided to step inside, since I was already here. And at first I saw nothing. Then something creaked, and I looked up. I can tell you, I got the fright of my life!"

It was a well-rehearsed account, and Rutledge nodded, still staring at the figure over his head.

Into his mind's eye came the image of the swan on Edgar Maitland's wedding cake, its wings spread, a ribbon in its mouth. The contrast was appalling.

"Where's the dog now? What did it look like?"

"I heard him, I didn't see him. There are several dogs at the Home Farm, and I'm told Mrs. Quarles has two King Charles spaniels."

Rutledge took out his own torch and shone it on the spectral winged body in the darkness above.

Quarles was dressed in street clothes, a dark suit, waistcoat, and white shirt. His arms were rigidly outstretched in an openwork cage that enclosed his entire body. An angel in a nativity pageant could easily conceal the white cage with a full-length robe and long flowing sleeves worn over it, giving the impression of floating in the shadows overhead. The thickly feathered wings attached somewhere at the back of the shoulders and partially outstretched, as if in flight, were a bizarre counterpoint to the dead man's ordinary clothing.

"He's a reasonably heavy man. Could one person pull him up to that height?"

"It's block and tackle. I've seen one man do it, for the pageant."

"Is there anyone who hated Quarles enough to do this to him? Because this is not just murder, there's viciousness at work here. Otherwise he'd have been lying on the floor."

Padgett sighed. "I shouldn't wish to speak ill of the dead, but he was a hard man to like. Cold-natured and unbending when he wanted his way. I'd bring my children here for the pageant, like the rest of the village and the surrounding farms, but only because they wanted to come and see the angel and the camel. I'd have stayed away, myself. I'll tell you straight out, I didn't have much use for Harold Quarles."

Padgett turned away, as if ashamed of his honesty. But something in his face told Rutledge that the man's feelings were too strong to conceal.

Hamish said, "He intended for you to hear it from him first."

"You've described the public man. Why did *you* dislike him so much?" Rutledge was blunt.

Padgett shrugged. "He could be callous. Almost to the point of cruelty. I don't like that in anyone."

Rutledge walked in a circle, trying to judge the body from every viewpoint. But only the man's front was visible. What else might be there, on the dark side, would have to wait until he was brought down.

"There's no blood on his shirt," Padgett offered. "We don't know if he was shot or stabbed."

"And no blood here on the floor."

"I had to leave him long enough to fetch Horton, and the lanterns. There was nothing else I could do," Padgett confessed.

"You were certain, before you left, that there was no one else here in the barn? Hiding behind one of the trestle tables?"

"I made sure of that. And besides, he was already dead. What harm could the killer do to him now?"

"He had time to clear away any evidence he'd left behind."

At that moment the door opened, and they turned as one man to see who was coming in.

Constable Daniels had returned, this time with a thin man wearing gold-rimmed spectacles. He appeared to have thrown his clothes on in some haste, and his hair hadn't been properly combed. Rutledge put his age at early forties.

"The doctor," one of the constables said under his breath.

"What's this about, Padgett? Daniels wouldn't tell me." O'Neil came briskly toward them, his gaze on the men staring back at him.

Padgett, almost reflexively, glanced upward, and O'Neil's eyes followed his.

"Good God!" he said in horror. "You aren't—that's *Quarles!*" He stood there for a long moment, as if unable to take in what he was seeing. "What the hell is he doing up there?" His gaze swung toward Padgett. "Is he dead? He must be dead!"

"To the best of our knowledge, he is. I didn't care to move him until you got here." Padgett crossed the flagstone floor to shake the man's hand, then presented Rutledge.

"Dr. O'Neil. Inspector Rutledge from London."

O'Neil looked Rutledge up and down. "Has he been up there that long? For you to be sent for? I should have been called sooner."

"I was in Dunster, attending a wedding, and word reached me quickly. We think he must have been killed earlier tonight. Last night. But that's your province."

"Indeed." His attention turned back to the dead man. "Who in God's name strung him up like that? He couldn't have done that to himself, could he? And how are we to get him down?"

Padgett nodded to Daniels, who was standing behind the doctor, his jaw fallen in shock. It was the first time he'd been allowed inside the barn. "Constable, you've used this apparatus. Let him down."

Daniels, startled, said, "Me? Sir?"

"Yes, yes, man, get on with it. You've done it often enough for the pageant."

Daniels reluctantly went toward the shadowed west end of the barn and fumbled at something on the wall. As he did, the man above their heads swayed, his hands moving, as if he still lived, and the lamplight picked out the whites of his open eyes as he seemed to stare balefully at his tormentors.

7

Inspector Padgett sucked in his breath and took a long step back.

Dr. O'Neil swore sharply, adding, "Have a care, man!"

The apparatus creaked as Daniels put his weight into it, and a feather, dislodged from one of the wings, drifted down from above, turning and spinning, holding all their eyes as it wafted slowly among them, as if choosing, and then coming to rest finally at Rutledge's feet.

The other men turned toward him, as if somehow he had been marked by it.

A shock swept through Rutledge, and he couldn't look away from the white feather. He prayed his face showed nothing of what he felt.

During the war, the women of Britain had handed out white feathers to anyone they felt should have joined the armed forces, challenging the man to do his duty or be branded a coward. It had got out of hand, this white feather business, to the point that the government had issued special uniforms for the discharged wounded, to spare them the mortification of explaining publicly why they were not now fit for active duty.

Every man there knew that story. And Rutledge could feel a slow flush rise in his cheeks, as if the feather had been earned, though in another time or place, by the charge of shell shock. That they recognized him, even without evidence, for what the world believed he was.

Padgett broke the spell, cursing Daniels under his breath. He started forward to help his constable and then thought better of it. "Horton."

Constable Horton hurried forward, his face tight, and in short order the two men got the apparatus under control. Bracing themselves against the dead man's weight, they began gently to lower Quarles into the circle of lamplight.

Rutledge saw, watching them now, that a single man could have manipulated the rope under less stressful circumstances. But Daniels, fearful of dropping Quarles, had found it impossible to work the rope smoothly.

Hamish said, "Ma' granny wouldna' care to see this," in a tone of voice that reflected his own feelings. "Witchcraft, she'd ha' called it."

It was as if Quarles flew down, landing easily first on his toes, the taut rope almost invisible against the darkness of the ceiling, the wings moving gently, as if of their own volition. And the watchers could at last see the other side of the body. The back of Quarles's head was matted with dark blood, staining the pale red of his hair

Attempting to tie off the rope, the two constables accidentally lifted the body again, and it seemed to the onlookers to have life in it still.

There was a brief hesitation, as if no one was eager to step closer. Then O'Neil said tersely, "Get him out of that wretched thing."

Releasing Quarles from the brace that had held him in the air was difficult. With a living person it would have been different, but the dead weight was awkward. And after that, detaching him from the wings hooked into the cage and the cloth at his shoulders and meant to appear from below as if they belonged where they were fastened, growing out of the man's own back, took several people. Rigor mortis hadn't set in, that much was apparent, as O'Neil quietly pointed out as they worked.

When at last Quarles slumped to the flagstone floor of the barn and the harness and cage had been dragged away, the doctor beckoned for the lamps to be brought nearer and knelt to begin his examination.

As O'Neil ran his hands over the body, a frown between his eyes, Rutledge got his first good look at the victim.

Quarles had pale red hair, a freckled complexion, and surprisingly regular features, although one eyebrow had a quizzical twist to it. A vigorous body, with a barrel chest and long legs. Rutledge judged him to be five feet ten inches tall, and put his age at either the late thirties or early forties. Without the force of his personality, he seemed oddly vulnerable, but the strong jaw and chin spoke of a man who knew what he wanted from life.

O'Neil was saying, "Nothing broken, as far as I can judge. No signs of a wound, other than what we can see on the back of his head. And that was the cause of death, if I'm not mistaken." He moved his fingers through the blood-soaked hair and then wiped them on his handkerchief. "There are several blows here. Lacerations on the scalp in two areas. I'll know more later, but someone wanted to make sure the first blow had done the job. And judging from the blood you can see in his hair, it hadn't. The aim was better the second time, because poor Quarles was semiconscious and not resisting."

"But both were struck from behind?" Rutledge asked. He had been studying the dead man's hands. They were badly scarred.

The skin was still tight and shiny in places, though the worst of the injury had faded with time.

Hamish said, "Aye, we've seen burns before. But look you, they're no' on his face."

Dr. O'Neil was regarding Rutledge, his expression puzzled.

He realized that the doctor hadn't taken his point. He clarified his question. "That is to say, do the blows indicate whether Quarles had turned away from someone he was talking with? Or was it a surprise attack, something he didn't see coming?"

"That's your task to work out, not mine. All I can say is that he might have been turning away. The first laceration is a little behind and to the right of the second. Or at the last minute he could have heard someone coming up behind him and started to turn to confront whoever it was. I can't tell you what was used to kill him. Or where he was killed. Unless there's blood on the floor that I haven't seen in this light?"

"Horton," Padgett said over his shoulder, "take one of the lanterns and go over the flagstones as carefully as you can. Pay particular attention by the mechanism of that rig."

The man set off, his light bobbing as he searched.

O'Neil stood, brushing off the knees of his trousers. "It's my opinion that he hasn't been dead very long. Hours, rather than days. Any idea who could have done this?"

"None," Padgett replied shortly.

"How did he come by those burns on his hands?" Rutledge asked.

O'Neil said, "He's had them as long as I've known him. I asked once, professional interest, but he just said it was an accident. It was clear he didn't want to talk about it. Which reminds me, has anyone thought to let Mrs. Quarles know that her husband is dead?"

"We preferred to keep this quiet until Rutledge got here." Padgett pulled out his watch. "They'll be stirring at the Home Farm soon, if they aren't already. It won't take long for someone to see the vehicles outside and come to find out what's happening. I suppose I ought to go to the house directly."

"If you'll lend me one of your men, I'll see to the moving of the body while all's quiet. Anything else you need from me?"

"Nothing at present—"

He was interrupted by Horton calling from the other end of the barn. "So far, there's no blood to indicate if he was killed in here, sir. We might do better in daylight, but I'll wager it wasn't in the barn."

Padgett turned to Rutledge. "Do you want to go to the house with me?"

Breaking bad news was not Rutledge's favorite duty, but someone had to do it, and it was just as well to meet the family now. Sometimes the way the household reacted to a death could be telling. He nodded.

"All right, Horton, you help the doctor. Daniels, you and Jenkins can see to this apparatus. Put it where it belongs and shut the chest on it. I don't want to see it again. As it is, I'll be hard-pressed to attend the pageant this year. Then I want the two of you to stand watch at the barn door. I'll leave my motorcar for Jenkins. Turn about, every two hours—"

Rutledge said, "Wait, let me examine that cage."

It was indeed wicker, as he'd thought, reinforced by wires, and the wings, he discovered, were attached as a rule to a brace that locked across the wicker frame, holding the Christmas angel safely in place. It was all in all a clever device, and must create quite a spectacle. But there was nothing on the harness or the ropes or the pulleys that offered him any clue as to who had used it for a dead man.

"Thanks," he said, nodding to the two constables, and turning to Dr. O'Neil, he asked, "Do you think Quarles was still alive when he was put into this contraption?"

"If he was attacked here, in the barn, I'd say he was dead before he was hoisted up into the rafters. The second blow rendered him unconscious, if he wasn't already, and he was dying. Beyond saving, in fact, even if his attacker had changed his mind. It must have taken several minutes to get him into that device. Very likely there was a cloth or coat around his wound, or you'd have seen where his head rested during the process. At a guess, that's why there's no blood to be found here. It's a deep wound, I could feel where fragments of bone have been driven into the brain. If he was brought here from somewhere else, he was dead before he got to the barn. And heavy as he is, he wouldn't have been easy to manage. But it could be done. I'd look for scuff marks—where he was dragged—outside. If we haven't obscured them with our own tramping about."

"Thank you, Doctor." Rutledge turned to follow Padgett, and O'Neil went with them as far as his own motorcar, to fetch a blanket.

Shielding his torch, Padgett studied the turf around the door. "He's right, too many feet have trod here. But there's no other way in; we had no choice."

Rutledge cast his light a little to one side, trying to find signs of torn grass. "How did the killer bring Quarles here? Motorcar? On his back?"

"If we knew that, we'd be ahead of the game, wouldn't we?" Padgett replied morosely. He climbed into the passenger seat while Rutledge was cranking the motor, and said to no one in particular, "I don't relish this. Mrs. Quarles is an unusual woman. As you'll see for yourself."

"In what way?"

"You'll see."

Rutledge turned the motorcar and went back through the trees. The mist had vanished, as if it had never been there. Where the track to the tithe barn met the farm lane, Padgett said, "We'll go through the main gates. Set me down as you get there, and I'll open them."

The drive ran through parkland, specimen trees and shrubs providing vistas as it curved toward the house. When it came out of the trees and into smooth lawns toward the southeast, it went on to loop a bed of roses in front of the door. In the light breeze of early morning, their scent was heavy and sweet, and dew sparkled like diamonds among the leaves.

The house was tall, perfectly set among gardens, its dormer windows on the eastern approach already touched with the first rays of bright gold as the sun rose. A very handsome property, Rutledge thought as he pulled up, the sort of house that spoke of old money and breeding.

For a long moment Padgett sat there, looking at nothing.

"Well," he said finally, "we must do our duty, and break their tranquility into shards."

"I don't see any dogs. Surely if they were loose, they'd be here to greet us," Rutledge commented as they mounted the shallow steps and Padgett lifted the brass knocker. "At the very least the one you might have heard."

Padgett, listening to the sound of the bell ring through the house, said, "I doubt the dog was hers. We'll ask at the Home Farm."

For several minutes no one came to the door. Then it swung open, and a housekeeper stood there, glaring at them before she recognized Padgett.

"Inspector," she said in wary acknowledgment. "What brings you calling so early?"

"I'd like to speak to Mrs. Quarles, if I may. If she isn't awake—"

"I doubt anyone's asleep after such a summons at this hour."

"It's rather urgent," Padgett replied, goaded.

"I'll ask if she'll receive you now."

Rutledge said, "I understand Mrs. Quarles has several small dogs."

The housekeeper stared at him, as if he'd lost his mind. "If it's the little dogs you've come about, they're asleep in Mrs. Quarles's bedroom, where they belong."

She shut the door in their faces, and Padgett repeated sourly, "*'I'll ask if she'll receive you.'* As if I'm a bloody tradesman come to settle my accounts."

"It's a matter of form," Rutledge said

"Yes, well, we'll see who's unwanted, soon enough."

When the housekeeper came to the door again, this time she swung it wide, to allow them to enter. "Mrs. Quarles will see you. If you'll follow me."

They walked into a spacious foyer. The black and white marble of the floor had been set in a chessboard pattern, and the walls were a pale green trimmed in white. A flight of stairs curved upward, and a small winged Mercury, gleaming in a shaft of sunlight from the fanlight above the door, balanced on his toes atop the newel post. Both men glanced at it, sharply reminded of the winged corpse in the tithe barn.

As he looked around, Padgett's face mirrored his thoughts: *Ostentatious.* But the foyer, while handsome enough, was by no means the finest the West

Country had to offer. Did Padgett know that? Rutledge wondered, or would it matter if he did? He seemed to resent everything about Harold Quarles.

The housekeeper led them to a door down the passage and tapped lightly.

"Come." The woman's voice inside the room was well bred and composed.

The housekeeper opened the door and said, "Inspector Padgett, madam."

The small sitting room was clearly a woman's morning room. A French gilt-trimmed white desk stood between the windows, and there was a pretty chintz on the settee and the two side chairs that stood before the hearth, the pattern showing a field of lupines on a cream background. The blue of the lupines had been picked up again in the draperies and the carpet.

Mrs. Quarles was standing with her back to the grate, her fingers pressing the collar of her cream silk dressing gown at her throat, her fair hair neatly pinned into place. She was a very attractive woman, perhaps in her middle thirties.

At her side was a tall man sitting in an invalid's wheeled chair, a rug over his knees. His dark hair was graying at the temples, and his face was distinguished, with dark eyes beneath heavy lids. He had an air of sophistication about him, despite his infirmity. Mrs.

Quarles's other hand fell to rest on his shoulder as Padgett introduced Rutledge.

"From Scotland Yard?" she repeated in a clear, cool voice, examining Rutledge. "Why are you here at this hour? Is something wrong? You haven't come about my son, have you?"

"There's been a death, Mrs. Quarles," Padgett said, taking it upon himself to break the news. "I'm afraid it's your husband—"

"Death?" Her eyebrows rose as if she couldn't quite understand the word. "Are you sure?"

"Quite sure. We've just found his body—that is, a few hours ago—" Padgett stopped, tangled in his own explanation. It was clear that he felt ill at ease in her presence, and that it annoyed him.

"Are you telling me that my husband *killed* himself?" she demanded. "I refuse to believe anything of the sort. Where did you find him, and what has happened to him?"

"We found him in the tithe barn—that is, I did, and summoned Mr. Rutledge here because of the unusual circumstances."

She said testily, "Please get to the point, Inspector."

Padgett bristled. "He was murdered, Mrs. Quarles." The words were blunt, his voice cold.

Rutledge silently cursed the man. He was letting Mrs. Quarles set the direction of the interview.

Her hand, resting on the man's shoulder, gripped hard. Rutledge could see the slender knuckles whiten with the force.

"Murder?"

The man raised a hand to cover hers.

Rutledge thought, they are lovers . . . there was something in that touch that spoke of years of companionship and caring. But here? In Quarles's house?

Mrs. Quarles recovered herself and said, "By *whom,* for God's sake? Are you quite sure it wasn't an accident of some sort? My husband was forever poking about the estate on his weekends here, and sometimes drove Tom Masters to distraction."

"We don't have the answer to that at present. Shall I send Dr. O'Neil to you directly? Or the rector?" It was noticeable that Padgett failed to offer the formal words of condolence.

"To me? I shan't need Dr. O'Neil. Or the rector." Her face showed shock, but no grief.

"We'll need to speak to the staff. And I should like to see Mr. Quarles's rooms if I may. I understand he'd come down from London for the weekend. Was he expected?"

The man in the chair answered for her. "Generally he sends word ahead. But not always. It's his house, after all. This time he arrived in the late afternoon Friday, and spent most of yesterday with Tom Masters, who sees to the

Home Farm. He came back around four, I should think, and told the staff that he intended to dine out. This was relayed to me when I came down before dinner."

Padgett asked, "Mrs. Quarles?" Sharply seeking confirmation.

"Yes, as far as I know, that's all true."

"Were you on good terms with Mr. Quarles during this visit?"

"On good terms?"

"Did you quarrel? Have words?"

He watched the first crack in her facade of cool reserve as she snapped, "We never quarrel. Why should we?"

"Most married couples do. Did you see him when he returned from his dinner engagement?"

"I was not waiting up for him, if that's what you're asking."

Rutledge stepped in before Padgett could follow up on that. "Did he dine alone?"

Mrs. Quarles turned to him, almost with relief. "How should I know? We go our separate ways, Harold and I."

"Then you would have no reason to worry if he didn't return at the end of the evening?"

"We live in different wings, Mr. Rutledge. By mutual agreement."

"Is there anyone on the staff who saw to his needs while he was here in Somerset? Someone who might have noticed that he was out later than usual?"

For an instant he thought Mrs. Quarles had misinterpreted his question. Then she answered, "He doesn't have a valet. My husband wasn't brought up with staff to look after him. He preferred not to be troubled now."

Rutledge turned to the man in the wheeled chair. She hadn't introduced him, by choice.

The man said with something of a smile, "I'm Mrs. Quarles's cousin. The name is Charles Archer. I live here."

"Can you shed any light on Mr. Quarles's movements during the evening? Or did you hear something that worried you? A dog barking, the sound of raised voices, lights near the drive?"

"My rooms overlook the main gardens. I wouldn't be likely to hear anything from the direction of the drive."

Mrs. Quarles added, "If he was killed near the road, anyone could have seen him walking there and attacked him."

"We don't know yet where your husband was killed. Did he have enemies, that you know of?" Padgett asked.

Mrs. Quarles's laughter rang out, silvery and amused. "Why ask me?" she demanded. "You yourself never liked him—nor he you, for that matter. And you must know that half the families in Cambury had fallen out with him in one fashion or the other. Stephenson, Jones, Brunswick—the list goes on."

Rutledge said, "Are you saying that these people felt strongly enough about your husband that they might have killed him?"

Mrs. Quarles shrugged expressively. "Walk down a street and point to any door, and you're likely to find someone who detested Harold Quarles. As for taking that to the point of murder, you must ask them."

"Why should they dislike him so intensely?"

"Because he's—he was—ruthless. He gave no thought to the feelings of others. He was very good at pretending he cared, when it suited his purpose, but the fact is—was—that he used people for his own ends. When people discovered his true nature, they were often furious at being taken in. By then it was too late, he'd got what he wanted and moved on. The wreckage left in his wake was nothing to him. When he couldn't simply walk away, he paid his way out of trouble. Most people have a price, you know, and he was very clever at finding it."

"Then why are you so surprised that he was murdered?"

"I suppose I never expected anyone to act on their feelings. Not here—this is Somerset, people don't kill each other here!"

Padgett, seeing his opportunity, said, "And you, Mrs. Quarles—do you number yourself among his enemies?"

She smiled at him, amused. "I have—had—a very satisfactory arrangement with my husband," she said. "Why should I spoil it by killing him? It wouldn't be worth hanging for. Though, mind you, there were times when he exasperated me enough that I might have shot him if I'd held a weapon in my hand. But that was the aggravation of the moment. He could be *very* aggravating. You should know that as well as I. All the same, I had nothing to gain by killing him."

"Your freedom, perhaps?" Rutledge asked. "Or a large inheritance?"

She regarded him with distaste. "Mr. Rutledge. I already have my freedom. And money of my own as well. My husband's death is an inconvenience, if you want the truth. I've been patient enough. If you wish to question my staff, Downing, the housekeeper, will see to it. Otherwise, I must bid you good day."

Padgett said, in a final attempt to irritate her, "Dr. O'Neil and the rector will confer with you about the services, when the body is released for burial."

"Thank you."

At the door, Rutledge paused. "I understand you have dogs, Mrs. Quarles."

"Yes, two small spaniels."

"Were they with you during the night?"

She glanced at Archer, almost reflexively, then looked at Rutledge. "They were with me. They always are."

But they were not here now . . .

"Are there other dogs on the estate?"

"I believe Tom Masters has several. They aren't allowed as far as the house or gardens."

Hamish was clamoring for Rutledge's attention, pointing out that Mrs. Quarles had not asked either policeman how her husband had died. She had shown almost no interest in the details—except to assume in the beginning that it was an accidental death.

And Padgett, as if he'd overheard Hamish, though it was more likely that he was goaded by a need Rutledge didn't know him well enough to grasp, said with venom, "Perhaps it would be best if we tell you, before you hear the gossip, Mrs. Quarles. We found your husband beaten to death, hanging in the tithe barn in the straps meant for the Christmas angel."

Charles Archer winced. Rutledge took a step forward in protest. He had not wanted to make such details public knowledge at this stage.

But Mrs. Quarles said only, "I never liked that contrivance. I told Harold from the start that no good would come of it."

A flush rose in Padgett's face, and he opened his mouth to say more, but Rutledge forestalled him.

"Thank you for seeing us, Mrs. Quarles. Padgett—" There was stern command in Rutledge's voice as he ushered the man through the door.

But before he could shut it, Charles Archer asked, "Is there anything we should do—?"

From the passage, Padgett interjected, "You must ask Dr. O'Neil about that, sir."

Rutledge felt like kicking him in the shins to silence him. But Padgett had had his say and let the man from London shut the door.

The housekeeper was waiting, and Rutledge wondered if she had been listening at the keyhole. Padgett said to her, "What is said here is not for gossip. Do you understand?"

"Indeed."

"We'll be back in the afternoon to speak to the staff. I don't want them talking amongst themselves before that."

Rutledge said, "Do you have keys to Mr. Quarles's rooms? I want you to lock them now, in our presence, and give the keys to me."

She was about to argue, then thought better of it. The two policemen followed her up the stairs and toward the wing that Quarles used on his visits to Hallowfields. Mrs. Downing made certain that each passage door was locked, and then without a word handed the keys to those rooms to Rutledge.

"These are the only ones?"

"Yes. I don't think Mr. Quarles wished to have just anyone going through his possessions." It was a barb intended for Padgett, but he ignored it.

"Who cleans his rooms?"

"That would be Betty, Inspector. But she has no keys. She asks me for them if Mr. Quarles isn't here. When he's at home, the rooms aren't locked."

"Are there any other rooms in the house that Mr. Quarles used on a regular basis?" Rutledge asked.

"Only the gun room, sir. He had his study moved up here some years ago, in the suite next to his bedroom, and put through a connecting door. For privacy. He said."

They thanked Mrs. Downing and went down the stairs. She followed, to see them out, as if expecting them to lurk in the shadows and steal the best silver when no one was looking. They could hear the click of the latch as she locked the door behind them.

8

Rutledge turned to Inspector Padgett as they crossed the drive to the motorcar. The anger he'd suppressed during the interview with Mrs. Quarles had roused Hamish, and his voice was loud in Rutledge's ears.

"What the hell were you thinking about? You were rude to the victim's widow, and you made no effort to conceal your own feelings."

"I told you. I hate them all. I wanted to see her show some emotion. Something to tell me that she cared about the man. Something that made her human."

"Next time we call on witnesses, you'll leave your own feelings at the door. Is that understood?"

Padgett said fiercely, "This is *my* turf. My investigation. I'll run it as I see fit."

"Not while the Yard is involved. Another outbreak like that, and I'll have the Chief Constable remove you from the case."

"No, you won't—"

"Try me." Rutledge walked down to the motorcar and turned the crank. He could hear Hamish faulting him for losing his own temper but shut out the words. Padgett had behaved unprofessionally, intending to hurt, and that kind of emotion would cloud his judgment as he dealt with the evidence in this case.

For an instant Rutledge thought Padgett would turn on his heel and walk to the tithe barn. Instead, sulking, he got into the motorcar without a word.

As they drove toward the gates, Rutledge changed the subject. "Who is Charles Archer? Besides Mrs. Quarles's cousin?"

"Gossip is, he's her lover. I've heard he was wounded at Mons. Shouldn't have been there at his age, but when the war began, he was researching a book he intended to write on Wellington and Waterloo. The Hun was in Belgium before anyone knew what was happening, and Archer fled south, into the arms of the British. He stayed—experience in battle and all that, for his book. Well, he got more than he bargained for, didn't he?"

"And he lives at the house?"

"Not the normal family arrangement, is it? But then rumor has it that there's not a pretty face within ten miles that Quarles hasn't tried to seduce. Sauce for the gander is sauce for the goose, I'd say."

"Any official complaints about his behavior?"

"Not as such."

"Mrs. Quarles mentioned a son. Are there any other children?"

"Just the one boy. He's at Rugby."

They reached the gates and turned into the lane that led to the tithe barn.

Harold Quarles's body had been taken away, and the barn had been searched again for any evidence or signs of blood, without success.

"Nothing to report, sir," the constable told Padgett, gesturing to the shadowy corners. "We've gone over the ground carefully, twice. And nothing's turned up."

Rutledge, with a final look around the dimly lit, cavernous building, found himself thinking that something must have been left behind by the killer, some small trace of his passage. No crime was perfect. If only the police knew where to look. Surely there must be something, some small thing that was easily overlooked . . .

Another problem. "Where did he dine?" he mused aloud. "And how did he get there?"

"We've only Mrs. Quarles's word that he went out to dine," Padgett pointed out. "It could be a lie from start to finish."

"I hardly think she would kill her husband in the house," Rutledge said to Padgett after dismissing the constable. "And he's not dressed for a walk on the estate. Let's have a look at that gatekeeper's cottage. I recall you told me no one lived there, but that's not to say it hasn't been used." He glanced around the tithe barn. "There's something about this place— it's not a likely choice for a meeting, somehow. If I'd been Quarles, I'd have been wary about that. But the gatehouse is another matter. Private but safe, in a way. Is it unlocked, do you think?"

"Let's find out."

Picking up a lantern, Padgett followed Rutledge out the barn's door. They walked in silence through the trees to the small cottage by the Home Farm gate.

There was a single door, and when they lifted the latch, they found it opened easily.

Rutledge took the lantern and held it high. There were only three rooms on the ground floor: a parlor cum dining room, a tiny kitchen, a bathroom hardly big enough to turn around in. Stairs to the upper floor were set into the thickness of one wall. There were two bedrooms, the smaller one possibly intended for a child, though someone had converted it into a workroom.

"When Jesse Morton lived here, he made gloves. He'd been a head gardener until rheumatism attacked his knees. That was before Quarles bought Hallowfields."

"Gloves?" Rutledge turned to look at Padgett.

"It's a cottage industry in many parts of the county, and especially here in Cambury. Hides are brought in from Hampshire and distributed to households on the list. Mr. Greer owns the firm here, and there are still a good many people who earn their living sewing gloves. My grandmother, for one. She raised three fatherless children, sewing for the Greers, father and son."

The furnishings—well-polished denizens from an attic, judging by their age and quality—weren't dusty, Rutledge noted, running his fingers over a chair back and along a windowsill. And the bedclothes smelled of lavender, sweet and fresh. Yet when he opened the armoire, there were no clothes hanging there, and nothing in the drawers of the tall chest except for a comb and brush and a single cuff link.

"Did you come here when the man Morton lived here? Has it changed?" he asked Padgett.

"Once, with my grandmother. I remember it as dark, reeking of cigar smoke, and there was a horsehair settee that made me break out in a rash. So I was never brought back."

"And you're sure that no one has lived here since then?"

"As sure as may be. What's this, then? A place of rendezvous?"

"It's been made to appear comfortable," Rutledge mused. "To give an air of—"

"—respectability," Hamish supplied, so clearly that the word seemed to echo around the solid walls.

But Hamish was right. There were lace curtains at the windows, chintz coverings on the chairs, and cabbage roses embroidered on the pillowcases. If Quarles had an eye for women, he could bring his conquests here rather than to an hotel or other public place. Or the house . . .

"—respectability," Rutledge finished. "Let's have a look at the kitchen."

It yielded tea and sugar and a packet of biscuits that hadn't been opened, along with cups and saucers and a teapot ready for filling from the kettle on the cooker.

"Who washes the sheets and sweeps the floor clean?" Padgett asked, looking round. "You can't tell me Mr. High and Mighty Quarles does that. Not for any woman."

"An interesting point," Rutledge answered. "We'll ask Betty, the maid who does his rooms at the house."

Both men could see at a glance that this was most certainly not the place where Quarles was killed. No signs of a struggle, no indication on the polished floor that someone had tried to wipe up bloodstains or dragged a body across it.

Rutledge said, "All right, if they met here, Quarles and his killer, then the confrontation was outside. Somewhere between this cottage and the tithe barn."

Padgett said nothing, following Rutledge out and closing the door behind them.

The sun was up, light striking through the trees in golden shafts, and the side of the cottage was bright, casting heavier shadows across the front steps. The roses running up the wall were dew-wet, today's blooms just unfurling.

A path of stepping-stones set into the mossy ground led to the shaded garden in the rear of the cottage. Flower beds surrounded a patch of lawn where a bench and a small iron table stood. Setting the grassy area off from the beds was a circle of whitewashed river stones, all nearly the same size, perhaps a little larger than a man's fist.

In the dark, Rutledge realized, the white stones would stand out in whatever light there was, marking where it was safe to stroll. Otherwise an unwary step might sink into the soft loam of the beds. He moved closer to examine them. None of them appeared to be out of place. Still, he leaned down to touch each stone in turn with the tips of his fingers. One of them, halfway round and half hidden by the bench, moved very slightly, as if not as well seated as its neighbors.

Padgett, watching, said, "You're barking up the wrong tree. There was a heavy mist last night, remember, hardly the weather for chatting under the light of the moon."

"And if Quarles was walking here, for whatever reason—coming home from a dinner party—it was a perfect site for an ambush."

"He'd have walked down the main drive."

"Who knows? He might have intended to go to the Home Farm."

"Far-fetched."

"Early days, that's all. I think we've done all we can here." Rutledge was ready to go on. But Padgett was staring now toward the house, which he couldn't see from here.

"If Charles Archer could walk, I'd wager it was him. *She* may have been content with the status quo, but if the man has any pride—well, it takes nerve to cuckold a man in his own house."

Padgett turned to walk back through the wood, and Rutledge, getting to his feet, heard Hamish say, "He's no' verra eager to help."

They went back to the tithe barn, where Rutledge's motorcar was standing. Padgett nodded to the constable guarding the tithe barn's door as Rutledge turned the crank.

They drove in silence, each man busy with his thoughts. As they reached Cambury, the High Street was empty, and many of the houses were still shuttered. Bells hadn't rung for the first service, and the doors of the church beyond the distant churchyard were closed.

Sunday morning. A long day stretched ahead of them.

Padgett was rubbing his face. "I'm dog tired, and you must be knackered. We'll sleep for a few hours then go back to Hallowfields. It's bound to be someone there. Stands to reason. They knew his movements."

Rutledge said nothing.

Padgett went on. "I sent Constable Daniels to bespeak a room for you at The Unicorn after he telephoned the Yard. It's just across the street there." They had reached the police station. As Rutledge stopped the motorcar in front, Padgett added, "Come in. We'll make a list of names, persons to consider. It won't take long."

With reluctance Rutledge followed him inside.

Padgett's office was tidy, folders on the shelves behind his desk and a typewriter on a table to one side.

Indicating the machine as he sat down and offered the only other chair to Rutledge, he said, "I've learned to use the damned thing. There's no money for a typist, but I find that most people can't read my handwriting. It's the only answer." He seemed to be in no hurry to make his list. Collecting several papers from his blotter, he shoved them into a folder and then turned back to Rutledge.

"Perhaps I should tell you a little about Cambury. It's a peaceful town, as a rule. We've had only two murders since the war. Market day is Wednesday, and there's always a farmer who has had a little too much to drink at The Glover's Arms. The younger men prefer The Black Pudding. They grew up wild, some of them, with no fathers to keep them in line. An idle lot, living off their mothers' pensions. But where's the work to keep them honest? A good many workmen congregate there too. It can be a volatile mix."

In an effort to bring Padgett back to the task at hand, Rutledge said, "Do you think either of these two murders has a bearing on Quarles's death?"

"On—? No, of course not. A young soldier killed his wife. We never got to the bottom of that, because he came here straightaway and confessed. Seems he was wild with jealousy over someone she'd been seeing while he was in France. Why he didn't kill the other man, God knows. And truth be told, I don't think he intended to kill *her*, but he knocked her down with his fist, and she struck her head on one of the firedogs. The other murder was family related as well—two brothers angry over the fact that the third brother inherited everything when the mother died. They shouldn't have been surprised. They'd walked out and left the boy to care for both parents while they were making their way in London. They didn't come home for the father's funeral and probably wouldn't have come for the mother's if there hadn't been property involved. There was a quarrel the night after her funeral, and it ended in the murder of the youngest. They claimed they'd already returned to London that morning, but there were witnesses to say otherwise."

"Who was left to inherit?"

"A cousin from Ireland. She's living in the house now, as a matter of fact. Her coming here set the cat amongst the pigeons, I can tell you. O'Hara is her name. Harold Quarles was taken with her. She told him what she thought of him, in the middle of the High Street." He grinned at the memory.

Rutledge was accustomed to dealing with the various temperaments of the local policemen he was sent to work with. Some were single-minded, others were suspicious of his motives as an outsider or protective of their patch. A few were hostile, and others were grateful for another set of eyes, though wary at the same time. Padgett seemed to feel no urgency about finding Quarles's murderer, and Rutledge wondered if he had already guessed who it might be and was busy throwing dust in the eyes of the man from London. And the next question was, why?

Hamish said, "Ye ken, he's dragging his feet after yon dressing down."

Rutledge had already forgotten that, but it wouldn't be surprising if Padgett was still smarting. There was arrogance behind the man's affability.

He asked, before Padgett could digress again, "Who might have had a reason to kill Quarles?" He took out his notebook to indicate that he was prepared to write down names.

"Consider half the population," Padgett replied with a broad gesture. "Mrs. Quarles said as much herself. I told you. I'm only one of many who will rejoice that he's dead."

"Hardly the proper attitude for a policeman?" Rutledge asked lightly.

"I'm honest. Take me or leave me."

"Quite." Rutledge added, "Did Quarles spend much time here in Cambury? Or was he most often in London?"

"He came down once a month or so. It depended on how busy he was in the City. Last year he came and stayed for nearly three months. That must have been an unpleasant surprise for the missus. She packed up and left for Essex, where Archer's sister lives."

"Speaking of Charles Archer, is it certain that he can't walk?" It was a possibility that shouldn't be overlooked.

"You must ask the doctor."

Rutledge wrote down O'Neil's name at the top of the page. "Let's begin with the household. What do you know about them? "

"Some of them come into Cambury on their day off. Generally they keep themselves to themselves. I daresay that's what's expected of them by the family. There's no butler, just the housekeeper, because they seldom entertain. If you're looking at the household, I'd put Mrs. Quarles at the top of that list."

"What about the townspeople?" When Padgett hesitated, Rutledge added, "The butcher, the baker, the candlestick maker. The rector. The doctor. The greengrocer."

"Quarles didn't get on with the rector. Rumor says he thought Heller was old-fashioned, out of step with the twentieth century. The living belongs to Hallowfields, and Quarles could replace him at will and bring in someone younger or more to his taste. The doctor he treated like a tradesman. The tradesmen he treated with outright contempt. Mr. Greer, owner of the glove firm, crossed swords with Quarles a time or two. According to Quarles, he was pushing up the cost of labor in Cambury, making it difficult for the local gentry to keep staff. The glove makers work at home, you see. It's not a bad thing for a woman with children or a man who can't do physical labor."

Rutledge had stopped taking notes. "The field is wide open, then. Still, it's hard to believe that this sort of bickering led to murder."

"There's Jones, the Welsh baker, if you want more than bickering. His daughter's head was turned by Quarles, and Jones had to send her away to his family in Cardiff. And Mrs. Newell was cook at Hallowfields until Quarles sacked her. Now, there's a woman who could have hauled Quarles into the rafters without any help. Arms like young oaks. Although in my view, she'd prefer a cleaver to a stone, for the murder weapon."

"Mrs. Quarles also mentioned the name Stephenson."

"Stephenson is a collector of rare books. He moved here from Oxford, when his health broke. He was born in Cambury. I never heard what lay between them. Money is my guess. He opened a small bookstore down the street, where his mother had had her millinery shop, and called it Nemesis."

Hamish said, "Ye ken, he didna' bring up the name himsel'."

Which was surprising. Would Padgett have mentioned Stephenson at all?

Still, Rutledge was beginning to form a mental picture of Harold Quarles. It appeared that he hadn't made an effort to fit into his surroundings. His own wife disliked him, come to that. Was he a contrary Londoner who irritated everyone he came in contact with, or did he feel that Somerset was too provincial to warrant courtesy? Yet Constable Daniels had claimed that Quarles wanted to be squire.

It could also be a sign of rough beginnings, this ability to rub everyone raw.

"What is Quarles's background? Did he come from money?"

"Lord, no. He worked his way up from scratch. His father went down the Yorkshire mines, but the boy was given a decent education through some charity or other, and rose quickly in the financial world. He'd tell you that himself, proud of his roots and making no bones about his beginnings. From what I gather, it was his honesty on that score that made him popular in London business circles. A diamond in the rough, as they say. If he hadn't managed that, they'd have turned their back on him. You know the nobs, they sometimes like brutal honesty. Makes them feel superior."

"But he must have also had the ability to make money for his clients, or they wouldn't have kept him very long. Rough diamond or not."

"I expect that's true." Padgett stood up with an air of duty done. "I'm asleep on my feet. I'm going home. You'll want at least an hour or two of sleep yourself."

Rutledge put away his notebook. "I'll be back here by twelve o'clock."

"Make that one."

They walked out together, and Padgett turned the other way, with a wave of the hand.

9

Rutledge could see The Unicorn from where he stood. It was a small hotel graced by a pedimented door and narrow balconies at the windows of the floors above. A drive led to the yard behind. He turned in there and went through the quiet side passage that opened into Reception.

At the large mahogany desk set in one corner, a young man was busy with a sheaf of papers, tallying the figures in the last columns. He put his work aside as he heard Rutledge's footsteps approaching and greeted him with a smile.

"Are you the guest Constable Daniels told us to expect?"

"I am."

The clerk turned the book around for his signature. "We're pleased to have you here, Inspector. The constable mentioned that there'd been a spot of trouble up at Hallowfields."

"Yes," Rutledge answered, signing his name and pocketing the key. The clerk was on the point of asking more questions, but Rutledge cut him short with a pleasant thank-you and turned away, picking up his valise as he crossed to the stairway.

The hotel had probably been a family home at some time, possibly a town house or a dowager house. The curving stairs to one side of Reception were elegant, with beautifully carved balustrades. Giving radiant light from above was an oval skylight set with a stained glass medallion of a unicorn, his head in the lap of a young woman in a blue gown, her long fair hair falling down her back in cascading tendrils. As romantic as any pre-Raphaelite painting, it must have given the house and subsequently the hotel its name.

His room was down the passage on the first floor and overlooked the High Street. Long windows opened into a pair of those narrow balconies Rutledge had noticed from the police station, the sun already warm on the railings. He was pleased to see that he'd been given such large accommodations, with those two double windows, their starched white curtains ruffled by the early morning breeze. He needn't fight claustrophobia as well as Padgett.

Hamish said, "Given to the puir policeman no doot to curry favor with them at Hallowfields?"

"Absolutely," Rutledge returned with a smile. "Which suggests the hotel is where he came to dine last night."

Hamish chuckled. "Aye, ye'll be sharing the scullery maid's quarters when the word is out he's deid and ye're no' likely to drop a good word in his ear about The Unicorn."

It was true—policemen on the premises more often than not were kept out of sight as far as possible, to prevent disturbing hotel guests. Which signified that word of the murder had not preceded Rutledge to the hotel, only the news that Quarles had business with him.

He sighed as he considered the comfortable bed, then set his valise inside the armoire and went down to ask about breakfast.

The dining room was nearly empty.

There was an elderly couple in a corner eating in silence, as if missing their morning newspapers here in the wilds of Somerset. There was a distinct air of having said all that needed to be said to each other over the years and a determination not to be the first to break into speech, even to ask for the salt.

And a balding man of perhaps forty-five sat alone by the window, his head in a book.

Rutledge ate his meal and then asked to speak to The Unicorn's manager. The elderly woman waiting tables inquired bluntly, "Was there anything wrong with your breakfast? If so, you'd do better speaking to the cook than to Mr. Hunter."

"It's to do with last evening."

She raised her brows at that, and without another word disappeared through the door into the lounge.

It was twenty minutes before the manager arrived, freshly shaven and dressed for morning services.

Rutledge introduced himself, and said, "It's a confidential matter."

"About one of our guests?" Hunter was a quiet man with weak eyes, peering at Rutledge as if he couldn't see him clearly. There were scars around them, and Rutledge guessed he'd been gassed in the war. "I hope there's nothing amiss."

"Do you keep a list of those who dine here each evening?"

Hunter said, "Not as such. We have a list of those we're expecting, and which table they prefer. And of course a copy of the accounts paid by each party. The cook keeps a record of orders."

"Were you here last evening?"

"Yes, I was. Saturday evenings are generally busy."
He glanced at the elderly couple. "Er—perhaps we
should continue this conversation in my office."

Rutledge followed him there. Hunter kept his
quarters Spartan. There were accounts on a cabinet
beside his desk, ledgers on the shelves behind it, and
a half dozen letters on his blotter. Nothing personal
decorated the desk's top, the cabinet, or the shelves.
The only incongruous piece was the glass figure of
a donkey, about three inches high, standing on the
square table by the door.

Hunter sat down and reached for a large magnifying
glass that he kept in his drawer. With it poised in one
hand, he asked, "Who is it you are enquiring about?"

"Harold Quarles."

Hunter put down the glass. "Ah. I can tell you he
didn't dine with us last evening." He frowned. "Were
you told otherwise?"

"We aren't sure where he took his dinner. The hotel
was the most logical place to begin. "

"Yes, certainly. Er, perhaps his wife or staff might
be more useful than I?"

"They have no idea where he went when he left the
house. Except to dine somewhere close by."

"And you haven't seen Mr. Quarles to ask him?"

"He's not at home at present."

Rutledge got a straight look. "What exactly is it you're asking me, Mr. Rutledge?"

Rutledge smiled. "It's no matter. If he wasn't here, he wasn't here." He rose. "Thank you for your time, Mr. Hunter."

"I saw Mr. Quarles last evening. But not here. Not at the hotel."

Rutledge stopped. "At what time?"

"It was close on to ten-thirty. Most of our dinner guests had left, and I stepped outside to take a breath of fresh air. I was looking up the High Street—in the opposite direction from Hallowfields, you see—and I heard raised voices. That's not usual in Cambury, but it *was* a Saturday night, and sometimes the men who frequent The Black Pudding go home in rowdy spirits. I stood there for a moment, in the event there was trouble, but nothing happened. No one else spoke, there was nothing more to disturb the night. As I was about to go inside, I heard footsteps coming briskly from Minton Street, and I saw Harold Quarles turning the corner into the High."

"Minton Street?"

"It's just past us, where you see the stationer's on the corner."

"Where does Minton Street lead?"

"There are mostly houses in that direction."

"No other place to dine, except in a private home?"

"That's right."

"And Mr. Quarles continued to walk past the hotel, as far as you know?"

Hunter said, "I had shut the door before he reached the hotel. I'm not on good terms with the man."

"Indeed?"

"He was drunk and disorderly in the dining room last spring. There was a scene, and I had to ask him to leave. It was embarrassing to me and to the hotel—and should have been to him as well. I haven't spoken to him since."

Padgett had said nothing about Hunter's encounter. He hadn't named the manager at all.

"Yes, I see that it would be uncomfortable. And so you have no way of knowing where Quarles went from Minton Street?"

"None." It was firmly spoken, his eyes holding Rutledge's.

"And he was alone? On foot?"

"Yes, on both counts."

"Do you know if there's anyone on Minton Street who might count Mr. Quarles among their acquaintance?"

"I would have no idea."

Rutledge thanked him and left Hunter sitting in his office, staring at the door.

At least, he thought, it put Quarles alone and on foot in town around half past ten. With perhaps another twenty or at most thirty minutes for his journey homeward. If that was where he was intending to go. Too bad Hunter hadn't seen which direction Quarles had taken.

Rutledge walked out of the hotel to the corner of Minton Street. Looking down it, he could see that the nearer houses were large and well kept, the sort of home that Quarles might have visited. It would be necessary to speak to each household, then, to find out. Or Padgett's men might be able to narrow that down.

There was a lane at the foot of Minton Street running parallel to the High Street, where cottages backed up to the fields beyond, a line of low hills in the distance. It wasn't likely that Quarles had dined in one of the cottages. Or was it? Had he chosen to walk into Cambury, to keep his destination private? Or was he to meet his chauffeur or retrieve the motorcar somewhere else?

Hamish said, "If it was the home of a woman?"

That too was possible.

Rutledge continued walking up the High Street, looking in the windows of closed shops as he passed. There were other small streets crossing the High—

Church Street and Button Row, James Street and Sedge Lane.

Beyond Sedge Lane stood the workaday world of the smithy-turned-garage and other untidy businesses that clung to the outskirts of a village struggling to become a small town, supplying the inhabitants whilst keeping themselves out of sight. Just beyond these, where the main road became Cambury's main street, was the cluster of cottages Rutledge had noted in the dark last night.

He turned back the way he'd come, crossing the High Street where a large pub, whitewashed and thatched, stood at the next corner, offering tables in the front garden under small flowering trees. The overhead sign showed a large kettle with steam rising from it, made of wrought iron in a black iron frame. The Black Pudding. It had the air of an old coaching inn and was one of the few buildings in Cambury that wasn't directly on the road, only a narrow pavement for pedestrians separating most of the house walls from the street.

He carried on to The Unicorn and went up to his room. This time he didn't resist the temptation of his bed, and stretched out as he was, his mind restless, Hamish lurking on the threshold of wakefulness until the ringing of the church bells roused him.

When services had ended, Rutledge retraced his steps to Church Street. Cambury had sprung into life while he slept, people stopping to speak to friends or herding their children toward home. St. Martin's was set in a broad walled churchyard that abutted a house of the same stone as the church. The rectory, then. A sign board gave the rector's name as Samuel Heller. The stonework of the church facade was old but well maintained, and the tall, ornate tower rose into a blue, cloudless sky. Last night's mist might never have been. Crossing the grassy churchyard, Rutledge saw the gate set into the wall and went through, into the front garden of the rectory.

He could hear birds singing in the trees scattered among the weathered gravestones, and a magpie perched on a shrouded marble cross watched him with a black and unreadable eye. Where there was shade the grass was still wet under his feet. On a gentle breeze came the sound of a cow lowing in a field beyond the houses.

The rector was at his breakfast and came to answer Rutledge's knock with his serviette still tucked under his chin. He seemed surprised to find a stranger on his doorstep, but smiled warmly and invited Rutledge to step into the narrow hall. Holding out his hand, he said, "I don't believe you're one of my flock. I'm Samuel Heller, rector of St. Martin's. How may I help you?"

"The name is Rutledge," he said, taking the rector's hand. The man's grip was firm and warm. "I'm from London, from Scotland Yard, and I need a few minutes of your time to speak to you about one of your parishioners."

"Oh, dear. That sounds rather serious. I was just finishing my toast," he said, taking out the serviette and wiping his lips. "Could I interest you in a cup of tea? The kitchen is a pleasant room, and my housekeeper doesn't come in on a Sunday, to chase us out of it."

Rutledge followed him back to the kitchen, and it was indeed a pleasant room, giving onto a garden, a small orchard behind it, and several outbuildings that by the look of them, their wood a pale silver, had served the rectory for centuries. The kitchen door stood open to the yard, letting in the warmth and sunlight and a handful of flies.

"I don't usually entertain in the kitchen," the rector went on in apology. "But the vestry meeting is in a quarter of an hour, and I am running a little late today."

He did look tired. Gesturing to a chair across the table from where he had been sitting, he brought Rutledge a fresh cup, then pushed the teapot over the polished wood toward him. Rutledge helped himself. It was strong tea, black and bitter, as if it had steeped too long.

"Now then, you were saying . . . ?"

It was hard to judge Heller—he was nearing middle age and thin, with an open face and calm gray eyes. Yet Padgett had included him in the list of Quarles's enemies.

"I believe Mr. Quarles at Hallowfields is one of your flock?"

There was a brief hesitation in the knife buttering Heller's toast, but his face showed nothing. "I include him in my flock, yes."

Which, as Hamish was pointing out, was not precisely a response to what Rutledge had asked him.

"How well do you know him?"

Heller put down his knife and looked at Rutledge. "Has he done something wrong, something that has drawn the attention of the police?"

He had answered a question with a question, almost as if he expected to learn that Quarles was on the point of being taken into custody and was reluctant to add to his troubles.

"*Do* you know him, Mr. Heller?" Rutledge asked bluntly.

"Sadly, not as well as I should like. I fear he's not what could charitably be called a member in good standing at St. Martin's. I expect I could count on one hand the number of times he's attended a service. Or that I have been invited to dine at Hallowfields." Heller smiled disarmingly. "But I'm stubborn to the bone, and I refuse to concede defeat. We asked Mr. Quarles to serve on the vestry, but he replied that it was not in anyone's best interest. I interpreted that to mean he's not often in Cambury and had no real knowledge of our problems here. But to give him his due, he takes a personal interest in Cambury, if not the church."

"In what way?"

"I think Mr. Quarles looks upon himself as squire, much to the—er—dismay of people in some quarters. We aren't strictly agricultural, you see, we've had cottage industries here for many years. Weaving, glove making. Even lace at one time. It changes one's perspective about such things. And there's the other side of the coin. What does a Londoner know about farming?"

The rector was nearly as good at skirting issues as Padgett. But he had confirmed Constable Daniels's remarks.

When Rutledge didn't comment, Heller said, "Now perhaps you'll be good enough to tell me why you are here. What is your visit in aid of? Why questions about Mr. Quarles on a bright Sunday morning?"

"I'm afraid that Harold Quarles was murdered last night."

"My dear Lord!" Shock wiped all expression from the rector's face. "I—we—don't often see murder. Surely it wasn't here—among us? That's why you're from the Yard, isn't it? The poor man died in London."

"I'm afraid someone met him near the Home Farm, and killed him there."

Heller sat back in his chair, staring at Rutledge.

"I must go to Mrs. Quarles at once," he said finally. "My meeting will have to wait." He frowned. "Near the Home Farm, you say? That's dreadful! It wasn't someone here, was it? I mean, it stands to reason that someone from London—" As soon as the words were out of his mouth, he glanced at Rutledge in consternation, as if he would recall them if he could.

"Why?"

"Why?" Heller blinked. "If he conducts himself in the City the same way he conducts himself here, it wouldn't be surprising. And I'm sure some of his business dealings are not always as successful as he might wish. I've heard of at least one where there was great disappointment in the outcome. Not the fault of Harold Quarles, I'm sure, investments can be volatile, but when someone has lost his savings, he tends to blame the messenger, as it were."

"Have people here in Cambury lost money through Mr. Quarles? For instance, Mr. Stephenson?"

"You will have to ask them, Inspector. I don't feel it's my place to say more about a man who is dead."

"If anything you know has a bearing on his murder, then you have an obligation to help the police get at the truth."

"Yes." The word was drawn out. Heller removed his serviette a second time, automatically folding it and setting it neatly by his plate. "You must forgive me, Mr. Rutledge. I shall have to speak briefly to my vestry and then go to Hallowfields. Thank you for bringing me the news personally." He stood up, and Rutledge followed suit.

"I would prefer it if you told no one else about Mr. Quarles for the moment."

"But—"

"We have many people to interview, and it would be best if we could see their reactions to the news for ourselves. But you may call on Mrs. Quarles, if she needs consolation."

"This is highly irregular—"

"Murder often is, Rector."

They walked together from the kitchen to the door. Rutledge said, "Whoever killed Harold Quarles, he or she may come to you for comfort of a sort. In a roundabout way, perhaps, but you'll sense when something is wrong. Be careful, then, will you? It's likely that this person could kill again." He saw once more the winged body in the shadows of the tithe barn's roof. Murder hadn't satisfied the killer—whoever it was had needed to wreak his anger on the dead as well. But in the cold light of day, as powerful emotions drained away, there could be a need to justify them, to feel that what had been done was deserved.

"I would hate to think that anyone I knew might be capable of murder." The rector had looked away, evading Rutledge's eyes.

"Let us hope it was not one of your flock. But the fact remains that someone was capable of it. Or Quarles would still be alive, and you'd be finishing your breakfast in peace."

Heller stopped at the door. "I don't believe in judging, Inspector. So that I myself need not fear judging."

With that remark, the rector swung the door shut.

Hamish said, "A verra' fine sentiment. But no' the whole truth."

Rutledge was halfway down the rectory path when he saw a man crossing the churchyard toward the north door, carrying a sheaf of papers under his arm. The man looked up, and for a moment their eyes met. Then he turned away and stepped inside the church. But there was something in that glance—

even at the distance between the two men—that held more than curiosity about a stranger. It had lasted long enough to be personal, as if weighing up an adversary.

Rutledge changed course as he went through the gate that separated the churchyard from the rectory. As he reached the porch and opened the door, he could hear music pouring from the church organ, the opening notes of Bach's Toccata and Fugue in D Minor. It was triumphant and sure, the instrument responding to the touch of trained hands. The great pipes sent their echoes through the sanctuary, filling it with sound, and the acoustics were perfect for such an emotional piece.

Hamish said, "His thoughts may ha' been elsewhere. He came to practice."

"I'd swear he knows why I'm here in Cambury. Not many people do. Yet."

"Ye ken, he must ha' seen you with yon inspector. And he's feeling guilty for anither reason."

Rutledge considered that for a moment, half of his mind on the music as it seemed to wrap around him there in the doorway. He hadn't mistaken that brief challenge. And he was certain the man knew Rutledge had taken it up and come as far as the church door.

Indeed, as he turned to go, he could feel the organist watching him in the small mirror set above the keys.

Let him wonder why the encounter had ended here. Or worry.

Outside, Rutledge stopped by the church board to see the name of the player. It was the third line down. One Michael Brunswick, and Mrs. Quarles had mentioned his name only four hours earlier.

10

It was past one o'clock when Rutledge walked into the police station. Padgett was on the point of leaving, and he frowned as Rutledge met him in the passage.

"I thought you might be sleeping still. I can tell you, I'd have stayed in my own bed if I'd been given the choice."

Rutledge said, "I went to speak to the rector."

Padgett's tone had an edge. "And was he any help in our inquiries?"

"Did you expect him to help?"

There was a twitch in Padgett's jaw. "Where's your motorcar? Still at The Unicorn? Constable Jenkins hasn't returned with mine."

As Padgett followed Rutledge across the High Street, he went on. "I've had time to think. I was all for blaming Mrs. Quarles. But I was wrong. This killing is most likely connected with London in some fashion. That's where Quarles lived and did business. We're wasting our time at Hallowfields."

"If that's true, why wasn't he killed in London?"

"Too obvious. There, the first people the police will want to speak to are his clients and business associates. You know the drill. But kill him in Somerset, and the police are going to look at his neighbors here, never thinking about London."

Rutledge smiled. "Which is precisely what someone here in Cambury may have been counting on—that we will hare off to London. Someone at Hallowfields may point us in the right direction."

Padgett had no answer to that.

Hamish said, "He wants you away to London. Ye ken, he'd like naething better than to find the killer himsel'."

But as the other inspector climbed into the motorcar, Rutledge found himself thinking that Padgett had other reasons to want to see the back of Scotland Yard.

They drove in uneasy silence back to Hallowfields.

Mrs. Downing summoned the indoor staff to her sitting room off the passage across from the kitchen, and they stood in front of the policemen in a ragged row, clearly uneasy. Rutledge counted them. The cook, her scullery maid, three upstairs maids and a footman, the boot boy, and the chauffeur.

All of them denied any knowledge of where Mr. Quarles had gone last evening. He had not called for the motorcar, nor had he taken it out himself. Aside from the message to the kitchen that he wouldn't be dining at home, no one had seen him after five o'clock.

Mrs. Blount, the cook, was a thin woman with graying hair. She added, "I was told not to expect Mr. Quarles for dinner, and that was that. It's not for me to question his comings and goings."

"Who gave you that message? Did you speak to Mr. Quarles yourself, or to someone else?"

"I believe it must have been Mrs. Quarles," Downing, the housekeeper, answered after no one else spoke up.

Lily, the youngest of the maids, softly cleared her throat. "I was coming to clear away the tea things when I heard him tell someone in the passage that he was dining out."

"Did you see who it was he was speaking to?"

"No, sir, I didn't."

"It was me he told." The woman standing behind the others spoke up.

"And you are . . ."

"My name is Betty, sir." There was strain in her
face. Rutledge put her age at forty, her pale hair and
pale eyebrows giving her a look of someone drained
of life, enduring all the blows that came her way with
patient acceptance, as if she knew all too well that she
counted for little in the scheme of things. "I look after
Mr. Quarles when he's to home." Her accent wasn't
Somerset. Rutledge thought it might be East Anglian.
A stranger among strangers.

"And no' likely to pry," Hamish put in. "Or gossip
with the ithers."

"No one saw him leave?"

Downing said repressively, "We have our duties,
Inspector, we don't hang about looking out the windows to see what our betters are up to."

"We was that busy in the kitchens," the cook added,
as if excusing the staff. "There was no one in the
front of the house just then. Mrs. Quarles had asked
for a tray to be brought up, and Mr. Archer was taking
his dinner alone in the dining room."

"Did any of you hear anything in the
night? Dogs barking, a motorcar on the drive,
shouting . . ."

They hadn't, shuffling a little as they denied any
knowledge of what had happened.

Betty said, "Please, sir. I've been told Mr. Quarles is dead. Mrs. Quarles called us all together to say so. No one will tell me anything else."

"I'm afraid it's true," Rutledge answered her. "Someone killed him last night."

He could see the horror reflected in every face, and in Betty's eyes, a welling of tears that were quickly repressed.

"I can't give you any more information at present," he added to forestall questions.

"It would help if you could think of anyone who might wish your master harm." Padgett, speaking for the first time, kept his voice level, without emphasis.

"Mrs. Newell," the footman offered, to an accompanying ripple of nervous laughter. "She was cook here before Mrs. Blount. She was always quarrelling with him over the cost of food, and the proper way to prepare it. In the end he sacked her after a mighty row."

Padgett caught Rutledge's eye, *I told you so,* in his expression. *Nothing of substance* . . . A wild-goose chase.

Rutledge thanked the staff and nodded to Mrs. Downing to dismiss them, then as Betty was about to follow the others from the room, he spoke quietly to her and asked her to stay.

Mrs. Downing pursed her lips in annoyance, as if in her view he was wasting his time and the staff's. But she made no move to leave.

"How long have you been with Mr. Quarles?"

Betty hesitated. "He brought me here at the start of the war."

"And you keep his rooms for him?"

"Yes, sir. I do."

"Did you also keep the gatehouse cottage tidy?"

"When it was asked of me. I was to have that cottage when I retire."

"Do you know if he chose to use that cottage himself?"

"It wasn't my business to ask, was it? He paid me well for my silence."

"Will you tell me where he went to dine last evening? Even if he asked you to keep his confidence, the situation is different now. You see, we must trace his movements from the time he left the house until he returned." Rutledge watched her face as he asked the question.

"I don't know. I asked if he wanted me to lay out his evening clothes, and he said he wasn't changing for dinner, he wasn't in the mood."

"Did any of his business associates come to visit at Hallowfields?"

"He seldom had guests," Mrs. Downing answered for her. "He was often invited elsewhere, but if he entertained it was in London. I don't remember the last real dinner I've served. He doesn't even invite Rector to dine."

Something a squire did with regularity. It was interesting that Quarles hadn't cared to exercise this particular duty. Or perhaps he was embarrassed to ask the rector to sit at table with his wife's cousin?

Rutledge thanked Betty and let her go. Then he said to Mrs. Downing, "Do you know Betty's background? Who employed her before she came to Hallowfields?"

"She was hired in London. I didn't interview her myself. She's a hard worker, though she mainly keeps to herself. We've had no trouble with her."

"We'd like to look at Mr. Quarles's rooms now, if you please."

As she led the two policemen through the passage door into the foyer, she said, "I'm not sure his solicitor would approve of this. It doesn't seem right to me that you should go through his things. I can't think why Mrs. Quarles allowed it."

"Is the solicitor a local man?" Rutledge asked.

"He's in London. Mrs. Quarles can give you his direction."

Rutledge handed her the keys. Mrs. Downing unlocked the door and stepped aside, as if taking no part in this desecration of a dead man's privacy.

The first of the suite of rooms had been converted into a study, as they'd been told, with a door through to a sitting room, and beyond that, the master bedroom.

The suite was handsomely decorated, and Padgett looked around him with patent interest.

The desk, a large mahogany affair, held mainly writing paper, pens, stamps, a map of the estate, and a folder of household accounts and another of farm business, none of it of interest to the police, and nothing personal, nothing indicative of the man.

There were several paintings on the walls, mostly landscapes. Rutledge wondered if they were Quarles's taste or if they had come with the house when he purchased the estate. The furnishings of the room were mid-Victorian and well polished. Betty's work, at a guess. If she cared for his rooms and his possessions, and kept any of his secrets, it was small wonder she'd taken his death personally.

Between the windows—which faced the front of the house—were shelves on which stood gray boxes of business papers, each with a white card identifying the contents. Duplicates of the papers Quarles had kept in London, or were these documents he didn't wish to leave there? Confidential reports, perhaps, for his eyes only. Was that why no one else cleaned these rooms? Betty appeared to be honest, without curiosity, a plain woman grateful for her position and not likely to jeopardize it by risking her employer's wrath. It was even possible that she couldn't read.

The perfect safeguard.

Rutledge ran a finger along the line of cards. He recognized one or two of the names on the outside. Portfolios, then. One box bore the single word CUMBERLINE.

They moved on to the sitting room, where there was little of interest—chairs in front of the hearth, more Italian landscapes, a table for tea, and another against the wall. The only personal touch was a blue and white porcelain stand holding a collection of walking sticks with ornate handles of ivory or brass or carved wood. Lifting one of them, Rutledge admired the ivory elephant set into the handle, the trunk providing a delicate grip. The workmanship was quite good, as was the silver figure of a sleeping fox capping another stick.

Padgett had moved on to the bedroom, and Rutledge followed him.

The armoire and chests yielded only the sort of belongings that were usual for a country house: walking clothes, boots, hats, two London suits with a

Bond Street tailor's label, and evening dress. Several books on a table by the bed had to do with business law and practices.

One of them was a leather-bound treatise on Africa, touting the wealth and opportunities that would open up when the war ended. Thumbing through it, Rutledge could see that the florid prose offered very little substance. Railroads, mining operations, river navigation, and ports were discussed at great length, along with large farms for the cultivation of coffee and other crops, suggesting that what Rhodes had accomplished in South Africa was possible in other parts of the continent.

Padgett, looking out the window across from Quarles's bed, said, "I can't see the gatehouse or the end of the drive or the tithe barn for the trees in between."

Rutledge came to join him. "You're right. Once Quarles reached that bend of the drive where the trees begin, he'd be out of sight. He might have met a dozen people at the gates, or entertained half of Parliament in the cottage, and no one would be the wiser. By the same token, if someone was waiting for him there, friend for dinner or killer in hiding, Quarles himself would have had no warning."

"Did you ask at The Unicorn if he'd dined there?"

"He hadn't. Hunter, the manager, saw him coming alone out of Minton Street around ten-thirty. But he doesn't know where Quarles went from there—toward home or toward another destination."

"You can't be sure Hunter isn't lying. They had a falling-out, he and Quarles. And it almost cost Hunter his position. Quarles was hell-bent on seeing him dismissed. It was Mr. Greer, who was dining there that night, who later smoothed the matter over." He added, "Didn't think to tell you this morning."

"Hunter didn't know that Quarles was dead."

"Or he didn't let on that he knew." Padgett took a deep breath. "But that's neither here nor there." He turned to survey the bedroom and the sitting room beyond. "If there are guilty secrets hidden in this wing, I don't know where to find them."

Rutledge agreed with him. But it was beginning to look like Quarles had no secrets to hide, personal or professional. None at least that might explain murder here in Somerset.

For that matter, if the man had been wise and clever, he'd kept no record of any misdeeds, so that they couldn't be discovered while he was alive or found after his death. An interesting thought . . .

The heavy dark woods and brocades of the master bedroom were almost melancholy, as if Quarles had spent very little time here, and even when he was in residence, he gathered nothing around him that might characterize the man underneath the successful facade. Was the estate itself all he needed to define himself? A measure of prestige, a visible statement that a man who had come from nothing had achieved everything? Old money, giving panache to the New. For some men it would be the crowning achievement of a lifetime.

Hamish said, "He was no' a countryman."

It appeared to be true, and that would explain why the house was treated as a symbol, not a home.

They locked the door behind them. Mrs. Downing waited for the keys to be passed to her. But Rutledge pocketed them, and her mouth thinned into a disapproving line.

On their way down the main staircase, they found themselves face-to-face with Mrs. Quarles, who was crossing the foyer. She looked up at them and said, "I see you've returned."

"Yes," Rutledge answered for both men. "Thank you for making your staff available to us. And if I may ask you one more question?"

She stopped, waiting.

Rutledge said, "Tomorrow—Monday—it will be necessary to notify your husband's solicitor and his business associates that he's dead."

"His solicitor is in the City. The firm of Hurley and Sons. As for his business associates, Davis Penrith was his partner until a year or so ago. He will be able to tell you who to contact." She hesitated and then asked, "Did Harold suffer?"

"You must ask Dr. O'Neil. But my impression was that he didn't."

"Thank you." She went on her way without another word. And he couldn't tell whether she was pleased or sorry.

From the house they went to the Home Farm, tucked in a fold of land and out of sight of Hallowfields.

It was a large, thatched stone house, and along the ridge of the roof, the thatcher had left his signature— the humorous vignette of a long-tailed cat chasing a mouse toward the chimney, while a second mouse peered out of what looked to be a hole in the thatch just behind the cat's heels. They had been created out of the same reeds that formed the roof and were remarkably clever.

Tom Masters opened the door to the two policemen, saying, "It's true, then? The scullery maid from Hallowfields told our cook not more than half an hour ago that Mr. Quarles was dead. I went up to the house, but no one answered the door. What's happened? I'm still in shock."

He was a square man, skin reddened by the sun, his dark hair streaked with gray. Rutledge could see the worry in his eyes.

"May we come in, Mr. Masters?" Padgett asked after explaining Rutledge's presence.

"Yes, yes, to be sure." He stood aside to let them enter and took them to a pretty parlor that overlooked the pond. "Sit down, please," he said, gesturing to the chairs across from the leather one that was clearly his. The worn seat and back had over the years taken his shape, and a pipe stand was to hand.

"Do you keep dogs, Mr. Masters?" Rutledge asked.

"We have two. They're out with my youngest son at the moment. What does this have to do with Mr. Quarles? Tell me what's going on."

"Last night, I was driving past Hallowfields and heard a dog barking," Padgett explained. "It was sharp, alarmed. When I stopped to investigate I found Mr. Quarles's body."

Masters frowned. "My dogs weren't roaming about last night. I know that for a fact. One sleeps with my son, and the other is in my bedroom at night. If they were out, I'd have known when I went up to bed." The frown deepened. "Are you suggesting that Harold Quarles simply dropped dead? No, I refuse to believe it. I'd have said he's fitter than I am."

"He was murdered." Rutledge watched as several expressions flitted across Masters's face.

"Murder? Dear God. I find that just as difficult to believe. Mrs. Quarles—how is she taking the news?"

"She's bearing up," Padgett said. "Did you see Mr. Quarles yesterday?"

"Yes, several times. The last time was just as my wife was bringing our tea. I saw him walking toward the house. I didn't speak to him then, but earlier we'd discussed several repairs that are needed about the estate. He seemed in the usual spirits at the time." Masters shook his head. "This is unimaginable. I'm having trouble grasping it."

"Can you think of anyone who might have wanted to harm Mr. Quarles?" Padgett asked.

A wary expression crept into Tom Masters's eyes. "I can think of a dozen people who couldn't bear him. That's not to say they could possibly kill him. To what end?" He hesitated. "Are you quite sure this was murder?"

"Quite," Rutledge responded. "How many people are in your household, Mr. Masters?"

"Er, my wife, two sons, and a daughter—the eldest is twelve—and four servants—a cook and two maids and a man of all work. He's married to the cook."

"Do they sleep in the house?"

"Yes."

"Can you hear anything from the direction of the cottage? Or the tithe barn? A dog in distress? A motorcar coming down the farm lane? A loud quarrel?" Rutledge asked.

"Probably not. Unless I was outside and the wind was in the right quarter." Alarm spread across Masters's face. "Are you saying we might have heard—come to his aid in time? My God, that's a terrible thought!"

"I doubt if you'd have been in time, whatever you heard."

They talked for another five minutes, but Masters appeared to have no information that could help the police in their inquiries. All the same, Rutledge had a strong feeling that the man wasn't being completely honest, that behind the pleasant face and forthcoming manner, there was a niggling worry.

Rutledge asked the farm manager again if he could name anyone who'd had a falling-out with Harold Quarles, and again he denied that he could.

"I shouldn't wish to make trouble for anyone. There's a difference between having words with a man and killing him in cold blood." He glanced toward Padgett. "I'm a farmer, not a policeman. The inspector, here, can give you better guidance on that score. I'd only be repeating gossip."

They left soon after that. Padgett said as they returned to the motorcar, "You could see he was hiding something. I might as well tell you what it is. His wife had a disagreement with Quarles. Over a horse, of all things. But she got the better of him, and that was that. All the same, with two policemen staring you in the face, it's hard not to think the worst. The wonder was Quarles didn't sack Masters. But then he's one of the best farm managers in the West Country. It would have been cutting off one's nose to spite one's face."

"Strange," Rutledge said, "how many people who readily tell us how much Quarles was disliked, stop short at making a guess about who could have killed the man. It's almost like a conspiracy of silence: you did what I'd have enjoyed doing, and now I'll thank you by not giving you away."

Padgett laughed. "You had only to know the man to hate him. But I've heard he was highly thought of in London. Imagine that—the nobs taking to him like one of their own. Here there were two problems with Harold Quarles. One was his pursuit of women, the other his belief that most people could be used."

"Or else," Hamish said quietly from the rear seat, "he didna' wish to be treated as one of the villagers."

Which came back to Quarles's simple roots.

It was late afternoon when they reached Cambury. Padgett stretched his shoulders and said, "Precious little came of interviewing anyone at Hallowfields. I expect you'll want to leave for London tonight and try your luck there."

"What do you know about the church organist? Brunswick."

"How did you come across him?" Padgett turned to stare at him. "Is there something you aren't telling me?"

"I saw him going into the church just before I came to meet you."

"Ah. He was practicing, I expect. He seems to prefer that to going home. Not that I blame him. His wife is dead. A suicide. She just went out and drowned herself, without a word to anyone."

"Why did Mrs. Quarles list him among those who hated her husband?"

"Yes, well, probably to throw you off the scent."

Rutledge stopped the motorcar in front of the police station, but Padgett made no move to step out. "You'd better hear the rest of it," he said after a moment.

"His wife worked for Mr. Quarles for three months, while he was rusticating here in Somerset. He needed someone who could type letters, keep records. When he went back to London, he gave her an extra month's wages and let her go. It wasn't long afterward that she killed herself. Brunswick jumped to the conclusion that something had happened between his wife and Quarles and that she couldn't live with the knowledge."

"Had something happened?"

Padgett shrugged. "I expect the only two people who can answer that question are dead. There was no gossip. There's always gossip where there's scandal. But you can't convince Brunswick otherwise. I kept an eye on him at first, thinking he might do something rash."

"And you didn't think he might wait until your guard was down and then go after Quarles?"

"He's not the kind of man who kills in cold blood."

But Rutledge had seen the look in the organist's eyes. And heard the passionate music pouring through the empty church.

He let the subject drop, and said instead, "We should speak to the doctor."

Padgett brought himself back from whatever place his thoughts had wandered. "Oh. Yes, O'Neil. We can leave the motorcar at The Unicorn and walk."

It was not far to the doctor's surgery, where James Street crossed the High Street. O'Neil lived in a large stone house set back behind a low wall, a walk dividing two borders of flowers. A pear tree stood by the gate to the back garden, and a stone bench had been set beneath it. The other wing of the house was the surgery, with a separate entrance along a flagstone path. The two men knocked at the house door, and after several minutes O'Neil himself answered it and took them through to his office.

In a small examining room beyond it, Harold Quarles lay under a sheet. He seemed diminished by death, as if much of what made him the man he was had been pride and a fierce will.

"I've examined him, and my earlier conclusion about the blows on the head stand. The first was enough to stun him. The second was deliberate, intended to kill. In my view, whoever did this wasn't enraged. Angry enough to kill certainly, but there are only two blows, you see. If the killer had been in a fury, he'd have battered the head and the body indiscriminately. You'd have marks on the face and the shoulders and back, even after the man was dead."

Rutledge asked, "You said the first blow was intended to stun."

"That's how it appears. You can see for yourself that he's a strong man, well able to defend himself. If the purpose of the attack was to kill, it would have been easier to accomplish if Quarles was down. If the murderer had stopped then, Quarles would have survived. Perhaps with a concussion and a devil of a headache, but alive."

"If he'd stopped, Quarles might have been able to identify him. Which could mean they were face-to-face, and then Quarles turned his back."

"What sort of weapon made these wounds?" Rutledge lifted the sheet.

"I couldn't begin to guess. Not angular, but not all together smooth. Solid, I should think. But not large. The edge of a spanner is too narrow. But that sort of thing."

"A river stone?" Rutledge gently restored the sheet.

"Possibly. But not exclusively that. An iron ladle? I'm not sure about a croquet ball. The brass head of a firedog? A paperweight, if it was a heavy one and there was enough force behind it. Surely it depends on whether someone came to do murder, or attacked the man on the spur of the moment. I couldn't find anything in the wound—no bits of grass or rust or fabric to guide us. I've given you all I can."

"Something a woman could wield?" Padgett suggested.

"I can't rule out a woman," O'Neil said skeptically. "But how did she manage to carry Quarles to the tithe barn, and then put him into that harness?"

"She had help. Once she'd done the deed, she went for help." It was Padgett speaking, his back to the room as he looked out the narrow window.

"Possible. But who do you ask to help you do such a thing to a dead man?"

"A good question."

Rutledge asked, "Is Charles Archer capable of walking?"

O'Neil's eyebrows flew up. "Archer? Of course not. I've been his physician for several years. He can stand for a brief time, he can walk a few steps. But if you're suggesting that he helped carry Quarles to the tithe barn, you are mad."

"What if Quarles was put into that invalid's chair of Archer's, and pushed?" Padgett interjected.

"I can't see Archer helping, even so. Of course I can't rule out the use of his chair."

"It's important to eliminate the possibility. We've been told that Quarles went out to dine last night. Did he in fact eat his dinner?" Rutledge asked.

"I haven't looked to see. Is it important?"

"Probably not. He was seen on the High Street around ten-thirty. That would indicate he'd spent the evening in Cambury." He turned to Padgett. "Did Quarles have friends on Minton Street, friends he might have dined with?"

Padgett said, "I'll have one of my men go door to door tomorrow. But offhand I can't think of anyone in particular. He was a queer man, not one to make friends here. Mr. Greer is his equal, that's to say, financially. You'd think they might have got on together. Instead they were often at loggerheads."

O'Neil said, "Are you saying it might be one of us? I can't think of anyone I know who would kill a man and then hang him in that infernal contraption."

"Perhaps the point of that was to make sure he wasn't found for some time. If Padgett here hadn't heard a dog barking and gone to investigate, it might have been a day or two before the barn was searched."

"Which would give the murderer time to get clear of Cambury and see to his alibi," Padgett said.

Soon after, they thanked O'Neil and left.

"I must telephone London," Rutledge commented as the two men walked back the way they'd come. "Someone may already have spoken to the solicitors and the partner."

He'd suspected that Bowles had put someone else in charge of the London side of the inquiry. Now he had an excuse to find out.

"I thought you were in charge," Padgett said.

"Here, yes."

Padgett paused by a bookshop. Rutledge looked up and saw that the name in scrolled gold letters above the door was nemesis. The shop was dark, but he could see the shelves of books facing the windows and a small, untidy desk on one side.

Padgett was saying, "You didn't tell me this." There was dissatisfaction in his voice. He'd hoped to be rid of the Yard.

If that was the case, why had he sent for them in the first place? Rutledge wondered.

With a sigh Padgett prepared to take his leave. "See what your London colleague has to say, and perhaps we'll have a better grip on what's to be done here. Tomorrow I'll send Constable Horton to Minton Street to discover where Quarles dined. We'll see if it holds with what Hunter told you at the hotel." He nodded in farewell and went on toward his house.

Rutledge watched him go. Hamish, in the back of his mind, said, "It wouldna' astonish me if yon policeman was the killer."

Surprised, Rutledge said aloud, "Why?"

"I dona' ken why. Only that he muddles the ground at every turn. And there's only his word that he found the body."

It was true. Padgett had offered a number of suspects for consideration, and then changed his mind. Others he'd neglected to mention.

"The invalid chair . . ."

"Aye, that's verra' clever."

"Such a suggestion would please the K.C. who defends the killer no end—what's more, it could have happened that way. We'd walked about too much to find the chair's tracks. If they were ever there. I wonder why Inspector Padgett dislikes the Quarles family so intensely."

At The Unicorn, Rutledge asked for the telephone and was shown to a small sitting room behind the stairs. He put in the call to London, and after a time, Sergeant Gibson came to the telephone instead of Bowles.

"The Chief Superintendent isn't here, sir. And I don't know that anyone's spoken to the solicitors yet," Gibson responded to Rutledge's questions. He added, "Inspector Mickelson is still in Dover, but he's expected to return tomorrow at one o'clock. He's taking the morning train."

Rutledge smiled to himself. Mickelson was Bowles's protégé.

"And what about the former partner? Penrith?"

"I was sent around to his house this morning, sir. Mr. Penrith isn't there. His wife's in Scotland, and the valet says he went to visit her. He should be home tonight."

"Did you tell his valet why you'd come to see Penrith?"

"It seemed best not to say anything, sir," Gibson answered. He was a good man, with good instincts and the soul of a curmudgeon And if there was gossip to be had at the Yard, Gibson generally knew it.

"Then I'd rather be the one to interview him."

"As to that, sir, if you're in Somerset, you won't be in London before one o'clock. I was present when Chief Superintendent Bowles told the inspector to make haste back to the Yard. Though he didn't say why, of course."

"I understand. Thank you, Sergeant."

"I do my best, sir." And Gibson was gone.

Hamish said, "Ye canna' reach London before noon."

"I can if I leave now," Rutledge answered.

"It's no' very wise—"

"To hell with wise."

11

In a hurry now, Rutledge strode out of the sitting room and went in search of Hunter, making arrangements for a packet of sandwiches and a Thermos of tea to be put up at once.

"I'll be away this evening. Hold my room for my return, please."

"I'll be happy to see to it. Er—did you find Mr. Quarles?"

"Yes, thank you," Rutledge answered, and went up the stairs two at a time. He took a clean shirt with him and was down again just as Hunter was bringing the packet of food and the Thermos from the kitchen.

The long May evening stretched ahead, and he made good time as he turned toward London. The soft air and the wafting scents of wildflowers in the hedgerows accompanied him, and the sunset's after-glow lit the sky behind the motorcar. When darkness finally overtook him, Rutledge was well on his way. But a second night without sleep caught up with him, and just west of London, he veered hard when a dog walked into the road directly in his path.

The motorcar spun out of control, and before Hamish could cry a warning, Rutledge had crossed the verge and run into a field. Strong as he was, he couldn't make the brakes grip in the soft soil, and then suddenly the motorcar slewed in a half circle and came to an abrupt stop as the engine choked.

His chest hit the wheel and knocked the wind out of him, just as his forehead struck the windscreen hard enough to render him unconscious.

It was some time later—he didn't know how long—that he came to his senses, but the blow had been severe enough to muddle his mind. His chest ached, and his head felt as if it were detached from his body.

He managed to get himself out of his seat and into the grass boundary of the field.

There he vomited violently, and the darkness came down again.

The second time he woke, he thought he was back in France. He could hear the guns and the cries of his men, and Hamish was calling to him to get up and lead the way.

"Ye canna' lie here, ye canna' sleep, it's no' safe!"

Rutledge tried to answer him, scrambling to his feet and running forward, though his legs could barely hold him upright. He must have been shot in the chest, it was hard to breathe, and where was his helmet? He'd lost it somewhere. He shouted to his men, but Hamish was still loud in his ear, telling him to beware.

He could see the Germans now, just at that line of trees, and he thought, They hadn't told us it was that far—they lied to us—we'll lose a hundred men before we get there—

Despair swept him, and Hamish's accusing voice was telling him he'd killed the lot of them. And the line of trees wasn't any closer.

The machine gunners had opened up, and he called to his men to take cover, but this was No Man's Land, there was no safety except in the stinking shell holes, down in the muddy water with the ugly dead, their bony fingers reaching up as if begging for help, and their empty eye sockets staring at the living, cursing them for leaving the dead to rot.

Rutledge flung himself into the nearest depression, but his men kept running toward the German line, and he swore at them, his whistle forgotten, his voice ragged with effort.

"Back, damn you, find cover *now.* Do you hear me?"

He dragged himself out of the shell hole and went after them, but they were determined to die, and there was nothing he could do. He watched them fall, one by one, and he tried to lift them and carry them back to his own lines, but his chest was aching and his legs refused to support him. He could hear himself crying at the waste of good men, and swearing at the generals safe in their beds, and pleading with the Germans to stop because they were all dead, all except Hamish, whose voice rose above the sound of the guns—cursing him, reminding him that each soul was on his conscience, because he himself was unscathed.

"Ye let them die, damn you, ye let them die!"

It was what Hamish had shouted to him the last time they'd been ordered over the top, and the young Scots corporal, his face set in anger, had accused him of not caring. "Ye canna' make tired men do any more than they've done. Ye canna' ask them to die for ye, because ye ken they will. I'll no' lead them o'er the top again, I'll die first, mysel', and ye'll rot in hell for no' stopping this carnage."

But Rutledge had cared, that was the problem, he'd cared too much, and in the end, like Hamish, he had broken too. He could hear the big guns firing from behind the lines as the Germans prepared for a counterattack, and firing from his own lines to cover that last sortie over the top. The Hun artillery had their range now, and he struggled to get what was left of his men to safety.

He'd had to shoot Hamish for speaking the truth, and that was the last straw—his mind had shattered. Not from the war, not the fear of death, not even the German guns, but from the deaths he couldn't prevent and the savage wounds, and the bleeding that wouldn't stop, and the men who lived on in his head until he couldn't bear it any longer.

Hamish's voice had stopped, and he knew then that he'd killed the best soldier he had, a good man who was more honest than he was—who was willing to die for principles, while he himself obeyed orders he hated and went on for two more years killing soldiers he'd have died to save.

Someone was grappling with him, and he couldn't find his revolver. His head was aching, blinding him, and his chest felt as if the caisson mules had trampled him, but instinct was still alive. He swung his fist at the man's face, and felt it hit something solid, a shoulder, he thought—

Hamish had come back—

His breath seemed to stop in his throat. Hamish's shoulder, hard and living, under his fist. If he opened his eyes—

A voice said, "Here, there's no need for that, I've come to help."

And Rutledge opened his eyes and stared in the face of Death. He slumped back, willing to let go, almost glad that it was over, and longing for silence and rest.

The farmer grasped his arm. "Where are you hurt, man, can you tell me?"

Rutledge came back to the present with a shock, blinking his eyes as the light of a lantern sent splinters of pain through his skull.

They were going to truss him up in that contraption, and hang him in the tithe barn—

And then the darkness receded completely, and he said, "I'm sorry—"

The farmer gruffly replied, "There's a bloody great lump on your forehead. It must have addled your brains, man, you were shouting something fierce about the Germans when I came up."

Rutledge shook his head to clear it, and felt sick again. Fighting down the nausea, he said, "Sorry," again, as if it explained everything.

"You need a doctor."

"No. I must get to London." He looked behind the farmer's bulk and saw the motorcar mired in the plowed field. His first thought was for Hamish, and then he realized that Hamish wasn't there. "Oh, damn, the accident. Is it—will it run now?"

"There's nothing wrong with your motorcar that a team can't cure. But I didn't want to leave you until I knew you were all right. There's no one to send back to the house. I saw your headlamps when I went to do the milking. You're not the first to come to grief in the dark on that bend in the road."

Rutledge managed to sit up, his eyes shut against the pain. "There's no bend—a dog darted in front of me, I swerved to miss him."

"A dog? There's no dog, just that bend. You must have fallen asleep and dreamt it."

It was a dog barking that had brought Padgett to the tithe barn . . .

"Yes, I expect I did." He put up a hand and felt the blood drying on his forehead and cheek, crusting on his chin. It was a good thing, he thought wryly, that he'd brought that fresh shirt with him.

He heaved himself to his feet, gripping the farmer's outstretched hand for support until he could trust his legs to hold him upright.

"I'm all right. By the time you get your team here, I'll be able to drive."

"Drive? You need a doctor above all else."

"No, I'm all right," he repeated, though he could hear Hamish telling him that he was far from right. "Please fetch your team. What time is it? Do you know?"

"Past milking time. The cows are already in the barn, waiting."

"Then the sooner you pull me out of here, the sooner they can be milked."

The farmer took a deep breath. "If that's what you're set on, I'll go. I don't have time to stand here and argue."

He tramped off, a square man with heavy shoulders and muddy boots. As the lantern bobbed with each step, Rutledge felt another surge of nausea and turned away.

Without the lantern, he couldn't see the motorcar very well, but as he walked around it, it seemed to be in good condition. The tires were whole, and the engine turned over when he tried it, though it coughed first.

Hamish said, "Ye fell asleep."

"I thought it was your task to keep me awake. We could have been killed."

"It was no' likely, though ye ken your head hit yon windscreen with an almighty crack."

Rutledge put his hand up again to the lump. It seemed to be growing, not receding, though his chest, while it still ached, seemed to feel a little better. He could breathe without the stabbing pain he'd felt earlier. His ribs would have to wait.

"It was pride that made you drive all night. To reach London before yon inspector."

He and Mickelson had had several run-ins, though the chief cause of Mickelson's dislike of Rutledge had to do with an inquiry in Westmorland last December.

"Aye, ye'll no' admit it," Hamish said, when Rutledge didn't reply.

The farmer was back with his horses, and the huge draft animals pulled the motorcar back to the road with ease, the bunched muscles of their haunches rippling in the light of the farmer's lantern.

"Come to the house and rest a bit," the man urged when the motorcar was on solid ground once more. "A cup of tea will see you right."

Rutledge held up the empty Thermos. "I've tea here. But thanks." He offered to pay the man, but the farmer shook his head. "Do the same for someone else in need, and we're square," he said, turning to lead his team back to the barn.

Watching the draft animals move off in the darkness, the lantern shining on the white cuffs of shaggy hair hanging over their hooves, Rutledge was beginning to regret his decision. But he could see false dawn in the east, and he would need to change his clothes and wash his face before finding Penrith.

The drive into London was difficult. His head was thundering, and his chest complained as he moved the wheel or reached for the brakes. But he was in his flat as the sun swept over the horizon. He looked in his mirror with surprise. A purpling lump above his eye and bloody streaks down to his collar—small wonder the farmer was worried about his driving on.

A quick bath was in order, and a change of clothes. He managed both after a fashion, looking down at the bruised half circle on his chest where he'd struck the wheel. His ribs were still tender, and he suspected he'd sustained a mild concussion.

Nausea stood between him and breakfast, and in the end, after two cups of tea, he set out to find Quarles's former partner. There was a clerk just opening the door at the countinghouse in Leadenhall Street, and Rutledge asked for Penrith.

"Mr. Penrith is no longer with this firm," the clerk said severely, eyeing the bruise on Rutledge's forehead.

Rutledge presented his identification.

The clerk responded with a nod. "You'll find him just down the street, and to your left, the third door."

"Are any of your senior officials here at this hour?"

"No, sir, I'm afraid not. They'll be going directly to a meeting at nine-thirty at the Bank of England."

Rutledge followed instructions but discovered that Mr. Penrith had not so far arrived at his firm at the usual hour this morning. "We expect him at ten o'clock," the clerk told Rutledge after a long look at his identification.

It took some convincing to pry Penrith's direction out of the man.

Armed with that, Rutledge drove on to a tall, gracious house in Belgravia. Black shutters and black railings matched the black door, and two potted evergreens stood guard on either side of the shallow steps.

The pert maid who opened the door informed him that she would ask if Mr. Penrith was at home.

Five minutes later, Rutledge was being shown into a drawing room that would have had Padgett spluttering with indignation. Cream and pale green, it was as French as money could make it.

Penrith joined him shortly, standing in the doorway as if prepared to flee. Or so it appeared for a split second. When he stepped into the room, his expression was one of stoicism. He didn't invite Rutledge to sit down.

"What brings the police here? Is it the firm? My family?"

Rutledge replied, "Mr. Penrith, I'm afraid I must inform you that your former partner, Harold Quarles, is dead."

The shock on Penrith's face appeared to be genuine. "Dead? Where? How?"

Rutledge's head felt as if there were salvos of French eighty-eights going off simultaneously on either side of him. "In Somerset, at his estate."

After a moment, Penrith sat down and put his hands over his face, effectively hiding it, and said through the shield of his fingers, "Of what cause? Surely not suicide? I refuse to believe he would kill himself."

Mrs. Quarles had said the same thing.

"Why are you so certain, sir?"

Penrith lowered his hands. "For one thing, Harold Quarles is—was—the hardest man I've ever met. For another, he was afraid of nothing. I can't even begin to imagine anything that would make him want to die."

"I'm afraid he was murdered."

He thought Penrith was going to fall off his chair.

"Murdered? By *whom*?"

"I have no answer to that. Not yet. I've come to London to find it."

"It can't be someone in the City. I can't think of anyone who would—I mean to say, even his professional competitors respected him." He stopped and cleared his throat. "He was generally well liked in London. Both his business acumen and his ability to deal with people took him into the very best circles. You can ask anyone you choose."

"I understand Quarles was from—er—different circumstances, in his youth."

"I know very little about his past. He was frank about being poor in his youth, and people admired that. Accepted it, because of his ability to fit in, like a chameleon. That's to say his table manners were impeccable, he knew how to dress well, and his conversation was that of a gentleman, though his accent wasn't. People could enjoy his company without any sense of lowering their own standards. They could introduce their wives and daughters to him without fear that he would embarrass them with his attentions."

His praise had an edge to it, as if Penrith was envious.

"Have you known him long?"

"He and I joined the firm about the same time, and we prospered there. In fact ended as partners. Still, I preferred to reduce my schedule in the last year or so, and left James, Quarles & Penrith to set up for myself.

He wished me well, and I've been glad of more time to spend with my family."

Penrith was fair and slim and had an air of coming from a good school, an excellent background if not a wealthy one. It was not likely that the two men had much in common beyond their business dealings. That would explain the stiffness in his answers.

"How is Mrs. Quarles taking the news?" Penrith asked. "I must send her my condolences."

"She's bearing up," Rutledge answered, and saw what he suspected was a flicker of amusement in Penrith's blue eyes before he looked down at his hands.

"Yes, well, this has been a shock to me. Thank you for coming in person to tell me. Will you keep me abreast of the search for his killer? I'd like to know."

"I was fortunate to find you at home at this hour."

"Yes, I've just returned from Scotland and it was a tiring journey. My wife is visiting there."

"I must call on his solicitor next. Do you know of any reason why someone would wish to harm Harold Quarles? You would be in a better position than most to know of a disgruntled client, a personal quarrel . . ."

"I've told you. His clients were pleased with him. As for personal problems, I don't believe there were any. He wasn't in debt, his reputation was solid, his connections of the best. But then I was his business partner, not a confidant."

"I understand in Somerset that he had a much different reputation—for pursuing women, with or without their consent."

A dark flush suffused Penrith's fair skin. "It's the first I've heard of it." His tone was harsh, as if Rutledge had insulted his former partner.

"He didn't have the same reputation in London?" Rutledge pressed.

"I told you. Not at all. Do you think he'd have been invited to weekends at the best houses if that were the case?"

"Thank you for your help. You can always reach me through Sergeant Gibson at the Yard."

"Yes, yes, of course." He got up and walked with Rutledge to the door. "This is very distressing."

Rutledge paused on the threshold. "Were you invited down to Somerset often?"

"Quarles and his wife seldom entertained after their separation. Over the years, I was probably in that house a dozen times at most, and then only when we had pressing business. I can count on one hand the number of times I dined there."

"Did you know of Mrs. Quarles's relationship with her cousin Charles Archer?"

"Yes, I did. By the time Archer came to live at Hallowfields, Harold and Maybelle were estranged. It made for an uncomfortable weekend there, if you must know. I never understood what the problem was, and Harold never spoke of the situation. One year they were perfectly happy, and the next they were living in different wings of the house. This must have been late 1913, or early 1914. He was angry most of the time, and she was like a block of ice. But I can tell you that after Archer arrived, wounded and in need of care, the house settled into an armed peace, if you can imagine that. I shouldn't be telling you this—it would be the last thing Harold would countenance from me. But he's dead, isn't he? And I shouldn't care for you to think that Mrs. Quarles was in any way involved in this murder."

In spite of his claim that he shouldn't have discussed the issue, there was an almost vindictive relish behind the words, as if Penrith was pleased that Harold's marriage was in trouble. A counterpoint to his own happy one?

Rutledge said, "I shall, of course, need to verify your claim to have been in Scotland."

Penrith seemed taken aback. "*My* claim? Oh—of course. Routine."

Rutledge thanked him and went out the door, feeling dizzy as he reached the motorcar. But it passed, and he went on to Hurley and Sons, Quarles's solicitors. The street was Georgian brick, and the shingles of solicitors gleamed golden in the morning light as he found a space for his motorcar.

A clerk in the outer office verified that Hurley and Sons had dealt with Mr. Quarles's affairs for many years, and showed Rutledge into the paneled office of Jason Hurley, a white-haired man of sixty. When he realized that his visitor was from Scotland Yard, he immediately suggested that his son Laurence join them. The younger Hurley was indeed his father's son—they shared a prominent chin and heavy, flaring eyebrows that gave them both a permanently startled expression.

Quarles's solicitors were shocked by the news—which Rutledge gave them in full—asking questions about their client's death, showing alarm when Rutledge told them that no one had yet been taken into custody.

"But that's monstrous!" the elder Hurley told him. "I find it hard to believe."

"The inquiry is in its earliest stage," he reminded them. "There's still much to be done. That's why I'm here, to ask who will inherit the bulk of Harold Quarles's estate."

Jason Hurley turned to his son. "Fetch the box for me, will you, Laurence?"

The younger man got up and left the room.

Hurley said, as soon as the door closed, "Was it an affair with a woman, by any chance? Mr. Quarles had many good qualities, but sometimes his—er—passions got the best of him."

"Did they indeed?"

"Occasionally we've been required to mollify the anger of someone who took exception to his pursuit. Mr. Quarles didn't wish his . . . pecadillos . . . to come to the ears of his London clientele."

"Who were these women? Where did they live?"

"In Somerset. I sometimes felt that perhaps this wasn't really an unfortunate passion as much as it was a way of striking back at Mrs. Quarles for the separation. You know her circumstances?"

"I've spoken to her," Rutledge answered the solicitor. "She was quite clear about how she felt."

"Yes, well, they had a quarrel the year before the war. I have no idea what it was about, but the result was a decision to live separately after that. Mrs. Quarles undertook the management of her own funds, and except for the house, for their son's benefit, they no longer held any investments in common."

"How did Quarles take the arrival of his wife's cousin soon after their separation?" Rutledge asked, curious now.

"He had very little to say about it. He'd already informed us that we would handle the legal aspects of the separation, and there was really nothing more to add. Certainly, Mr. Archer was on the Continent when the marriage fell apart, for whatever reason. He couldn't be called to account for that, whatever his later relationship with Mrs. Quarles might be."

"Was it before or after Mr. Archer came to live at Hallowfields that Mr. Quarles's—er—pursuits began?"

"To my knowledge, well afterward. Which is why I drew the conclusions I have. As far as the separation went, Mr. Quarles was scrupulous in his handling of it."

"Aye," Hamish interjected, "he could show his vindictiveness then."

An interesting point, and Rutledge was on the brink of following it up when the solicitor's son returned with the box.

Hurley opened it and looked at the packets inside before choosing one. "This is Mr. Quarles's last will and testament." He unfolded it and scanned the document. "Just as I thought, the only bequest to Mrs. Quarles is a life interest in the house in which she now resides—the estate called Hallowfields. The remainder of his estate is held in trust until Marcus's twenty-fifth birthday.

A wise decision, as it is a rather large sum, and Marcus is presently at Rugby."

"Nothing unusual in that arrangement," Laurence Hurley put in. "Considering their marital circumstances."

"Yes, I agree. What about his firm? Did he leave instructions for its future? Does anyone gain there?" Rutledge asked.

"There is provision for junior partners to buy out his share. A very fair and equitable settlement, in my opinion. When he made out his will, Mr. Quarles told me that he couldn't see his son following in his footsteps. He felt Marcus would be better suited to the law if he wished to follow a profession. He held that money could ruin a young man if not earned by his own labor, even though his son will be well set up financially."

"Can you think of anyone who might have clashed with Mr. Quarles, over business affairs or personal behavior? Enough to hate him and want to ridicule him in death?"

Laurence Hurley said, "By indicating that he was no angel? Or that he pretended to be an angel? I don't quite see the point, other than to hide his body for as long as possible. His murderer would have had to know about that apparatus, wouldn't he? That smacks of someone local."

Jason Hurley frowned at his son's comments. "To be honest with you, I can't conceive of anyone. No one in London, certainly. He was respected here."

Rutledge asked, "If he was—unhappy—about his wife's situation, how did Mr. Quarles react to what he might have viewed as his partner's defection? Was there retaliation?"

"Even when he and Davis Penrith dissolved their partnership, it appeared to be amicable. Although I couldn't help but think that Mr. Penrith would have been better off financially if he'd continued in the firm. Not that he hasn't done well on his own, you understand, but the firm is an old one and has been quite profitable over the years. It would have been to his advantage to stay on."

"I understand from Mr. Penrith that he wished to spend more time with his family than the partnership allowed."

"Ah, that would explain it, of course. Mr. Quarles was most certainly a man who relished his work and devoted himself to it. I sometimes wondered if that had initiated the rift with his wife. His clients loved him for his eye to detail, but it required hours of personal attention."

"Was there anyone else who might have crossed Mr. Quarles? Who later might have felt that there were reprisals?"

Both father and son were shocked. They insisted that with the exception of his matrimonial troubles, Mr. Quarles had never exhibited a vengeful nature.

"And marriage," Laurence Hurley added, "has its own pitfalls. I daresay he could accept the breakup, perhaps in the hope that it would heal in time. When Mr. Archer joined the household, hope vanished. Mr. Quarles wouldn't be the first man to suffer jealousy and look for comfort where he could."

Hamish said, "Ye ken, he's speaking of his ain marriage . . ."

There was nothing more the senior Mr. Hurley could add. Quarles had left no letters to be opened after his death, and no other bequests that, in Hurley's terms, "could raise eyebrows."

"Except of course the large bequest to a servant, one Betty Richards," Laurence Hurley reminded his father.

"Indeed. Mr. Quarles himself explained that she had been faithful and deserved to be financially secure when he was dead. I haven't met her, but I understand there was no personal reason for his thoughtfulness, except the fact that she was already in her forties and as time passed would find it hard to seek other service. He was often a kind man."

"In the will is there any mention of the gatehouse at Hallowfields?"

Hurley frowned. "The gatehouse? No. There's no provision for that. I would assume that it remains with the house and grounds. Were you under the impression that someone was to inherit it?"

Hamish said, "He's thinking of yon man in the wheelchair."

Archer . . .

"The gatehouse came up in a conversation, and I wondered if it held any specific importance to Mr. Quarles."

Laurence Hurley said, "None that we are aware of."

"What do you know of Mr. Quarles's background?"

"He came from the north, coal country, I'm told. He arrived in London intending to better himself, and because of his persistence and his abilities, rose to prominence in financial circles. He made no claim to being other than what he was, a plain Yorkshireman who was lucky enough to have had a fine sponsor, Mr. James, the senior partner of the firm when Quarles was taken on."

Which meant, Hamish suddenly commented in a lull in Rutledge's headache, Hurley knew little more than anyone else.

"How did he burn his hands so badly?"

"It happened when he was a young man. There was a fire, and he tried to rescue a child. I believe he brought her out alive, though burned as well."

"In London?"

"No, it happened just before he decided to leave the north."

"Is there any family to notify?"

"Sadly, no. His brothers died of black lung, and his mother of a broken heart, he said. It was what kept him out of the mines—her wish that he do more with his life than follow his brothers. He said she was his inspiration, and his salvation. Apparently they were quite close. He spoke sometimes of their poverty and her struggle to free him from what she called the family curse. It was she who saw to it that he received an education, and she sold her wedding ring to provide him with the money to travel to London. He was always sad that she died before he'd saved enough to find and buy back her ring."

It was quite Dickensian. The question was, how much of the story was true? Enough certainly for a man like Hurley to believe it. The old lawyer was not one easily taken in. Or else Quarles had been a very fine spinner of tales . . .

Rutledge left soon after. The morning sun was so bright it sent a stab of pain through his head, but he had done what he'd come to London to do, and there was nothing for it but to return to Somerset as soon as possible.

Hamish was set against it, but Rutledge shrugged off his objections. He stopped briefly to eat something at a small tea shop in Kensington, then sped west.

It was just after he crossed into Somerset, as the throbbing in his head changed to an intermittent dull ache, that he realized Davis Penrith had not asked him how Harold Quarles had died.

12

As Rutledge came into Cambury, he pulled to one side of the High Street to allow a van to complete a turn. The sign on its side read CLARK AND SONS, MILLERS, and it had just made a delivery to the bakery. A man in a white apron was already walking back into the shop after seeing it off. Welsh dark and heavyset, he reached into the shop window as he closed the green door, removing a tray of buns.

Was he the Jones whose daughter had been sent to Cardiff after receiving Harold Quarles's attentions?

Very likely. And to judge from the width and power of his shoulders, he could have managed the device in the tithe barn with ease.

Rutledge went on to the hotel, leaving his motorcar in the yard behind The Unicorn, then walked back to the baker's shop. A liver and white spaniel was sitting patiently outside the door, his stump of a tail wagging happily as Rutledge spoke to him.

Jones was behind the counter, talking to an elderly woman as he wrapped her purchase in white paper. His manner was effusive, and he smiled at a small witticism about her dog and its taste for Jones's wares. Watching her out the door, he sighed, then turned to Rutledge.

"What might I do for you, sir?"

Rutledge introduced himself, and Jones nodded.

"You're here about Mr. Quarles, not for aniseed cake," he replied dryly. "Well, if you're thinking I'm delighted to hear he's dead, you're right." At Rutledge's expression of surprise, Jones added, "Oh, yes, word arrived with the milk early this morning. Bertie, the dairyman, had heard it at the Home Farm. Great ones for gossip, the staff at the Home Farm. Tell Bertie anything, and he's better than a town crier for spreading rumors. But this time it isn't rumor, is it?"

"No. And you'll understand that I need to know where you were on Saturday evening. Let's say between ten o'clock and two in the morning."

Jones smiled. "In the bosom of my family. But I didn't kill him, you know. There was a time when I'd have done it gladly, save for the hanging. I've a wife and six children depending on me for their comfort, and even Harold Quarles dead at my hands wasn't worth dying myself. But I say more power to whoever it was. It was time his ways caught up with him."

"I understand he paid more attention to your daughter than was proper."

Jones's laughter boomed around the empty shop, but it wasn't amused laughter. "You might call it 'more attention than proper.' I called it outright revolting. A child her age? Filling Gwyneth's head with tales of London, telling her about the theater and the shops and seeing the King morning, noon, and night, to the point she could think of nothing else but going there. She was barely sixteen and easily persuaded into anything but working here in the shop, up to her elbows in flour and dough in the wee hours while the ovens heat up, taking those heavy loaves out again, filling the trays with cakes and buns before we opened at seven. It's not easy, but it's what kept food on my table as a boy and food on hers now. She was my choice to take over when I can no longer keep it going, but after Quarles had unsettled her, she'd no wish to stay in Cambury. I don't see her now, my own daughter, but once in three months' time. I can't leave here, and I can't bring her back, and she's the apple of my eye. But she isn't the same child she once was. He cost her her innocence, you might say."

It wasn't unusual for a girl Gwyneth's age to change her mind every few months about what she wished to do with her life. It was a time for dreaming and pretending that something wonderful might happen. Quarles had precipitated her growing up in a way that Jones was not prepared to accept.

Reason enough to kill the man.

But Jones seemed to read his mind, and he said before Rutledge could pose the next question, "I would have done it there and then, not wait, if I was to kill him. I could have put my hands around his neck and watched him die in front of me. I was that angry. If you're a father, you understand that. If you're not, you'll have to take my word for it. Rector helped me see sense. I'm chapel, not Church of England, but he made me think of my family and where I'd be if I let my feelings carry me into foolishness."

The words rang true. Still, Jones had had time to think about what he'd say to the police when someone came to question him. Since early morning, in fact.

Jones was adding, "My wife was here as soon as she'd heard. I didn't tell her, it was going to come out soon enough anyway. She asked me straight out if I'd done this. And I told her no. But I could see doubt in her eyes. Thinking I might have gone out after she went to sleep. I didn't."

In his face was the hurt that his wife's suspicion, her need to come to him at once for assurance, had brought in its wake. Which to Rutledge indicated just how much hate this man must have harbored.

"Did you know that Quarles was in Cambury this past weekend?"

"Not at first. Then I saw him with Mr. Masters on their way to the ironmonger's shop. That was Saturday morning."

"We'd like you to make a statement, Mr. Jones. Will you come to the police station after you close the shop and tell Constable Daniels what you've just told me?"

"I'll do it. And put my hand on the Bible to swear to it."

The door of the shop opened, and two women came in.

"If there's nothing more, I'll ask you to leave now," Jones said quietly. "It won't do my custom any good for me to be seen talking with the police. Now that the news is traveling."

Rutledge nodded and went out while the women were still debating over lemon tarts and a dark tea bun with raisins in it.

He walked along the High Street, listening to Hamish in his head until he reached the police station. Constable Horton was there, reading a manual on the use of the typewriter.

He looked up as Rutledge came in, smiling sheepishly. "I hear him swearing in his office. I wondered what the fuss was all about. Looks easy enough to me, once you know where your fingers belong." Setting the manual aside, he added, his eyes carefully avoiding the red and swollen abrasion on the Londoner's forehead, "The inspector isn't here, sir, if it's him you're after."

"I need the direction of the Jones house. I just spoke to Mr. Jones in the bakery. I'd like to talk to his wife next."

"Inspector Padgett thought you'd gone up to London."

"So I have," Rutledge answered, and left it at that.

Horton explained how to find the Jones house, and Rutledge thanked him, leaving on the heels of it.

The Jones family had a rambling home at the bottom of James Street, apparently adding on with the birth of each child. There was no front garden, but the window boxes were rampant with color, and the white curtains behind them were stiff with starch.

Rutledge tapped on the door, and after a moment a woman answered it, a sleepy child on her hip.

She had been crying, her eyes red-rimmed.

Rutledge introduced himself, showing her his identification. She hesitated before inviting him into the
house, as if trying to come up with an excuse to send
him away. In the end she realized she had no choice.

The parlor, with its horsehair furniture and broad
mantelpiece, was spotlessly clean. Mrs. Jones settled
the child on her lap, and asked quietly, "What brings
you here, Mr. Rutledge?"

Her Welsh accent was stronger than her husband's.
Her hands, red from Monday's washing, brushed a
wisp of dark hair back from her face, and she seemed
to brace herself for his answer.

"You've heard that Mr. Quarles was killed over the
weekend?"

"The news came with the milk. I was sorry to hear
of it."

But he thought she wasn't. She couldn't spare any
thought or emotion for Harold Quarles, when she
could see her whole world crumbing into despair if her
husband was the murderer.

"I've spoken to your husband. I need only to verify
what he told me, that he spent Saturday evening with
you and the children."

Her eyes flickered. "He did that. It's the only time
we have as a family, to tell the truth."

"And he didn't go out after you'd gone up to bed?"

"That he didn't. The next youngest, Bridgett, had a little fever, and we were worried about her."

Her hands shook as she smoothed the dress of the little girl in her lap. "We've six girls," she said, then immediately regretted speaking.

"I understand that the oldest daughter is living in Cardiff."

She was reluctant to answer, as if not certain what her husband might have said. "Gwyneth's with my mother. A real help to her, she is, and there's no denying it."

"I also understand that it was Harold Quarles's fault that your daughter had to be sent away."

"The whole town knows of it," she answered, on the verge of tears. "We can't go anywhere without some busybody asking after her, as if she was recovering from the plague. That tone of voice, pitying, you see, but with a hint of hunger about it, hoping we had had bad news. A baby on the way."

"I'm sure it has been difficult for you—"

"And if you're thinking that Hugh had anything to do with what happened to that devil," she said fiercely, "you'd be wrong." The child in her lap stirred with her intensity, an intensity in defense of the husband she herself doubted, protecting her family if she must perjure her soul.

How many wives had done the same, time out of mind? Yet would Mrs. Quarles have protected her husband this fiercely? he wondered. But Hamish reminded him that there was a son, Marcus.

"How can you be so certain?" Rutledge asked Mrs. Jones. "He must have felt like any father would feel, that the man ought to be horsewhipped."

"He wanted to use his fists on him, true enough, but there was us to think about. Too high a price, he said. And it wasn't as if the devil had touched Gwyneth, only talking to her in such a way that she believed he would take her away to London. It was foolishness, but her head was turned, wasn't it? And she's so pretty, it makes your heart ache to think what can happen to one so young—" She stopped, something in her face, an anguish that she tried to stifle, alerting him.

To think what can happen . . . not *what could have happened.*

But before he could question the difference in tenses, she began to cry, a silent weeping that was all the more wrenching to watch, tears rolling down her face, and her arms encircling the sleeping child as if to keep her safe from all harm. He had to look away from the grief in her eyes.

After a moment Rutledge said, "What's wrong, Mrs. Jones? Shall I bring someone to you—your husband—"

"Oh, no, please don't let him see me like this!" She tried to wipe her eyes with the dress the little girl was wearing, but the tears wouldn't stop. It was as if he'd opened floodgates, and there was no way to put them right again.

Hamish said, "It's no' yon dead man she's crying for."

And not Hugh Jones, either.

What's more, her husband hadn't appeared to be upset.

"What's happened? What is it your husband doesn't know?"

He crossed the room and took the child from her arms, and went down the passage to the kitchen where a crib stood under the windows looking out over the back garden. The child sighed as he lowered her to the mattress, and she put her thumb in her mouth.

Rutledge went back to the parlor and sat down next to Mrs. Jones, offering her his handkerchief.

"I couldn't tell him," she said, sobbing. "I didn't know *how*." Her fingers fumbled in the pocket of her apron and drew out a sheet of paper.

He saw that it was from a letter.

The scrawled writing was tear stained and nearly indecipherable, but he managed to read the pertinent sentences.

—she must have waited until I was asleep, and left then, in the middle of the night, with only the clothes on her back, and I'm at my wits' end what to do or where to look—ungrateful child after all I've done—

Gwyneth, it appeared, had run away from her grandmother's house.

And if any man had an excuse for murder, Hugh Jones did now.

"Are you certain he doesn't know?" Rutledge asked, folding the letter and putting it back into Mrs. Jones's hand.

"I can't think how he could—but he loves Gwyneth, she's our firstborn and he's been set on her since she first saw the light of day. He may have felt it in his bones, that she was in trouble. I've been so frightened, with nowhere to turn—for three days it's nearly eaten me alive, and then Bertie this morning spilling out the news as if he knew—*knew* she had run away and was certain Hugh must know as well."

Had the girl come to that gatehouse to look for Harold Quarles, and somehow the baker had discovered that she was there?

But Mrs. Jones was right—how *could* he have learned she had left Cardiff?

Yet she herself had answered her own question—*He may have felt it in his bones, that she was in trouble—*

True enough, but surely not to the extent of going to the Hallowfields gatehouse to see.

Hunter had reported that he'd heard voices quarreling, just before Quarles turned the corner.

Had Jones confronted Quarles, demanding to know where his daughter was? Then followed him home to Hallowfields, to see for himself if she was hiding in the gatehouse? And when he couldn't find her, he lost his temper.

It was possible. All too possible. Rutledge could understand Mrs. Jones's fears. But that would have meant he knew . . . it kept coming back to that.

Unless Jones had found the letter where she'd hidden it from him. One of Gwyneth's sisters might have told him that the post had brought with it a letter that made Mama cry.

Hamish said, "It's no' likely. Still—"

Rutledge comforted Mrs. Jones as best he could, then went to make tea for her. The child was still sleeping, face flushed a little with the morning heat of the kitchen, and silky dark eyelashes sweeping her cheeks, her dark hair curling about her neck. She would be a beauty, he thought, when she was grown. Like her sister?

But now there was no Harold Quarles to tempt her. She was safe.

He found cups in the Welsh dresser, and before he could carry the tea back to the parlor, Mrs. Jones had come to stand in the door, shame written on her face.

"I am that sorry to put you to such trouble," she began, but Rutledge cut her short.

"Drink this, if you will," he said, setting the cup on the table and pulling out a chair for her to sit down.

"But the cat's out of the bag," she said wretchedly. "Now Hugh will know, and everyone else. And what am I to do about Gwynie? I can't go to Cardiff, and I can't send Hugh, and she's been gone for *days*—" Her face changed, her eyes suddenly haunted. "Do you think she wrote to *him*, Mr. Quarles, when she ran off? I'd not have thought it of her, but I haven't seen that much of her since we sent her away. I might not know what's in her *heart* now."

A mother's nightmare staring her in the face.

For an instant he thought the flood of tears would begin again, but she had cried herself out, and slumped in the chair at the table, so forlorn he felt pity for her.

What could she do?

"I'll speak to London," he promised her, "and have the police in Wales alerted. We may be able to find her."

It was all he could promise, and she was pathetically grateful. Reluctantly he left her there, staring into her teacup, as if the leaves in the bottom held the answer to her worries.

And for all he knew, they did.

When Rutledge left the Jones house, he turned toward the church, intent on finding out where the organist, Brunswick, lived.

Just before he reached his destination, he came to a pretty cottage where masses of apricot roses climbed cheek by jowl with honeysuckle, framing the windows of the south corner and drooping in clusters above the door. The stonework was very much like that of the church and the rectory in style and age, and he thought it might once have served as a church-warden's house.

He was admiring it, unaware at first of the woman kneeling in the front garden, setting out small plants from a nursery tray. She glanced up as Rutledge stopped but didn't speak. He glimpsed dark, flame red hair, a freckled nose, and intense blue eyes before she bent her head again to her gardening.

Was this the Miss O'Hara who had come to Cambury and set the cat amongst the pigeons, as Inspector Padgett had claimed?

Still digging in the pliable earth, she said with a soft Irish accent, "You needn't stare. You must be the man from London."

"As a matter of fact," he replied, "I was admiring the house and the roses."

She looked up again, and this time her smile was derisive. "Of course you were."

He could feel himself flush, and she laughed, a low, sultry chuckle.

"While I've interrupted you, Miss O'Hara," he said, ignoring the embarrassment he'd felt at her accusation, "I might as well ask where you were on Saturday night between ten o'clock and two in the morning?"

"Because I've had words with Harold Quarles? He thought he was a great flirt, but I didn't care for his attentions, and told him as much. End of story. And if you must know about Saturday evening, my cat and I were in bed asleep. You can ask him if you need corroboration." She gestured toward the cottage door. "He's there, in the sitting room, curled on a cushion. You can't miss him."

"A man has been murdered, Miss O'Hara. It's not a matter of jest."

She sobered in a flash. "I know something about murder, Mr. Rutledge, and I never consider it a matter of jest. But Mr. Quarles's death doesn't touch me. I didn't know him except to see him on the street. If you expect me to weep over his passing, I'm afraid I can't accommodate you."

Turning back to her plants she said nothing more, expecting him to walk on.

But Rutledge was not so easily dismissed. He said, "Why did Quarles single you out for his attentions? Did he have encouragement?"

"Encouragement?" He had angered her. "Indeed he didn't. And it's rude of you to suggest it."

"Still, the question remains."

She stood up, and he realized she was tall, nearly as tall as he was. "If you want the answer to that, I suggest you speak to Mrs. Quarles."

"Why should she have the answer?"

"Because he flirts with women to embarrass her. She must live here, while he appears to spend most of his time in London now. And he bears no shame for what he does, it's like a game to him. I don't know how she deals with it. I don't care. It's her business, isn't it? The people who suffer are the families of the women he's singled out."

"That's very callous of him," he said, surprised at her perception. He'd heard much the same suggestion from the elder Hurley.

"He's a man who doesn't care what others think of him. If it had been Mrs. Quarles who was killed, I would believe him capable of it."

He quickly reassessed his initial opinion of this woman.

Hamish said, "Aye, she'll turn your head if you're no' careful."

"Do you think he hated her that much?"

"I don't think it was hate, precisely. But she walked away from him, and for that perhaps he wanted to punish her." She smiled. "I've had experience of flirtatious men. I can tell the difference between one who is trying to attract my notice and one who is making a show of his interest."

"Do you know Mrs. Quarles?"

"I've seen her occasionally in the shops. She strikes me as a strong woman who knows her own mind. What I don't understand is why she married the man in the first place."

A very good question.

"I'm told he could be very pleasant if he wished."

"That may be so, Inspector, but I'm sure most of Cambury would wonder if he knew the meaning of the word. If that's all you have to ask me? The roots of these nasturtiums are drying."

"That's all for now, Miss O'Hara." He touched his hat and walked on. But he could feel her gaze following him. The temptation to turn was strong, but he refused to give her that satisfaction.

He stopped briefly at the church, but it was empty.

Rutledge went on, past the churchyard to the outskirts of Cambury, where beyond the last of the houses, he could see farms scattered across the fields. They could have been ten years old or two hundred, crouching so low that they seemed to have grown from seed where they were. Splashes of color dotted the view—washing hung out to dry, flowers blooming in gay profusion here and there, the different green of kitchen gardens, the bare earth of barnyards, and the fruit trees in small squares of orchards, like soldiers on parade, all a patchwork laid over the slightly rolling landscape. Somerset at its prettiest.

Turning around he chose another route to the High Street, not wanting to give Miss O'Hara another reason to taunt him. Hamish chuckled in his mind.

He was halfway to The Unicorn when Inspector Padgett came out of a shop and stopped short.

"I thought you'd be in London today."

"I was. There's nothing unusual about Quarles's will. Except for the bequests to staff, everything is left to his son, to be held in trust until he's twenty-five. His wife will have a life interest in the house, after which it reverts to the boy. Which tells me that Quarles never really put down roots here. If he had, he'd have made certain Mrs. Quarles was evicted."

"Interesting idea. Did you speak to the partner? Penrith?"

"Former partner. He parted with Quarles more than a year ago and now has his own firm."

"Any hard feelings when they parted company?"

"None that I could see. Penrith told me that Quarles wasn't pleased, possibly because they'd made so much money as partners. But he didn't fight the dissolution of the partnership."

"That's disappointing to hear. What about trouble with former clients?"

"He couldn't recall any."

Padgett had been staring at the lump on Rutledge's forehead. "What happened to you?"

"A misstep," Rutledge answered shortly.

"It must ache like the devil."

It did, but Rutledge wasn't giving him the satisfaction of admitting to it.

"All right, you're back in Cambury. Have you been to question anyone? Or are you just taking the air?"

"I spoke to Mr. Jones, the baker. And his wife. They both swear Jones never left his house on Saturday night. Miss O'Hara was asleep with her cat. I was just about to call on Mrs. Newell, the former cook at Hallowfields. I went to the police station. Constable Horton told me you weren't in."

Padgett looked down, as if studying the road under his feet. "Yes. Well, I went home. You didn't tell me you were going to London. I found out quite by chance."

"I left in the night. I wanted to be there before Penrith went to his office." And before Mickelson returned from Dover.

"Fair enough." He turned to walk with Rutledge. "I'm on my way to speak to Stephenson at Nemesis. The bookseller. A waste of time—I don't think he could have managed the cage. But then you never know, if he were angry enough, what he might carry off. Are you certain you found nothing in London to turn the inquiry in that direction?"

"Not yet," Rutledge said. "Early days."

Padgett grunted. "Come with me, then. We'll clear Stephenson off our list."

Rutledge went on with him, but when they reached the bookshop, the sign on the door read CLOSED.

"He never closes," Padgett said, putting up his hand to shade his eyes as he peered into the dark shop. "Celebrating Quarles's demise, you think?" The sun hadn't reached the windows, and the shelves for Stephenson's stock prevented what light there was from traveling too far into the interior. "No sign of him. That's odd. There's a girl who comes in when he's off searching for estate sales."

Hamish said something in the back of Rutledge's mind.

Padgett was on the point of turning away when a movement caught his eye. "Oh—there he is." Tapping on the glass, he put his face up against it to attract the man's attention. Then he said abruptly, "Good God— *Rutledge—*"

The tone of his voice was enough. Rutledge wheeled and pressed his face to the glass as well before shoving Padgett aside and kicking open the door. As it flew back, the flimsy lock shattering, Padgett was ahead of him, bursting into the shop.

Beyond the desk, in a small alcove where Stephenson kept a Thermos for his tea and a stock of wrapping paper, the man was hanging from a rope attached to a hook in the ceiling where he had once run a cord to bring the lamp nearer. The lamp was dangling beside him now, and it was the swaying of the glass shade that Padgett had glimpsed through the window glass as the bookseller jumped.

The odor of spilled lamp oil filled the small space.

For a mercy, Stephenson had not broken his neck in his fall, but his face was suffused with blood and his hands were flailing, as if to stop them from rescuing him. The chair he'd used had tipped over almost directly under him, just out of reach.

Rutledge turned it up, shoved a stack of books on it, and had it under Stephenson's feet in a matter of seconds, catching first one and then the other and forcing them down to relieve the pressure on his neck. His hands went on thrashing about, in an effort to jerk away.

Padgett had clambered up the shelves in the alcove, pushing aside the rolls of wrapping paper and tipping over the Thermos in his haste to reach the dangling man. Rutledge spied a knife used to cut the wrapping paper just as it spun to the floor, and releasing one of Stephenson's ankles, he reached up to hand it to Padgett. Stephenson tried to kick him in the face with his free foot, but Rutledge caught it again, just as a toe grazed the lump on his forehead. He clamped the foot down hard, his grip reflecting his anger.

The rope was heavy, heavy enough to do the work of killing a man, but Rutledge had Stephenson's wriggling feet securely pinned while Padgett cursed and sawed at the rope from his precarious perch.

The strands of hemp parted so suddenly that all three men fell to the floor in a tangle of limbs, the books from the chair clattering around them. Rutledge fought his way out of the knot of hands and feet, stretching across to lift the rope from Stephenson's neck.

A ring of red, scraped flesh showed above his collar as Stephenson clawed at it and gasped for breath, the air whistling in his throat before he could actually breathe again.

"Damn you!" he whispered when he could muster enough breath to speak. And after much effort, gulping in air, struggling to say something, he managed to demand, "Why didn't you let me finish it—and save the cost of the hangman?"

"Because, you fool, we want some answers first," Padgett shouted at him in furious relief. "You can't go doing the hangman's work and leave me to wonder if you were the killer or if someone else is still out there."

Rutledge turned to the desk, looking to see if there was a note, but he found nothing. His head was thundering again, and Hamish was busy in his mind.

"Where does he live?" Rutledge asked Padgett as they got to their feet.

"Above the shop."

Leaving Padgett to minister to the distraught man, Rutledge found the stairs and went up to the first floor. It was mostly used for stock, with a clutter of empty boxes, wrapping paper, a ladder, and other odds and ends that had no other home. After one swift glance Rutledge went on to the second floor. There he found modest living quarters, a bedroom and a sitting room, a kitchen to one side. On the walls were framed lithographs, the only touch of color except for a red tablecloth in the kitchen.

There was no sign of a note.

So Stephenson wasn't intending to confess, but to leave doubts in all their minds, just as Padgett had accused him of doing.

Hamish said, "But it doesna' prove he's guilty."

Rutledge hurried back down the stairs and found Padgett trying to get Stephenson to drink some tea from the mercifully undamaged Thermos. The man clenched his jaw, his eyes closed, his abrupt return to life leaving him shaken.

Rutledge squatted beside Padgett and, when he looked up, shook his head.

Padgett nodded.

They waited for five minutes before questioning Stephenson.

Padgett said, "What in God's name did you think you were doing?"

As the heavy flush faded from Stephenson's still-puffy face, Rutledge recognized him as the man he'd seen reading a book in the hotel dining room the morning he'd questioned Hunter about Quarles.

Stephenson said in a strained voice, "I knew you'd be coming. When Bertie told me about Quarles being murdered, I knew it was only a matter of time. And when I saw you walking down the High Street, I couldn't face it any longer."

A confession? Rutledge waited grimly.

"Face what?" Padgett demanded testily. "Here, drink this tea. I can hardly hear you."

He pushed the cup aside. "I thought everyone knew. It's why I came back to Cambury. It's why I named the shop Nemesis."

"Well, you're wrong."

"I wanted to kill him, you see, but lacked the courage. I hoped that if I came back here, having to see him, unable to hide, one day I'd be able to do it." He ran his hand through his thinning hair and went on bitterly, "You can't imagine what it's like to want to kill someone. It eats away at you until there's nothing of you left. It's like a hunger that can't be satisfied, and in the end it destroys you too. The shame of it is like a knife in your brain."

"What had he done to you, that you hated him?" Rutledge asked.

Stephenson moved restlessly, his face turned away. "It's none of your business."

"It is now. If you hadn't tried to hang yourself, we'd have done nothing more than question you. Now you're a suspect, and a suspect has no secrets," Padgett said roughly. "Not from the police."

His words were met with a stubborn silence.

Finally Padgett said, "Very well, I'll see you to Dr. O'Neil's surgery. Can you walk that far?"

"I don't intend to walk that far or anywhere else."

"That's as may be, but you'll see the good doctor if I have to fetch a motorcar and drive you there myself."

"Fetch one," Rutledge replied. "We don't want to give the gossips more than needful."

With a grunt, Padgett went away to the police station.

Rutledge could see the man before him sink into himself, his face still red, coughing racking him. He refilled the cup with tea, and Stephenson swallowed it painfully, almost strangling on it.

They waited in silence, the bookseller looking inward at something he couldn't face, and Rutledge listening to Hamish in the back of his head.

When Padgett came back, Stephenson stood up shakily, a martyr ready to face the lions. "Oh, very well, let's be done with it."

"Are you going to try this again?" Rutledge asked, gesturing toward the rope.

"To what end?" Stephenson replied wearily. "Fear drove me to desperate measures. You're here now. It serves no purpose to die."

13

Padgett led Stephenson out the door and Rutledge shut it firmly behind them. The broken latch held, just, and Rutledge left the sign reading CLOSED.

There were a number of people on the street, and they turned to stare as Rutledge assisted Stephenson into the vehicle.

A young woman rushed up, asking, "What's wrong? Where are you taking him? Mr. Stephenson, what's happened? You look so ill."

Stephenson, unable to face her, mumbled to Rutledge, "My part-time assistant, Miss Ogden."

She was very frightened. Rutledge was suddenly reminded of Elise, for the women were about the same age. Yet the differences between the two were dramatic. Elise with her confidence, her willingness to take on a marriage that would challenge her, had the courage of her convictions if not the patience. Miss Ogden was gripping her handbag so tightly that her knuckles were white, and she was on the verge of tears, looking from one man to the other for guidance. She struck Rutledge as timid, willing to serve, perfectly happy to be buried among the dusty shelves of a bookstore, and helpless in a crisis, expecting others to take the first step and then reassure her.

"We're driving Mr. Stephenson to Dr. O'Neil's surgery," he told her gently. "He'll be fine in a day or two. There's nothing to worry about."

"Could it be his heart?" she asked anxiously. "My grandfather died of problems with his heart. Please, ought I to go with you? Or should I keep the shop open?"

Others were attracted by the fuss, clustering across the street from the motorcar, trying to hear what was being said. Halting as they came out of shops, several women put their hands to their mouths, their small children staring with round, uncertain eyes as they sensed the apprehension gripping the adults: two policemen appearing to take poor Mr. Stephenson into custody—

Rutledge could almost feel the rising tide of speculation rushing toward him, on the heels of word that Quarles was dead.

He answered Miss Ogden before Padgett could put a word in.

"Mr. Stephenson had an accident and should see Dr. O'Neil, but there's no danger of his dying. We were lucky to find him in time. Perhaps we ought to leave the shop closed for today and let him rest." He knew how to make his voice carry so that onlookers heard him as well.

She turned to Stephenson for confirmation. He nodded wretchedly. With a long backward glance, she stood aside to let them leave.

Rutledge got into the rear seat with the bookseller, swearing to himself. Padgett drove off without acknowledging the people on the street, not interested in what they were thinking.

"Did you not consider that that woman would have been the one to find you, if we hadn't?" Rutledge demanded of Stephenson. "It was an unconscionably selfish thing you did. Next time you want to kill yourself, choose a more private place."

Stephenson said, "I was wretched—I only wanted to die." His voice had taken on a whine. "You don't know what I felt, you can't judge me."

But Rutledge did know what he felt. Disgusted with the man, he tapped Padgett on the shoulder. "Let me out just there. If you have no objection, I'll call on Mrs. Newell as planned." He tried to keep the revulsion he was feeling out of his voice.

"Go ahead. I'll be kept some time with this fool." There was irritation in the inspector's voice as well as he pulled over to let Rutledge step down. He offered begrudging instructions on how to find the former cook from Hallowfields, and then was gone almost before Rutledge had swung the rear door shut.

Rutledge watched them out of sight on their way to O'Neil's surgery, then set out for Mrs. Newell's small cottage.

Hamish said, "Ye've lost your temper twice now. It's yon blow to the head. Ye'll no' feel better until ye gie it a rest."

Rutledge ignored him, though he knew it to be true.

He was just passing the greengrocer's shop, its awning stretched over the morning's offerings: baskets of early vegetables and strawberries and asparagus. A motorcar drew up beside him, and Rutledge turned to see who was there. He found himself face-to-face with Charles Archer seated behind a chauffeur, one of the servants Rutledge had met in the Hallowfields kitchen.

Archer's invalid's chair was lashed to the boot in a special brace made for it.

"My apologies. I can't come down. Will you ride with me as far as the green?"

"Yes, of course." Rutledge got into the rear of the motorcar and nearly stopped short when he realized that there was no room for Hamish to sit. But that was foolishness. He shut the door and turned to Archer. The man shook his head. Silence fell until the motorcar pulled to the verge next to the green. There Archer said to the chauffeur, "Leave us for a few minutes, will you? A turn around the green should be sufficient."

When the man was out of earshot, Archer continued. "I've just come from Doctor O'Neil's surgery. I'm told you haven't—er—finished yet with Harold's remains. But I wanted to see the body for myself. He refused to let me, even though I was there to identify it."

"In due course."

"I haven't told Mrs. Quarles what I came to do. She will insist on carrying out that duty herself. But there's no need."

"If you'll forgive me for saying so, Mr. Archer, she doesn't seem to be distressed over her husband's death. I doubt you're sparing her, except in your own mind."

"She married the most eligible of men. It was seen as a good match in spite of his background. Only she discovered too late that the facade didn't match the man. I don't know what precipitated the break between them, but she has said she had very good reasons for turning her back on him."

"Then why not a divorce, to end the match once and for all?"

"I don't know. It isn't money. She has her own. I think it was in a way to prevent him from marrying anyone else. God knows why that mattered to her."

Hamish noted, "He's verra' plausible . . ."

"Perhaps to prevent another woman suffering as she has done?" Rutledge suggested.

"That's too altruistic. I love Maybelle, in spite of the fact that I'm her cousin. I'd have married her myself, if she hadn't met Quarles while I was away in Switzerland for some time. My mother was ill and the mountain air had been recommended for her. I stayed there six years, watching her die. When I came home, it was to an invitation to a wedding. And I couldn't talk her out of it. You saw Quarles dead, I imagine. You never knew him when he exerted that wretched ability to make people agree to whatever he wanted. It's what made him a successful investment banker."

Remembering what Heller had hinted, Rutledge said, "Did any of his advice go wrong? I mean very wrong, not just an investment that didn't work as it had been promised to do."

"He was damned astute. That was his trademark. Nothing went wrong that he hadn't balanced in one's portfolio to take up the risk, should the worst happen. People were very pleased. That was, until Cumberline."

"Cumberline?" He'd seen the box with a label bearing that name in Quarles's study.

"Yes, it was an adventure stock. A South Seas Bubble sort of thing, as it turned out. Do you remember Cecil Rhodes's great concept of a Cairo to Cape Town Railway driven through the heart of Africa? The same sort of thing, but here the railroad would run from Dar Es Salaam to the Congo River, with goods coming by ship from the southern Indian Ocean to the East African coast, carried by train overland to the Congo, and then put on ships again for the passage north. It was expected to save the journey through the Red Sea and the Mediterranean and was to bring out ivory and other goods from East Africa as well. Zanzibar spices, Kenyan coffee, wild animals for the zoos of the world, and anything that expanded scientific knowledge. Labor would be cheap, and using the river cut the costs of such a railway nearly in half. On paper, it was exotic, and many men who had made money in the war were in search of new enterprises. Especially with Tanganyika in our hands now."

"I must have been in France while this was talked about. It sounds feasible, but then I don't know much about the Congo, other than that the Belgians fought the Germans from there. As did Britain in Kenya. How deep is the Congo where a train could transfer goods?"

"I've no idea. Neither did the promoters or the investors. It turned out to be a case of the sly fox being tricked by sharper wolves. Quarles had mentioned it to a few of his clients but for the most part didn't promote it. And it was just as well there were only a few clients involved, because the project collapsed. Gossip was soon claiming that he'd chosen men he was happy to see fall. That it was a matter of revenge, and he knew all along that the project was doomed."

"Certainly an excellent way to make enemies," Rutledge agreed.

"Quarles went to ground here in Cambury until the worst was over. The odd thing is, it was a nine days' wonder. His reputation for honesty prevailed, and the general opinion was, the men who complained were making him the scapegoat for their own poor judgment."

"Did any of those clients live here in Cambury?"

"I have no way of knowing that. But I should think that if one of the investors was out for revenge, he wouldn't have waited all this time. Nearly two years."

"I wonder. Did Quarles manipulate this scheme? Did he for instance collect investment funds but never transfer them to Cumberline, knowing it was likely to fail?" Rutledge had read parts of the treatise on Africa in Quarles's bedchamber. Surely a man as astute as he was said to be could see through the promises made in it?

Archer turned to look at him. "What a devious mind you have."

"It won't be the first time that such a thing was done."

"Quarles has a partner. One Davis Penrith. I hardly think he could have perpetrated such a scheme without the knowledge of his partner. And Penrith is not the sort of man who could carry off such trickery, even if Harold could. He came into the firm to lend respectability. He has that kind of face and that kind of mind." Archer hesitated. "Although it was soon after the Cumberline fiasco that Penrith went his own way."

"Interesting."

"Yes, isn't it? But for Penrith, I'd almost be willing to believe in your suggestion. I don't particularly like the man, for reasons of my own. Still, Quarles has been scrupulously careful—a man of his background has to be. That's the way the class system works."

The chauffeur had made his circuit of the pond and now stood some distance away, awaiting instructions. The High Street was busy, people taking advantage of a fine afternoon. From time to time they gathered in clusters, heads together. The likely topic of gossip today was Harold Quarles and his untimely death. Or possibly the news of Stephenson driving off with Padgett was already making the rounds. A number of people cast quick glances at Charles Archer seated in his motorcar, deep in conversation with the man from London. Speculation would feed on that as well, as Rutledge knew.

He made to open his door, but Archer said, "Er—you will have noted the arrangements at Hallowfields. I wasn't cuckolding Harold, you know. I'm no longer able to do such a thing. But I would have, if I could. I've found that being with someone you love, whatever the arrangement, is better than being alone. I sank my pride long ago, in exchange for her company."

"You needn't have told me this."

"I read your expression when you saw us together. I want you to understand that what lies between Mrs. Quarles and myself didn't lead to murder. Harold's death won't change our arrangement in any way. She won't marry me. I'm honest enough to accept that."

"Why not?"

"Because she knows that pity is the last thing I could tolerate. As it is, we are friends, and it is easier to accept pity from a friend. Not from a lover."

"Thank you for being honest. I will not ask where you were late Saturday night. But I must ask if you can tell me with certainty that your invalid chair was in your sight for the entire evening and into the night."

Archer considered Rutledge. "You're saying someone moved the body. He wouldn't have been a light burden."

Rutledge said, "Yes." The full account of the nightmarish hanging in the tithe barn would be out soon enough.

"For what it's worth, I give you my word that to my knowledge the chair never left my bedside."

Rutledge got down, and as he closed the door, Archer signaled to his driver.

As the motorcar moved on toward Hallowfields, Rutledge stood on the street, looking after him.

Hamish said, "Do ye believe him?"

"Time will tell. But he made his point that neither Mrs. Quarles nor her lover had any need to murder her husband. Now the question is, why? To help us—or to hinder the investigation?"

A boy came running up, pink with exertion and hope. "A message for you, sir."

Surprised, Rutledge put out his hand for it.

The boy snatched the sheet of paper out of reach. "Mr. Padgett says you'd give me ten pence for it."

Rutledge found ten pence and dropped it into the boy's hand. The crumpled sheet was given to him and then the boy was off, racing down the High Street.

The message read:

I'm about to speak to Mrs. Newell. Care to join me?

Rutledge swore, turned on his heel, and went back to the police station, where Padgett was on the point of setting out.

"I'm surprised you got my note. I saw you hobnobbing with Archer when you'd been heading for Mrs. Newell's cottage. Anything interesting come of it? The conversation with Archer, I mean?"

The suggestion was that Rutledge had lied to the local inspector.

"He'd gone to the surgery to offer to identify the body. O'Neil put him off."

"Now, Dr. O'Neil didn't tell me that. Did Archer ask you to arrange for him to see Quarles?"

They were walking down the High Street. At the next corner, Padgett turned left onto Button Row. It was a narrow street, with houses abutting directly onto it.

"Not at all. I don't think he was eager to do his duty, but he wished to spare Mrs. Quarles. He also wanted me to understand his relationship with Mrs. Quarles."

"And did you?"

"It's unusual, but clearly acceptable to all parties. That's the point, isn't it?"

"He went to the surgery to protect Mrs. Quarles, if you want my view of it. She could have struck her husband from behind, then finished the job when he was out of his senses. It would be like her not to leave the body there, a simple murder, but to make a fool of him in death."

"Could she have dealt with that apparatus on her own?"

"Given time to get the job done? Yes. If you let the pulleys work for you, you can lift anyone's weight.

That's the whole point of it, to make the angel fly without dropping her on top of the crèche scene." He smiled. "Though I'd have given much to see that a time or two. Depending on who flew as the angel that year. The question is, would she have had the stomach to touch her husband's corpse as she put him into the harness? If she hated him enough, she might have."

Hamish said, "He doesna' like yon dead man and he doesna' like yon widow. Ye must ask him why."

Until Quarles and his wife came to Cambury, there was no one to make him feel inferior, Rutledge answered silently. They weren't born here, he didn't like looking up to them, and at a guess, both of them expected it.

Hamish grunted, as if unsatisfied.

Rutledge changed the subject. "How is Stephenson?"

"O'Neil says he'll be in pain for several days. The muscles in his neck got an almighty yank when he kicked the chair away. By the time we reached the surgery, he was complaining something fierce. Dr. O'Neil is keeping him for observation, but I don't think Stephenson will be eager to try his luck a second time. At least not with a rope."

They were coming up to a small whitewashed cottage in a row of similar cottages. This one was distinguished by the thatch that beetled over the entrance, as if trying to overwhelm it. In the sunny doorway sat a plump woman of late middle age, her fair hair streaked with white. She was making a basket from pollarded river willows, weaving the strands with quick, knowing fingers.

She looked up, squinting against the sun. "Inspector," she said in greeting when she recognized Padgett.

"Good afternoon, Mrs. Newell. I see you've nearly finished that one."

"Aye, it's for Rector. For his marketing."

"You do fine work," Rutledge said, looking at the rounds of tightly woven willow.

Behind her in the entry he could see another basket ready for work, this one square, the top edge defined and the tall strands of willow that would be the sides almost sweeping the room's low ceiling. The sleeves of Mrs. Newell's dress, rolled up past the elbows, exposed strong arms, and her large hands, handling the whippy willow as if it were fine embroidery thread, never faltered even when she looked away from them.

"Where do you get your materials?"

"I pay old Neville to bring me bundles when he and his son go to fetch the reeds for their thatching over by Sedgemoor. These he brought me a fortnight ago are some of the best I've seen. My mother made baskets. Lovely ones that the ladies liked for bringing cut flowers in from the gardens. It's how I earn my bread these days. And who might you be, sir? The man from London come to find out who killed poor Mr. Quarles?"

Bertie and his milk run had been busy.

"Yes, my name is Rutledge. I'm an inspector at Scotland Yard."

She studied him, still squinting, and then nodded. "I've never seen anyone from Scotland Yard before. But then Mr. Quarles was an important man in London. And he let the staff know it, every chance he got."

A ginger cat came to the door, rubbing against the frame, eyeing them suspiciously. After a moment, he turned back inside and disappeared.

"Can you think of anyone who might have wished to see Mr. Quarles dead?" Rutledge went on.

She laughed, a grim laugh with no humor in it. "He could charm the birds out of the trees," she said, "if he was of a mind to. But he had a mean streak in him, and he rubbed a good many people the wrong way when he didn't care about them. Sometimes of a purpose. If you wasn't important enough, or rich enough, or powerful enough, you felt the rough side of his tongue."

"Rubbed them the wrong way enough to make them want to kill him?"

"You'll have to ask them, won't you?"

Padgett took up the questioning. "You worked at Hallowfields for a good many years. Was there anyone among the staff or at the Home Farm who had a grievance against Mr. Quarles?"

She glanced up from her work, staring at him shrewdly. "What you want to know is, could I have killed him? Back then when he let me go, yes, I could have taken my cleaver to him for the things he said about me and about my cooking. The tongue on that man would turn a bishop gray. I'm a good cook, Mr. Rutledge, and didn't deserve to be sacked without a reference. Where was I to find new employment? It was a cruel thing to do, for no reason more than his temper. And I've paid for it. For weeks I thought about what I'd like to do to him, from hanging him from the meat hook to drowning him in the washing-up tub. But I never touched him. I didn't relish hanging for the likes of Harold Quarles."

"Perhaps someone else in the household believed it was worth the risk. How did they get on with the man?"

"I can't see Mrs. Downing touching him neither, however provoked she is. She's all bluster when it comes to trouble. Besides, she's Mrs. Quarles's creature."

"Would she kill for her mistress?"

Mrs. Newell shook her head. "She could hardly bear to see me kill a chicken."

"What about Mr. Masters at the Home Farm?"

"They had words from time to time, no doubt of it, and I've heard Mr. Masters curse Mr. Quarles something fierce, when he thought no one was in hearing. There's many a house like Hallowfields that would like to hire him away from Mr. Quarles. But he stays, in spite of the wrangling."

"Why?"

"Because nine days out of the ten, he's on his own, with no one looking over his shoulder. And he can do as he pleases."

"Mrs. Quarles herself?" Padgett asked next.

"I doubt she would dirty her hands with him."

"I understand there was no love lost between the two of them," Rutledge put in.

"But it wasn't murderous, if you follow me. It was a cold hate, that. Not a hot one. I'd put my money," she said, warming to the theme, "on Mr. Jones, the baker. Quarles was after his daughter. Such a pretty girl, raven dark hair and green eyes, and only sixteen when Quarles spotted her on the street. He gave her no peace and offered her the moon, I'll be bound, for one night. Her pa sent her to Wales, out of reach. And not before times, I heard, because Mr. Quarles offered to take the girl to London and set her up in style. I think she'd have run off with him then, if her pa hadn't got wind of it."

This was a richly embroidered version of the story, very different from what Mr. Jones or Mrs. Jones had claimed. Mrs. Newell's fingers were twisting the willow strands viciously as she spoke, and Rutledge could see how strongly she still felt, whatever she was willing to admit to.

"He was probably old enough to be her father," Rutledge pointed out.

"Ah, but lust doesn't count itself in years. And what young pretty thing in a town like Cambury wouldn't see stars when she pictured herself in a fine London house with a large allowance all her own."

"How did Mr. Jones discover what was happening?"

"It was Miss O'Hara who put him wise. She overheard something in the post office that concerned her, and despite not caring for making herself the center of attention again, she went to the baker. It seems Mr. Quarles had asked the girl for a decision by week's end."

Hamish was asking if she'd told the unvarnished truth or seen her chance to get her own back on Quarles, even after he was dead. Or because he was.

"A near run thing," Rutledge agreed with Mrs. Newell. "But if Mr. Jones was angry enough to kill Quarles, why not there and then?"

"We're none of us eager to hang, Mr. Rutledge. There's some say that vengeance is a dish better taken cold." She spoke with quiet dignity.

"Yes, I see your point."

"Anyone else who might have quarreled with the dead man? Been cheated by him? Believed he'd seduced a wife?" Padgett asked.

"That's for you to discover, isn't it? I told you what I thought. Gossip is always rampant with the likes of Harold Quarles. But gossip doesn't always end in murder."

"Nor is gossip always true," Rutledge said. "What do you know about Mr. Brunswick, the organist at St. Martin's?"

Her eyes narrowed. "What of him?"

"His name came up in another context."

"Oh, yes? Then let that other context of yours tell you what you want to know. I've nothing to say against Mr. Brunswick."

They spoke to her for another five minutes, but to no avail. And Rutledge found it frustrating that she was so reluctant to talk. She knew both the household at Hallowfields and her neighbors in Cambury. But

cooks were an independent lot, master of their do-
mains, often arbiters of staff matters, and even though
she had been shown the door and was now reduced to
making baskets, Mrs. Newell kept her opinions to herself. It had been ingrained in her to keep the secrets
of a household. Whatever her feelings toward Quarles,
old habits die hard.

As they walked away, Rutledge said dryly, "As a
rule, people rush to deny they are capable of murder.
Here, everyone—including yourself—admits to having
a reason to commit murder."

"Refreshing, isn't it?" Padgett commented with
relish. "If we find the murderer, half the village will be
up in arms to protect him. Or her."

"Very likely. But I'm beginning to think that you've
encouraged one another in this pastime of disparaging
Quarles to the point that someone finally decided to
do something about it. Or to put it another way, found
himself or herself faced with a tempting opportunity
that seemed foolproof, and took advantage of it."

"For the public good?" But Padgett's humor was
forced this time. After a moment, he went on, "You've
spoken to Jones and his wife. Anything there to
support Mrs. Newell's suggestion?"

"I don't know. He swears he was prepared to
kill Quarles, and then remembered that he was the

sole breadwinner of a large family. So far he has the strongest motive, if Quarles had meddled with his daughter. But both of Gwyneth's parents deny that anything happened. To protect Gwyneth? Or is it true? What I'd really like to know is what triggered the actual killing. Why have old grievances all at once erupted into murder? How does one measure hate, I wonder?"

As they turned into the High Street again, a woman was coming toward them walking her little dog on a lead, and Rutledge remembered what had happened the night before, when he'd seen a dog in the middle of the road, and the farmer claimed he'd seen nothing of the sort but had drifted to sleep just before he reached the bend.

He said to Padgett, "You've told me you heard a dog barking, and went to investigate. But so far, we haven't found a dog that was running loose that night. Are you certain it was a dog, and not a fox?"

Padgett, caught off guard, said, "I told you it was a dog. There's the end of it." He was short, unwilling to consider another possibility.

Hamish said, "I'll gie ye a hundred pounds he's lying."

But Rutledge wasn't ready to confront Padgett. He let the subject go.

It was late, the sun low in the western sky, his head was thundering, and he'd had no luncheon. "Let's call it a day," he said as they approached The Unicorn.

"Suit yourself," Padgett said, as if Rutledge was failing in his duty. "I wonder you didn't call on a few of Quarles's clients while you were in London. To get the feel of the man in his own den."

"At a guess, many of them don't live in London. When we've found evidence pointing in that direction, we'll go back and have a look. Have you discovered where Quarles went to dine on Saturday?"

"I decided to put my men to asking if strangers were seen about the village on Saturday. So far no one's noticed anyone they didn't know by sight," he admitted grudgingly. "That simply means whoever was here wisely stayed out of sight. I wonder if he—she—was waiting in the gatehouse cottage for Quarles to return. Whoever it was couldn't be seen from the house or the farm, but he could watch the road."

"Not if Quarles returned by the main gate to Hallowfields."

"But he didn't come back by the main gate."

"Why would he use the Home Farm lane?"

Padgett was smiling. "Perhaps he heard the dog I heard."

They were sparring, taking each other's measure, pointing out each other's flaws, neither giving an inch, because they had more or less rubbed each other the wrong way from the start.

Rutledge recognized it for what it was, but he didn't think Padgett did.

Hamish said, "Aye, but watch your back."

Rutledge bade him a good evening and went up the steps into the hotel. Padgett, still standing in the street, watched him go with an unreadable expression on his face.

14

It was a long night. Rutledge's head was still aching, and he was unable to sleep, tired as he was. Hamish, awake and in a surly mood, haunted his mind until at one point Rutledge got up and sat by the window for a time, trying to shut out that persistent, familiar voice.

Still, Hamish gave him no peace. First the war, then the drive to London, then back to the war again, before shifting the theme to Meredith Channing.

That brought Rutledge up out of numbed silence.

"I canna' think why she seeks you out."

Rutledge said, "You don't know what you're talking about."

"Oh, aye? She kens ye're no' comfortable when she's there, but she doesna' avoid ye."

"I don't think she knew I'd be at the wedding. I didn't expect to see her there."

"Yon bride stayed with her when she went to London. Ye're a fool if ye believe she didna' tell the lass that Maitland chose ye for his groom's man."

"All right. What was she to do, beg out of the wedding?"

Hamish chuckled. "Would ye ha' begged off, if Maitland had told ye she was coming?"

There was no answer to that. He would have had to explain why, and he couldn't. And it would have aroused Edgar's suspicions.

"Why did ye no' ask someone about her, since everyone knew her?"

He'd been too busy struggling with his fear of what she'd see in his mind. Whatever she said about her ability to read thoughts, mocking it as a parlor game to entertain friends, he knew too well that she could read his. He could feel it.

"Or ye didna' want to know."

And Edgar Maitland had tried to stir Rutledge's interest in that direction. It had been the perfect opportunity to ask her history. Instead he'd brushed off the suggestion that they were suited to each other, unsettled and embarrassed.

"She's no' sae bonny as the Irish lass."

Rutledge swore. How did Hamish expect him to answer that? And then realized that he needn't answer at all.

He tried to shut the voice out of his mind, but it was nearly impossible to ignore it. Finally, as the church clock struck four, he drifted into sleep, and Hamish of necessity was silent.

Morning found the lump on his forehead a variety of shades of blue and purple. But the dizziness and the throbbing had gone. He shaved, dressed, and went down to breakfast, discovering to his surprise that it was close to nine o'clock.

As he ate he tried to piece together the parts of the puzzle facing him: who could have killed Harold Quarles?

Someone in London? Or someone here in Cambury? Hamish, bad-tempered this morning, reminded him that he hadn't gone to see the organist, Brunswick.

He finished his breakfast and went to remedy that shortcoming. Padgett was in the police station but declined accompanying him.

"There was a housebreaking last night, and I must deal with it. I know the culprits, and this is the first serious trouble they've been in. If I don't stop them now, they'll find themselves in prison. And who'll run the farm then? Their mother's at her wits' end. They're good lads, but there's no hand at the helm, so to speak. Their father's drunk, day in and day out."

Hamish said, "It could wait. He doesna' wish to come wi' ye."

It was probably true.

Rutledge left the police station and soon found himself at the small stone house close by the church where Padgett had told him that Michael Brunswick lived.

Brunswick himself answered Rutledge's knock. They stared at each other in silence. Something in his face told Rutledge he'd been waiting for it for some time.

Rutledge introduced himself and showed his identification, but Brunswick brushed it aside.

"I know who you are." He stepped back to allow Rutledge to enter.

There was a piano taking pride of place by the window of the sitting room, and books of music were scattered about. Untidy the room was, but it had been well dusted and cleaned, as if keeping up standards. Rutledge remembered that this man's wife had died, a suicide.

"Then you know what I'm here to ask. Where were you Saturday night?"

"At home, asleep. I don't go out of an evening since my wife's death."

"I've been told that you're among the people I should speak to in regard to what happened to Harold Quarles." It was not a direct accusation, but close enough, Rutledge hoped, to elicit a response. It wasn't what he'd expected.

"He's dead. That's all that matters to me."

"Then I'm forced to include you among my list of suspects. I think you knew that the first time I saw you. What I'd like to know is why? When only a handful of people were aware of why I was here." Rutledge considered him—a tall man, fair hair, circles under the eyes that spoke of sleepless nights. His fingers were long and flexible, trained to play an instrument. And he was strong enough to move a body if he had to.

Brunswick said, "Include me if you like. It makes no difference to me."

"Why should you be glad a man's been murdered? Most people are repelled by the thought of that."

"You know as well as I do that Harold Quarles was a man who made his own fate. He didn't give a damn about anyone as far as I know, and in the end that invites what happened to him Saturday night. You can't walk around oblivious to the pain you cause, and expect no one to retaliate. There's always a line that one crosses at his own risk. Beyond it, ordinary rules don't apply."

"Whatever most people might feel, whatever they dream about doing in the dark of night when they can't sleep, in the daylight there are obstacles. They fear for their souls, they fear the hangman, they fear for those they love. And Harold Quarles would still be alive."

Brunswick laughed. "I've lost God, I've lost those I loved. Why should I fear the hangman when he comes to put the rope around my neck? I don't have much to live for."

"If you didn't kill the man, who did?"

"Someone who is fool enough to believe he won't be caught. Inspector Padgett brought the Yard in, didn't he? Why do you think he did that?"

Hamish said, "Aye, it's a guid question."

"To avoid having to arrest someone he knew," Rutledge replied, and was pleased to see that his answer had taken Brunswick aback.

"You think so? He's had as much reason to hate as any of the rest of us."

"If you know what that reason is, you must tell me."

Brunswick shook his head. "You're the policeman. You'll have to ask him."

"Then tell me instead about your wife's death."

Brunswick's color rose into his face. "She's dead. Leave her in peace."

"I can't." He could hear Hamish objecting, but he pressed on. "I'm told she drowned herself. Did she leave a note, any explanation of why she took her own life?"

"There was no note. Nothing. Leave it alone, I tell you."

"Do you think Harold Quarles played any part in her decision?"

"Why should he have?"

"Because you hate him. It's the only conclusion I can draw, Mr. Brunswick. And the only reason I can think of for Mrs. Quarles to include your name in her list of those who might have killed her husband."

That shook him to the core.

"Did she also tell you that my wife spent weeks at Hallowfields, working for her bastard of a husband?"

"Perhaps it's time you gave me your side of the story."

Brunswick was up, pacing the floor. "She went there against my wishes. She said we needed the money. He'd left London, rusticating, he said. Hiding from angry clients, if you want my view. He worked in his study at the house, and after a time, he let it be known he needed someone to type letters for him. She applied, and he took her on, two hours in the morning, and three in the afternoon. One week after she left Hallowfields, she was dead. What would *you* make of it, if she'd been your wife?"

"What sort of mood was she in that week?"

"Mood? How should I know? She wouldn't talk to me. She wouldn't tell me what had happened, nor would she explain why she sat here and cried that first morning she didn't go back to him."

"And so you suspected the worst."

"Wouldn't you? She couldn't live here in this cottage after spending her days at Hallowfields. She couldn't accept me, after she'd had her head turned by that bastard. Do you think I didn't guess that something had happened? She'd gone to Dr. O'Neil that morning, first thing. She must have thought she was pregnant. We'd tried, we couldn't have a child. That's why she wanted the money, to go to a specialist in London and find out why. After she was dead, I went to Dr. O'Neil myself and demanded to know what he'd said to her. I asked him straight out if she was pregnant. And he said she wasn't, that he'd wanted her to talk to someone in Glastonbury. It was an ovarian tumor, he said. But the truth was, he didn't want me to know what my wife couldn't tell me—that the child she was carrying wasn't *mine*. He didn't want me to live with that for the rest of my life. But I knew. I *knew*."

He turned to face the wall, his back to Rutledge and his head raised to stare unseeingly at the ceiling. "Get out of here. I've never told anyone, not even Rector, what I just told you. I don't know why I'd confess my shame to a stranger, when I couldn't even confess to God."

Hamish said, as Rutledge shut the door behind him, "Do ye believe him?"

Rutledge replied, "More to the point, I think he believes what he told me. And that's the best reason I've heard so far for murdering Harold Quarles and then hanging his body in that infernal contraption. It goes a long way toward explaining why simply killing Quarles wasn't enough."

He walked back to the hotel, to his motorcar, and drove out to Hallowfields.

Mrs. Quarles agreed to receive him, though she kept him waiting for nearly a quarter of an hour before Downing came to take him to the same room where he'd met her the first time. And she was alone.

"Are you here to tell me you've found the man who killed my husband?"

"Not at present. I've come to ask you if you know what the relationship was between your husband and Mrs. Brunswick."

"Hazel Brunswick? She came to do clerical work for him. There was no relationship, as you call it."

"Her husband believes there must have been."

"Only because of Harold's reputation. I can assure you there was nothing between them."

"Why should he make an exception of Hazel Brunswick, if he didn't draw the line at seducing a girl of sixteen?"

"Gwyneth Jones? He wouldn't have touched her, either. He wanted me to believe he would—he wanted me to be torn apart by jealousy and so shamed by his behavior I'd do anything to stop it. And then when I came crawling back, he'd have the satisfaction of rejecting *me*. But you see, I was married to him all those years. I learned to see through him. Once the scales fell from my eyes, I realized what sort of man he was, and how he punished people who got in his way. Davis Penrith knows that as well, but he blinds—blinded—himself to what Harold's true nature was. He didn't want to see. Or perhaps was afraid to see, afraid to recognize the man he'd worked with for so long."

"Gwyneth's father was worried enough to send her away to Wales."

"Believe me, if Harold had been seriously interested in Gwyneth, sending her to Wales wouldn't have stopped him from following her. My husband got what he wanted, most of the time. That too was in his nature."

"And in the process, he tormented a girl and her father, a woman and her husband, and who knows what other victims. Was there nothing you could do to stop the game?"

"You haven't understood my husband." She had kept him standing, as if he were a tradesman. "How do you move someone like that? Ask Samuel Heller, not me. Though I doubt very much that Harold had a soul. I know for a fact that he didn't have a conscience."

"Are you aware that sometimes he entertained someone in the gatehouse by the Home Farm lane?"

"I've been told that sometimes the lamps burned there late into the night. But no one, so far as I know, had the courage to find out what he did there. It was talked about, you see, there was speculation. And when I went into Cambury, I had no way of knowing whether the girl who waited on me in a shop or in the hotel dining room was one of his conquests or not. But if you look for the truth, you'll probably discover he never brought anyone there. Betty might tell you, she cleaned those rooms. Still, the gossips of Cambury were agog with curiosity. And so for the most part, I never went into town at all."

Rutledge wondered if she really knew what her husband was doing—whether she had simply convinced herself of his spite or used it to excuse her relationship with Charles Archer. Physically or emotionally, a tie was there.

"Why do you hate your husband so much?" he asked. "Is this because of Charles Archer? Did you marry the wrong man? Or were you late in discovering the sort of man your husband was?"

"I was in love with Charles Archer, and he with me, before he took his mother to Switzerland for treatment of her tuberculosis. They'd told him she was dying, but she lived six more years. I never saw him during those six years. He never left her side. He cared for her, and he stayed with her to the end. While he was away, I met Harold Quarles, and he swept me off my feet. He was attentive, charming, caring, and he was *there*. There were flowers and gifts, invitations to dinner, invitations to the opera, invitations to go riding. He was just a clerk at the house where he was employed, but already he was making a reputation for himself—a reputation of another sort, as a man who could manage money and was astute in business dealings. And he asked me to believe in him and marry him, and he would see that

I continued to live as well as I did then, if not better. I thought I was in love with him, and I knew I was lonely. I could hardly recall what Charles looked like— certainly not the man in the photograph he'd given me before leaving for Switzerland. I told myself he was never coming back, that the doctors had been wrong before, and that his mother would live forever, and I'd be a spinster by that time. And so I married, and the first years were wonderful. Harold kept every promise he'd made me, and I was happy—" She broke off. "Why in God's name am I telling you all this? It's none of your business!"

"What went wrong?" he asked gently. "What changed your feelings?"

"I will never tell you that. You can hang me if you like, but I will never tell you. I have a son, and I would rather face death than break his heart."

"Have you told him that his father is dead?"

She turned away and walked to the window. "No. I haven't found the words. I'm leaving tomorrow to bring him home."

"How did you explain Charles Archer to your son?"

She wheeled to face him again. "I didn't have to. There's nothing to tell, except that he's an old friend and I have brought him here to heal."

"You were lovers before Charles Archer was wounded at Mons."

Her face flamed to the roots of her hair. *"How dare you?"*

"It's there in the way you put your hand on his shoulder for strength and for courage," he said, his voice gentle. "Is your child Harold's son or Charles's?"

"Get out!"

"I must ask that, you see, because it could explain why you killed your husband. He's old enough, your son, to hear rumors, to make guesses, to read into your look or your touch when you're with Archer more than you expect him to see."

"Get out!" she said again and reached for the bell pull, almost yanking at it.

"I'm sorry if I've upset you. But for your own protection, you need to tell me the truth. Your son has lost one parent—"

She strode to the door, opening it herself.

Rutledge said "I'm sorry" again, and left the room, passing her so close that he could smell the fear on her.

But not, he thought, as he went to find Mrs. Downing, fear for herself.

Betty was in the laundry room sorting sheets, her long face flushed with the work, her eyes red from crying.

She made a move when she first saw him coming through the door, like a startled child who didn't know where to turn and couldn't find its mother's skirts. And then she straightened, bracing herself, waiting for him to speak to her.

Rutledge said, "I'm here to ask a few more questions, that's all. Tell me about the cottage at the end of the Home Farm lane. Do you know who came there with Harold Quarles?"

"I never asked. It was none of my business," she said again.

"Were there women who stayed there—for an evening, for the night?"

"I don't know."

"You must. You kept the rooms clean, and the beds. There would be signs."

"I made an effort not to pry. I did my duty and saw only what I wanted to see." Pushing at her sleeves, she went back to work. Her arms, though thin, were strong, the bones large.

"He's dead, Betty."

"I know he is. And where am I to go now, without him to care for? What's ahead for me, how will I manage? I was safe here, and I was needed. Where will I find that again?"

He was startled by her vehemence.

"Mrs. Quarles will keep you on. Or give you a reference if you wish to leave." It was not his place to tell her that Quarles had taken care of her future.

"You don't understand. I'm tired, I can't go on doing the heavy work a maid of my age is given. Like these sheets. I never had to work this hard when Mr. Quarles was alive. There was only his rooms and the gatehouse. And he wasn't here all that much. Now I'm told to help out generally. Earn my keep. He'd promised me the gatehouse. But they won't let me have it. I know they won't. And I'm at my wits' end for knowing what I'm to do."

Indeed, she looked tired and ill.

"If Mr. Quarles promised to look after you, he will have done. And there is no one who can change what he decided to give you."

She laughed, a dry, hard sound that seemed to carry all her pain with it.

"I'll believe it when I see it."

"Do you fear this family so much?"

She looked surprised. "Fear them? No, of course not. It's just that I have come to trust Mr. Quarles, and he was *young*—I thought the years ahead would be safe, and I've never been truly safe before, not in my whole life. You don't know what that's like. And there's nothing left now."

He did understand. Whatever she'd suffered before coming to Hallowfields, she'd been given a taste of a different life. Now she believed that it was being stripped from her, and she couldn't find the strength to cope alone.

Quarles had used her to keep his secrets, and she still did. The bequest would serve to seal her lips for the remainder of her life. It was a large sum, unexpectedly large for a servant. But it would buy silence. That was what it had been designed to do.

There was nothing more Rutledge could learn from her. Not now, when her worries went beyond catching a murderer. But he asked one last question.

"You knew Mr. Quarles better than most of the staff. People tell me he's vicious, he's kind, he's callous, he's cruel, he's respected in London and hated in Cambury—"

"He came from a hard world. He'd had to make his way where he was treated like the working-class man he was, expected to touch his cap to his betters, step out of their way, and do what he was told. Until you've known that, you don't know what it's like. He knew what they thought about him, what was said behind his back. But he was blessed with a good mind, and he prospered, in spite of the past. And he was proud of that. To keep it, he told me he'd had to fight from the day he left Yorkshire, and he'd had to use whatever tools came to hand, not being born with them to start with. Not six months ago, he said to me, 'There's no one to save the likes of you and me, Betty. Except ourselves. You remember that, and you'll do fine.' "

But she hadn't gained strength from the man; she'd used his instead.

Rutledge thanked her and left her to the folding of the heavy sheets, her back bent to the labor, her eyes concentrating on keeping the folds sharp and smooth. Sprinkling lavender among the folds, her rough hands gentle, she looked into a stark future and found it frightening.

Rutledge went back to the gatehouse and walked through the wood to the tithe barn, nodding to the constable on duty as he opened the door and went inside.

It was different in the daylight. Empty, a smoky light spilling in from the door, the rafters ghostly shapes over his head. The barn was as long and as tall as he remembered, and he could almost see Harold Quarles above him, the outspread arms, the white-feathered wings.

"It's no' something you forget," Hamish said quietly, but his voice seemed to echo in the vastness.

Rutledge walked the length of the barn and back again.

Why go to the trouble to put Quarles in that abominable harness and lift him to the rafters? To hide the body until someone thought to look for him here, not in Cambury, where he'd gone to dine? To make a mockery of the man who seemed to care so little for the feelings of others? Or to show the world that even Harold Quarles was vulnerable?

If Mrs. Quarles had killed her husband, would she have done this? Not, he thought, if she cared for her son. Murder Quarles, yes, ridding herself of him without the shame of a divorce. Or the truth coming out in a courtroom. But making a spectacle of his death? Rutledge had come to understand her pride, and now he could see that she had nothing to gain by such a step.

Hamish said, "Yon organist might have wanted to make a spectacle o' him."

Rutledge could readily believe that.

Would Inspector Padgett try to cover up Brunswick's guilt? Because the man seemed to know more about the inspector than was good for him. An interesting possibility. Padgett hadn't been eager to interview the man.

Rutledge walked the length of the barn again, trying to feel something here, to sense an angry mood or a cold hatred. But the barn had nothing to say to him. The silence of the past lay heavily around him, smothering the present. Harold Quarles was only a fragment of this great barn's history, and although his end here was appalling, it would be forgotten long before the roof fell in here and the rafters that had held the angel up cracked with age.

A sound behind him made him whirl, but there was nothing to be seen. He stood there, without moving, listening with such intensity that he heard the sound again.

A mouse moved out of the shelter of one of the columns that supported the roof, whiskers twitching as his dark, unfathomable eyes examined the two-legged intruder. He sat up on his hind legs and waited for Rutledge to make the first move. But when the man from London stood his ground without a threatening sound or motion, the mouse ran lightly to the wall of the barn and disappeared into the shadows.

Had he been here when a murderer had brought Harold Quarles into the barn and went to take the apparatus out of its box? What had he seen?

Hamish said, "It was no' a stranger."

And that was the key to this barn. In the mist that night a stranger would have had trouble seeing it at all, if he hadn't known it was here. Rutledge himself hadn't until he was almost on it. And even if the killer had wanted to make certain the body wasn't found straightaway, the cottage was closer than the barn. In here, in the darkness—even with a torch—it would have taken time to pull the ropes and pulleys out of their chest and lay them out, when Quarles could just as well have been stowed behind one of the trestle tables or a section of the stable roof. No matter how much had been written about the Christmas pageant, understanding the mechanism—even if someone knew it was there—was another matter.

Hamish said, "Better to put the body in yon chest."

"Exactly." He'd spoke aloud, and the constable at the door peered in. Rutledge said, "Sorry. Bad habit, talking to myself."

The man grinned and shut the door again.

Whatever Padgett might want him to believe, Rutledge now had evidence of a sort that the murderer must be here, in Cambury.

The journey to London to spike Mickelson's guns had probably been an act of vanity, nothing more.

15

Rutledge found Padgett in the police station completing his report on the housebreaking. Even before he reached the office, he could hear the ragged tap of typewriter keys and an occasional grunt as something went wrong.

Padgett looked up, his ill temper aggravated by the interruption.

Rutledge said, not waiting for Padgett's good humor to return, "You wouldn't accompany me when I went to see Brunswick. It would have been wise if you had. He believes you had something to do with Harold Quarles's death. He told me to ask you why you hated the man."

Padgett's reaction was explosive. He swore roundly, his face red with anger.

"While you were exchanging confidences, did he tell you that at the time I suspected him of drowning his wife? And I've yet to be satisfied that her death was a suicide. There's no love lost between us."

"He believes she was Quarles's lover, and that the child she might have been carrying at the time of her death wasn't her husband's. Reason enough for murder."

"Well, she wasn't carrying a child at the time of her death. Not according to O'Neil. But she did have a tumor the size of a small cabbage. Brunswick believes the doctor is covering up the truth. They had words just before the funeral. Of course he—Brunswick—wouldn't care to think he'd killed his wife for no reason other than his own jealousy."

"Could she have borne children, if the tumor was safely removed?"

"Probably not. She wasn't drowned at home, mind you, but in one of those streams on Sedgemoor. A dreary place to die. A dreary battlefield in its day, for that matter. She ought to have survived—if she'd changed her mind, she might have saved herself. The stream wasn't all that deep. The only reason I didn't take Brunswick into custody was that simple fact. But I've kept an eye on him since then."

"What was your quarrel with the victim? You might as well tell me," Rutledge said, "it will have to come out sooner or later."

He could see the defiance in Padgett's eyes as he surged to his feet and leaned forward over the desk, his knuckles white as they pressed against the scarred wooden top. "I see no reason to tell you anything. I'm a policeman, for God's sake. Do you think I killed the man? If so, say that to my face, don't go hinting about like a simpering woman."

Rutledge held on to his own temper, knowing he'd provoked the anger turned against him and that the angry man across from him hoped to use it to deflect him from his probing.

"Padgett. I'll speak to the Chief Constable if I have to. And don't push your luck with me. My temper can be as short as yours."

" 'Ware," Hamish warned Rutledge. "He's likely to come across yon desk and throttle ye."

But at mention of the Chief Constable, Padgett got himself under control with a visible effort.

"Leave the Chief Constable out of this!"

"Then talk to me."

"I'm not a suspect. I don't have to give you my private life to paw over."

Rutledge was on the point of taking Inspector Padgett into custody and letting him think his position over in one of his own cells.

But Hamish warned, "Ye ken, it will only set him against you more. There's shame here, and it willna' come out, whatever ye threaten."

Rutledge took a deep breath. "Padgett. You found the body. There's no other witness. You could have hauled Quarles up to the beams yourself, as a fitting revenge for whatever he did to you. It doesn't look good."

Padgett started for the door, intending to push Rutledge aside. "If that's what you want to believe—"

"It's what the killer's barrister will claim, to throw doubt on the evidence we collect for trial. And then whatever you're hiding becomes a matter of public record forever after. I shouldn't have to tell you this. Think about it, man!"

Padgett stopped in midstride.

"Look, set your feelings about Quarles aside and consider the case clearly. If it were Mrs. Quarles—or Jones, the baker—or even Brunswick who had found the man's body by the side of the road, and you knew the history of their relationship with the victim, that person would be suspect almost at once. An unexpected confrontation, a temper lost, an opportunity taken. You'd have no choice but to investigate the circumstances."

"I'm an honest man, a good policeman." Padgett's voice was tight, his face still flushed with his fury.

"No doubt both of these are true. Do they put you above suspicion? You may not be guilty—but you must be cleared, any question of doubt put aside so that you don't cast a shadow over the inquiry."

"Are you going to take me off the case? I don't see how we can work together now."

"I'm not removing you. But you must give me your word you didn't kill Quarles."

"What good is my word, if I'm a murderer? Do you think I'd stop at perjuring myself to escape the hangman?"

"Your word as a policeman."

It was the right thing to say. Padgett's ruffled feathers relaxed, and he swore, "As God is my witness, then. I give you my word as a policeman."

Hamish said to Rutledge, "Aye, all well and good, but he didna' swear to stop interfering."

"I was looking for the truth, not trust," Rutledge answered him grimly.

They went on to Dr. O'Neil's surgery, to interview Stephenson.

The doctor greeted them, and if he saw any stiffness in their manner, he said nothing about it. Taking them to the narrow examination room where he'd put the bookseller, he added, "He's recovering well enough. Physically, if not emotionally. But that's not unexpected, given the circumstances. Be brief, if you want to question him."

"Before we go in," Rutledge said, "can you tell me if Michael Brunswick's wife was diagnosed with a tumor? Or was she pregnant at the time of her death?"

O'Neil sighed. "Brunswick has convinced himself that I lied to him. I didn't. If he killed Quarles, he'll be coming for me next. He's one of those men who can picture his wife in another man's arms if she so much as smiles at a poor devil in the post office or the greengrocer's. The fact is, I believed it to be ovarian from the start, because she'd had no symptoms until the tumor was well advanced. And I told her as much, warning her to prepare herself. I did prescribe tests, to confirm my diagnosis. Her mother had died of the same condition. Sadly, she knew what to expect. And if by some miracle of surgery she survived the cancer, there would be no children."

"How did you do the tests?" From what Rutledge had seen of the small surgery, he was certain Dr. O'Neil didn't have the facilities for them here.

"I sent her to Bath, to a specialist there. Quarles lent her his motorcar and his chauffeur. She was in her last week of employment at Hallowfields the day she came to me, and when she told Quarles she was glad she was nearly finished, because it appeared that she was ill, he arranged to send her. It was a kind gesture. But Mrs. Brunswick made me promise to say nothing to her husband about that—she said he would disapprove."

Rutledge thought, It could have been that Brunswick found out—

But that wasn't the murder he'd come to Cambury to solve.

"Why the interest in Mrs. Brunswick?" O'Neil asked, clearly busy putting two and two together.

"It could offer a reason for her husband to kill Quarles," Padgett answered, following Rutledge's thinking. "Early days, no stone unturned, and all that."

"I've finished with Quarles, by the bye. And he did eat dinner the night he was killed."

"Then let his wife bury him," Padgett said. "The sooner the better."

O'Neil looked at Rutledge for confirmation, and he nodded.

The doctor opened the door to Stephenson's room. The man looked up, sighed wearily, and visibly braced himself for what was to come.

Rutledge said, "I'm happy to see you feeling a little better."

"There's better and better," Stephenson said without spirit.

"Why kill yourself, if you've done nothing wrong?" Rutledge asked. "It's a waste of life."

"My reasons seemed to be sound enough at the time—"

He broke off and turned his face toward the wall, tears welling in his eyes.

"Do we clap you in gaol as soon as Dr. O'Neil here gives us leave?" Padgett demanded irritably. "You as much as confessed that you wanted to kill Harold Quarles. Did you or didn't you? You can't have it both ways."

"But he can," Rutledge put in quietly. "If he paid someone to do what he couldn't face himself."

"That would be betrayal. I wouldn't stoop to that. By rights," he went on, "an eye for an eye, I should have killed *his* son. I couldn't do that, either."

"If you didn't kill Quarles, why were you so certain we were about to take you into custody for this murder? Certain enough to kill yourself before we could." He added in a level voice, no hint of curiosity or prying, merely trying to clarify, "Just what did Quarles have to do with *your* son?"

"I don't want to talk about it. I'm still shaken, hardly able to believe I'm still alive. I expected never to see this world again. I thought I was well out of it." His face was hidden, his voice rough with tears. "For God's sake, go away and leave me alone."

"In the end, you'll have to clear yourself by telling us the truth."

"I don't have to do anything of the sort. You can't threaten me with hanging. I know how the noose feels about my neck, and what it's like to plunge into the dark. The next time will be easier, and it won't be interrupted. *I really don't give a damn.*"

"If you want to die so badly," Padgett reminded him, "you'd have to convince us first that you deserve to. What you're feeling now is self-pity, not evidence. Do you think you're the only man who's lost a son? I can find you a dozen such fathers without leaving the parish."

"He was my only child—my wife is dead. I never thought I'd be grateful for that, until the day the news came."

Rutledge shook his head, warning Padgett to leave it as he was about to reply. Reluctantly Padgett turned and walked away, shutting the door behind him. Rutledge said to Stephenson, "Consider your situation. If you want to claim this crime even though you didn't commit it, go ahead. That's not vengeance, it's martyrdom. And in the final moments before the trapdoor drops, you'll find martyrdom isn't a satisfactory substitute for what you'd promised your son to do."

Not waiting for a reply, Rutledge turned on his heel, leaving Dr. O'Neil alone with his patient.

As they walked down the passage, he could hear Stephenson's voice: "I loved him more than anything, anything."

Outside, Padgett said, "Why did he call that bookstore of his Nemesis, if he wasn't waiting for his chance to kill Quarles? Whatever lay between them, it must have been a fearsome hate on Stephenson's part."

They had just reached the High Street when the boot boy from The Unicorn caught up with them. "You're wanted, sir, if you're Inspector Rutledge. There's a telephone call for you at the hotel. I was told at the station you'd be with Inspector Padgett."

"And who would be calling the inspector?" Padgett asked, inquisitiveness alive in his face.

"London," Rutledge answered. "Who else?" He handed the flushed boot boy a coin, nodded to Padgett, and walked away toward The Unicorn.

Hunter was waiting for him at Reception, and escorted him to the telephone room. "They promised to call again in fifteen minutes." He took out his pocket watch. "That's half a minute from now."

On the heels of his words, they could hear the telephone bell, and Rutledge went to answer it.

It was Sergeant Gibson, who asked him in a formal tone to wait for Chief Superintendent Bowles to be summoned.

The tone of voice, as always with Gibson, reflected the mood of the Yard.

Bowles, when he took up the receiver, shouted, "You there, Rutledge?"

"Yes, sir, I'm here."

"What's this I hear about your questioning Mr. Penrith and speaking to Hurley and Sons?"

Mickelson was back in London and complaining.

"It was in the course of—"

"I don't give a fig for your excuses. I sent you to Cambury to find a murderer, and I've had no report of your progress. Davis Penrith has been on the horn to the Yard, expressing his concern, wanting to know if we've taken anyone into custody. Have we?"

"Not yet. I reported the death of his former partner to Penrith, and asked who among the victim's business connections might have a grievance against the man dead. I asked Hurley and Sons who benefited from the will. It's the usual procedure. You gave me no instructions not to follow up in London."

In the background Rutledge could hear Hamish derisively mocking his words.

"This was an important man, Rutledge. Do you understand me? Inspector Padgett was quite right to call in the Yard, and if you aren't capable of dealing with this inquiry, I'll send someone down who can."

"We're interviewing—"

"You're wasting time, Rutledge. I can have you out of there in twenty-four hours, if you don't give us results. Do you hear me?" The receiver banged into its cradle with a violence that could be heard across the room. Rutledge smiled. Mickelson must have been very put out indeed.

As he turned around to leave, Rutledge saw that Padgett had followed him to the hotel and was standing in the doorway. He must have heard a good part of the conversation. From the look on his face, most assuredly he'd heard the receiver put up with force.

He said blandly, "I was just coming to inquire. Do you want to tell Mrs. Quarles that she can bury her husband, or shall I?"

Rutledge wiped the smile from his lips. "Yes, go ahead. I think she'll be glad of the news."

"Yes, sooner in the ground, sooner forgotten. Shall I tell the rector that he'll be posting the banns for a marriage, as soon as the funeral guests are out of sight?"

"Sorry to disappoint you. I don't think she'll marry Archer. Now or ever."

"Care for a small wager?" Padgett asked as he turned away, not waiting for Rutledge's answer.

Hamish said, agreeing with Rutledge. "She willna' marry again. There's her son."

Rutledge went up to his room, surprised at how late in the afternoon it was. He felt fatigue sweeping over him, and knew it for what it was, an admission that Padgett and Chief Superintendent Bowles had got to him.

Hamish said, "You were in great haste to get to London before yon inspector returned from Dover. You canna' expect to escape unscathed."

It was nearly four-thirty in the morning when someone knocked at the door of Rutledge's room.

He was sleeping lightly and heard the knock at once. "I'm coming."

The only reason he could think of for the summons was another murder, and he was running down a mental list as he pulled on his trousers and opened the door.

It wasn't Inspector Padgett or one of his constables. Standing on the threshold was Miss O'Hara, her hair tousled, and a shawl thrown over hastily donned clothes.

"You must come at once," she said. "I've got Gwyneth Jones at my house. She just came home, and her father's at the bakery, firing up the ovens, her sisters asleep in their beds."

He turned to find his shoes and his coat. "Is she all right?"

"Frightened to death, tired, hungry, and looking as if she's slept in her clothes. Mrs. Jones told me you knew her story. The question now is, what to do? Gwyneth's father is going to be furious, and her mother is on the point of having a fit."

"Have you told the girl that Quarles is dead?" Rutledge asked as they went toward the stairs.

She shook her head. "No, nor has her mother. Gwyneth explained to her mother that she was homesick, but she told me that she missed Cambury and wanted to work in the shop again, rather than dance to her grandmother's tune."

They opened and shut The Unicorn's door as quietly as possible, so as not to disturb the night clerk sleeping in his little cubicle.

"How did you know which room I was in?" he asked as they stepped out into the cool night air and walked briskly toward Church Street.

"How do you think? I looked in the book at Reception."

Rutledge found himself reflecting that if the story got around Cambury that he was seen escorting a disheveled Irishwoman out of the hotel and back to her house at this hour of the morning, gossip would be rampant. And Padgett would have much to say about it. The one bright point was that Gwyneth had been sent to Miss O'Hara's house while it was still dark. They could at least keep her arrival quiet for a while.

As if she'd read his mind, Miss O'Hara suppressed a laugh. "We'll have to avoid the man who brings round the milk. Bertie. He's the worst rumor monger in Cambury. If you wish to have your business discussed over the world's breakfast table, confide in him."

The first hint of dawn was touching the eastern sky, and the coolness of evening still lurked in the shadows. It would be light enough soon for anyone looking out a window to see them.

"Why did Mrs. Jones bring her to you?"

"If the other children had seen their sister, there'd be no keeping the news from their father. I was the only woman living alone she could think of."

"What do you know about the situation?"

"Enough to realize that if she'd fled Wales, and her father got wind of it, he'd kill Harold Quarles."

"How did the girl get home?"

"Begging lifts from anyone she thought she could trust. She had a little money with her, but not enough to pay for a train or omnibus."

They had reached the O'Hara cottage and quickly slipped inside.

Gwyneth Jones was sitting dejectedly in the kitchen, her hands wrapped around a mug of hot tea, her face as long as her tangled dark hair.

All the same, he could see that she was a lovely girl, with curling black hair and dark lashes, dark eyes, skin like silk. But whatever spirit she might have possessed was now sunk in gloom and fear.

She started to her feet like a cornered wild thing when she saw that Miss O'Hara had brought someone with her.

Rutledge said quickly, "You needn't be afraid. Your mother has told me about you. I'm a policeman—from London. Inspector Rutledge, and you can trust me. Miss O'Hara did the right thing, asking me to help you sort out your troubles."

"A policeman?" She frowned. "My mother says I can't come home—she wants to send me directly back to Wales, and she refuses to let me see my da. It's as if I've done some terrible thing, and no one wants me anymore."

She sounded like a terrified and bewildered child.

Miss O'Hara went to her and put a hand on her arm, urging her to sit down again. Instead, Gwyneth threw her arms around the older woman and began to cry wretchedly.

"Miss Jones. Gwyneth," Rutledge began. "Listen to me. There's been some trouble here in Cambury, that's why I'm here. Rather—um—serious trouble."

His hesitation as he searched for a less threatening word than *murder* was enough. The girl broke free of

Miss O'Hara's embrace and turned to stare at him, her tear-streaked face appalled. "My father's dead. *That's why they won't let me go to him.*"

"No, its not your father—"

"Then it's Mr. Quarles who's dead, and you've got my father in custody for it."

"He's only one of several suspects, Gywneth. No one has been taken into custody—"

"I tried to tell him, Mr. Quarles isn't a monster, whatever the gossips say. But he believed them, just like she did." She pointed to Miss O'Hara, then added, "Mr. Quarles was nice to me, he told me that I could choose my own life. I don't have to follow my father in the bakery if I don't want to. I don't have to be the son my father never had—"

His eyes met Miss O'Hara's over the girl's head. "Gwyneth. Did Quarles offer to take you to London, and help you find this new life?"

"Of course he didn't. He told me I must learn to do something well, to make my living. To cook or to bake or to make hats, it didn't matter. He told me not to go into service. His sister did, and she was wretched to the end."

"Where does his sister live?" Rutledge asked, thinking that she could provide him with more information about Quarles than anyone else.

"She's dead. All his family is dead. They have been for years. He doesn't have anyone but his son."

"You're certain Mr. Quarles didn't try to convince you to run away from home? Or encourage you to leave your grandmother's and come back to Cambury?" Miss O'Hara asked.

"Of course not. My father thought he was flirting with me, but he wasn't. He said he hated to see such a pretty girl waste her life in Cambury, when she could live in Glastonbury or Bath and marry better than the young men I know here. And he's right, I don't like *any* of them well enough to marry them."

It was a different story from the one Jones himself had told Rutledge. But taking that with a grain of salt, Rutledge could see that Jones was jealous, wanted his favorite child to stay with him and inherit the bakery, not find work and happiness away from Cambury. He'd seen Quarles as the snake in his Eden, tempting his young daughter with tales that turned her head. And he'd read what he wanted to believe in the older man's attentions.

Who knew what was in Harold Quarles's mind—whether he wanted to help her or hoped to lead Gwyneth astray, perhaps take advantage of her when she was older and lonely and far from home.

She *was* extraordinarily pretty. But would she be any happier in a larger town? Would she find this young man of her dreams—or would she be trapped by someone who had other reasons for befriending her, and in the end, ruin her? Quarles hadn't troubled himself over Gwyneth's inexperience.

Rutledge could see and understand a father's anger. He could also see—if it were true—that Quarles might have discovered in Gwyneth more than Cambury had to offer and tried to show her that she could reach higher than her parents had, her mother with six children, her father content with his fourteen hours a day in his bakery.

It didn't matter. Quarles was dead, and Hugh Jones had a very good reason for killing this man who was interfering with his family.

Rutledge said, "Did your father know you were running away?"

She looked down, as if ashamed. "I've written to him since March, begging to come home. I told him I was wretched and couldn't bear to be there, away from everyone. He knew I was unhappy. Still, he said I must stay for now. And so I didn't tell him I had decided to run away—he'd have come to Wales and stopped me, if he'd had to lock me in my bedroom. And so I slipped away without a word."

"Didn't you think your grandmother would be frantic with worry?"

"No. She doesn't like me. She says God didn't intend for a woman to be as pretty as I am, and it's a burden for her to keep an eye on me, and the devil works through a pretty face, and—" She burst into tears again.

Even if Jones had no idea his daughter was going to run away, he knew she was unhappy, and he must have missed her greatly himself. Tormented by the need to keep her away from Quarles, he could well have decided to take matters into his own hands and rid them both of the man who had caused the family so much grief.

Either way, the baker had much to answer for.

"Did you write to Mr. Quarles, to say you were leaving Wales?"

She looked up, shocked. "Oh, no, if I did that, Da would never let me come home again!"

Rutledge said to Miss O'Hara, "I think you should put her to bed straightaway, and keep her out of sight until I've had time to sort this out." And to Gwyneth, he said, "You must stay here for a day or perhaps two, and keep out of sight. Do you understand?"

"I want to go home to my mother and my sisters."

"I'm afraid you'll have to pay that price for leaving your grandmother's house without permission. Miss O'Hara has been put to a good deal of trouble taking you in like this, but she's done it for your mother's sake, and for your father's as well. If you don't listen to her, and gossips connect your unexpected return with Mr. Quarles's death, there could be long-lasting suspicion about your father's guilt even after we've found the killer. The bakery could suffer as well. You owe your parents this consideration."

"I understand," she answered petulantly. But she was young and, in the end, might not be ruled.

He waited until Miss O'Hara had taken the girl upstairs and put her to bed, then thanked her for her help.

She looked tired, and strained. "I know something about being hunted," she said. "That's why I took Gwyneth in. Her mother was at her wits' end. I think Mrs. Jones must be a little afraid of her husband."

"Perhaps not afraid, precisely. But she's feeling guilty about her role in hiding Gwyneth's return. Did the girl tell you more about how she managed to get this far on her own? She took an enormous chance."

Miss O'Hara smiled. "She dirtied her face and teeth, to make herself seem less attractive. Now you must go, before the neighbors begin to talk. I can hear Bertie in the next street." In fact the clink of milk bottles and Bertie's whistle were ominously close.

He smiled in return. "Thank you. Tell Mrs. Jones that patience will serve her better, and silence."

"Do you believe that this child's father killed Quarles?"

"God knows. For Gwyneth's sake, and her mother's, I pray he didn't."

Bertie had other gossip to carry with the milk that morning. Someone had told him the way in which the body had been found, and the shocking news turned the town on its ear.

It met Rutledge over his breakfast.

Rutledge said, irritated, "Who let slip this information?"

Hamish answered, "I wouldna' put it past yon inspector, in retaliation."

That was not only possible, but likely. It served two purposes. It annoyed Rutledge, and it made it more difficult for him to do his job properly. Often what the police held back was a key to tripping up a killer.

Padgett would be satisfied with both outcomes. Whether he himself was guilty of murder or not, he was in no haste to prove that someone on his patch had done such a thing. By the same token, if it could have been laid at Mrs. Quarles's door, Padgett would have been pleased enough.

Glancing out the window as he drank his tea, Rutledge saw the Quarles motorcar passing down the High Street.

Mrs. Quarles on her way to fetch her son from Rugby?

He pitied the boy. The whole ugly story of the murder was common knowledge now, and there would be no way to protect him. It would have come out in the course of the trial, and the newspapers were bound to make much of the circumstances. But that was months away, not now while the boy's grief was raw.

Padgett came to find him before he'd finished his tea.

Rutledge swallowed his ire with the last of his toast and waited.

"We're not slack in our duty in Cambury," Padgett said, sitting down. "My men have been busy. It appears one Harold Quarles dined with Mr. Greer on Saturday evening. But not until seven o'clock."

"I'm surprised that he didn't come to us with that information himself."

"You're free to ask him. That brings us to another problem. Where was Quarles between the time he left Hallowfields and his arrival on Minton Street? It doesn't take that long to walk in from the estate, now, does it?"

Half an hour at most, in a leisurely stroll. Which would mean he could have reached the High Street as early as six o'clock.

Where was Quarles for nearly an hour? At the estate still? Sitting in the gatehouse cottage, waiting for someone? Or had he come into Cambury?

"He met someone on the way," Rutledge answered Padgett. "It's the only explanation that makes sense."

"He was *expecting* to meet someone on the way. Or he'd have left later than he did."

"Point taken. Why did he dine with Greer? I thought they disliked each other."

"They do."

Rutledge pushed his chair back. "I'll want to pay a visit to Mr. Greer."

"I thought you might." Padgett, grinning, followed him out of the hotel.

The owner of the glove firm lived in a large house next but one to the High Street, with black iron gates and a handsome hedge setting it off.

Greer was just stepping out his door, on his way to his office, when the two policemen lifted the gate latch and started up the short walk.

Greer said, "We will speak here, at the house," as if he'd called the meeting, not the reverse.

A man of middle height with graying hair and an air of confidence, he waited for them to pass through the door before him and then shut it behind them. "This way."

He led them to a study at the back of the house, overlooking the side gardens. A bench in the grassy lawn stood beside a small pool, and a frog perched on the pool's edge. Set apart by trees, this appeared to be a retreat, and one of the long study windows opened on to it.

Greer took his chair behind the broad maple desk and gestured to the other two placed across from him.

"Well. This is to do with Harold Quarles. What is it you want to know?"

"He dined at your house on Saturday evening. What time did he arrive?"

"We had another guest, a Mr. Nelson. They came in together promptly at seven." There was something in his tone of voice that told Rutledge he was not pleased about that.

"Did Mr. Nelson bring Quarles in from Hallow-fields?"

"As to that, I don't know."

"Did they leave at the same time?"

"No, Mr. Nelson remained here for another hour or more. He had a business proposition to put before

us. Neither Quarles nor I approved of it. We both preferred to see Cambury stay as it is, rather than bring
in new industry to the area. Mr. Nelson believed that
the village could support two business enterprises and
wanted our backing in presenting his concept to the
town fathers."

"And so he stayed on to try to convince you?"

"Quarles was adamant in his position. He said what
he had to say early on, and then left. I expect Mr.
Nelson had already put as much effort into persuading
Quarles as he did afterward with me."

"What sort of new industry?" Padgett wanted to
know.

"He felt that gloves had seen their day, and that the
up-and-coming field would be leather goods of a different sort. Valises, wallets, diaries—a long list of items.
I think if Quarles had believed it would benefit me
in any way, he'd have been against change on general
principles. But I disliked the idea as well. For once,"
he said, smiling wryly, "we were actually in agreement
about this matter."

"You felt that Nelson met Quarles first, possibly
driving him here, in order to bring him around to his
position?"

"As Quarles left first and on foot, it's a natural
assumption."

"How did you know he left on foot?"

Greer flushed. "I asked my butler."

"As he was leaving, did Nelson follow Quarles into the street to finish the conversation between them?"

"No, of course not, I told you he'd stayed. He joined me in a glass of port, and continued to try to persuade me."

"Do you think Mr. Nelson had any reason to wish Quarles harm? That he might have followed him back to Hallowfields, talked to him again, and in a fit of anger, attacked him?" It was Padgett's question now, and Greer turned to him in disgust.

"That's absurd. Nelson mentioned three villages he's interested in for his factory. We were the first he spoke to, because of my glove firm. He still had two others to visit. One of them has nearer access to the railway. It would suit his purpose much better. But there's less competition in Cambury, and I think that held a great appeal." He shrugged. "Labor would be cheaper here, you see, versus the convenience of the railway for shipping."

"Is it possible that Quarles agreed with Mr. Nelson after all, and you went out as Quarles left and had words with him?" Rutledge asked.

"I don't pursue my guests into the street to harangue them."

"But you failed to inform us that you'd seen the victim on the evening he was killed," Rutledge said.

"I saw no reason to present myself at the police station just to tell them I'd had a dinner guest who later died. You found me soon enough, and as you can see, I was in no way involved with what happened to Harold Quarles."

"Has your staff told you that not only was Quarles murdered, he was also put into the Christmas angel harness and hauled into the rafters of the tithe barn?"

No one had. They could see the shock in Greer's eyes, and the graying of the skin on his face.

"My good God!"

Rutledge waited, saying nothing.

After a moment, Greer went on, "You suspect Nelson of having done such a thing? But how could he know the harness existed? He lives in *Manchester*." Greer stirred uneasily, as if thinking that should it benefit Nelson to kill one of the objectors to his project, why not make it a clean sweep and kill both?

He reached for the telephone on his desk and asked to be connected to Manchester, and the firm of one R. S. Nelson.

They waited, and in due course, Nelson was brought to the telephone at the other end.

There was a brief conversation, as if Nelson thought Greer was calling to change his position. Then Greer said, "No, I just wanted to ask if you'd spoken to Harold Quarles after you left me on Saturday evening?"

There was a reply at the other end.

Greer said, "No reason in particular. I could see that he was not going to budge. I wondered if you'd felt otherwise."

After a moment, grimacing, he said, "Well, if you must know, Quarles was murdered that night. And the police are here asking if you or I know anything about that, as apparently we're the last people to have seen him alive."

He listened, then said, "I see. I'll wish you a good day."

Hanging up the receiver with some force, Greer said, "He informed me he had no need to turn to murder to see his business prosper, and he'd judged Quarles as the sort who resisted change for the sake of resisting. And he accepted that, because, and I quote, 'I grew up in the north myself, and know a stubborn bastard when I see one.'"

He spoke the words with distaste. "I had no desire to work with that man on Saturday evening, and even less desire to do it now. If you will excuse me, I'm late at my office, and I think there's nothing more I can do to help the police in their inquiry." He stood up, dismissing them.

Rutledge said, "Thank you for your time. You'll still be required to make a statement about events of that evening. If you will give Inspector Padgett the direction of Mr. Nelson in Manchester, he'll ask the police there to take his."

That seemed to please Greer and make up for the unpleasantness of having to present himself at the police station.

He followed them out, and as he closed the gate behind them, he said, "I never liked Harold Quarles, and I've made no pretense of anything else. But I don't resort to murder to settle my differences. I would not have willingly invited the man to dine, most certainly not on a social occasion. Because he doesn't entertain at Hallowfields, it was left to me to invite both men here. I can tell you that my wife didn't join us. It was not that sort of evening."

He nodded and left them standing there.

"Pompous ass," said Padgett, watching Greer walk up the street.

"But he filled in that hour for us. What's left is to find out who argued with Quarles before he reached the corner of the High Street, where Hunter tells us he was alone."

"You believe him then?" Padgett asked. "And Nelson as well?"

"It doesn't appear to be a motive strong enough for what happened at the tithe barn. I hardly see this man Nelson killing someone he had never met before just to rid himself of an obstacle to the site for his factory. Do you?"

"No," Padgett returned grudgingly. "But by God, I'll see to it we have both statements in our hands."

They had reached the High Street themselves now, and in the distance Greer was just walking through a door. "His place of business?" Rutledge asked.

"Yes. Beyond Nemesis, in fact. You know, it could have been Stephenson who spoke to Quarles on the street. Or Brunswick. But probably not the baker, Jones. He would have been home at that hour, not prowling the streets. But my men tell me that sometimes Stephenson is restless and walks about at night."

"We'll have to ask him—"

Rutledge broke off. The rector, Samuel Heller, was coming toward them, distress in his face.

When he reached Rutledge he said, "You misled me."

"In what way, Mr. Heller?"

"You told me that Mr. Quarles was dead. But not the manner in which he was found. My housekeeper informed me this morning. Is it true? And if so, why did you keep it from me?"

"It was a police decision," Rutledge replied. "I didn't want that part of Quarles's death to be public knowledge until I was ready."

"And so we all have learned such terrible news with our morning tea, and from a servant! It's not proper."

"Would it have made any difference in what you told me?" Rutledge asked. "As I remember, you were not eager to judge others."

Heller had the grace to flush. "And I would still tell you the same thing. But this is—I don't know—I can hardly find the word for it. Blasphemous. Yes. Blasphemous suits it best. To use that angel in such a fashion. What drives another human being to that sort of barbarity?"

"If you remember, I warned you to beware of a confession that might mean someone is looking for absolution for what he'd done."

"Yes, Mr. Rutledge, you warned me, and I have been on my guard. But no one has come to confess. Though I have heard from Dr. O'Neil that Mr. Stephenson from the bookshop might have need of my counseling.

Apparently he's distraught, working himself up into an illness."

"Any idea why?" Rutledge asked.

"He lost his only child in the war. And he feels that he himself is partly responsible for the boy's death."

"In the war?" Padgett asked. "Quarles didn't have anything to do with it?"

Heller lifted his eyebrows. "Harold Quarles? I should think not. If there's anyone to blame, it's the Army. Or the Kaiser. What made you suggest Mr. Quarles?"

"Because Stephenson admits to hating him, indeed, he told us he wanted to kill the man. Where's the connection, if he's haunted by the son and hates Quarles?" Padgett asked.

"In his own poor imagination, I expect," Heller said with some asperity. "A man who is in great distress, great agony of spirit, sometimes blames others for his misfortunes, rather than face them himself."

"I'm a greater believer in connections than in spiritual agony, thank you all the same, Rector," Padgett said.

Heller smiled grimly. "I would never have guessed that, Mr. Padgett," and with a nod to Rutledge that was brief and unforgiving, Heller turned away and strode back toward his church.

"I think," Rutledge said slowly, "we ought to have another chat with Stephenson."

"What's the use? He's not ready to tell us anything. And I have work to do. You might contact the Army, to see if there's any truth in what the rector was told."

Changing the subject, Rutledge asked, "Has Mrs. Quarles made any decision about her husband's burial?"

"Yes, oddly enough. She's taking him back to Yorkshire."

"I can understand that she might not want him here, although that might be his son's choice. But why not London?"

"She said that he deserved to return to his roots," Padgett answered him. "Whatever that might mean."

Rutledge considered the matter. "Then whatever turned her against him might also have to do with his roots."

"She knew what he was when she married him."

"Yes, she's honest about that. But what did she learn later that made her judge him differently and demand a separation? Apparently Quarles didn't fight it, and it's possible he didn't want whatever it was to become open knowledge. For that matter, why was she searching his background in the first place? Was she looking for something—or did she stumble over it? And I don't believe it was Charles Archer wounded in France that upset the marriage."

"You can't be sure of that," Padgett objected.

Rutledge gave him no answer. He was already in a debate with Hamish over the subject, Hamish strongly supporting the need to find out more about Quarles's past while his own pressing concern at the moment was the bookseller.

Padgett said, "Well, I'll leave you to your wild goose chase. I'll be at the station, if you want me."

Hamish was saying now, "What about yon lass? Ye canna' leave her much longer."

"Let her sleep. Then we'll see what to do about her. I'll have to tell her father. And that should answer a lot of questions."

He walked on to the doctor's surgery, found that Dr. O'Neil was busy with another patient, and asked his nurse if he could speak to Stephenson without disturbing the doctor.

She was willing to allow him to see the patient, she said, if he promised not to upset the man. "We've got five people in the waiting room, and I don't want a scene."

"Has Stephenson been upsetting the household?"

"Not precisely, but his state of mind is delicate. I was asking him just this morning if there was anyone we might send for, a cousin or something, to help him through his distress, and he began to howl. I can't describe it as a cry, and the doctor's wife came running to see what was the matter."

Small wonder that O'Neil had sent for the rector.

Rutledge gave her his word and hoped that he could keep it as he was led back to the room where Stephenson was sitting on the edge of his bed, his face buried in his hands.

He looked up as Rutledge came through the door, then dropped his head again, saying, "What is it you want? Can't you leave me alone?"

"I'm worried about you," Rutledge said easily. "I think there's something on your mind that you can't let go. Is it the fact that Quarles is out of reach now, and there's no one else to hate? Except yourself?"

His words must have struck a chord. Stephenson lifted his head again, his eyes showing alarm. "What have you found out? What do you know?"

"Very little. You mourn for your son. You hated Harold Quarles. There has to be a link somewhere. And if you hate yourself, it was because you feel you let your son down in some way, when he needed you most."

Stephenson began to cry in spite of himself. "Yes, yes, I should have put him on the first ship out of England, and let him go somewhere—anywhere—safe. But I didn't. He was so young, and I wanted to keep him with me. He was so like his mother, so gentle and sweet-natured. I couldn't let him go—and so I killed him."

Alarmed, Rutledge said, "When?"

"Damn you, not literally. I'd never have laid a finger on him."

"Then how is Quarles involved? I'm tired of playing solve the riddle."

Stephenson, burdened by his shame, buried his face in his hands again, unable to look anyone in the eye.

Rutledge, considering what Stephenson had just told him, asked, "Was your son called up in the draft and afraid to go to war?" It was hazarding a guess, but he was surprised at the reaction.

Stephenson rose to his feet to defend his son, gathering himself together to shout Rutledge down. He could see it coming.

And so he added, "Or was the coward you?"

Stephenson gasped, his features changing from pure blazing anger to such self-loathing that Rutledge had to look away.

But he thought Stephenson was lying when he said, "Yes, it was I. I couldn't bear to see him brutalized by the army, shoved into the battle lines, told to kill or be killed. I couldn't live with that."

It was the *boy* who'd been afraid, who had wanted to take ship. And the father who was determined to keep him in England. The boy, not the man.

"What could you do about it?"

"I went to the only person I could think of important enough to help me. I went to Harold Quarles—I'd grown up in Cambury, my mother was still living here—and I begged him to find a way to get my son out of the army. I told Quarles what would happen if I let him go, and I promised him anything, that I would do anything he asked, however difficult it was, if he would go to the Army and tell them not to send Tommy across to France."

"And what did Harold Quarles promise you?"

Stephenson's face twisted in grief. "He wouldn't even hear me out. He refused to help. I tried to tell him that they have all sorts of units. Quartermaster, signals, radio, enlistments—none of them having to do with actual fighting—and I told him Tommy could do those. He was cold, unyielding, and told me that he would not speak to the Army for me or anyone else. And so Tommy went to be trained as a soldier, and he was shipped to France, and on his first day at the Front, he waited until the trench had emptied and bent over his rife and pulled the trigger. The letter from his commanding officer called him a coward and said that he had disgraced the company. All I could think of was that he was dead, and that surely there had been some way for a man as powerful and well thought of as Harold Quarles to stop him from going abroad."

He was silent in his grief now, and that was all the more telling as he stared into a past he couldn't change. Rutledge rested a hand on his shoulder.

"I wanted to kill his commanding officer, then I realized those were only words, they didn't matter. It was Quarles who was to blame, and I wanted to make him suffer as I had done. I came here to haunt him, I wanted him to think about Tommy every time he passed the shop or saw me on the street, and remember his own child. I made a point to find out when he was returning to Cambury, and I put myself in his way as often as I could. And when I had wrought up my determination, I was going to kill him. But like my son, I couldn't find the courage to do anything. Like my son, I couldn't bring myself to kill, and yet I wanted it as I'd never wanted anything before or since, save to keep Tommy alive."

Stephenson saw himself as failing Tommy twice, Rutledge realized. In not saving him in the first place and then in not being able to avenge him in the second. And as long as Harold Quarles was alive, the opportunity to kill him still existed. Once Quarles was dead, it was too late for vengeance. And so the bookseller had punished himself by putting that rope around his neck. It wasn't so much a fear of the police that had driven him; it was the knowledge that when he was questioned, his shame would be exposed to the whole world. Tommy the coward, son of a coward.

But the story *was* out now.

As if Stephenson realized that, he lay back on his cot, his arm over his face, and his face to the wall.

Rutledge said, "Thank you for telling me. Whatever you feel about Harold Quarles, the fact remains that we must find out who killed him. It's a question of justice. As for his failure to help you and your failure to help your son, there are times when no one can help and a man's life has to take its course. Tommy wasn't the only one in that battle who was afraid. Most of us in the trenches were terrified. It would have been unnatural not to be."

Stephenson said, "He was the only one who didn't go over the top that morning. He was the only one who used his weapon against himself rather than the enemy. He let all the world see his fear and judge him for it. I think of that often, how awful his last hours— minutes—must have been, with no one to tell him he was loved and must live. I wasn't there, I wasn't *there*."

The final failure, in the father's eyes.

"Nor was God," Rutledge said, and sat with the grieving man for another quarter of an hour, until he was calmer.

16

Rutledge went back to the O'Hara cottage and tapped lightly on the door. He had the distinct feeling that every window overlooking where he stood was filled with people waiting to see how he was received.

Miss O'Hara answered his knock, her finger to her lips. "She's asleep. I can only hope her mother is resting as well. What are we to do? Have you spoken to her father?"

"Not yet." He followed her into the pretty room he had hardly had time to notice that morning. There were comfortable needlepoint cushions everywhere, a row of small framed photographs on the mantel, and surprisingly, a pair of revolvers mounted on a polished board. As he glanced at them, she said, "My father's."

There was defiance in the words, as if Rutledge might think she had no right to them.

Certainly they were incongruous in this very feminine setting, but he had no intention of rattling her pride.

She offered him tea, but he declined, adding, "You've been up most of the night, I think. Sit down. We'll have to work this out between us. The rest of the family, Gwyneth included, will be too emotional to choose what's best."

"What *is* best?" she countered.

Rutledge took a deep breath. "I don't believe Gwyneth could have killed the man. I don't think her mother, much as she hated what Quarles had done to her family, would have carried the murder to such extremes—"

"Yes," she interrupted with a little shiver. "I've heard the tale of the Christmas angel. It's barbaric. Mrs. Jones might well have killed him, but not that. I agree."

"Which leaves us with Gwyneth's father, and whether or not he knew about the letter from her grandmother."

"Does it really matter? The child's complained to him enough. He might have decided to bring her home the only way he could."

"Coincidence?" Rutledge shook his head. "I don't know. It will not be easy talking to him. But I don't think Mrs. Jones will be able to cope when he comes home this evening. It will spill out somehow—a child asking why Mummy cried all day, a neighbor wanting to know why she was here in your house at such an ungodly hour—and she will break down and tell him the truth."

"She's stronger than you realize. But his suspicions will be aroused."

There was a short silence. He said, "You told me you knew something about murder. And about being hunted."

"That I did. It's why I'm in England, the last place on earth I'd like to be. I was caught in the middle of the Easter Rebellion in 1917. I did what I had to do, to save myself and my family. And after that I had to leave. Do you want to take me up for that?" He could feel her anger and resentment.

"It's not my jurisdiction," he answered mildly. "If it has no bearing on Quarles's death, then I have no business interfering."

"Thank you for being so damned condescending," she flared, her voice rising a little before she could control it.

"Condescending?" He smiled, and it touched his eyes. "Hardly. It's you who is still sensitive. I'm merely putting your mind at ease."

She had the grace to laugh lightly. "You were in the trenches, I think. You know what war is like. Well, it was war in Dublin. And elsewhere. We were under siege, and we were afraid of what would happen if we lost. What sort of retribution there would be for us and, more urgently, our families. I went to the fighting to bring my father's body back, and I had to kill someone to do it. I don't regret it, he doesn't invade my dreams, and I'd do it again if I had to."

She would have been an easy target, with that flame red hair. It had been a brave thing to do to go after her father, and it could have ended horribly. Right or wrong, his cause or not, Rutledge could respect her courage.

Returning to what had brought him here, Rutledge said, "May I leave Gwyneth in your care for a little longer? I'll be gone for some time. Don't let her leave, for any reason."

"No, I've kept the door locked until 1 look to see who's knocking. I've said my prayers for that family. I hope God is listening."

As he rose to leave, Miss O'Hara said, "She won't go back to her grandmother's. I can tell you that. She was wretched, and the old woman used her unmercifully. The tyranny of the weak. And then she had the unmitigated gall to tell the poor lass that she was the devil's get whenever Gwyneth failed to please her."

"I don't think the family knew."

"They must have. But they closed their eyes because there was no other way to keep her out of the man's clutches. Quarles had much on his soul when he went to God, and the names of Gwyneth and her family are engraved on it."

Rutledge went out the door and waited until he'd heard the click of the key locking it before turning toward the Jones's house.

Hamish was saying, "Ye ken, you were taken in."

"By what?"

"That one, the Irish lass. Ye absolved her of the killing withoot a single proof that what she said was true."

"It's not my jurisdiction," he said, a second time.

"Oh, aye? She's done you a guid turn and bought your silence."

"It doesn't matter right now. The girl does."

"She admits to a murder," Hamish admonished him. "What's to say that the second killing wasna' easier? And the lass has a temper. When he spoke on the street, she gave him short shrift. But who is to say what happened next between them?"

It was true.

"But it will have to wait," Rutledge said. "Hugh Jones must be sorted out first. Before he learns that Gwyneth is back in Cambury."

Hamish said, still not satisfied, "She holds on to a guid deal o' anger, that lass. She would ha' put him in the rig to be a lesson, even if only for her ain pleasure. Yon murderer felt the same anger. It's no' a thing most of the village could ha' done."

"I don't see Stephenson dragging Quarles to the tithe barn and manhandling him into that cage. But then it might explain his strong sense of guilt."

"Ye ken, ye havena' delved into yon dead man's past. Is it to put yon inspector's nose oot of joint that ye cling to this village? Just as ye went in sich a great hurry to London, to spike the guns of the ither inspector?"

"That's nonsense!" Rutledge snapped, and then realized he'd spoken aloud.

He wasn't aware that during his conversation with Hamish he'd been standing outside the Jones house. Going up to the door, he hoped it would be Mrs. Jones who answered, not one of the children. But she was quick, before he'd knocked, as if she'd been watching for him to come. She could see the O'Hara house from the south window of her parlor.

The little girl wasn't on her hip today, and she glanced over her shoulder as she opened the door, as if to be sure there was no one about.

"Do come in," she said softly, and as soon as they were shut into the little parlor, she went on. "How is she? I was that worried—she was in such a state when I opened the door. God alone knows she took an awful risk, all alone on those roads! I knew she was unhappy . . ."

Her voice trailed off.

"She's sleeping. It's what she needs. But she won't go back to Cardiff. You do see that, don't you? The next time she may not be as lucky."

"Well, she won't have to now, will she—" And she broke off, her hand to her mouth, as if to stop the words, but it was too late.

"With Quarles dead?"

"He was an awful man. I can't wish him alive again. And I want my girl home to stay. Her gran's getting on. She wasn't always such a terror. But what choice was there, I ask you!"

Her eyes were pleading with him to tell her that everything would be all right, that this nightmare would resolve itself without trouble for anyone she loved. But he couldn't, and after a moment, she looked away, sadness pulling her face down. "What are we to do about Gwyneth? She must come home. I want her here, not at a stranger's house."

"Mrs. Jones, I must ask you again. Can you be absolutely certain that no one in the house told your husband about the letter from Wales?"

"I don't see how anyone could have done. The post came when only the baby was here, and she wouldn't know. And I kept it safe in my apron pocket, where no one would look."

But he could read the uncertainty in her face now. The fear that she hadn't done enough.

"Would you have killed Harold Quarles to keep your daughter safe?" he asked bluntly. "I have to know."

She looked at him then. "If it was to be Gwynnie or him, I'd choose Gwynnie. But what about the rest of them, what are they to do without me, if I'm gone? Besides, I've heard what was done to him. Much as I wanted him away from Gwynnie, I couldn't have brought myself to touch him . . ."

On the whole, Rutledge thought that was true. She wasn't the sort of woman to take pleasure in her vengeance. It would be enough for the man to be dead, out of her daughter's troubled life.

"I must go now and tell your husband. Will you do nothing until I've seen him?"

"When he comes home tonight, what will he say? That's what frightens me. He'll *know* I kept secrets. As well, he'll be angry with me for keeping Gwynnie from him."

"I can't promise you he won't be angry."

"You think he's done this thing."

"I don't know, Mrs. Jones. And that's the truth."

"He *could* have pulled him up on that rig. He's done it before for the Christmas angel . . ."

He was shocked that she would admit it. At first he wondered if she was trying to shield herself, the mother, the protector of her children. And then he realized that she was thinking aloud, that she had forgotten he was there in the agonizing drain of her own worry.

He said good-bye, and she nodded absently, her mind so wrapped up in the question of whether the man she'd married and given six daughters to was capable of murder, that he wasn't sure she knew when he left.

The walk to the bakery was silent. Hamish had finished what he wanted to say. But Rutledge's thoughts were heavy. If he took Jones into custody, who would keep the bakery open? Not his wife. And not the girl, despite her training up to fill his shoes. What would become of this family?

It was the duty of a policeman to be objective. He'd told Padgett that. And yet sometimes it was impossible to ignore the different personal tragedies that murder brought in its wake. Few of those touched by violent death walked away unscathed.

Hamish said, startling him, "There's yon widower, as well."

"Brunswick. Yes, I know. If indeed he killed his wife, would that have satisfied his jealousy? Or did he bide his time and wait for the opportunity to stalk Quarles? Or—if he didn't kill his wife, if her death was a suicide—he might well kill Quarles and put him in that contraption, to have the final word. And Stephenson's case hinges on whether he scraped up the courage to act on behalf of his dead son."

They were just passing Nemesis, the bookshop. Rutledge wondered if it would ever reopen. The CLOSED notice was still in the window. But then people were surprisingly resilient sometimes. The shop might be all the man knew to do, and the only haven from torment. Books were a great comfort, because they didn't stand in judgment. He would feel safe among them.

The bakery was just ahead now, Jones bowing a well-dressed woman out, a white box in her hands and a smile on her face. Then he looked up the High Street and saw that Rutledge was coming his way. As the woman moved on, Jones stood there, and something in his posture told Rutledge that he knew—or guessed—what was coming. He straightened his apron, as if girding his loins for battle, and waited.

When Rutledge reached him, Jones said, "Come inside, then."

Rutledge followed him into the bakery. It was redo-
lent with cinnamon and baked breads, swept clean, the
shelves sparkling like diamonds in the sun coming in
the windows. At present the shop was empty. It wasn't
time for the tea trade to come.

"Will you have something?" Jones said, to put off
the inevitable. "Are you a man with a sweet tooth?"

"Thank you, but it's important for us to talk before
someone comes in."

Jones nodded to two wrought-iron chairs, painted
white and the seats covered with a rosebud-patterned
fabric. It was where women could wait until their
orders were ready. Incongruously now it served as a
place of interrogation.

As he sat down, Jones said, "I didn't kill the man.
But you don't believe me." There was strength in his
voice and certainty. "That's how it stands now."

"But there are new extenuating circumstances to
answer to, Mr. Jones."

The Welshman was wary now, as if half afraid
his wife had confessed. Or that Rutledge had discovered something Jones believed hidden too deep to be
found.

"Your daughter ran away from her grandmother's
house—"

"*When?*" His voice was taut with fear.

"Several days ago."

Jones surged from his chair and started for the door. "Close up behind me, I'm on my way to Wales. This business of Quarles can wait. There's my daughter to be thought of."

"Wait—*we know where she is.*"

Jones stopped in his tracks. "What do you mean, you know?"

"She's been found. She's safe."

But the man was not satisfied. "I'll see her for myself. If that man talked her into anything rash, I'll go to the doctor's surgery and cut out his liver, dead or not, see if I don't!"

There was such rough menace in his voice that Rutledge could believe he would do just that.

"Sit down, man, and let me finish," he said curtly.

Jones stood where he was by the door, grim and determined.

"I said, sit down, Jones, or you'll learn nothing more." It was the voice of a man accustomed to being obeyed on a battlefield. Jones didn't move for an instant longer, then grudgingly came to sit down, his body so tense Rutledge could see the cords standing out in his neck.

"She's safe. And she's had no dealings with Quarles. She's said as much, and I believe her. Homesickness made her run away, and a grandmother who berated her for being pretty."

He growled, like an animal, deep in his throat. "She wrote she was unhappy, but I didn't want to believe her. I didn't want to see what the old woman was capable of. I wanted her safe, that's all."

"Let go of your hate and think about your daughter. And what this means in terms of your own guilt."

"*My* guilt?" There was something in his eyes that Rutledge couldn't read. But he could see that Jones's mind was moving swiftly and in a direction that was unexpected. Yet he said nothing, and sat where he was.

"If you knew Gwyneth had run away, it would make the case for your killing Quarles strong enough to bring in a verdict against you. At least at the inquest. If you found out she'd left Wales and decided to make certain this time that your daughter could remain in Somerset, the next logical step would be confronting Quarles. There would certainly be words between you, and if in his usual callous way he turned his back on you, it would surprise no one if you lost what was left of your temper and killed him. It's an explanation I'm bound to tell the inquest. But is it right—or wrong? I must make a decision, Jones, and you will have to give me the unvarnished truth in order to make it."

Jones looked him in the eye. "How did you learn all this about my daughter running away? Who knew, to tell you?"

"At the moment—"

"It was my wife, wasn't it? It has to be. Did Gwynnie write her a letter?"

Rutledge could answer that. "No."

"Gwynnie's mother's been crying. I could see it when I came home at night. Redness that she said was from soap in her eyes or the baby's fist striking her while she was nursing. But it was a letter, wasn't it? From Gran, then, if not from Gwynnie."

He had come to the truth in his own fashion. A man with a mind that was as sharp as the knives with which he cut the dough on his board, he had let himself be blinded by his love for his daughter. But now he was thinking clearly and about to protect his wife.

Rutledge cut him short. "Your wife couldn't have put Quarles in that apparatus—"

"Oh, yes, I heard about that. But I could have come along behind her and done it, couldn't I? To throw suspicion away from her. That's how it'll be seen. Well, I won't have it. I killed the accursed Harold Quarles, and I ran him up into the rafters like a rat on a string. And if you let me see my daughter one last time, I'll go with you to the station and sign my statement. I give you my word."

"And what," Rutledge demanded, irritated, "will become of the bakery and your family? Had you forgotten?"

Jones blinked, as if he'd been slapped in the face. "I've trained my girl, she can run it for us."

"Damn it, man, she's still half a child. How is she going to manage? And at her age, what will this do to her, slaving the hours you do, even if your custom stays with you. Coming home at night tired and dispirited, with nothing to look forward to but another morning baking bread for people who stare at her and remember you were hanged."

Jones took a deep breath.

It was extraordinary, Rutledge thought, to watch two people trying to protect each other, out of sheer fright. And neither had the courage to ask the other for the truth.

"No, don't tell me again that you're guilty. Go home and speak to your wife, man, and between the two of you, try to make sense. We don't need martyrs, we want to find a killer."

Jones said staunchly, "I told you, I killed Harold Quarles."

"And not a quarter of an hour ago, you were prepared to tell me you hadn't. Talk to your wife. Afterward I'll take you to Gwyneth. Your daughter shouldn't be there until you've come to grips with yourselves. In the interim, stay here and think about what you're asking of your wife and your daughter. Cambury has a long memory, Hugh Jones, and you'll find if you confess to murder, even the murder of someone as unpopular as Harold Quarles, there will be people who turn against you. It's how people are."

He got up to leave. There was no fear of flight in this case, he thought, Jones wouldn't leave his family to face their nightmare alone.

Jones called to him as Rutledge was reaching for the door. "She couldn't have done it. It's not in her nature to kill."

But Rutledge thought he was trying to convince himself, not the man from London, as he spoke the words. Sometimes doubt was the deadliest of fears. It grew from nothing more than a niggling concern until it overwhelmed trust and shone a new light on small inconsistencies, white lies, honest mistakes, and human frailty. And as it distorted perspective, it could also distort the truth. Words taken out of context loomed terrifyingly large, and in the end, doubt could convince a loving husband or wife that their partner was capable of the unthinkable.

Both Hugh Jones and his wife were in the throes of doubting, and they would never quite be the same again.

Outside on the High Street, Rutledge swore. It hadn't gone well, this business with the baker. But it had been doomed from the start, because the girl had run away. Would Jones persist in his assertion that he'd killed Quarles? Or would his wife persuade him to let the police do their work unhindered.

And in the meantime, what was he, Rutledge, to do if one of that family *was* a murderer?

Padgett was just coming out of the station.

"You look like a man who wished he hadn't seen a ghost," the inspector said in greeting.

Rutledge was in no humor for the man's badgering. "I want to know what it is you held against Harold Quarles. And I want to hear it now. If not in the station, we can walk on the green."

"I told you—"

"I know what you told me, and I'm damned well running out of patience. What did Quarles do? Threaten to have you dismissed? It's the only reason I can think of, other than insulting your wife, for your refusal to give me the truth."

"It's none of—"

"—my business. But it is. This is your last chance. Talk to me, or I'll know the reason why."

Padgett walked away, as if turning his back on Rutledge. Then he whirled around, his face twisted with fury. "I gave you my word I hadn't killed him."

"Other people in Cambury are having to watch their most private affairs being aired in public. Why should you be different? Whether you killed him or not, I want to know what lay between the two of you. I want to make my own judgment call. I can tell you, if I'm recalled to London, you'll fare less well with the man who will take my place. At least you know you can rely on my discretion."

"All right. Let's be done with it. You won't be satisfied until you know. There were two occasions when the bastard swore he was going to speak to the Chief Constable and have me dismissed. And he could do it. Rich and powerful as he was, he could do it. The Chief Constable doesn't like to be disturbed. That's why I called London myself, instead of going to him. Anything for peace, that's his belief."

"What happened with Quarles?"

"One such occasion was when Hunter was having trouble with him at the hotel. It was while Quarles was rusticating here. I stepped in and Quarles told me flat out that he would see the Chief Constable the next day. He did, and I was dragged on the carpet for upsetting an important man. Told to mind my manners and get along with my betters, and stop this nonsense."

"That must have stung."

"You have no idea," Padgett said trenchantly.

"And the other occasion?"

"It was shortly after Quarles moved into Hallow-fields. I had to remind him that the two dogs he had at that time—not the spaniels, but two large brutes—couldn't be allowed to run free and attack the sheep of nearby farms. He told me they'd done no such thing. I replied that I had eyewitnesses and would pursue the matter. He told me he'd have the Chief Constable teach me my manners. And I was called to account. I referred the Chief Constable to the farmers who'd complained. And when he spoke to them, Quarles had paid them off without my knowledge. They denied losing a single sheep. But the dogs were penned at night after that, and I was left to look the fool."

"Where are they now? The dogs?"

"They were old, they died some time ago. They weren't eating the sheep, just chasing them and killing them, for sport. I never found out what price he'd paid the farmers, but they blandly lied on his behalf and left me hanging out to dry. Lazy he may be, but the Chief Constable has a long memory, you'll find. And that's why I couldn't have you going to him. It would be the last straw. I'd lose everything."

It could, Hamish told Rutledge, explain the bark of the dog outside the tithe barn that attracted Padgett to investigate: a well-honed lie that had about it the sweet taste of vengeance.

"You heard a dog the night Quarles was murdered."

"So I did. You can't disprove it."

"Nor do you seem to be able to prove it."

Padgett said, "I've told you. Now the matter is closed. Do you hear me?"

"You still haven't grasped the fact that by your own admission you're a suspect. Don't you see? Whether you like it or not, whether I wish to pursue it or not, you had a very good reason to kill that man. Don't expect favors from me. I will treat you as fairly as I do everyone else."

"Is that why you've held information back from me? Do you really think I've killed Harold Quarles?" There was something in his eyes, a measuring look, that made Rutledge want to step back, away from Padgett.

"It doesn't matter what I feel. I'll want to find your statement ready for me tomorrow morning. About finding the body. Whether I use it or not, I must ask for it. And whether you want to give it or not, personally and professionally, you have no choice."

"Damn you." Padgett turned and went back into the police station, slamming the door behind him.

Rutledge let out a long breath.

But the question now was, how had Brunswick learned of Quarles's two attempts to have Padgett sacked? Had he been present, that night in the hotel dining room? And had someone—his wife?—told him about the earlier event? There must even have been talk in the village at the time, forgotten though it might be now.

Hamish said, "Ye must ask yon clerk why he didna' tell ye that the inspector was present when there was trouble."

That was easily dealt with. Rutledge crossed the street to the hotel and went in search of Hunter.

The manager was working in his office behind Reception. He rose when Rutledge came through the door, wariness in every line.

Rutledge greeted him and got to the point. "You didn't tell me, when you described the problem you had with Harold Quarles here in the hotel dining room, that you had called the police in."

"Inspector Padgett was here that night, a diner. He and his wife were celebrating her birthday. He came to my assistance when Quarles turned nasty, and intervened."

"Did you know that Quarles had spoken of this to the Chief Constable, in an effort to have Padgett dismissed from his post in the police?"

Hunter's eyes slid away. "Yes. I heard later. It was talked about. I didn't wish to bring it up. It wasn't my place. If you want to know more, you should speak to Inspector Padgett."

"If you've misled me about this, how do I know that you've told me the truth about Quarles arguing with someone—Quarles turning the corner out of Minton Street, and the fact that you have no idea where he went from there."

Hunter said, "I told you the truth. My truth. I thought it was best that Inspector Padgett explain his role and the consequences of his actions."

"Because this information could involve him in the murder?"

Smiling wryly, Hunter said, "That's not my problem. It's yours. It seems he's told you. Or someone has. Either you've leapt to conclusions about the Chief Constable being approached, or you know what transpired there. I don't. I kept my position and Mr. Padgett kept his. That was what mattered."

"Who else was here that night? Do you remember?"

"The dining room was quite busy that evening. I can't recall everyone who was here. Mr. Brunswick.

Mr. Greer. The rector, dining with a curate he knew from another living. Others. It was a matter of face, you see. Mr. Quarles was intent on saving his, and Inspector Padgett was trying to calm a volatile situation. Quarles insisted that I be sacked from the hotel, but fortunately for me, the owner had no intention of being bullied. Hardly, you'd think, a reason to kill a man."

"In your case, possibly not. But this was relevant to my inquiries. What else have you neglected to tell me?"

"Nothing. To the very best of my knowledge, I've spoken only the truth."

"A truth with holes in it."

"There are no other holes. I swear to you."

Hamish said, "Ye ken, he didna' need to kill the man. Only lie for someone else."

Padgett?

Was that who had quarreled with the victim on Minton Street after he'd left the Greer house? And had Hunter shut his eyes—or his ears, in this case, and told the police he hadn't recognized the voice of the other person?

Murder was a strange business, as Rutledge had learned from years of meticulous detective work and well-honed intuition. The smallest clue could change a case from the most straightforward appearance of truth to a tangled web of lies. Or vice versa. There could be no small mistakes, no withholding of evidence to spare someone—or to condemn someone.

Had Hunter lied for Padgett?

On the whole, Rutledge thought not. There appeared to be no real connection between the two men. No depth of commitment that would make one protect the other. After all, neither had lost their positions, in spite of Quarles. Padgett had been shamed by his superior and in front of his fellow villagers. And so had Hunter. But in a vastly different sense.

Padgett depended on his standing in Cambury for his authority and influence as a policeman.

Rutledge said, "If there are any more omissions you'll like to mend, you know where to find me." And he walked out of the office, leaving Hunter chewing his lip.

From the hotel, Rutledge went to Miss O'Hara's house. Gwyneth was still sleeping, and he told Miss O'Hara about the interview at the bakery.

"Mrs. Jones is afraid he killed Quarles—he's used that apparatus—and he's afraid she has, though he knows she wouldn't have thought of hanging him in the beams of the tithe barn," he ended.

"But he's going to confess to protect her?"

"He's confused, worried about his wife, worried about his daughter, and in the end, to protect both of them, he's willing to step forward."

"Is it a smoke screen, though?" she asked, twisting her long slim fingers into knots. "Is he hoping you'll refuse to hear his confession and leave him in the clear after all?"

"There's that. I've told him to go home and talk to his wife. She may tell him his daughter is here, and she may not. I want you to be prepared."

"It will be a tearful reunion." She sighed. "All right, I'll do my best to keep them from foolishness, if they come here first. But look at this, Mr. Rutledge. He never swore to you that he didn't see that letter. If it were kept in her apron pocket, it could have fallen out. He could have seen it. He wouldn't tell her if he had."

"True."

She looked at him thoughtfully. "You don't want the killer to be one of the Jones family, do you?"

"If the fates are kind . . ." He smiled.

"Did you think he might be afraid that Gwynnie killed Quarles?"

"She couldn't have put him in that harness."

"But if she had killed him, her mother, whatever the qualms on her own account, might have gone back to the scene and tried to hide the body. She might have thought of the cage. She might have reasoned that if Quarles could just go missing for a day or two, she could smooth over her family's anguish regarding Gwyneth's whereabouts and make it all come out right."

"Mrs. Jones might have tried to hide the body, but she'd have been in a great hurry to get back to Gwyneth, for fear she'd do something foolish. The rig would have taken too long. No. I saw her after she'd got the letter, and she was frantic, she didn't know where her daughter was. Besides, the girl reached Cambury after Quarles had been found."

Miss O'Hara said, "Yes, that's true. Look, you've got me spinning motives in my head. I don't know what to believe."

"Do you want me to take the girl away? Is she too much for you?"

"Here she's safe from talk. Let her stay."

He thanked her and left. He was almost on the point of going on to the Jones house to tell Mrs. Jones how her husband had reacted to the news of his daughter's return but decided against it. Let the man and his wife work out their own problems first, and the girl's next. After that it was more likely that the truth would come out. One way or another.

Padgett. Jones. Brunswick. Stephenson. Mrs. Quarles.

What was it about this case that he couldn't put his finger on? Why didn't he have that instinctive sense of where an inquiry was going?

It all came back to that damned cage. Who knew about it? And why would someone want to put a dead man in it, and leave him to hang among the shadowy beams of a medieval tithe barn?

What was the truth behind not the murder but the hatred that launched it?

17

In the event, Hugh Jones sent for Rutledge almost a quarter of an hour after he'd closed the bakery and come home.

Rutledge had spent some time talking to the War Office on the telephone, asking for the military record of one Thomas Stephenson. After several delays as he was sent to one desk after another, Stephenson's description of his son's death was confirmed. The officer reading it was cold, unsympathetic, and Rutledge wondered if he had ever served in France or merely kept the accounts of those who had and considered himself an expert on trench warfare.

He wasn't ready to confront the tangle of Hugh Jones and his family. But he walked there, and when no one answered his knock, he let himself in.

"I couldn't wait," Jones said as Rutledge came though the parlor door. "I shut the bakery early. My wife's not here, there's a neighbor caring for my girls, and nobody knows where Gwynnie is. I asked her sisters. They haven't seen her."

"She's with Miss O'Hara. I expect your wife has gone there against my advice. Your daughter slept most of the day. This will be the first opportunity her mother has had to speak to her."

Jones heaved himself from the horsehair sofa. "Then we'll go to the Irish woman's cottage."

Rutledge walked a little ahead of him, and when they reached the house, he could hear raised voices inside. Miss O'Hara opened her door, and it was plain that she'd had enough.

Like parents everywhere, Mrs. Jones's fright and worry had dissolved into anger, and as her daughter stood before her, hangdog and crying, she was berating her for causing the family such grief.

Gwyneth looked up to see her father coming into the room, and she stood poised for flight, like a startled animal knowing it was cornered and had nowhere to go. Mrs. Jones, whirling, gasped and fell silent.

Jones stood where he was, taking in the situation at a glance.

"You did a bad thing," he scolded his daughter. "You caused us much grief and your mother's tears." His voice was stern.

"But you wouldn't let me come home. You did *nothing*," the girl cried.

"And whose fault is that, and now the man is dead, and we're being looked at by the police. Because you couldn't mind your father or listen to your mother. *Girl, you're going to be the death of me.*"

His voice broke on the last words, and he stood there, his mouth open, nothing coming out, and his face was filled with all the things he wanted to say and couldn't.

Gwyneth turned and ran back through the house, to the room where she'd been sleeping. Her mother, with a swift glance at Jones, started after her. But Rutledge stopped her.

"No. She's better off out of this. Mrs. Jones, I've come to take your husband into custody. I'd promised that he could see his daughter first."

"You'll do no such thing," she said, fighting through her emotional turmoil. "I killed that man."

"Don't be a fool, woman—" Jones began, but she turned on him next.

"And what have you done but thunder and threaten to kill the devil yourself, and fumed with frustration that your daughter had to be sent away while he still lorded it over the village? I heard you a thousand times and, yes, so have your children and, for all I know, your neighbors. Where there's the power of words, you are a murderer. And God help me, so am I, because in my heart I wanted to see him dead."

They stared at each other.

Out of the corner of his eye, Rutledge saw Miss O'Hara step out her own door and move into her garden, her hands clasping her elbows and hugging her arms to her chest.

Jones had turned to Rutledge and was repeating what he'd claimed earlier. "I killed the man. Let it be done with."

"You're a stubborn Welshman, Hugh Ioan Jones. Do you hear that?" his wife accused.

He said, for the first time showing gentleness, "What would you have me do, love, let you hang in my place?"

She began to cry. "I just want things to be the way they were. I want to go back to when we were safe and the only worry was how to feed the next mouth."

He crossed the room and gathered her in his arms. "I'd do anything for you, love. Die for you, even."

She was not a woman of beauty. Time and child-bearing had worn her down, and worry had added lines to her face and drawn the color from it.

"There were times I wondered," she said, then pushed him away. "Go to your daughter, Hugh Jones, and then come home to your dinner. I doubt it's edible now. But we'll eat it anyway."

He held her for a moment, then without a word went down the passage to find Gwyneth.

Mrs. Jones looked up at Rutledge. "We're a sorry lot, bragging of being murderers. And you still aren't sure, are you?"

Rutledge asked wryly, "Are you?"

She said simply, "If he'd killed Harold Quarles, he wouldn't have touched me. He'd have gone directly to Gwynnie, for fear he'd break down."

It was a woman's reasoning, but Rutledge nodded. Whether or not it cleared Hugh Jones was another matter.

She sighed. "I'll go fetch the children and set out our dinner. I doubt any of us will swallow more than a spoonful."

He let her go, and waited. After a time, Hugh walked into the parlor without his daughter.

"She'll come home in her own time. I'll ask Miss O'Hara if she minds keeping her a little longer."

He walked past Rutledge and went out the door.

Rutledge waited, and in ten minutes, her face washed and her hair brushed, Gwyneth Jones stepped shyly into the parlor.

The resilience of youth, he thought.

"The selfishness of the young," Hamish countered. "*She* got what she wants, even if no one else did."

She was indeed a pretty girl, despite the dark circles beneath her eyes and the strain in them only just easing. In a small voice she apologized to Rutledge for being so troublesome, and then looked around for Miss O'Hara.

"She's in the garden. She wanted to give your family a little privacy."

Gwyneth nodded and went out.

After a time, Miss O'Hara walked back in her own house and shut the door behind her.

"Well," she said, hands shoved into the pockets of the short jacket she was wearing, "all this drama has made me hungry. You'll take me to The Unicorn to dine. I'll expect you in half an hour, and let the gossips be damned."

He found himself laughing.

And then realized that she was quite serious.

The next morning, Padgett met Rutledge at the dining room door as he was leaving after his breakfast.

Padgett followed him into Reception and said, "The rumor mill has been busy. I hear you had dinner with the lovely Miss O'Hara. Won't look good in London, will it, if you have to take her into custody for murder."

"I doubt she killed Quarles because he flirted with her in the street."

"Oh, ho! She's already in the clear—" He held up a hand before Rutledge could make the retort that Padgett saw coming. "Never mind. We've got a far different problem. The baker, Hugh Jones, is in the station wanting to make a statement."

Rutledge swore silently. "Let him make whatever statement he cares to write down and sign. But we'll not take any action on it until I'm satisfied he isn't lying."

"His girl's come home. He thinks that makes him your favorite suspect."

"And it does. But I haven't yet been able to show he knew she'd left her grandmother's. If Jones killed Quarles without knowing she was leaving Wales, it was coincidence."

"She'd written him that she was unhappy there. He just told me as much. He might have been clearing the way for her to come."

Rutledge considered Padgett. "Do you really think Hugh Jones is our murderer?"

"Better him than me," Padgett said tersely. Then he added, "I don't see him leaving his family destitute. And he would. Still, if Quarles goaded him, who knows what he might have forgotten in the heat of the moment? He's a strong man, mind you."

"There's something else I want to speak to you about. Let's walk."

They went outside where they couldn't be heard. Rutledge said, "This business with Brunswick leaves me unsatisfied."

"Whether he killed his wife or she killed herself?"

"In a way. Sunday, when we were discussing past murders here in Cambury, you told me about a young soldier returning from the war who believed his wife had been unfaithful. He knocked her down and killed her."

"Yes, he claimed it was in a fit of temper."

"Who was the man he suspected of sleeping with her?"

Padgett frowned. "We never knew. He told me he'd killed his wife, and there was the end of it. Gossip claimed it was a lorry driver who'd been seen about the place from time to time, but he turned out to be her brother. And after killing her, the husband wasn't about to besmirch her good name. Odd business, but for all I know, the war turned his mind, and it was all in his imagination. There was no talk about her before he came home."

"Could the other man have been Harold Quarles? There's a rumor about a mistress. Was she this woman? Or is his mistress just wishful thinking on the part of busybodies?"

Padgett's eyebrows flew up. "Quarles? Somehow I don't see it. And nor did the gossips. But there's her farm, and this business of him playing squire when he first came to Hallowfields. It could have begun that way. What put you on to that possibility?"

"Thinking last night about Brunswick and his wife."

Padgett shook his head. "The soldier's wife was quite pretty. But water over the dam, now. Nothing we can do about it, even if it was Quarles."

"It might explain why Brunswick was so certain his own wife was unfaithful. There was precedent."

"I put that down to his naturally jealous nature. But you never know. Dr. O'Neil is releasing Stephenson today. With orders not to open the shop for the rest of the week."

"I've spoken to the Army. Stephenson's son died in France of a self-inflicted gunshot wound. Has the rector been to see him?"

"Yes, according to O'Neil, Mr. Heller was there for nearly an hour. And he said that afterward,

Stephenson appeared to be in a better frame of mind. We seem to be at a standstill. Do you think we'll find our man?" He was serious now, and his eyes were on Rutledge's face, trying to read his thoughts.

"We'll find him," Rutledge answered grimly. "Whoever did this went to great lengths to leave behind no evidence we could collect or use against him. But there's always something. When we have that, we'll have him."

Padgett was silent for a moment. Then he said, "You're the man on the spot. I'll see to Jones. And I'll have a brief chat with Brunswick as well."

He nodded and walked away.

Rutledge stood looking after him with mixed feelings.

Almost without conscious thought, Rutledge went to the hotel yard and got into his motorcar. He hadn't planned to drive out to Hallowfields, but he found himself drawn again to the tithe barn, restless in his own mind, unable to pinpoint what it was that niggled at the corners of this inquiry, why it was he couldn't seem to draw all the edges together and make a whole.

He had watched Mrs. Newell do that with her willow strands, the basket taking shape under her deft fingers, the certainty with which she worked demonstrated by the steadily rising levels on the basket sides, the way the willows, whippy and straight, bent and wove to her fingers, and the simple grace with which it all came together.

Would, he thought, driving down the High Street toward Hallowfields, that murder inquiries had the same subtle texture and execution.

He left the motorcar by the main gate and walked from there to the gatehouse at the Home Farm, then stood in its little garden, trying to put himself in the darkness of Saturday near midnight, and the confrontation in this place that must have led to murder. After a moment he went across to the one stone that had been slightly dislodged from its neighbors. No blood or hair would have adhered to it. Whoever had used it would have seen to that. But he hefted it in his hand and felt the smooth weight of it, the neatness with which it filled his palm and the size, which allowed him a firm grip.

It was made for murder, he thought, as perfect a weapon as even an ancient warrior could have found, before he learned how to shape a tool for killing.

Hamish said, "It's whimsy, this."

Rutledge smiled and put it back in its place beside its neighbors.

He looked up at the gatehouse, across to the tithe barn, no longer guarded by one of Padgett's constables, and then down the lane toward the Home Farm.

Was there nothing here to re-create that scene of murder?

Pacing on the grassy verges of the lane, he tried to shut his mind to someone calling somewhere in the distance and the sound of a tractor rumbling into a barn.

At the end of his next turn, he looked up, following the flight of a bird, and realized that the parkland on this side of the road, part of the estate, had a matching stretch of wood on the far side, perhaps thirty feet deep, and overgrown. Whether or not it belonged to the estate, he didn't know, but seedlings must have escaped from the park over the decades and found fertile soil there, making themselves a poor reflection of their better grown neighbors.

Walking over the road, he stepped into the bushy tangle of wildflowers and brambles that marked the verge, and went about ten feet into the wood, so that he could look back at Hallowfields from a different perspective.

He realized he had a better view of the Home Farm lane from here than he did from the estate property, and moved another half dozen steps among the trees until he could see both gates—that to the farm, and the drive to the house.

Changing his angle a little, he nearly stumbled over a length of halfrotten wood from a fallen tree.

He turned to look down at it, and what struck him then was how out of place it appeared, even here amidst all the other tangled debris of winter.

Curious, he began to walk in a half circle, and about ten feet away he found the rest of the tree the length had come from. Lichen covered the stump from which the tree had split, and in its fall it had broken into two sections. The longest half was disintegrating where smaller branches lay half covered in last year's leaves. Just where the shortest length should have been was a mossy depression. That section had been lifted out and moved to a better vantage point.

No animal could have done that.

He walked back to the length he'd seen first and measured it, and then looked once more at the empty space where it had been removed from the rotting trunk. Yes, a perfect fit.

This wood wasn't dense. Anyone walking here could easily be seen from the road. But in failing light or in the dark, when there was no movement to attract the eye, no light to pick out shapes or brightness of skin, someone could sit on that short length of trunk and wait, with a perfect view of the entrances to Hallowfields.

How had he come here? By foot? Bicycle? Motorcar? Where would he have hidden a motorcar?

Rutledge left the wood and walked on up the main road, just as a lorry came roaring past, leaving him in a cloud of dust.

The wall of the estate ran on for some distance, but there was a rutted track some fifty or sixty yards away from the gates where a team and farm equipment could pull in and turn around. It was used often enough— the grass was matted and torn, muddy in places, deep grooves in others.

In the distance he spied a small farm, the barn's roof towering over the house, and a team standing in the yard while a man bent over the traces.

Between the track and the farm was plowed land, already a hazy green with its spring crop.

A vehicle sitting here on a Saturday evening would be invisible in the darkness.

Hamish said, "Yon inspector told ye there were no strangers in the village."

"Yes. But if someone drove through, without stopping, it would make sense."

"Aye, but why not afoot? Quarles was on foot."

"That limits where he came from—and where he could go afterward."

"Ye're searching for straws. Gie it up."

"Someone waited there."

"Sae ye think. But ye canna' say *when*. And how did he know what was in the tithe barn?"

Rutledge began to walk back to the wood. "True enough."

What about the man Nelson? Had he waited here for Quarles? No, Quarles left the Greer house and would have been well home and in his bed before Nelson came this way again. If Greer was telling the truth.

Who argued with Quarles outside the Greer house? Who had known to look for him there? Had the argument not been resolved, and so he had come ahead of Quarles to pursue it again?

Padgett? He admitted to being on this road the same night . . .

It had been some time since the incident in the dining room of The Unicorn—why should Padgett suddenly attack Quarles? Why *now*? That was a sticking point.

Was there something that had happened more recently? Tipping the scales, trying a temper that was already on a short leash?

Padgett hadn't been very forthcoming. It could be true.

No one would notice a policeman passing along this road. It was regularly patrolled, because of Hallowfields. It wouldn't be reported that Padgett had come this way—if he hadn't taken over his man's last run, if he hadn't found the body, who would have known he was here waiting?

Rutledge reached the log again and sat down carefully, so as not to ruin his trousers. But this bit of wood was dry, and his feet sank comfortably into a slight depression that appeared to be made for them.

It would be possible to sit here for some time . . . hours if need be.

Who? And how many weekend evenings had someone waited here, to catch Harold Quarles unawares?

Standing up, he found a few long twigs and set them up around the log, put his coat over them to resemble a man, his hat on the log itself, and went back across the road.

In the daylight, he might well have seen the coat, looking for it. But it didn't strike the eye at once, and if there was no movement, he'd have missed it. Even with the sun out.

Rutledge went back to retrieve his clothing, and cranked the motorcar.

Hamish said, "What does it prove?"

"Nothing. We still have the problem of the apparatus."

Coming into Cambury, he was reminded of something Hamish had accused him of earlier, that he hadn't looked into Quarles's past.

And then one name leapt out at him. The partner, Davis Penrith.

He hadn't asked how Quarles had been killed.

Rutledge hesitated, nearly pulled into The Unicorn's yard to make a telephone call to London. And instead he gunned the motor and drove through the village without stopping.

Hamish called him a fool. "It's no' what's wise."

"I couldn't think straight Monday morning. I didn't have any reason then to question him further. It wasn't until I'd left London that I realized he showed no curiosity about his partner's death. If they worked together for nearly twenty years, there would have been *some* interest in the man's demise. Even if they disliked each other after the breakup of the partnership."

"Excuses," Hamish grumbled, and settled into a morose monologue for the rest of the journey.

It was late when Rutledge reached the city. Nevertheless, he went straight to Penrith's house.

The footman who answered the door at this late hour was dubious about disturbing Penrith.

"He's entertaining a guest," he informed Rutledge, "and told me he'd ring when the guest was leaving. He didn't want to be disturbed, meanwhile."

"Yes, I understand. But this is police business, and it comes first."

The young footman stood there uncertainly for a moment, then replied, "I'll go and ask."

He came back five minutes later. "Can this wait until tomorrow?"

"It cannot."

The footman went away again, and when he returned, he led Rutledge into a small room at the back of the house that appeared from the way it was decorated to belong to Penrith's wife. The furnishings were feminine, painted white and gold, the chairs delicate, and the hangings at the windows trimmed with tassels.

Penrith was standing there, a frown on his face, when Rutledge walked through the door.

"I hope you've come to tell me that you've caught Harold's murderer."

"In fact, I haven't," Rutledge said easily. "I've come with questions I should have asked you on Monday."

"This is not the time—"

"I'm afraid your business with your guest will have to wait."

It was interesting, Rutledge thought, watching the man, to see that a stern front made him back down. If the partnership was to have succeeded for many years, it would have been Quarles who was the dominant force. Penrith couldn't have controlled the other man.

Hamish said, "But ye didna' know him alive."

Rutledge nearly answered aloud but caught himself in time. To Penrith he said, "This may take some time. I suggest we sit down."

Penrith sat at the small French desk, and as Rutledge took the armchair across from him, Penrith said, "I don't care for your tone."

"For that I apologize. But the fact is, time is passing and I need to confirm several pieces of information before I can move forward."

At this Penrith seemed to relax a little, marginally but noticeably. As if he was more comfortable with a simple request for information.

"In the first place, why did you and the victim sever your business ties?"

"I've told you. I wished to spend more time with my family. I'm not a greedy man, I've made enough money to live comfortably for the rest of my life. Why spend every hour of my day grubbing for more?"

"Surely you could have stayed within the partnership and simply cut back on your appointments. In fact, you appear to have one this evening."

Penrith picked up the pen by his wife's engagement book. "You didn't know Harold Quarles. There was no such thing as half measures for him."

"Did your decision to leave have anything to do with the Cumberline debacle?"

The pen snapped in Penrith's fingers.

"Where did you hear of Cumberline?"

"I saw the box in the victim's study. And there is some talk in Cambury about his 'rusticating' there. I put two and two together. Something went wrong, and you left the firm."

"I didn't intend to defraud anyone, if that's your insinuation." As an afterthought he added, "And I don't think Quarles did, either."

"But he made no attempt to prevent a handful of people from investing in a foolhardy scheme that was bound to fall through."

"Some people think they know best. There's nothing you can do to educate them or protect them. Some of those who made a great deal of money during the war were hot to double it. I found that distasteful. But I didn't try to trick them."

"Did you have your own money in Cumberline?"

"A little—" He broke off. "Why am I being questioned like this?"

"Because your partner is dead and there's no one else I can ask. Let's suppose, for the sake of argument, that you disagreed with Quarles's methods in dealing with Cumberline, and in order not to be tarred by that brush, you decided the time had come to leave James, Quarles and Penrith."

He didn't need to hear confirmation of his question. It was written in Penrith's face.

"And I'd like to suggest to you that you haven't always seen eye to eye with your partner."

"Here," Penrith said, leaning forward, "you aren't suggesting that I killed the man!"

"I'm trying to get to the bottom of Harold Quarles. If his own partner didn't care to be associated with him any longer, and if his wife has made her own arrangements to deal with the problems in her marriage, I want to know more about the man and who else might have hated him."

"I didn't *hate* him—"

"I think it more likely that you feared him."

Penrith got to his feet. "I won't hear any more of this."

"We are speaking of Quarles, not of you. If you feared him, why didn't his wife?"

That caught Penrith off guard. "I—don't know whether she feared him or not."

"It seems that a few years into their marriage, she learned something about him, what sort of man he was, that caused her to separate from him legally. Not just a move to another part of the house, but terms drawn up by their solicitors. Just as you did financially."

There was worry in Penrith's eyes now that he couldn't conceal.

"I don't know what their relationship was—or why. She stopped coming to London, and they stopped entertaining. And Quarles became a different man, in some ways. He never spoke of his wife to me after that. I told myself it might be because of Archer . . ." He stopped. "Does she tell you she feared him? That he might have made her come to regret her decision?"

There was intensity in the question that Penrith couldn't keep out of his voice.

"Whatever it was that came between them, she appears to feel a deep and abiding emotion of some sort. I think, if you want the truth, that she acted to protect her son."

Light seemed to dawn behind Penrith's eyes. "Yes," he said slowly. "I begin to see what you are saying."

"Then what was it that turned Maybelle Quarles against her husband?"

Penrith sat down heavily. "I don't know what it was."

"But you must have some suspicion. It wasn't only Cumberline that turned you away from the firm the two of you had built together. The immediate cause, perhaps, but not the long-standing one."

That hit its mark, but Penrith said nothing.

"What is there in Harold Quarles's background that could have brought someone to Cambury to kill him?"

"Considering the reputation he had for being overbearing and dictatorial in the village, I should think you would find enough suspects there to satisfy any police inquiry," he retorted.

"The more I question the villagers, the more I hear one thing: whatever their grievances, people tell me that Harold Quarles wasn't worth hanging for."

Hamish said, "He didna' mention the women . . . It was you."

But then, not living in Cambury, he might not know, Rutledge answered silently.

When Penrith made no reply, Rutledge said, "You never asked me how he died."

Surprised, Penrith said, "Didn't I? Of course I did."

"He was struck in the head with one of the white stones that ring the iron table in the Home Farm's gatehouse garden."

Penrith turned away. "That's terrible." But the words lacked feeling.

"Did you know that Quarles provided a Christmas pageant in the tithe barn on his property, for the entertainment of the village?"

"I was the one who went out and found that confounded camel," Penrith told him with some force. "It took me the better part of a week."

"Why were *you* sent on such an errand? Why not one of the house clerks?"

"Quarles was threatening to sack everyone in sight. God knows why he wanted a camel—I expect it was something his son asked for."

"We know very little about Quarles's life before he came to London, only that he'd worked in the mines, came south to make his fortune, and so on. You must know more than that."

Penrith was suddenly wary. "His background? I don't think he spoke of it, except for that early story about his mother's ring. He was an odd sort. He'd dredge up stories about going down for coal, and they rang true. People believed him. And five minutes later, he was a Londoner through and through. The time came when I didn't really know what to believe. Whether he used the coal face to promote himself, or whether he really did go down. He said once that his parents' house had been eaten by the coal. That he had nothing to go back to but bad memories."

"No one came from Yorkshire to visit him? No one stopped him on the street to beg a few pounds from an old friend? No one wrote to him?"

"He told me his family was dead. I had no reason to think that was a lie," Penrith said defensively "After all, I didn't really give a damn about his past."

"You were a curate's son, I believe?"

"Yes. How did you know that?"

"Someone told me that you gave respectability to the firm, after Quarles took over from the James family."

Penrith flushed. "If you say so. I had no prospects when I—when I came to London. Like most young men, I was grateful to find a position. I had no expectation of rising in it."

"Where was your father's living?"

"In Hampshire. Why?"

"You didn't know Quarles before you were thrown together in London?"

"That's right. I don't see where this is going."

Neither did Rutledge. He was looking for anything, a crack in Penrith's armor, a small piece of information that he could move ahead with. But his sixth sense, his intuition, told him that something was not right. Penrith seemed to alternate between fears for his own standing and distancing himself from Quarles.

"Look, I've left my guest for long enough. If you will come again at a more convenient time, I'll be happy to continue this conversation."

Rutledge stood up. "Thank you. I will."

Penrith was waiting for Rutledge to precede him through the door. But as Rutledge came up to him, he stopped and said, "What village was that in Hampshire?"

Penrith stiffened. "I thought perhaps you would prefer to know where in Yorkshire Harold Quarles had come from."

"I think that door is shut. Quarles himself closed it a long time ago. Thank you for your time, Mr. Penrith."

He walked by the man and down the passage the way he had come. Penrith followed him as far as the entrance to the house, as if to be certain he was gone.

When Rutledge had reached the street, he looked back, and Penrith was still standing there.

Hamish said, "Ye're a fool if ye drive far again tonight."

"I'll go to the flat," Rutledge answered, cranking the car.

He was caught in London traffic, and on the spur of the moment he turned toward the Yard in the hope of seeing Gibson leaving, but no such luck. He was looping back toward the west end, and as he pulled into the swirl around Trafalgar Square, he saw Mrs. Channing trying to hail a cab. It was late, a busy evening, and she looked tired.

Without thinking he maneuvered the motorcar to the lions, nearest where she was standing, and called, "Can I give you a lift?"

He would have done the same for his sister, Frances, or for Maryanne Browning.

She looked up, smiling in recognition. "Ian. How lovely! Yes, I'd be glad of a lift."

He waited for her to slip in next to him, and she said, light and dark flitting across her face as he drove on, "I was at St. Martin-in-the-Fields with friends. A memorial service. "

"At this hour?"

"It was especially arranged for this hour, actually. An evening concert in his memory. The music was wonderful. His family arranged it—they do every year, on the Thursday evening closest to his birthday. A rejoicing for his life, short as it was."

He wanted to ask who the friend was but refrained. "You're on your way home, then."

"Yes. I had a letter from Elise. They're having a lovely time."

"That's good to hear."

The conversation dwindled as he turned toward Chelsea, as if neither of them knew quite what to say next. A few drops of rain spattered on the windscreen. Mrs. Channing saw them and said, "Well, I'm doubly grateful to you now, Ian." Her last words were lost in a downpour, and she laughed. "It's quite like Dunster, isn't it?"

The thunder soon followed, and she moved a little nearer so that her voice would carry, one gloved hand pulling her coat closer against the chill of the sudden storm. "Mrs. Caldwell telephoned me. We're having lunch together next week. I think she's planning a little dinner party for the bridal pair when they return."

He had forgot Elise Caldwell's father, and his invitation to call. Caldwell was in the same business as James, Quarles and Penrith.

Meredith Channing was still speaking, and he realized he'd missed half of it. Just ahead was her house, and as he drew up to the walk, he said, "I think there's an umbrella somewhere—"

"It's not far, don't bother. I should ask you to come in for tea or coffee, but I'm tired tonight. Another time?"

"Yes, thank you."

She got out, shut her door, and with a quick wave dashed to the house. Her maid was there to let her in almost at once.

As the door closed behind her, he sat where he was, the motor ticking over, and wished he'd asked her where the Caldwells lived.

18

It wasn't difficult to find out where Caldwell & Mainwaring was located in the City, and Rutledge was there as the doors opened the next morning.

He sent in his card, and Caldwell himself came out to greet him. "This is a pleasant surprise. What brings you to our part of the city? Not murder, I hope?"

"As a matter of fact, it is," Rutledge said. "I'm here about the death of Harold Quarles."

Caldwell frowned. "Yes, I've just heard. Disgraceful business. I hope you find whoever did it and quickly. What can I do to help?"

Caldwell led him to a corner office where the heavy Turkey carpet set off the elegant mahogany desk and the suite of chairs arranged in a half circle near the windows. Gesturing to Rutledge to be seated, Caldwell rang and asked for tea to be brought. Then he joined Rutledge. Pointing to the portrait over the mantelpiece, he said, "My father. He was a man you'd have liked. The son I lost was his image. It was like losing my father twice."

"I can imagine how it must have been."

It was evident Caldwell was waiting for the tea to be brought, and when they were settled, and his clerk had withdrawn, he said, "Now, to business. You must have come for information. I hope I have it."

"What do you know about the background of either partner, Quarles or Penrith?"

"Not much more than everyone else. Penrith's father was a curate in Sussex—"

"Sussex? I thought I was told Hampshire."

"No, Sussex it was. I'm nearly certain of that."

Then Penrith had lied.

"Go on . . ."

"Quarles came from somewhere around Newcastle. Coal mining, which he was lucky enough to escape, according to the accounts he gave. I met him several times when he was clerk to Mr. James the younger. There was something about him—and this will sound to you quite discriminating on my part, but it isn't—that didn't seem to march well with his story. I had the feeling that there was more to him than met the eye. And that was it, something in his eyes, as if the real person were locked away behind them. I had the feeling that he could be quite ruthless if he chose."

"An interesting point."

"Yes, and I said something to my father about it. His reply was that I had no way to measure how rough the man's life had been, or how he had managed to escape the fate of his brothers. The story was that they'd died in a mining accident and he didn't want to do the same."

"There appears to have been some ruthlessness on his part aside from working his way into a prosperous business," Rutledge said, thinking about Cambury.

"Nevertheless, Quarles quickly changed from the rough diamond he claimed himself to be to a rather polished one. He married well, and he had a reputation for scrupulous honesty—"

"Even when it came to Cumberline?"

"Ah. That was an odd story. I think it was seven men who paid dearly for investing in that disaster. Quarles swore he'd put some of his own money into it, but I find that hard to believe. He was too astute."

"Do you know who these seven men were?"

"I don't. But there should be files of transactions somewhere. We're required to keep track of such things."

Rutledge saw again in his mind's eye the box marked cumberline on the shelf in Quarles's study at Hallowfields.

"What else can you tell me about him?"

"Nothing, I'm afraid. Oh, there was one thing, rather strange I thought at the time, but I can't remember why it disturbed me. We were standing outside a restaurant in the Strand, and a young woman came up to us, asking if we'd like to subscribe a sum for the memorial that was being erected to the men missing on the Somme, those who were never found. We all gave her money toward the cause—how could you not? All save Quarles. He turned away from her and said something to the effect that he was not an army man, that he'd sent in his subscription for the navy dead instead."

"It seems to me the simplest thing was to make a donation and let it go," Rutledge responded.

"Yes, but the young woman was asking to write our names down on the subscription list, to go into a book they were intending to place in the memorial."

Rutledge could almost hear Stephenson's voice, breaking as it recounted how he'd pled with Quarles to speak to the Army on his son's behalf. And Quarles refusing to even entertain the idea.

"He was too old for the war," Hamish said, without warning. "And his son is verra' young still."

Both comments were true. But Rutledge had taken up enough of Caldwell's time, and the teacups were empty. Courtesy required that he leave.

"Is there anything else you can think of?"

"No. I don't care to speak ill of the dead. If you weren't a policeman, and someone I trust to use the information wisely, I would never have told you as much as I have."

"Thank you, sir, for your trust. It isn't misplaced."

They shook hands, and Rutledge left.

Outside in the street, he mulled over the fact that Penrith had lied.

Why?

He found a telephone in a hotel and called a friend of his who had been an Anglican priest. Anthony Godalming had lost his faith and retired to his family's home in Sussex. He rarely went out and seldom spoke to old friends. But Rutledge reached the man's sister, told her it was urgent, and in time Goldalming came to the telephone.

His voice was neither friendly nor unfriendly—it seemed to hold neither warmth nor coldness. But Rutledge could tell his call was not welcomed, a reminder of too much that still had to be put behind, for sanity's sake.

"Anthony, thank you for speaking to me. I'm looking for someone, a curate in Sussex some years ago. Twenty perhaps? Longer, even. His name was Penrith. He had one son."

"Penrith?" The man on the other end of the line seemed to dredge deep in memory and come up short. "I don't recall anyone of that name down here. Are you sure it was Sussex?"

"Before your time, then?"

"It could be. Does it matter greatly?"

"Yes. I need to find the father, if he's alive. And the son as well, if anyone knows where he may be. London, possibly."

There was a long silence. "Very well. Tell me how to reach you."

Rutledge gave him instructions to call The Unicorn in Cambury.

"Has this to do with the war, Ian? Tell me honestly." There was strain in Godalming's voice now.

"No. To my knowledge, neither man was young enough to serve with us. This has to do with a murder inquiry. That's why I'm searching for information. Otherwise, I wouldn't have asked you."

"Surely the police have ways to find these men."

"I don't think they do. You have the only fact I've been able to dig up, and that's little enough."

Rutledge heard a grunt that might have been in disagreement.

"Thank you, Anthony."

"Not at all." There was a click at the other end.

Driving fast as he reached the outskirts of London, Rutledge headed for Somerset, his mind sifting through what Penrith and Caldwell had had to say to him.

It had been, for the most part, a very unproductive journey. Penrith's relationship to Quarles had not been worth pursuing, or so it seemed, and yet that one lie about where his father had been curate still rankled. Why had he felt the need to lie?

"It doesna' mean," Hamish said, taking up the thread of Rutledge's thoughts, "that he's a murderer."

"It's possible he has his own secrets to conceal. His own background. Was it really Penrith who initiated the separation from Quarles? Or the other way around?"

But that didn't make sense. A man like Quarles would have made it his business to know any secrets that Penrith possessed. It was in his nature, as it was in Penrith's to bury his head in the sand.

What had broken up Quarles's marriage? And what had broken up Quarles's partnership?

This occupied Rutledge's mind all the way to Somerset, and late as it was when he arrived, he drove straight to Hallowfields and knocked on the door.

It was several minutes before someone answered his summons. Mrs. Downing, still in her black dress with the housekeeper's keys on a chain at her waist, the symbol of her office even in this modern age, was not pleased with him.

"It's late, Mr. Rutledge, and you've disturbed the household. Mrs. Quarles is not here."

"Yes, I understand she's gone to Rugby. I need to look at something in Mr. Quarles's study, and you don't need her permission to allow me to do that."

"Can't this wait until the morning?"

"I'm afraid not."

Reluctantly she let him into the foyer, and then when the door was securely locked once more, she led him up the stairs.

Charles Archer, in his dressing gown, was rolling down the passage toward them, coming from the other wing as Rutledge reached the first floor.

"Is there trouble?" he asked anxiously, but Rutledge shook his head.

"I've something I wish to see in the study Mr. Quarles used here at the house. I'm sorry to call so late, but it's rather urgent."

"To do with what? I thought you'd inspected his rooms."

"To do with his business in London."

"Ah. Then I can't help you. Downing will see to it for you." He turned away but stopped and swung around. "The man who brings the milk and the gossip told the staff you were on the point of taking the baker, Hugh Jones, into custody for Harold's murder. Is this true?"

"I can't comment on that tonight."

"It's nonsense, Rutledge. The man's no killer. He has a family to consider."

"Then who would you put in his place?"

Archer had the grace to look away. "I'm not offering you a sacrificial lamb."

"What can you tell me about Quarles's former partner, Davis Penrith?"

"Penrith? I hardly know him. He's been to the house a time or two, dining here with his wife at least once. He never seemed comfortable in Harold's company. I always thought that odd, since they'd worked together for years."

"They didn't appear to have much in common, other than their business dealings."

"That's not unusual, is it? Business seems to attract opposites sometimes. It's not a requirement to share interests." Archer turned toward his rooms. "Good night, Rutledge. I hope you find what you're after."

Mrs. Downing, standing silently by and listening to the conversation, waited for instructions. Rutledge said, "It's the study I need to see."

She led the way, took his keys, and unlocked the door for him. From a passage table she took up a lamp and lit it for him to use.

It took only a matter of two minutes to locate the first Cumberline box and lift it from the shelf. He took it to the nearest chair, sat down, and opened it.

All that was inside was a thick sheaf of papers, and he thumbed through them quickly, interested not in what they referred to but in names of investors.

He found that there were groups of paperwork, clipped together to keep them separate, and each had a name at the top.

Seven of them. No, eight.

He went to the desk, found paper and pen, and began to jot the names down.

Mrs. Downing, her face disapproving, said, "I'm not sure this is regular, Mr. Rutledge. I've had no communication with Mr. Quarles's solicitors, and Mrs. Quarles is away. I can't, in good conscience, allow you to remove anything from—"

"I'm not removing these papers, Mrs. Downing. I need the names listed on them." He continued to work, then double-checked what he had done, to make certain he had all the names down.

Finishing with the file, he put it back where he'd found it and thanked Mrs. Downing.

She followed him out of the rooms and she locked them again, then returned the keys. On the way down the stairs she said, "Young Marcus will be here soon, with his mother. I hope it won't be necessary for the police to be tramping about, asking questions and disturbing the family at all hours. It won't be good for the boy."

"The police have work to do, Mrs. Downing. It can't be helped. But I'll keep in mind that the boy will be in residence."

They had reached the door, and Mrs. Downing opened it for him. Then, as he stepped out into the night, she said, "If you want my opinion, it's Mr. Brunswick who killed Mr. Quarles. I never liked the man, he treated his wife something terrible. Jealous and overbearing and always looking for the worst in people. I saw him a time or two, prowling about, looking to see if he could catch his poor wife in something. If he didn't want her here, why didn't he put his foot down?"

Rutledge stopped. "You didn't tell me any of this before."

"No, and for a very good reason," she said. "Hazel Brunswick confided in me. She took her tea in my rooms, not with Mr. Quarles, and she talked sometimes about her life. I kept her confidences. All he wanted to spend money for was music. The house was bursting at the seams with it, and she was tone-deaf; she couldn't hear anything he played. That's why she came to work here, to provide for herself and the children to come. She defied him, if you want the truth, and Mr. Quarles thought it was all a game, but I knew it wasn't. He struck her once—"

"Quarles?"

"God save us, no, it was Mr. Brunswick struck his wife. And that's when she decided to find work, because she said he would respect her more if she could stand up to him and didn't have to beg for whatever she wanted. But once is never the end of it, is it? Once becomes twice, and twice thrice, and it's on its way to being a habit, isn't it?"

"Surely the people at St. Martin's Church knew? The rector?"

"He never hit her in the face, you see." There was something in her gaze that looked back to another woman and another past. "I was married to one such, I know their ways. He was killed in a mill fire, and I was glad of it."

Rutledge believed her. "Did you know Mrs. Brunswick was ill?"

"She told me what she thought it might be. It crushed her. All her hopes and plans gone for naught.

She said he didn't care for sick people, that he'd turn away from her and wait for her to die."

"Do you think Brunswick killed her, or that her death was a suicide?"

"I can't answer that. But Mr. Brunswick had the nerve to come here. He followed Mr. Quarles home one night, just after she died, and called him a murderer. I'd been to the Home Farm to take a lemon cake to Mrs. Masters, and I heard them down by the gatehouse. He was shouting, you couldn't help but hear, asking for money to pay for her burial, asking for compensation for turning his wife from him."

"What did Mr. Quarles say to that charge?"

"He laughed and told Mr. Brunswick not to be tiresome. I thought they'd come to blows, but just then I saw Mr. Quarles striding up the lane, and I went the other way, so as he wouldn't think I was eavesdropping."

"I've heard Mr. Brunswick play. He's a very fine organist."

"He has to work hard at it, he's not gifted. Hazel told me that was the sorrow of his life, and why she pitied him. He wanted to play in a cathedral, and all he was fit for was St. Martin's Church, in a small living like Cambury."

"I wish you'd spoken to me before—" he said again, but she shook her head.

"I had to weigh up what I felt I could say. Mrs. Quarles wants to see this inquiry closed quietly, for the boy's sake, and if you arrest Mr. Brunswick, Hazel Brunswick's unhappiness and her suicide will be dragged up again and talked about, and the gossip about Mr. Quarles and her being lovers as well. It wasn't true, Hazel Brunswick wasn't that kind of woman. Now my conscience troubles me. I should have done more to help her than I did. I should have told Mr. Quarles about the beatings, or Rector. And if her husband killed her, and then killed Mr. Quarles, then justice must be done. I hope Mrs. Quarles will understand."

"Who met Mr. Quarles in the gatehouse, Mrs. Downing? Someone did. You have only to walk through it to guess what its purpose was."

She gave him a pitying smile. "It was where he would have brought his mother, if she'd lived. Though he'd go and sit there sometimes, brooding."

Rutledge could hear Hamish's voice in the darkness as they had walked through the small, tidy rooms. *Respectability*—

"There was never a mistress who waited for him there?"

"He'd have liked the world to think so."

"Why wouldn't his mother have lived here, in the house? If he cared so much for her?"

"He'd have passed her off as his old nanny, no doubt. I ask you," she replied spitefully. "He was ashamed of his roots, didn't you know? He bragged about them, and he used them, but he didn't want to be what he was. He'd buried his past so deep even he couldn't remember the half of it."

She shut the door in his face, and Rutledge stood there, remembering what someone had told him, that Mrs. Downing was Mrs. Quarles's creature. She might not have killed for her mistress, but could she be counted on to veil the truth or twist it in a different direction to serve another purpose? He'd have to keep that in mind.

Still, servants were often guilty of snobbery. They took their standing and their self-worth from the man or woman they worked for. And Mr. Quarles had never lived up to Mrs. Downing's standard—how could he, when she perceived his social level to be so much lower than her own?

He turned back to his motorcar, feeling the miles he'd driven, and the lateness of the hour. But Hamish was saying, "Ye canna' leave it."

"Her charges against Brunswick? No. But tomorrow is soon enough."

"If he followed him once, he followed yon dead man again and again."

"Very likely that's why the log was moved."

"And when Quarles turned away, this time a weapon was to hand."

Rutledge stopped as he was getting into the motorcar, listening to the silence of the night and the quiet ticking over of the motor.

"I wonder why Brunswick was chosen as her scapegoat? Because he's guilty? Or because he's vulnerable?"

Hamish was silent.

Rutledge drove back into Cambury and left his motorcar in the yard behind The Unicorn. The hotel was quiet, and there was no sign of the night clerk. As Rutledge turned to the stairs, he thought he could hear him snoring gently on his cot behind Reception.

As he reached his room, he saw the small message slipped into the brass number on his door.

Anthony Godalming had telephoned and asked that Rutledge return his call at his earliest convenience.

Rutledge glanced at his watch. It was close to midnight.

He would have to wait until tomorrow.

Rutledge was on his way down to breakfast when Constable Daniels met him in the lobby.

" 'Morning, sir. I think you'd better come . . ."

"What is it?" Rutledge asked.

"I was stopped on the street and told the bakery hasn't opened this morning," the constable said. "So I went to have a look for myself, bearing in mind what happened to Mr. Stephenson."

"Quite right, Constable." As he followed the man out the door, he said, "Did you look in the windows?"

"The shades are still down, sir. Usually at this hour you can smell the bread baking." They were walking briskly down the High Street. "But I don't think the ovens have been fired up."

"Under the circumstances, he may have chosen to stay home."

"He didn't close the bakery when his girls were born," Daniels said. "It's most unusual."

They had reached the shop now, and Daniels was right, the shades had not been raised and the door was firmly closed. What's more, there were no trays of fresh baked goods in the window.

Rutledge said, "Go to the Jones house. Don't alarm his wife, man, just find out if he's still at home."

The constable trotted back the way he came, and Rutledge moved forward to knock at the door. But no one answered.

Hamish said, "He's no' there."

Rutledge used his fist now, hammering at the door, and behind him he could feel people on the street stopping to see what he was about. He had just raised his fist again before walking to the back of the shop when the door moved an inch or two and Rutledge could just see Jones's face in the shadows.

"We're closed—" Jones began, but recognizing Rutledge, he opened the door wide and said, "Come in. Quickly."

Rutledge stepped inside and stopped, appalled.

The once tidy bakery was a scene of chaos. Flour and sugar were scattered around the shop, eggs flung everywhere, their broken shells crunching under Jones's feet as he stepped back. Handfuls of sultanas and spices and other ingredients were smeared on the walls, and a stone jar of lard lay on its side, cracked. The smell of cinnamon and allspice, ginger and nutmeg filled the air, almost overwhelming to the senses. Even the pretty chairs where Rutledge and the baker had sat talking had been caked with water and flour.

"Gentle God," Rutledge said.

"Someone believes I killed him," Jones was saying, defeat in his voice. "That's what it must be."

"You can't be sure of that—"

"Oh, yes. In all the years I've lived here, I never gave short measure to my neighbors. What's more,

they never repaid me like this. Never." He gestured
to the destruction of his bakery. In the past twenty-
four hours he had been through emotional turmoil,
and he had not expected it to touch his livelihood in
this way.

"Did you give a statement to Inspector Padgett?"

"I did that. I put down the truth, and I signed it."
He shrugged. "I talked to my wife. She made me see
reason. But the police can still claim I knew Gwyneth
was coming home and went to Hallowfields. My word
against theirs. You know that as well as I do." He was
speaking of Padgett but not by name. "I'm not out of
the woods, and if they try to bring my wife into it, I'll
do what I have to for her sake. By backing off, I gave
her peace of mind for a bit, that's all. And I daren't tell
her about *this*, and ask her help clearing away, can I?"

"Who in Cambury would come to Harold Quarles's
defense?"

"I never expected anyone would do that. I thought
he was roundly disliked." He glanced around his shop
again. "It's petty, this. Thank God nothing is broken.
The glass, the ovens, the trays. But my stock . . ."

There was no way to rescue the ruined spices, the
flour, the sugar, the sultanas, or the spilled milk and
eggs. Even after cleaning up, the bakery would have
to close for several days until such things could be

replenished. And more than one household would go without bread for its meals and cakes for its tea.

"Let me send for Gwyneth. This is work she can do."

"No. I'll see to it myself."

There was a knock at the door.

"Send them away," Jones said. "I haven't the heart to face them."

But it was only the constable, returned from the Jones house. Rutledge let him in.

"I asked the woman come to help his wife clean the carpets if he was at home—"

Daniels broke off, whistling at his first glimpse of the ruined shop, then glanced at his boots, as if half expecting them to be ruined as well.

Rutledge, righting the stone crock that held lard, said, "The sooner you start, the sooner it will be cleared away. The chairs can be cleaned, the walls and floor as well. It will take longer to see to the shelves and the counters, but it can be done. I don't believe Miss Ogden would talk, if you asked for her help. The bookshop is closed for now."

"Clear away? In aid of what?" Jones asked, his voice flat. But he went for a broom and bucket, then set to work, his heart not in it.

"Who did this?" Constable Daniels asked quietly, looking to Rutledge. "And why?"

"We don't know," he answered shortly. "Stay here, Constable, keep an eye on the shop and on Mr. Jones. I want to have a chat with Inspector Padgett."

Daniels, standing aside to let him pass, said, "It's the sort of damage a child might do. We don't lock our doors, anyone can come and go." He hesitated, then added, "The Quarles lad. Marcus. Constable Horton saw the motorcar just after two this morning, bringing him home along with his mother. If he heard the servants gossiping or the tales flying about just now, he's of an age where this sort of thing might help the hurt a little."

"Do you know the boy well? Is he like his father?"

"He's away at school. I haven't seen him much of late."

Rutledge nodded and went out the door.

It was still too early to telephone Godalming in Sussex, and Inspector Padgett wasn't in his office. Rutledge went back to The Unicorn and encountered Padgett just coming out of the hotel's dining room. He turned around and followed Rutledge to his table. Sitting in the sunny window, Rutledge quietly filled him in.

Padgett shook his head when Rutledge told him what Mrs. Downing had claimed to have seen and heard.

"Much as I'd like to believe it's Brunswick, you must consider the source. Like you, I wouldn't put it past Mrs. Quarles to get her housekeeper up to this. Or Archer, for that matter. The family is scrambling to give the man a better reputation in death by seeing this inquiry is over with as soon as possible."

"If it's Brunswick, Quarles comes out of the trial as a saint, not a libertine."

I come to bury Caesar, not to praise him . . .

"It would also support your theory that Brunswick killed his wife," Rutledge went on. "And if he killed Hazel Brunswick, the odds are good that he killed Quarles. I've found a place in the wood opposite the gatehouse where someone waited just out of sight."

"Yes, well, that could have been anyone. And at any time. We can't prove it was Saturday night." Padgett reached over and helped himself to a slice of Rutledge's toast, heaping a spoonful of marmalade on it. It was intended to irritate, but Rutledge said nothing.

"My wife detests marmalade. I never get it at home." He wiped his fingers on his handkerchief. "The Chief Constable sent down a message that he's awaiting word we'd settled on a murderer."

Rutledge dropped the subject of Brunswick. "Last night someone wrecked the bakery. Jones found it this morning when he came in. Constable Daniels is there now."

Padgett swore. "Some months ago, Jones gave me the names of two boys who had stolen tarts when he wasn't looking. I expect they wanted revenge, and since the town's gabbling about the man's guilt, they must have decided this was as good a time as any. I'll have a word with them."

Rutledge held his tongue. In another ten minutes he could make the telephone call to Godalming.

But Padgett sensed something in the texture of the silence and said, "What are we to tell the Chief Constable?"

"Whatever you like," Rutledge answered and stood up. "I've got something to attend to. Then I'm going back to speak to Brunswick."

"Suit yourself." Padgett got to his feet. "I'll be at the station."

Rutledge waited until he had gone out, then went to the telephone room to make his call.

Godalming himself answered, and Rutledge asked, "Did you find our man?"

"A curate by the name of Penrith had the living for some years in a village northeast of Chichester. He died of typhoid early in 1903. He had one son and no money to educate him. The boy went into the army. He never came back to see his father. Whether that means he's dead as well, or that he knew his father was no longer living, I can't say."

"And that's all you've turned up?"

"It isn't enough?" There was a weariness in the voice coming down the line that had nothing to do with fatigue.

"Yes, thank you, it is. I was—hoping for more."

"Yes. We all do, don't we?"

And the connection was broken.

A dead end. Whatever reason Penrith might have had for lying about his father, it appeared to have nothing to do with Quarles. There might be other skeletons that filled that particular closet. Penrith could be illegitimate, for one, and the curate took him in. Or because their names were the same, Davis Penrith might have tried to provide himself with more respectable antecedents than a serving girl sacked because someone had tired of her.

Hence the lie to Rutledge . . .

He had learned through his years in the police that no detail was so small it could be safely ignored.

And so he put in a call to London, to Sergeant Gibson, who was not on duty at the Yard that day, if he cared to leave a message . . .

Rutledge did. It was brief. "Find out if one Davis Penrith served in the British Army between 1898 and 1905. If so, where, and what became of him." Let them sort it out. It would take time, and he'd already given two hours to the War Office on behalf of Stephenson's son.

The voice on the other end of the line, laboriously writing out the message, said, "1898 and 1905?"

"That should be inclusive. If it isn't, we'll look again."

"My father was in the Boer War," the voice said. "Saw a bit of fighting, and came home with a lion's head mounted for the wall. Drove my mother mad hanging it where it could be seen, coming down the stairs. We were the only family on our street with a real lion's head. I used to charge my mates a farthing a look. Very good, sir, I'll see he gets the message on Monday morning."

Rutledge fished in his pocket for the list he'd made in Harold Quarles's study. Then he put in his third and final telephone call, this one to Elise Caldwell's father.

"Sir, can you tell me anything about these men?" he asked after Caldwell's greeting. He read the list of eight names.

"I know six of them. They made their fortunes from the war. Butler is dead, of course—an apoplexy. Simpleton went to Canada, as I recall. Talbot and Morgan live in London, as does Willard. MacDonald is in Glasgow. Hester and Evering are new to me. Here, are these by any chance a list of investors in Cumberline?"

"Yes, they are."

Caldwell chuckled. "Well, well. I've always wondered. If you're thinking of the six I know in terms of the murder of Harold Quarles, then you're barking up the wrong tree. While I wouldn't trust them with my purse, I can tell you they aren't likely to avenge themselves with a spot of murder. They'd rather lose a second fortune than admit to investing unwisely. And they seldom sue, because there's the risk that a canny barrister might find that their own coattails are none too clean."

"Would they be likely to hire someone to do the deed for them?"

"Not likely at all. Of course I can't speak for this man Hester, or Evering. What can you tell me about them?"

"Hester is from Birmingham. A manufacturer of woolens—I have the name of his firm. Broadsmith and Sons."

"Ah. He's Willard's son-in-law. You can strike him off the list as well."

"That leaves Evering. He lives in the Scilly Isles. No firm given."

"Don't know him at all. You'll probably find your murderer closer to home," Caldwell informed him. "I wouldn't worry about these eight men."

"Thank you, sir. This has saved a great deal of footwork."

Caldwell said, "Any time, Ian. Good hunting."

19

Rutledge decided to walk to Brunswick's house. The morning was fair. The streets were filled with people doing their marketing, and a farmer was bringing in half a dozen pigs, their pink backs bouncing down the middle of the street as motorcars and lorries pulled to one side.

Brunswick didn't answer his door, and Rutledge walked on to the church, thinking that the organist might have gone to practice for the Sunday morning services. In fact, as he crossed the churchyard, he could hear music pouring out the open door. He stepped inside.

As his eyes adjusted to the dimness, he saw that there were two women kneeling by the front of the church, arranging flowers in tall vases, and somewhere the rector, Mr. Heller, was deep in conversation with a young man, their voices carrying but not their words.

The church was larger inside than it appeared to be outside, with a wagon roof and no columns. As Rutledge passed by, Heller caught his eye and nodded but continued with his conversation. Brunswick, in the organ loft, paused between hymns, but was playing again by the time Rutledge had climbed the stairs and come to stand by him.

"I'm busy," Brunswick said over the crash of the music.

Rutledge's posture was that of a man content to wait through the next five hours if necessary.

After a time, Rutledge said, "My mother was a pianist, quite a fine one in fact. Your interpretation of that last piece was very different from hers."

With an abrupt gesture of annoyance, Brunswick lifted his fingers and feet, letting the pipes fall silent. Everyone in the church looked up, the two women and the two men, as if after the music, the sudden stillness was deafening.

"If you've come to take me into custody, get on with it. Otherwise you're breaking my concentration."

"Do you wish to talk to me here, where everyone can hear, or elsewhere?"

Brunswick got to his feet, stretching his shoulders. "We can walk in the churchyard."

They went down to the door and into the sunlight, warmer outside after the chill trapped within the stone walls of the church.

"The talk of Cambury is that Mr. Jones is your man. Why should you need to speak to me?"

As they walked among the gravestones, Rutledge said, "I've often wondered if a guilty man ever spares a thought for the poor bastard who is sacrificed in his stead. If you were the killer, would you speak up to set Jones free?"

"I don't see that this is something I need to consider. Unless of course you aren't confident of your ability to judge who is guilty and who isn't," Brunswick countered.

Rutledge laughed. "Meanwhile," he went on, "I've learned a great deal more about your relationship with your wife. It appears not to have been a very happy one. At least for her."

"I thought you'd come to Cambury to find out who killed Quarles, not to chastise someone who has already said everything that can be said to himself. I wasn't a very good husband."

"If you killed one," Rutledge put it to him, "the chances are very good that you killed the other. Or conversely, if you were wrong about one of them, then the odds are you were also wrong about the other."

"Prove that I killed either one."

Rutledge was silent for ten yards or more. "I don't think your quarrel with the dead man has anything to do with jealousy. I believed you at first, and you must have believed it yourself in a way. It can't explain all the evidence I'm looking at, and I'm beginning to believe there's more to this than meets the eye. You abused your wife because you were already angry. You accused Quarles because you knew your wife was vulnerable to kindness after your own behavior, and her shocking death made you want to blame *her*, not yourself. I think you're relying on the general public's view of Harold Quarles, to call him a monster and excuse yourself from blaming him for all your ills because that's easier than facing the truth. I think it's time you took a long look in your mirror."

There was an inadvertent movement beside him.

"The police must look at hard fact. What we feel, what we think doesn't matter. There appears to be enough fact lying about. And Inspector Padgett would like nothing better than to connect one death with the other. If your conscience is clear over your wife's suicide, then so be it. It's my responsibility to determine what part you played—if any—in Harold Quarles's murder. But once that is done, Padgett will search for connections, and see them where there may be nothing at all."

"All right, I wanted him dead. I make no secret of that. Look at it any way you care to. Why is my own affair."

Touché, Rutledge thought to himself. "What you wanted isn't at issue. You can't be hanged for that. What counts is whether you lifted your hand with a weapon in it, and struck Harold Quarles on the back of his head."

Brunswick turned to look at Rutledge, his face unreadable. "I would have watched him die. I would have wanted him to see whose hand it was. And I'd have probably throttled him, not struck him."

Rutledge said, "It doesn't always work out that way. When the chance arises, sometimes the choice of weapon depends on where you are and why you aren't prepared."

"I've told you I was in my bed. Either take me into custody or leave me alone. I'm not giving you the satisfaction of a confession of my sins so that you can sort them out and pick the one that will hang me."

Rutledge said pensively, "I think Quarles pitied your wife. It's one of the few decent things we've learned about him, that he tried to get her to proper medical care."

Brunswick wheeled to face him, his voice savage, his eyes narrowed with his anger. "You know nothing about my wife. And you know damned little about Harold Quarles. Well, I've made a study of the man. Where did he come from? Do you know? I went to Newcastle to see for myself. There's a Quarles family plot, right enough, but it's long since been moved to a proper churchyard some twenty miles away. The village where they lived is so black with coal dust it's almost invisible, roofs fallen in, windows gone. The mine's closed, the main shaft damaged beyond repair. The owners got as much coal as they could out of it and the miners they employed, and simply abandoned both. The sons followed Quarles's father into the mines and died young, lung rot and accidents. The father was already dead by that time. The mother was dead by 1903. Nobody remembers Harold. Isn't that strange? It's as if he never existed. But one old crone who'd lived in the derelict village told me she thought perhaps there was another boy who ran away to join the army and never came home again. So who is our Harold Quarles, I ask you? And if he doesn't exist, how can anyone kill him?"

Rutledge took a step back, the vehemence of Brunswick's attack unexpected.

Hamish, busy at the edges of Rutledge's mind, was a distraction as he tried to assimilate what Brunswick had told him.

If Penrith hadn't returned home after he joined the army—and now it appeared that Quarles might have done the same thing—was that where they'd first met? And forged a friendship that took them from lowly beginnings to a very successful partnership? In war men were thrown together in circumstances that brought them closer than brothers, cutting across class lines, age, and experience. In their case, the Boer War?

He and Hamish were examples of that: men who might have passed each other on a London street without a second glance, but in the context of the trenches they had seen each other as comrades in the battle to survive. They had learned from each other, trusted each other, and protected their men in a common bond that in fact hadn't ended with death.

Rutledge said to Brunswick, "It's all well and good to make a study of the man's life. But that still leaves us with his death. There's no one left in the north who cares if he lived or died. You've just pointed that out. So we're back to Cambury."

"You aren't listening, are you? Did it ever occur to you that Harold Quarles is a mystery because he's got something to hide? There are almost no traces of him, anywhere you look. He has a wife and a son, and I'll wager you they know less about him than I do. He was a liar, he was secretive, he used people for his own ends. What made him that way? That's what I wanted to know. He owed me for what happened to my wife, and he didn't care."

Rutledge remembered what Heller, the rector, had said to him. He repeated it now. "It's not our place to judge. The police can only deal with laws that are broken. If he has never broken a law, then we can do nothing."

Brunswick put a hand to his forehead, as if it ached. "I've always tried to live my life as a moral man. And where has it taken me? Into the jaws of despair. If you want to hang someone, hang me and be done with it. Let Harold Quarles, whoever he may be, claim one last victim."

He turned on his heel and walked back toward the church.

As Brunswick went in through the church door, squaring his shoulders as if shaking off their conversation, Rutledge thought, Stephenson couldn't bring himself to act. In his eyes, it was an appalling failure. This man is ridden by different demons.

Hamish said, "Aye. He doesna' know what he wants."

"On the contrary. I think he may have a taste for martyrdom, and hasn't discovered it yet. Dreamers often do."

"He didna' kill his wife."

"I'm beginning to believe he didn't. But that's neither here nor there. Why was he so obsessed with Harold Quarles's past? To excuse his murder by claiming the man was evil to start with?"

The rector was coming across the churchyard toward him, a frown on his face.

"What did you say to Michael? He's sitting there in front of the organ, not touching the keys."

Rutledge said, "It's my responsibility to speak to anyone who might have had a reason to kill Quarles."

"But Michael hasn't killed anyone, has he? It's only because he admits how he felt about the man that you believe he might have. Inspector Padgett has convinced you that Michael murdered his wife, and therefore he wanted to kill Quarles as well. But many of us don't see it that way. It was a tragedy, and he was out of his mind with grief and distress when she died. He didn't understand her suicide. It was a betrayal to him, an admission of guilt. It was the only reason he could think of for her to leave him, you see. That someone had turned her away from him."

"Apparently he didn't behave very well toward her when she was alive."

"Yes, it could be true, though I never saw evidence of it. I do know they weren't very happy together long before Hazel went to work for Quarles. So you see, if he'd intended to take matters into his own hands and kill Harold Quarles, he'd have done it then and there, in that confused and bitter state of mind. And he didn't. That's to his credit, don't you see?"

"If he didn't intend to kill him, why has Brunswick spent a good deal of his spare time of late looking into Quarles's past? What good is it?"

Heller was surprised. "Has he been doing such a thing? He's never said anything about it to me. What is he looking for, for heaven's sake?"

"I don't know. I don't know that he himself understands what he's after."

"Yes, well, that may be true." Curiosity got the better of him. "Has he found something?"

"Very little. I don't think Quarles wanted his history to be found. Well enough to boast about its simplicity, but not to have the truth about it brought into the open. The poor are not necessarily saints. And sinners do have some goodness in them. Isn't that what the church teaches?"

Heller took a deep breath. "Back to Michael. Do give him the benefit of the doubt. There's much healing left to do."

"I'll bear that in mind," Rutledge answered mildly. He turned to walk back toward the church, and Heller followed him. "We aren't going to solve this dilemma, Mr. Heller, until we have our killer. And to that end, I must go on questioning people, however unpleasant it must be."

Heller said nothing, keeping pace beside him, his mind elsewhere. As they parted at the corner of the churchyard, he broke his silence. "I will pray for you to be granted wisdom, Inspector."

"It might be more beneficial to your flock if you prayed for wisdom for Inspector Padgett as well."

Heller smiled. "I already do that, my boy." He glanced upward, where a flight of rooks came to perch on the pinnacles of the church tower. After a moment he said, "I've been told that Mrs. Quarles is home again, with her son. They're to collect her husband's body and take it north for burial. I did wonder why Mrs. Quarles hadn't asked me to preside over a brief service here, before her husband was taken north. But that's her decision to make, of course."

"Perhaps here in Cambury, you know him better than Mrs. Quarles wishes."

Heller sighed. "I can tell you how it will be. Once Mr. Quarles has left the village, it will be as if he never was. We'll not talk about his irritating qualities, because of course he's dead. There will be a family bequest to the church, and we'll name something after him, and forget him. It's a poor epitaph for a man who was so forceful in life."

"Did you know that Quarles's partner, Davis Penrith, was the son of a curate?"

"Actually I believe Mr. Quarles brought that up once in a conversation. He seemed to find it amusing."

"Because it wasn't the truth, or because Penrith didn't live up to his father's calling?"

"I have no idea. But Mr. Quarles did say that he didn't have to fear his partner, because the man would never turn against him. Or to be more precise, he said the one person he'd never feared was his partner, because Penrith would never have the courage to turn against him."

"When was this?" Rutledge asked.

"I don't remember just when—I think while Mr. Quarles was living here in Cambury for several weeks. I was out walking one afternoon, and he was coming back from one of the outlying farms. He stopped to ask me if he could give me a lift back to town, and I accepted. We got on the subject of enemies, I can't think how . . ."

"That's an odd topic for a casual encounter."

"Nevertheless, he made that remark about Penrith, and I commented that loyalty was something to value very highly. He told me it wasn't a matter of loyalty but of fact."

Yet Penrith had walked away from their partnership. And as far as anyone knew, Quarles hadn't felt betrayed. Had, in fact, done nothing to stop him.

"They were an unlikely pair to be friends, much less partners," Rutledge mused.

"Yes, that's true. I thought as much myself from Mr. Quarles's remarks. But there's no accounting for tastes, in business or in marriage, is there? Good day, Mr. Rutledge."

He watched the rector striding toward the church door, his head down, his mind occupied. As Heller disappeared into the dimness of the doorway, Hamish said, "There's no' a solution to this murder."

"There's always a solution. Sometimes it's harder to see, that's all."

"Oh, aye," Hamish answered dryly. "The Chief Constable will ha' to be satisfied with that."

Miss O'Hara was just coming out her door with a market basket over her arm as Rutledge passed her house. She hailed him and asked how the Jones family was faring.

"Well enough," he told her.

"We ought to find whoever killed Quarles and pin a medal on him. They do it in wars. Why not in peace, for ridding Cambury of its ogre."

"That's hardly civilized," he told her, thinking that Brunswick might agree with her.

"We aren't talking about civilization." She drew on her gloves, smiled, and left him standing there.

Rutledge could still see her slender fingers slipping into the soft fabric of her gloves. They had brought to mind the uglier image of Harold Quarles's burned hands, the lumpy whorls and tight patches of skin so noticeable in the light of Inspector Padgett's lamps as the body came to rest on the floor of the tithe barn.

Like the coal mines, those hands were a part of the public legend of Harold Quarles. Neither Rutledge nor Padgett had thought twice about them, because they had been scarred in the distant past.

He turned back the way he'd come and went on to Dr. O'Neil's surgery.

The doctor was trimming a shrubbery in the back garden. Rutledge was directed there by the doctor's wife, and O'Neil hailed his visitor with relief. Taking out a handkerchief, he wiped his forehead and nodded toward chairs set in the shade of an arbor. "Let's sit down. It's tiresome, trimming that lilac. I swear it waits until my back's turned, and then grows like Jack's beanstalk."

They sat down, and O'Neil stretched his legs out before him. "What is it you want to know? The undertaker has come for Quarles, and I've finished my report. It's on Padgett's desk now, I should think."

"Thank you. I'm curious about those scars on Quarles's hands."

"You saw them for yourself. The injuries had healed and were as smooth as they were ever going to be. It must have happened when he was fairly young. I did notice that the burns extended just above the wrist. And the edges were very sharply defined, almost as if someone had held his hands in a fire. You usually see a different pattern, more irregular. Think about a poker that's fallen into the fire. The flames shoot up just as you reach for it. You might be burned superficially, but not to such an extent as his, because in a split second you realize what you've done, drop the poker, and withdraw out of harm's way. What I found remarkable was that Quarles hadn't lost the use of his fingers. That means he must have had very good care straightaway."

"Were there other burns on his body? His neck, for instance, or his back. I'm thinking of bending over a child, protecting it with his own body as he runs a gantlet of fire."

"I wasn't really looking for old wounds."

"If he'd had other scars like those on his hands, surely you'd have noticed them."

"Yes, of course. Burns do heal with time, if not too severe. A wet sack over his back might have been just enough to prevent permanent scars. Where, pray, is this going?"

"Curiosity. I'm wondering if there were other enemies besides those we know of in Cambury."

O'Neil said slowly, "If someone had held his hands to a fire, it would have been Quarles who wanted to avenge himself."

"Yes, that's the stumbling point, isn't it?" Rutledge smiled wryly.

O'Neil said, "Sorry I can't help you more."

"Do you by chance know anything about these Cumberline funds that Quarles nearly lost his reputation over?"

O'Neil laughed. "A village doctor doesn't move in such exalted circles." The laughter faded. "Sunday night as I was trying to fall asleep, I kept seeing those wings outstretched above the dead man. It occurred to me that after someone hit him from behind, they desecrated his body. The only reason I could think of was that Quarles died too easily, that perhaps he was expected to die slowly up there with the wings biting into his back. Terrible thought, isn't it?"

And that possibility, Rutledge thought, spoke more to Michael Brunswick than it did to Hugh Jones.

Constable Horton spent a wet Saturday evening in The Black Pudding. It was not his first choice, but his friends drank there from time to time, and he went in occasionally for a pint to end his day.

Tom Little was courting a girl in the next village but one, and full of himself. He thought she might say yes, if he proposed, and his friends spent half an hour helping him find the right words, amid a good deal of merriment. The landlord had occasion to speak to them twice for being overloud.

Constable Horton, trying his hand at peacemaking, joined the group and steered the conversation in a different direction. He was finishing his second glass when a half-heard comment caught his attention. He brought his chair's front legs back to the floorboards with a thump and asked Tommy Little to repeat what he'd just said.

Little, turning toward him, told him it would cost him another round. Constable Horton, resigned, got up to give his order, and when everyone was satisfied, Little told him what he'd seen on the road beyond Hallowfields.

It was too late to rouse Inspector Padgett, but Constable Horton was at his door as early in the morning as he thought was politic.

Padgett went to find Rutledge as soon as he'd finished his breakfast.

"Here's something we ought to look into. Horton brought me word before I'd had my tea at six. It seems that one Thomas Little and a friend were on their way back to her home last Saturday evening. He's courting a girl from a village not far up the road, and she'd spent the day with him in Cambury. This was nine-thirty, he thinks, or thereabouts. They'd ridden out of Cambury on their bicycles just as the church clock struck nine. As they were nearing Honeyfold Farm— that's about two miles beyond Hallowfields, on your left—they saw Michael Brunswick coming toward them on a bicycle. He passed without a word, and they went on their way, laughing because he'd looked like a thundercloud. Unlucky in love, they called him, and made up stories about the sort of woman *he* was seeing. Then they forgot all about him until Little made a remark about him last night in The Black Pudding."

Rutledge, standing in Reception, said, "That would put Brunswick at Hallowfields before Quarles left the Greer house. And if he'd been away, he wouldn't have known that Quarles was dining in Cambury. There wouldn't have been any point in waiting for the man."

"Yes, I'd thought about that. But where did Brunswick go when he reached Cambury? Home? To The Glover's Arms?"

"He told me he was in bed and asleep."

"Hard to prove. Hard to disprove."

"The early service this morning isn't for another three-quarters of an hour. I should be able to catch Brunswick before he goes to the church."

Rutledge walked briskly toward Brunwick's house, and when he knocked, the man opened the door with a sheaf of music in his hand. He regarded Rutledge with distaste and didn't invite him inside. "What is it now?"

"We've just learned that you were seen on the road near Honeyfold Farm last Saturday evening at nine-thirty. You said nothing about it when we asked your whereabouts the night that Quarles was killed."

"Why should I have? It had nothing to do with his murder."

"Where had you been?"

"To Glastonbury."

"Can anyone confirm that?"

"I went to dine with a friend who stopped there on his way back to London. He was tired, the dinner didn't last very long, and I came home." There was an edge to his voice now. "If you must know, I'd had more to drink than was good for me, and I had spent a wretched two hours listening to this man crowing over his triumphs. He's a musician; we'd studied together. I wished I'd never gone there. I wasn't in the best of spirits when I left him."

Which explained the comment that he'd looked like a thundercloud when he passed Tommy Little and the girl he was courting.

"When you reached Cambury, what did you do?"

"I undressed, when to bed, and tried to sleep. Harold Quarles was the last person on my mind then."

Rutledge thanked him and left.

"It's no' much," Hamish said.

"I didn't expect it to be. He would have been too early to see Quarles leaving Minton Street and turning toward Hallowfields. They must have missed each other by a quarter of an hour at the very least."

"If he didna' lie."

"There's always that, of course. But Little seems to feel very confident of his times." Rutledge stopped and turned to look over his shoulder. Brunswick was hurrying toward St. Martin's, his black robe streaming behind him. Rutledge watched him go.

Would a man in Brunswick's state of mind go meekly to bed in the hope of sleeping, after being humiliated by a more successful friend? Especially if he'd had a little too much to drink? Of course there was the long ride to Cambury to cool his temper and wear him down. But Tommy Little had seen the man's face, and it appeared he was still smarting from the visit.

Looking up at the Perpendicular tower of St. Martin's, Rutledge realized that the rectory overlooked the church on its far side. He went back to The Unicorn and bided his time until the morning services were over.

When he reached the rectory an hour after noon, Rutledge found Heller dozing in a wicker chair in his garden, a floppy hat over his face. He woke up as he heard someone approaching, and sat up, pulling down his vest and smoothing his hair.

"Is this an official call?" he asked, trying for a little humor, but the words were heavy with worry.

Rutledge joined him in the shade, squatting to pick up a twig and twist it through his fingers.

"It's about Michael Brunswick," he said after a moment, not looking up at the rector. "I believe it's customary for him to practice your selections for the Sunday services on Saturday morning. Do you recall if he did that on the Saturday that Quarles died? He was meeting a friend in Glastonbury. There might not have been time for him to play beforehand."

Heller was caught without an answer. He sat there, studying Rutledge, then said, "He did indeed come into practice that morning. A little earlier than usual, as I recall. I was there and heard him. We talked about the anthem I'd chosen. It's a favorite of mine."

"And so there was no need for him to play the organ that evening, after his return?"

Heller sighed. "No need. But of course he did. The windows were open, I could hear him from my study. He wasn't playing my selections. It was tortured music. Unhappy music. I did wonder if it was his own composition. And it ended in a horrid clash of notes, followed by silence." He looked back at the rectory, as if he could find answers there in the stone and glass and mortar. "He's a wretched man. He wants more than life has chosen to give him. He plays perfectly well for us during services. We are fortunate to have him. Why should he feel that he needs to reach for more? If God had intended for him to be a great organist, he wouldn't have brought him to us at Cambury, would he have? There is much to be said for contentment. And in contentment there is service."

Rutledge stood up, without answering the rector.

Heller said, "You mustn't misunderstand. Michael Brunswick's music isn't going to drive him to kill. It's eating at *him*, he's the only victim."

Rutledge said, "Perhaps his music is the last straw in a life full of disappointments. What time did he finish playing?"

"I don't know. Perhaps it was twenty past ten. If you remember there was a mist coming in. Hardly noticeable at that time, but an hour later, it was thick enough that strands of it were already wrapping around the trees in my garden. I was worried about Michael, and looked to see if his house was dark. It was, and so I went to bed myself."

"If there had been lights on?"

"I'd have found an excuse to go and speak to him. To offer comfort if he needed it. Or if not, to assure myself that he was all right." He took a deep breath and examined his gardening hat to avoid looking at Rutledge. "You mustn't misconstrue what I've told you. It would be wrong."

"It would be wrong to let someone else take the blame for Quarles's death. Mr. Jones has already suffered for his daughter's sake."

"Yes, I heard what had happened at the bakery. Mr. Padgett believes it was boys acting out of spite, but I think someone is grieving for Quarles. A woman, perhaps, who cared for him and believes the gossip about Mr. Jones. You warned me once, Mr. Rutledge. You told me someone might come to me frightened by what they'd done and I must be careful how I dealt with them. In return I warn you now. Rumor has always maintained that Harold Quarles had a mistress in Cambury. I don't know if it's true or not, but if it is, she's not one of the women he flirts with in public, she's someone he visited quietly, I suspect, when no one was looking. If she exists, I say, she's had no way to grieve openly while everyone in sight is gloating over Quarles's death. Alone, lonely, she must be desolate, and it will turn her mind in time. Just beware."

It was an odd speech for a man of the cloth to make to a policeman.

"Surely you can guess—"

"No. I've never wanted to know whose wife or sister or daughter she may be. I can do nothing for her until she comes to me. This is just a friendly warning."

"Thank you, Rector. I'll bear it in mind." But he thought that Heller was intending to turn his attention away from Michael Brunswick by using village gossip to his own ends. He was a naïve man in many ways. And he might consider a small white lie in God's cause no great problem for his conscience.

"Ye ken," Hamish said, "he doesna' want to lose his organist. It's why he defends him sae fiercely."

He turned to walk away, but Heller stopped him. "I told you that I refused to judge, lest I be judged. It's good advice, even for a policeman."

But the fact remained, Rutledge told Hamish in the silence of his mind, that there was proof now that

Michael Brunswick could have crossed paths with Harold Quarles.

To test it, he stood on the street just above Michael Brunswick's door and looked toward the High Street. The angle was right, as he'd thought it might be. Coming home from St. Martin's, Brunswick would have had a clear view of Minton Street and the corner that Quarles would have turned on his way back to Hallowfields.

The mist hadn't come down then. And Brunswick, needing someone or something on which to expend his anger and frustration, might have watched Quarles walk up the High Street alone. He could have cut across the green without being noticed, followed at a distance, and let the trees shield him on the straight stretch of road that marched with the wall of the estate.

"Why did the dead man no' go through the gates and up the drive?"

"Because it must be shorter to come in by the farm gate and cut across the parkland."

Rutledge went to fetch the motorcar and drove out to Hallowfields, leaving it by the main gate. Then he paced the distances from there to the house, and again from the Home Farm lane to the house. Because of the twists and turns of the drive, allowing for vistas and specimen trees set out to be admired, it was nearly three hundred yards longer. If he was tired, it would have made sense for Harold Quarles to choose the shorter distance.

Brunswick might have called to him, or challenged him. And if Quarles had turned away in rejection of what he wanted to say, that act could have precipitated the murder.

"Listen to me . . ."

"I'm tired, I want my bed. You have nothing to say to me that I have any interest in hearing . . ."

Those white stones stood out—Brunswick needn't have thought to bring a weapon—and in a split second, without a word, Quarles would have been knocked down. It was the second blow that mattered. Had Brunswick intended it as the death stroke? Rutledge could see him still caught up in that fierce need to hurt as he'd been hurt, stepping back too late, shocked by the suddenness of death.

It would have been easy to convince himself that Quarles had brought on the attack by his callous indifference. To feel no responsibility for what he'd just done.

And then the slow realization that the man had got off too lightly, a quick death compared to Hazel Brunswick's drowning, must have triggered his next actions.

The facts fit together neatly.

Then why, Rutledge wondered, was he feeling dissatisfied, standing there on the lawns of Hallowfields, looking for holes in his own case?

He walked on to the house and this time knocked at the door, asking for Mrs. Quarles when Downing opened it.

"She's with her son. Come back another day."

"If she could spare me a few minutes, I'd be grateful." His words were polite, but his voice was uncompromising.

She went away, and in a few minutes conveyed him with clear disapproval to the formal drawing room. Mrs. Quarles came in after him, dressed in deep mourning. She was very pale, as if the ordeal of breaking the news to her son had taken its toll.

Against the backdrop of the drawing room, pale blue and silver, she was almost a formidable figure, and he thought she must have intended to impress him after his impudence in demanding to see her.

"What is it you want to know, Mr. Rutledge? Whether I've turned into a grieving widow?"

"There are some questions about your husband's past—"

"That could have waited. I bid you good day."

He stood his ground. "I think you're probably the only person who knew your husband well. With the possible exception of Mr. Penrith."

"I have no idea what Mr. Penrith thinks or knows about my late husband. I have never asked him. Nor will I."

"There are some discrepancies that I'd like to clear up. We've learned that Mr. Quarles removed the remains of his family from the village where they lived and died to another churchyard. But no one who lived in the old village has any recollection of him as a child."

"You have been busy, haven't you? I can't speak for anyone who does or doesn't recall his childhood. He did move his family, but that was after our son was born. Or so I was told. He never took me north with him, it was a painful chapter in his life, and I was content to leave it closed."

"We would also like more information about his enlistment in the Army. Did he see action during the Boer War, or was he posted elsewhere in the empire?"

Her face changed, from irritation to a stillness that was unnatural. "Was he in that war? He never spoke of it to me." Her voice was crisp, dismissive, and her eyes were cold.

"Was that when he met Davis Penrith?"

"I have no idea. It was my impression they met at the firm where they were employed."

"Can you tell me anything about the burns on your husband's hands? They were quite severe and possibly inflicted by someone else. If so, they may have a bearing on his murder."

She moved swiftly, reaching for the bell. "Good day, Mr. Rutledge."

Behind him, Downing opened the door, and Mrs. Quarles nodded to her.

Rutledge turned to the housekeeper. "I don't believe we've finished our conversation. Thank you, Mrs. Downing."

The housekeeper looked to her mistress for guidance. But Mrs. Quarles walked past Rutledge without a word or a glance and left him standing there.

He could hear her heels clicking over the marble of the foyer and then the sound of footsteps as she climbed the stairs.

Mrs. Downing was still waiting. He let her show him to the door.

From somewhere in the house, he could hear a boy's voice, calling to someone, and lighter footsteps approaching.

But the door was shut so swiftly behind him that he didn't see Marcus Quarles after all.

20

Walking back to where he'd left the motor-car along the road, Rutledge pondered his conversation with Mrs. Quarles.

Most of his questions had been based on a little knowledge and good deal of guesswork. Nevertheless, the dead man's widow had been disturbed by them.

Oddly enough he was beginning to see a pattern in Harold Quarles's actions.

The man had removed his family from their original grave site and reburied them in a place where they weren't known. Only the headstones in the churchyard identified them, and no one in this other village would have any memory of them or the boy who wasn't—yet—laid to rest among them.

And there was the story to explain his burns, lending an air of heroism to the other tales he'd spun. Of course there had to be an explanation. The scars were obvious to anyone who met him or shook hands over a business agreement. But Rutledge thought that Mrs. Quarles had a very good idea how he'd come by them, whatever the rest of the world believed.

As for the army, Quarles's service had been quietly put behind him. Either because he hadn't particularly distinguished himself or his service record was dismal. And Davis Penrith had done the same thing.

With any luck, London would have those records for him in another day. And a telephone call to Yorkshire would confirm the removal of the graves.

Harold Quarles had created the face he showed his business associates with great care. What was behind the mask? Brunswick was right, something must be there.

Hamish said, "Ye ken, he's the *victim*."

"That's true," Rutledge answered, turning the motorcar back toward Cambury. "But where there are secrets, murder sometimes follows. Or blackmail. Was that what Brunswick had been moving toward? Take the bookseller, Stephenson. Quarles wouldn't tell him why he refused to contact the Army on the son's behalf. It must have seemed unbelievably cruel to a desperate father. And Stephenson brooded over it to the point that he wanted to kill the man. Who else is out there nursing a grudge and waiting for the chance to do something about it?"

"A straw in a haystack," Hamish said.

"Yes, well, the Yard is often very good at finding straws."

But Hamish laughed without humor. "It doesna' signify. If the murderer here isna' the baker nor the bookseller, ye're left with the man who plays the church organ."

He hammered on for the next hour as Rutledge sat by the long windows overlooking the High Street and wrote a report covering everything he'd learned so far.

There were loose ends. There were always loose ends. Murder was never closed in a tidy package.

Who had wrecked the bakery? How could anyone prove that Brunswick had indeed seen Quarles leaving the Greer house and turning for home? Who had argued with Quarles there? Brunswick himself? Greer?

Rutledge left the sheets of paper on the table and went out again, crossing the High Street and walking on to knock on Brunswick's door.

The man was haggard, and short-tempered as well. "What is it this time?"

"I need to find some answers that are eluding me. When you stopped playing the organ that Saturday night a week ago, when Quarles was killed, did you leave the church at once, or sit there for a short period of time?"

Brunswick blinked, as if uncertain where Rutledge had got his information and what it signified. "I—don't recall."

"If you travel from the church to this house, for a small part of that journey, particularly when you're on foot, you have a clear view of Minton Street. At just about the time you might have done that, perhaps ten-thirty, Harold Quarles was coming out of the house where he'd dined. Between there and where Minton meets the High Street, he encountered someone who argued with him. Their voices were loud. They may have carried this far. I need to know the name of that man or woman with him."

Brunswick stood there, his gaze not leaving Rutledge's face.

It was a turning point, and the man was well aware of it. If he admitted to seeing Quarles, he was admitting as well that he could have killed the man.

He had only to say: "I must have walked home earlier than that. I didn't see Quarles at all, much less hear him talking to someone on Minton Street."

Or "I didn't leave the church for another quarter of an hour or more. I couldn't have seen him—the clock in the tower was striking eleven."

And it would have been impossible, whatever the police suspected, to prove otherwise.

Rutledge waited.

Finally Michael Brunswick said, "I didn't see Quarles."

"You must have heard his voice."

"No."

Hamish said, "He's afraid to tell ye."

After a moment Brunswick went on. "If Quarles was there, he'd already gone."

"All right, I'll accept that. The timing wasn't perfect. Who was still there? Who had been with him only a matter of seconds before?"

"It was Davis Penrith."

Brunswick had condemned himself with four words.

Davis Penrith had been in Scotland that weekend, staying with his wife.

Rutledge was torn between going to London himself and asking the Yard to request a statement from Penrith regarding his weekend in Scotland. In the end, he compromised and telephoned the man at his home.

Penrith was distant when he came to take Rutledge's call. But as the reason for it was explained, he said,

"Here, this is ridiculous. I've a letter from my wife. Let me fetch it."

He came back to the telephone within two minutes.

"It's dated the Thursday after my return. I'll read you the pertinent passage: 'Mama was so pleased you could come, however short the visit. And Mr. and Mrs. Douglas were delighted you were here to dine with them. We have become dear friends. Shall I invite them to stay with us in June, when they'll be in town?'"

"Where does your mother-in-law live?"

"In Annan. That's just over the border from Carlisle."

Rutledge knew that part of Scotland. If Penrith had been there for the weekend, he couldn't have reached Cambury and returned to Annan without losing the better part of two days—the journey was close on three hundred miles each way.

"When did you leave for the weekend?"

"My staff can tell you—I left here Thursday evening and I set out from Annan just after our luncheon on Sunday. As you may remember, you found me at home on Monday morning because I got in so late."

"Will you go to Sergeant Gibson at the Yard and give him a written statement to that effect? Show him the letter as well."

"If it will help to find Harold's killer."

Rutledge thanked him and broke the connection.

Sitting there by the telephone, he considered his next step. He had sufficient evidence for several inquests. He could show a very good case for Hugh Jones, Stephenson, and now Brunswick. They would undoubtedly be bound over for trial. His duty done?

Why of all people had Brunswick named Penrith?

To shield someone else?

Or to make a point?

Hamish said, "He told ye he didna' care."

Rutledge crossed the room and opened the door before he answered Hamish. "Why did Brunswick look into Quarles's past?"

"Aye. It's a sticking point."

"A different kind of revenge? To bring the man down, and make him watch the dissolution of everything that matters to him?"

"It doesna' suit the man's temperament."

Rutledge wasn't satisfied. "In an odd sort of way, it does. If he thinks there's no chance for a conviction—despite his pleas to be hanged—his name and photograph will be in every newspaper in England as he talks about his wife and his music and what sort of man Harold Quarles was."

"He could ha' tried blackmail. And it didna' serve."

Hadn't Mrs. Downing said Brunswick had come to Quarles for money, after his wife's death? Was that why he was so angry that his wife wasn't carrying a child when she died? It would have made a better case . . .

"Yon bookseller also asked to be hanged."

"Yes, because he had nothing to live for. Brunswick's wife failed him, his music has failed him, and he would like nothing better than to make someone else pay for his trouble."

Rutledge was walking through Reception. "If we'd found Brunswick dead, I'd know where to look—at Harold Quarles."

"The Chief Constable is waiting," Hamish answered. "And Old Bowels as well."

There was nothing for it now but to cross the High Street and report his findings to Inspector Padgett.

Padgett was not as pleased as Rutledge had expected him to be. He was idly making designs on a sheet of paper, frowning as he listened, his gaze on his pen rather than Rutledge's face.

"I'll speak to the Chief Constable, of course. But are you sure? He doesn't like a muddled case. There's Jones, the little family notwithstanding. And as far as we know, he could have wrecked his own bakery in an effort to elicit sympathy. You said yourself that nothing of great value was broken. Did I tell you? I did bring in the two most likely vandals, and their parents can account for their whereabouts that night."

"I saw his face. Jones hadn't done it."

"Yes, well. We've looked at this before. Who grieves for Harold Quarles? Not his wife. The mistress that everyone would like us to believe in? As far as I'm concerned, if she exists, you were right about it being the little wife killed quite by accident by her soldier husband. I've even asked my wife if she knew who the mistress was. And her answer was telling—that Quarles hadn't started the rumor, other people had. His son? The boy *was* home, wasn't he, when this happened? And fourteen is a wild age, emotions hot and temper hotter, but I daresay his mother never let him out of her sight."

"If you disagree with my conclusions, tell me so."

"It's not that I disagree. I don't like any murder on my patch, and most particularly not one that attracts the notice of London."

Padgett had been vacillating since the beginning. Rutledge was losing patience.

"Then I shall speak to the Chief Constable—and leave you out of it."

"No, I'll do it. I told you. What's this business about Penrith?"

"Brunswick named him as the person arguing with Quarles outside the Greer house. I'm not sure it wasn't for a very good reason."

"No one saw a strange motorcar in Cambury that night. Nor did they see a strange man wandering about."

Rutledge had already considered that question.

"Penrith is known to many people in Cambury. He came here from time to time, when he and Quarles were partners. Would they have considered him a stranger?"

"I expect they wouldn't."

"Yet the evidence is clear. He was in Scotland."

Padgett capped his pen and threw it down on the desk. "Brunswick's a coldblooded chap. That fits the fact that the body was moved and trussed up in that rig. It's not everyone's cup of tea, touching someone they've just killed."

Rutledge said, "Tell me again why you acted so quickly to summon the Yard while Quarles was still up there in the harness? Before you'd even had time to consider the evidence."

Inspector Padgett smiled. "I wanted to walk away with clean hands. The man put me in the wrong with the Chief Constable twice over. Third time's unlucky. No one can say I didn't follow the rules to the letter. Even his widow. I got my own back there. I'm satisfied."

21

It was late. The day had worn on to the point that clouds had rolled in and the sunset was lost behind them.

Rutledge walked in the churchyard for a time, unable to bear his room—when he had come back to it, it had felt close, claustrophobic, as if storm clouds were moving in. He had left at once and, without conscious thought, found himself in the grassy paths that wandered among the headstones.

Hamish, reflecting his own mood, was giving Rutledge the rough edge of his tongue. Reminding him that barely a year before he'd been a broken man in the clinic to which his sister, Frances, had removed him. Rutledge couldn't recall much of that change. The new surroundings had confused him, and Dr.

Fleming, looking for a handhold on his new patient's sanity, was probing into things best left buried deep and covered over with layer upon layer of excuses.

He hadn't expected to survive. He hadn't cared much either way, except when he saw his sister's troubled face, the strain and exhaustion almost mirroring his own as she sat with him hour after hour, day after day, seldom sleeping, sometimes taking his hand, or when he couldn't bear to be touched, talking softly to him about the distant past. About anything but the war. Or Jean, who had walked away and never looked back.

Now he was pacing a Somerset churchyard, debating his own wisdom.

To Rutledge's surprise, Padgett hadn't taken Brunswick into custody. Still, he was preparing to present their findings in the case to the Chief Constable in the morning and ask for an inquest to be held. And afterward Rutledge would be free to leave for London.

Rutledge cut across what Hamish was saying, the soft Scots voice, heavy with accusation and condemnation, finally falling silent.

"Who wrecked the bakery? I'd feel better about the case if that had been cleared up."

There was no answer from Hamish.

"There has to be a reason for it. A hand behind it. But whose?"

Silence.

"No one's shed a tear for the man—"

But that was wrong. One person had. The maid, Betty, who cleaned Quarles's rooms and kept the gatehouse tidy. Who had been left a bequest of money when all she wanted from her employer was the promise of a roof over her head when he died.

Rutledge had almost forgot her. She was a pale figure on the fringe of the group of servants, a tired woman folding the sheets, feeling her years, wondering what was to become of her.

Rutledge turned back to The Unicorn's yard and retrieved his motorcar. As he did, a few drops of rain splashed the windscreen, leaving dusty blotches.

By the time he reached Hallowfields, it was coming down in earnest, and a rumble of thunder sounded in the distance. He dashed through the rain to the door and knocked loudly. The footman who answered seemed not to know what to do about the policeman on the steps, and Rutledge said, "I'm here to see one of the maids. Take me to the servants' hall, if you please."

The man stepped back and let him enter. Rutledge walked briskly toward the door leading to the servants' stairs and found the staff gathered in Mrs. Downing's sitting room, listening to the Sunday evening reading from the Bible. Heads turned as he stood in the doorway.

Mrs. Downing said, "We're at prayers."

"I'll wait in the passage."

He shut the door and walked a dozen steps away, listening to the soft murmur of voices. After five minutes or so, Mrs. Downing came out of her sitting room, her face severe.

"What is it this time?"

"I'd like to speak to Betty. The woman who took care of Mr. Quarles's—"

"Yes. I know who she is. Give me a minute."

She went back into her parlor and dismissed the staff, keeping Betty with her. When they had gone about their duties, she herself left the room and held the door open for Rutledge to enter.

Betty was waiting, apprehension in her face.

Rutledge asked her to sit down, then told her they had very likely found her employer's murderer. It would be only a matter of days before it was official.

Her hands clenched in her lap, she said, "Who is it?"

"I'm not at liberty to tell you that. But it isn't Hugh Jones, the baker."

He could read her emotions as they flitted across her face. Surprise. Bewilderment. Shame.

"They were talking in the servants' hall," she said. "The man who brings the milk told the scullery maid that he'd confessed."

"Mr. Jones gave the police a statement. It wasn't a confession. He won't be arrested."

"Why are you telling me this? And not the others?"

"Because I think you know. Did you go to the bakery in the middle of the night? Was it you who destroyed everything you could lay hands to?"

Tears filled her eyes but didn't fall. "He's been good to me. M—Mr. Quarles. No one else cared, but I did. I wanted to punish whoever had killed him. I wanted to make him as wretched as I was."

"You succeeded in making Mr. Jones wretched. He didn't deserve it."

"But they talk, the servants. I hear them. His daughter had come home, and he was distraught. Everyone said he was the only one who could have put Mr. Quarles up in that wicker cage. They said he'd done it to show that Mr. Quarles was no angel, that he'd tormented the Jones family until they couldn't stand it any longer."

"Yes, I know. The police nearly made that same mistake. But it wasn't true. You owe him an apology, and restitution."

"How can I pay for what I've done? I only have my wages." She was gripping her hands together until the knuckles were white. And then she looked at Rutledge. "He said terrible things about Mr. Quarles when he sent his daughter away. What does *he* owe for that?"

"You aren't Mr. Quarles's defender. He has a wife and a son to protect his good name."

"His wife hated him as much as the rest did. But the boy, Marcus, is a good child. He would have made his father proud. It's hard to think of him father- less. If they hang this man you've decided killed Mr. Quarles, I'd like to be there."

"Why do you think his wife turned against him? It was a happy marriage for some time, or so I was led to believe."

"And so it was. I was never told what it is she holds against him. But she said once, when she didn't know I was there, if she knew a way, she'd wash the very blood out of Master Marcus's veins if it would do any good. Mr. Archer called that a cruel thing to say, but she answered him sharply. 'You can't imagine what cruelty is, Charles. I can't sleep at night for remembering what was done.'"

"You've known Mr. Quarles for some years. What was his wife talking about?"

"He was a hard man, but not half the things said about him are true. I think she wanted an excuse to live with Mr. Archer, to make it right in her own eyes.

I think she believed he'd feel better about living under her roof if he thought she was married to a monster." She wiped her eyes with the back of her hand. "He was good to me. That's all I know. No one else ever was."

The next morning, as Rutledge was packing his valise, he was summoned to the telephone.

It was Sergeant Gibson. "I've had a bit of luck, sir. Remember the constable you spoke with on Saturday, when you left me a message?"

"Yes, I do." The lion's head and a small boy charging his mates a few farthings to look at it.

"That was Constable Wainwright, sir. Over the weekend he spoke to his father about fighting the Boers. His father saw a good deal of action. And he remembers Private Penrith. Described him as a fair, slender chap, a quiet one keeping to himself for the most part. Said he was reminded of the young Prince of Wales, sir. This was in Cape Town, just before Corporal Wainwright was to sail home. Penrith was quite the hero, according to Wainwright. He walked miles back to a depot for help, after the Boers ambushed the train he was taking north. There was talk of a medal, but Penrith himself quashed that idea. He says he was too late, all the men were dead by the time rescue reached them. He blamed himself."

"He was the sole survivor?"

"According to Wainwright's account, yes, sir. He was knocked about when the train came to a screeching halt, and dazed. But his rifle had been fired, though he couldn't remember much about the action."

"Hardly a record to be ashamed of."

"No, sir. Shall I go on looking at Mr. Penrith's military career?"

"No. Yes. When did he leave the army? And where else did he serve? Did Corporal Wainwright mention one Harold Quarles?"

"I don't believe he did, sir."

"Include him in your search. And, Gibson, I want to be sure who and what this Davis Penrith is. One source has told me his father lived in Hampshire, another that his father lived in Sussex. I want that cleared up."

"Yes, sir. I believe one Davis Penrith came in this morning to make his statement about a journey to Scotland. Is this the same man, sir?"

"It is."

"Wouldn't it be simpler to send a constable around to ask him these questions?"

Rutledge said, "He's already answered one of them. But not to my satisfaction."

Sergeant Gibson said neutrally, "Indeed, sir."

Rutledge broke the connection, absently rubbing his jaw with his fingers.

So Penrith was apparently all he claimed to be. No one, however, had so far explained the confusion between Hampshire and Sussex. But it might be nothing more mysterious than being born in one county and growing up in the other.

For the moment he put Penrith out of his mind and went in search of Hugh Jones.

The bakery was still closed on this Monday morning, but it was ready for use as soon as fresh supplies arrived. Jones said, as Rutledge came through the door, "I managed to bake bread this morning for my regular customers. Only twenty loaves, but a start. It was all the flour I had."

"I think I've found the person who did this damage. An elderly maid at Hallowfields. She'd served Quarles, seen only his best side, apparently, and she was told that you had killed him. Hence the vandalism."

Jones sighed. "He still makes trouble for me, even in death. I'm grateful Mrs. Quarles took him away from here to bury him. Else I'd fear to walk through the churchyard of a night."

"Inspector Padgett is satisfied that we've found Quarles's killer. He'll be taken into custody sometime this morning."

"Who is it?"

"You'll hear soon enough. The evidence points strongly to Michael Brunswick."

"Another family Quarles destroyed. Ah well. I'm sorry for him. He's a man haunted by disappointment. But I never saw him as a murderer."

"Inspector Padgett believed Brunswick could have killed his wife."

"There was a lot of talk at the time. No one paid much attention to it. Thank you for telling me about what happened here."

Rutledge left the baker and walked on to the police station. Padgett had just returned from his meeting with the Chief Constable.

"He agrees, there's enough evidence to make an arrest. We'll see what the lawyers can make of it now. I expect you're wanted back in London. I'll deal with Brunswick. He's at the church, playing the organ. I spoke to Rector on my way in, and he told me. He wants to be present. I think he's afraid Brunswick will do something foolish. I don't see it that way."

Rutledge went there himself and stood in the open door at the side of St. Martin's, listening to the music for a time. Brunswick was practicing an oratorio, struggling with it, going over and over the more complicated sections until he got it right and locked into his memory. It was a long and frustrating session. When he'd finished, he launched into a hymn he knew well, and the difference in the two pieces was telling. Brunswick had ability but not the soaring skill that great musicians strove for.

Hearing voices approaching, Rutledge went back to the hotel to fetch his valise. Coming down the stairs again, he stopped by Reception.

Hunter was there to bid him farewell and a safe journey.

Half an hour after he'd driven out of Cambury, the telephone in the small parlor beyond the stairs began to ring.

The staff was busy with the noonday meal, and no one heard it.

It was an uneventful drive to the city. Rutledge arrived late and went directly to his flat.

The next morning, he called on Davis Penrith at his home.

"We've found your former partner's murderer. He was taken into custody yesterday and charged. The inquest will find enough evidence to bind him over for trial."

Penrith's face was still. "Who is he?"

"The organist at St. Martin's. He believed his late wife had an affair with Quarles. She killed herself."

Penrith searched for something to say. "I'm sorry to hear it."

"There's one small matter to clear up with you."

Penrith smiled wryly. "I told you my father was curate in Hampshire. Only for five years, before moving on to Sussex. My mother was alive then, it was a happy time. The living in Sussex was cramped and wretched. I tend not to think of it if I don't have to. I hope it didn't cause you any trouble."

"None at all," Rutledge answered blandly.

"Well, then, thank you for telling me about this man Brunswick. I'm glad the matter is cleared up, for the sake of Mrs. Quarles and Marcus."

Penrith prepared to show Rutledge out, walking to the study door.

"Actually, that wasn't the matter I wished to bring up."

Surprised, Penrith stopped, his hand on the knob.

"I can't think of anything else that needs to be clarified. I made my statement. You'll find it at the Yard."

"Thank you. No, what I wanted to clarify are several names I have here on my list. Mr. Butler is dead, I believe. Mr. Willard and Mr. Hester, Mr. Morgan and

Mr. Simpleton, and Mr. MacDonald were investors in the Cumberline fiasco."

Wary, Penrith said, "Where did you find those names?"

"They were in a box marked CUMBERLINE in Harold Quarles's study."

He could see the anger and frustration in Penrith's face. "Indeed. And what else of interest did you find in his study?"

"Very little. We've managed to look at these seven men and determine that they had no reason to attack and kill Mr. Quarles."

"No, of course they wouldn't. They are men of some reputation, they value their privacy, and they aren't likely to wait almost two years for a paltry revenge."

"If you consider murder paltry."

"That's not what I meant. I'm sure they would have preferred taking the matter to court, ruining us, and making Harold Quarles and myself laughingstocks. They are ruthless businessmen. It's the way they settle matters such as Cumberline. But they saw that in taking our firm to court, their own business practices might come under scrutiny. I can tell you that these men lost no more than they could afford to lose. They knew from the start that it was a risky investment, but they also had Cecil Rhodes in their sights, and their greed won over their common sense."

"Was this other investor, a man named Evering—"

Penrith must have been prepared for the question, but it still nearly splintered his carefully preserved calm. "Evering was one of Harold's clients. He made the decision to include the man."

"Was Cumberline the reason you broke with Quarles?"

Penrith fiddled with the fob on his watch chain. "All right, yes. It was. I thought Cumberline was risky from the start. I thought Quarles was taking a direction we'd never taken before with the firm. I thought his judgment was failing him. But he had his reasons for offering Cumberline, he said, and it would do us no harm. Financially, he was right, though it was a close-run thing. I felt that the good name of the firm—and more important, the good will of James, Quarles and Penrith—was tarnished."

"What was his reason, did he ever tell you?"

"Not in so many words. Most of these men had made their money in the war, cutting corners, shoddy goods, whatever turned a penny. He said the poor sods in the trenches didn't count for anything, if a shilling could be made from their suffering. And it was the same greed that made Cumberline so attractive to such men."

"Was Evering also profiting from the war?"

"I have no idea. You'd have to ask Quarles. And he's dead." Penrith took out his watch. "I really must go. I have matters to attend to in my office."

He held the door for Rutledge, and there was nothing for it but to thank Penrith and leave.

Rutledge drove to the Yard, and reported to Chief Superintendent Bowles, who appeared to be less than happy to hear there was a successful conclusion to the inquiry.

It was two hours later when Sergeant Gibson came to his office and said, "The Penrith in South Africa was born in Hampshire, his father lost his living there and went on to Sussex, where he didn't prosper. His son joined the army for lack of funds for a proper education, and served his time without distinction save for one heroic act—"

"—when the train was attacked. What else?"

"That's the lot. He never went back to Sussex. Instead he made his way in the City, and most recently set up his own investment firm after leaving James, Quarles and Penrith."

"And Quarles?"

"Almost the same story. Survived the attack, was badly injured, and didn't go back to his unit until they were ready to sail. He was from Yorkshire, but like Penrith, settled in London. Both men served their time, and that was that."

"All right, leave your report on my desk. A wild-goose chase."

"Why," Hamish wanted to know, "did Penrith deny they'd served atall or knew each ither before London?"

Rutledge reached for the report and went through it again, looking for what injuries had sent Quarles to hospital for such a long recovery.

He found it, a short notation in Gibson's scrawl: *burned in attack, nearly lost hands.*

Mrs. Quarles must have discovered this as well, if she hadn't already known about her husband's service in South Africa. Hardly sufficient reason to demand a separation. And even if Brunswick had learned of it, few people would care, even if he shouted it from the rooftops.

Hamish said, "It doesna' signify. Let it rest."

Rutledge turned to the paperwork on his desk, concentrating on the written pages before him. In his absence there were a number of cases where he would be expected to give testimony, and he marked his calendar accordingly. Then he read reports of ongoing inquiries where the sergeants in charge were collating evidence and passing it on for a superior to inspect.

He made comments in the margins and set the files aside for collection. Three hours later, he'd come to the bottom of the stack, and the report that Sergeant Gibson had prepared about the military backgrounds of Quarles and Penrith.

The sergeant had summarized the material in his usual concise style, and his oral report had matched it. Rutledge tossed the folder back on his desk for collection and filing, and sat back in his chair, rubbing his eyes.

Hamish was restless, his voice loud in the small office, rattling the windows with its force. Rutledge warned, "They'll hear you in the passage," before he realized he was speaking aloud.

But Hamish was in no mood to be silent.

Rutledge reached for a folder again, realized it was Gibson's report, and tried to read it word for word in an effort to shut out Hamish's tirade. Gibson in his thoroughness had attached a copy of Penrith's military service record to support his notes.

It was nearly impossible to concentrate, and Rutledge shut his eyes against the thundering noise in his head. The last line on the page seemed to burn into his skull, and he flipped the folder closed, shutting his eyes and trying to concentrate.

It was several minutes before his brain registered anything more than pain.

He wasn't even certain he'd seen it, but he lifted the report a last time and tried to find it, first in the summation, and then in the military record itself.

And almost missed it again. Lieutenant Timothy Barton Evering.

The name of the officer in charge when the train was attacked.

Gibson, for all his thoroughness, had had no way of knowing that it mattered. Rutledge had been searching for different information, and it was only because the sergeant was not one to leave any fact undocumented that the name was even included.

Rutledge stood up, the sheet of paper still in his hand, and went to find Gibson. But the sergeant had gone out to interview a witness for one of the other inspectors.

Rutledge went back to his desk, took up the file, reached for his hat, and left the building.

He found Davis Penrith in his office. Brushing aside a reluctant clerk, Rutledge opened the door instead and strode in

Without waiting for Penrith to take in his abrupt appearance, Rutledge said, "I thought you told me you didn't know an Evering. That he was Quarles's client."

"I don't—"

"The officer in charge of the train ambushed out on the veldt was Timothy Barton Evering."

Penrith's mouth dropped open. It took him several seconds to recover. Then he fell back on anger. "What are you doing, searching through my past? I'm neither the murder victim nor a suspect in his death. You'll speak to my solicitor, Inspector, and explain yourself."

"Timothy Barton Evering."

"He's *dead,* man! There were no other survivors."

"Then who is Ronald Evering? His son?"

"I don't know any Ronald Evering. I told you, the investors in Cumberline were Quarles's clients, not mine. Now get out of my office and leave me alone!"

Rutledge turned on his heel and left. Back at the Yard, he left a message for Chief Superintendent Bowles that he would not be in the office for the next three days, went to his flat, and packed his valise.

It was a long drive all the way to Cornwall. Rutledge had sufficient time to wonder why it mattered so much to tie up a loose end that in no way affected the outcome of a case that was already concluded. All the same, action had improved his headache, and that in itself was something.

Penrith had given incomplete answers three times. Once about where his father had been curate, once about Quarles's background, and again about Evering. Whatever it was that Mrs. Quarles knew and Brunswick had been determined to ferret out, Davis Penrith must know as well.

There was a secret somewhere, and whether it had a bearing on this murder or not, it connected three people who on the surface of things had nothing in common.

Hamish said, "Do ye think the three acted together? If so, ye're a fool."

"Why has Penrith felt compelled to lie to me? If I'd gone to Hampshire looking for his past, I'd have found only a five-year-old boy. If I'd gone to Sussex, I'd have discovered that the grown man had served in the Army. And there was nothing in the legend of Harold Quarles about his military career, short as it was. He'd have used it if it had in any way served his purpose."

"They were no' deserters, they didna' need to hide."

"Precisely. Constable Wainwright's father called Penrith the sole survivor of that massacre on the train. Yet Quarles survived as well."

"It was Penrith who was pointed oot to him."

"Yes, the handsome young soldier who reminded Wainwright of the Prince of Wales: slender and fair and a hero. What was Quarles doing while Penrith was being a hero? Why wasn't he one as well? His wounds were serious enough to keep him in hospital for a long time. And back in London, why didn't Penrith's heroics become as famous as Quarles's escape from the mines? It would have stood him in good stead in many quarters." He drove on. "What will one Ronald Evering have to say about his own investment in the Cumberline stocks, and his father's dealings with Penrith and Quarles?"

22

The sea was rough, and the mail boat bucketed through the waves like a live thing, fighting the water every foot of the crossing. Rutledge, shouting to the master over the noise of the sea and the creaking of the boat, asked him to point out St. Anne's.

"That one, you can barely see the top of it from here. It's our third port."

"Do you know the Everings?"

"These many years. Visiting, are you?"

"An unexpected guest," Rutledge said, watching the little island take shape. But it was another hour and three-quarters before they reached the tiny bay that was St. Anne's harbor, and their voices were suddenly loud as the wind dropped and the seas smoothed in the lee of the land.

"Evering must not have got word you were coming today," the master said, lighting his pipe. "The house usually sends down a cart for visitors."

"Are there often visitors?"

"Not often. Ronald Evering's the last of the family, and not much for entertaining."

Rutledge watched as the man maneuvered the small craft toward the stone quay and efficiently secured it to the iron rings that held it against the fenders.

"Off you go," he said to Rutledge, nodding to the path that ran down to the harbor. "Up there, cross the road, and when you see the arbor, follow the path to the house. Would you mind carrying up the mail? It would save me a trip."

Rutledge took the packet that was held out to him.

"Will you be going back today?"

"Most likely."

"Then I'll come for you."

Rutledge stepped out onto the quay and waved to the departing mail boat as he reached the path. It ran up the sloping hillside in looping curves, as if a goat had been the first to climb here. As he went, the wind reached him again, and he carried his hat in his hand to keep it from flying off. Halfway up he could see the Scilly Isles spread out before him like a map, the four or five larger ones showing signs of habitation, the smaller ones dotting the sea like afterthoughts. On the northern exposures the bare rocky slopes of the nearest islands were covered with what appeared to be heather, while the sunnier southern parts of the islands were green.

It was a very different world from London or indeed from Cornwall.

The sun began to break through the clouds, watery and halfhearted, as Rutledge reached the road and crossed it to the Evering house. It was beautifully situated, facing the south, and protected from the north by a higher slope than the one on which it stood. He came to the arbor, opened the lovely swan-neck gate, and took the shell path up to the door.

The master of the mail boat told him that there had been shipbuilding on the largest island in the last century, but here on St. Anne's were fields of flowering bulbs and perennials. He could see that the daffodils were already dying back, their yellow and green leaves covering long beds.

The brass knocker on the door was shaped like a pair of swans, like the top of the gate in the arbor.

A middle-aged woman came to answer the door. She seemed surprised to see a stranger there, and craned her neck to look beyond him toward the harbor. The mail boat was just rounding the headland.

"Ronald Evering, please. My name is Ian Rutledge."

She stepped aside to let him come into the foyer, and said doubtfully, "I'll ask if Mr. Evering will see you." Disappearing down a passage, she glanced over her shoulder, as if to see if he was real or had vanished when her back was turned.

After several minutes, she led him into a small parlor that overlooked the sea. Which, he thought, every room in this house must, save for the kitchen quarters.

Evering was standing by the cold hearth and regarded Rutledge with some interest. "Do I know you? We seldom have visitors on St. Anne's, but sometimes people come to see the seals or watch the birds. We let them camp near the headland."

"I'm here to ask you about your father."

"My father?" Evering was at a loss.

"Yes. Lieutenant Timothy Barton Evering."

Ronald Evering said without inflection, "My elder brother. He's dead. Why should you be interested in him?"

"Because he served in South Africa. Can you tell me the circumstances surrounding his death?"

"They are painful to me. I prefer not to discuss them. Why are you interested in him?" he asked again. "Are you writing a book on that war? If so, my brother's death was a footnote, no more. There is more interesting material to be found, I'm sure."

Rutledge changed his ground. "It's my understanding that you were one of the investors in the Cumberline stock scheme. Is that true?"

Evering was very still. "Who are you? And what do you want here?"

"I'm Inspector Ian Rutledge, from Scotland Yard, Mr. Evering." He held out his identification. "Harold Quarles has been murdered—"

Evering turned away toward the mantelpiece, his hands gripping the mahogany edge, his head bowed. "I hadn't heard. I'm sorry. When did this happen? Where?"

"In Somerset, where his country house is located. Some ten days ago."

Evering took a deep breath. "I hope you've found his killer."

"Yes, he's already in custody. It was when I was searching Mr. Quarles's rooms that I came across your name in connection with Cumberline. In his study he kept a file on the transactions."

Evering turned to face Rutledge. "And how did you learn about my brother?"

"We were looking up Harold Quarles's service records, in an effort to find out what role, if any, his past played in his death."

"I can't see how South Africa matters? Or the Cumberline stocks. Surely neither of those could be connected to murder?"

"Not to my knowledge. But it pays to be thorough, Mr. Evering. How long have you known Mr. Quarles?"

"Not very long. I invested a sum of money with him, and it didn't prosper."

"Did you know when you invested your money that Quarles had served under your brother in the Boer War?"

Evering glanced toward the windows, where a shaft of errant sunlight had turned the sea from gray to deep green. "The War Department gave us very little information about my brother's death. He died on active duty and served his country well. That's what my father was told in the telegram. I was very young at the time, and if he learned more, he never spoke of it."

"And so it was quite by chance that you should choose an investment offered by two men who served in your brother's company."

"Neither Mr. Quarles nor Mr. Penrith ever mentioned the fact. If they recognized the name or knew my relationship to Timothy, I didn't realize it."

"Did you deal with both partners? Penrith and Quarles?"

"Yes, I talked to Mr. Quarles first, and then he brought in Mr. Penrith."

It sounded straightforward, told without hesitation or attempt to conceal.

"Is that all you came to ask me, Mr. Rutledge?"

"I'm informed that Penrith and Quarles were the only survivors of the Boer attack. Do you know if that's true?"

"I've told you—I know very little about how Timothy died. The fact of his death was enough. My parents never recovered from the shock."

"Yes, I can understand."

"Were you in the Great War, Mr. Rutledge? If you were, you can appreciate that many details of what happens in a battle are not reported. My brother's commanding officer wrote a very fine letter to my father, and it said very little beyond the fact that Timothy died bravely and didn't suffer. That he was an honor to his regiment, showed great promise as an officer, and would have had a fine career in the army if he'd lived. How many such letters does an officer write? He could say the same thing to a dozen grieving families, and who would be the wiser?"

"It is meant well. Sometimes the details are—distressing."

"Yes, I'm sure that must be true. For my mother's sake, I was grateful. She died not knowing whether he suffered or not. Which is what really mattered, in the end." Evering gestured to the chairs that stood between them. "Won't you sit down, Mr. Rutledge? I'll ring for tea. It will be some time before the boat returns."

"Thank you." Rutledge took the chair indicated and waited until Evering had given the order for tea to the woman who'd answered the door.

"One of the reasons I'm following up on the South African campaign is that something that happened in Harold Quarles's service out there—he served nowhere else, you see—disturbed his wife to such a degree that there was a serious breach with her husband. It lasted until his death."

Evering considered Rutledge for a moment and then said, "I don't know what to say. I've never met Mrs. Quarles or spoken to her. Does she think this—whatever it was—had to do with my brother?"

"I have no way of knowing what it is. I'm here to learn as much as I can about the only serious action Quarles saw during the war."

"It's a mystery to me. But if she tells you anything that I ought to know, please send me word. I'd be grateful."

The tea came, and they drank it in silence. Rutledge's mind was occupied, and Evering seemed to have little conversation, as if living alone in this empty, silent house had shaped his spirit.

But as he set his teacup down, Rutledge asked, "And so, as the only surviving son, you inherited this house?"

"My father's family was one of the earliest settlers here. Generations ago. We are as close to 'native' here as anyone can be. You either love or hate it. My brother joined the army because he wanted adventure and excitement, both in short supply here on St. Anne's. My mother called it a need to be a man, and persuaded herself that in due course he'd come home, marry, and settle here for the rest of his life. As the elder son, that's what was expected of him. Instead he died in a place none of us had ever heard of and couldn't find on a map. Look, there's the mail boat. No passengers to hold it up today. You should be there when it comes in, Mr. Rutledge."

"I almost forgot." Rutledge reached into his pocket and brought out the packet of mail. "I was to give you this." He glanced at the return address on the top envelop but said nothing.

Evering thanked him and sent for the maid to bring Rutledge's coat and hat. "I'm afraid it will be a wet crossing. Those clouds on the horizon spell rain. Thank you for coming, Mr. Rutledge. I'm sorry I couldn't be more helpful."

But Rutledge, as he went out into the wind, smelling now of rain, thought that on the whole Ronald Evering had not been sorry at all.

By the time the boat reached the mainland, they were caught in a downpour, and in spite of his useless umbrella, Rutledge managed to start his motorcar without drowning.

Cutting across Cornwall in the direction of Dunster, Rutledge spent the night there with the Maitlands, newly returned from their wedding trip and delighted to see him. They would have kept him longer, but he was up before dawn the next morning, and by first light was well on the road again, heading for Cambury.

He drove straight through the village when he reached the High Street, and out to Hallowfields.

Mrs. Quarles was in mourning, he was told, and not seeing anyone.

"Tell her I know about Evering," he said, and in three minutes, he was face-to-face with Harold Quarles's widow in the formal drawing room. She was not happy to see him, and the two small dogs at her feet growled as he entered.

"I thought we were fortunate in not having to deal with Scotland Yard any longer," she told him shortly. "And here you are again." She didn't ask him to sit down.

"I'm afraid that I'm rather tenacious when it comes to making certain that the man I hang is indeed the killer I was looking for."

"You have doubts about Brunswick? But I was told he confessed."

"For reasons of his own—which may or may not be the right reasons. It's Evering I'm interested in, and how he died."

"Who told you about Evering? Was it Penrith? If you tell me it was, I won't believe you."

"Penrith would as soon keep the matter quiet. He's lied to me enough to make me suspicious, and that wasn't very clever of him."

"Then you'll hear nothing from me."

"Mrs. Quarles, I'm very close to stumbling on the truth. If you know Evering's name, then you know what it is I'm after. And I warn you, it's very likely that Michael Brunswick knows more than I do, and that he'll use what he knows at his trial, to disgrace your husband publicly."

"There's no way Brunswick could know anything. I wouldn't have learned the truth myself if Harold hadn't been so drunk one night that he talked in his sleep. It was as if he were having a waking nightmare. I've never seen anything before or since to match it. The next morning I confronted him with it, and at first he told me I was imagining things. And then he swore he'd see me dead if I said anything to anyone. I knew then that it was true. And I left him, because I couldn't stand to be in the same room with him or feel those hands—"

She broke off.

"You might as well tell me, Mrs. Quarles. I won't walk away until I know the whole truth about your husband. If it has nothing to do with his murder, I will never speak of it. You can trust my word on that."

She stared at him. "What use to me is your word?"

"It's better that I find out than someone else trying to pry into the past."

Walking past him to the door, Maybelle Quarles opened it quickly, as if expecting to find Mrs. Downing there with her ear pressed to the panel. But the passage was empty. She closed it again and went to the window, looking out. When she spoke, she had pitched her voice low, so that it barely reached his ears.

"You are a persistent man, Mr. Rutledge. Very well. I will tell you what you want to know. Not because of the persistence, but because by your digging, it's possible that other people will get wind of the truth, and we will never have peace in this family again."

Turning back to him, she said baldly, "My husband burned Lieutenant Evering alive, after shooting the wounded on that train."

"Gentle God," Rutledge said softly. "In heaven's name, why?"

"I don't know. I wish I did, it would make my own nightmares easier to bear."

"Does Penrith know? Surely—"

"He must know. The soldiers who reached the train misread what they saw, and Penrith made no move to correct them. They must have thought Harold was burned trying to save the lieutenant. They believed the Boers had come into the train and killed the wounded. My husband was delirious, he couldn't tell them what had happened after Penrith went for help."

"It could well be true."

"In that nightmare, he relived listening to Evering die. He relived shooting the wounded. He lay there, writhing on the bed, and begged God to help him after he'd burned his hands to make it appear he'd done his best. He'd kept that secret so long that it was tormenting him, and that night, he confessed to God or the devil, I don't know which, and I sat there, afraid to call for help, *listening to it all.*"

Rutledge had only to look at the torment in her face to believe her. To understand why she hated the man she'd married and couldn't bear to live with him. And yet she'd never divorced him . . .

"Why did you stay with Quarles?"

"I have a son. Harold would have taken him from me if I'd told anyone else. I'm not a fool, Mr. Rutledge, I knew the danger of living under the same roof with a murderer. But I did it for Marcus, and God saw fit on that Saturday night to release me from my prison. And I have thanked him on my knees for it."

"Why didn't you consider killing him yourself, if you felt afraid?"

"And leave my child without a father or a mother? I think not."

He left soon after. There was nothing more he could say to the woman standing by the empty grate staring down into flames that she could see only in her mind. And there was no comfort he could give her. It was beyond any words he could utter, and it would be patronizing to try.

Hamish said, as Rutledge pointed the bonnet of the motorcar down the drive, "It doesna' change the murder or who did it."

"Quarles was a strange man. A killer at heart, ruthless and coldblooded, and yet he could be kind as well. What was it Miss O'Hara said? That someone should be given a medal for ridding Cambury of the ogre?"

All at once he could hear shouting in the distance and stopped the car to listen. It appeared to be coming from the Home Farm. He got out, walked a little way across the lawns, and saw that Masters and one of his men were wading into the pond just beyond the barns and outbuildings. Something was in it, a long blue streak in the middle of water already turning muddy from the hurried thrashing of their feet. He raced toward the farm, watching the scene play out like a drama on a stage. Masters was close now to what appeared to be a blue gown, and he was reaching out, trying to drag it nearer, then trying to right the figure as it began to lash out wildly.

It was a woman, and she wasn't trying to cling to her rescuers, she was struggling to free herself. Rutledge, out of breath, got to the water's edge just as Masters succeeded in dragging the woman to shallower depths.

It was Betty Richards, the elderly woman who had served Quarles, and in his name tried to destroy the bakery.

Her hair was down, gray streaked and straggling, half covering her face, and she was crying, trails of tears spreading into the muddy stream running from her hair and into her eyes.

Masters, his breathing tumultuous, was shaking her, demanding to know in broken sentences what the hell she thought she was doing.

Rutledge said, "She was trying to drown herself, man. Get her inside and fetch some blankets. Tea as well, and towels to dry her hair."

Masters let her go, turning to Rutledge. "What are you doing here? I thought you'd found your killer."

"In more ways than one." He reached out and put a hand on Betty's shoulder, comforting her as best he could.

"There was nothing else I could do," she said, sobbing into the wet skirt she held to her face. "I had nowhere else to go, nothing left."

Rutledge asked sharply, "Did Mrs. Quarles give you notice?"

She tried to shake her head but her hair was a heavy mass down her back. "It was Mrs. Downing. She said they'd be cutting back staff now, and I'd not be needed any longer. Mr. Archer told her I could take care of his rooms. But she said it would be up to Mrs. Quarles, and I mustn't hold out any hope."

Rutledge swore. Hadn't they read the will? Hadn't they seen the bequest to this poor wretch?

As if in answer, Betty said, "Mrs. Downing never liked it that I wasn't under her. But I wasn't and never was meant to be. She was told that from the start."

Mrs. Masters had come with blankets and they wrapped Betty in them as water ran from her clothes and she began to shiver. Rutledge let Mrs. Masters take over, guiding Betty toward her kitchen, making soothing noises.

Masters said, "I never liked that woman."

"Betty?"

"Not Betty, I hardly knew her. No, Mrs. Downing. She creeps around the house, listening at doors and spreading gossip. I don't know how Mrs. Quarles can stand her."

"I don't think she sees that side of her housekeeper. Will Betty be all right with your wife?" He watched Mrs. Masters close the kitchen door behind them.

"She'll see that Betty is taken care of. I've half a mind to take her on myself, to get her out of Mrs. Downing's clutches. But I don't need more staff."

"Then you might spread a little gossip of your own. Harold Quarles left a sizeable bequest to that house-maid. She'll never want for anything again."

"Why on earth should he do that?"

"I don't know. But I think Mrs. Downing might. I'll have a word with her."

Rutledge walked back the way he'd come, and leaving the motorcar where it was, he went on to the house and knocked again at the door.

Mrs. Downing opened it to him, and he stepped inside before she could prevent him.

"Has there been a reading of the will?" he asked, and her eyes flickered.

"It was read privately. The staff wasn't invited to hear. Afterward, we were told by Mrs. Quarles how we were to be provided for."

"Was nothing said to you about a bequest to the woman who had served Mr. Quarles by taking care of his rooms?"

"Not to me. I wasn't told anything at all."

"But you overheard something, didn't you? When Mrs. Quarles spoke privately to Betty."

"She never did—"

Rutledge said, "Bring her down here to me. I want to speak to Mrs. Quarles."

"I can't—"

But he ignored her and called Mrs. Quarles's name. She came to the top of the stairs, her face flushed with her anger. "What do you think you're doing?"

"Come down here, or I'll come up there."

Without a word, she came down the stairs and walked past him to the small sitting room. He followed.

"What is it you want?" She stood there, cold and straight, as if nothing more could touch her.

"There was a bequest in your husband's will. To the housemaid who looked after him. Betty Richards."

"What business is that of yours?"

"She was never told, after the will was read. I want to know why."

"I didn't think it was an appropriate bequest. She's not capable of handling that much money—"

"Tell me the truth. Or I'll see to it that you're taken into Cambury police station for theft."

"It's not theft," she retorted. "It's my husband's money—"

"And he left it to that woman."

"That woman, as you put it, is his widowed sister. He kept her here as a maid, and let the world think he was kind to take her on. But he did it to keep the rest of us out of his rooms and his affairs. He knew he could trust her. She's not fit to be my son's aunt, and I won't have her in this house any longer."

"Then give her the money he left to her, and let her go."

"For all I care, she can starve. She's a Quarles and I hate them all!"

She went past him out of the room, slamming the door behind her. Any sympathy he'd felt for her had vanished. He pulled open the door and called to Mrs. Downing.

"You'll pack Betty Richard's things and send them to Cambury to the house of Miss O'Hara. She'll be staying there until someone from the solicitor's office can be summoned. I want them there within the hour, do you hear me?"

Mrs. Downing said, "I'll see to it—"

But he was out the door. As he looked back at the house on his way to his motorcar, he saw a face staring at him from the window. A boy, he realized, in Harold Quarles's rooms.

It was Marcus Quarles, a bewildered, frightened expression on his face.

Rutledge drove to the Home Farm and asked Tom Masters and his wife to send Betty Richards to Cambury as soon as she'd recovered.

"She's sleeping now, poor thing," Mrs. Masters told him. "Let her rest. It will be soon enough to take her there tomorrow."

"You may find yourself in trouble if you take her in," he warned. "I'll go ahead and tell Miss O'Hara that she's to have a guest."

Miss O'Hara frowned when he told her. "I'm not a boardinghouse. But if you insist, then I'll keep her safe."

"She won't be staying long. You'll be hearing from Mr. Hurley. A solicitor. He'll have instructions for her."

"Yes, well, that may be. You owe me another dinner, then."

Rutledge smiled. "I'll remember."

He didn't stop at the police station. He had nothing to say to Inspector Padgett. But on his way to speak to Miss O'Hara, he'd noticed the board outside St. Martin's Church.

Someone had covered the name of MICHAEL BRUNSWICK, ORGANIST.

In London, Rutledge went directly to the house of Davis Penrith.

He said to the man as he was shown into the study, "You have lied to me more times than I care to count. About your father. About Quarles. About Evering. I know about South Africa now. Almost the entire story."

"You can't possibly know."

"About Evering burning alive? About the wounded who were shot? About the fact that you never turned Quarles in to the authorities?"

"I had no proof!"

"Of course you did. You knew how many wounded there were, or you'd have never walked across the veldt alone to find help. You and Quarles would have left that train together to find help, because there was nothing the Boers wanted from it then. But he stayed behind. I want to know why."

"I tell you, I didn't know."

"What was it, cowardice? Did you and Quarles get cold feet when the Boers attacked, and hide under the carriages? Was that why you survived? They were dead shots, the Boers. How was it that neither you nor Quarles was wounded, and yet everyone else on that train died?"

"I don't remember. When the train was stopped, I was knocked down. *I don't remember.*"

"How did Quarles burn his hands? If he was in that carriage with Evering, why were only his hands burned?"

"I wasn't there."

"But you knew when you walked away and left Quarles there—with no wounds, mind you—that Evering was alive. Wounded, perhaps, but alive. The Boers didn't burn men to death."

"It was the lantern in the last carriage. It was hit and broken. I don't know why it burned, but it did."

"You surely knew Ronald Evering was the brother of the man Quarles killed. Why did he come to you to invest his money?"

"I can't answer that. Coincidence—one in a thousand odds—"

"I think he must have learned something, and he came to you to find out the rest." It was a battering of questions, and Rutledge could tell that Penrith couldn't sustain it.

"He couldn't have known anything, no one did. We never told anyone we'd been in the army. Not even Mr. James."

"What were you trying to hide, if it wasn't cowardice?"

"We were hiding nothing. Nothing."

"Why did you write a letter to Ronald Evering, just in the last few days? It arrived on St. Anne's the same time I did, and I carried it to the house myself."

"I—he'd said something about wanting to invest with me again. I told him that the opportunities he spoke of had not turned out the way he'd hoped, and I thought he would be wise to look elsewhere."

"How odd, that after Cumberline, he would wish to trust you again with any sum of money."

"Yes, I thought the same—" Penrith broke off. "That's to say, I found it odd myself."

"You've lied to me about many things. Why did you lie to me about Scotland?"

It came out of nowhere, a shot in the dark from Rutledge that shook Penrith to the core. "I *was* in Scotland. I swear to you I was! There's the letter from my wife."

"But not that whole weekend. She says something about it being such a brief visit, and that you'd arrived just in time to dine with the Douglases. I think you reached Scotland on Sunday afternoon, not on Friday. And you're letting an innocent man hang in your place. You were in Cambury on that Saturday night. You quarreled with your former partner first on Minton Street, where you'd followed him from Hallowfields, and then you went ahead of him, knowing he was on foot. And you killed him, because you were afraid of him, and what he knew about your past. He was doing things that you didn't approve of, that you feared would ruin both of you. The Cumberline stocks, his outrageous behavior in Cambury, refusing to listen to you—"

"It wasn't that way, you've got it wrong—"

"Why did you strike your partner down, and then carry his body to the tithe barn and hoist him to the ceiling in that angel's harness, where no one would think to look for him? Did you hope that this would give you time to reach Scotland before anyone could accuse you of killing him?"

"I never put him in that harness—you're lying—"

"But that's how he was found. And someone did it. If it wasn't you, then who would do such an ugly thing?"

"I never put him in anything—"

"An innocent man is going to hang," Rutledge said again. "And it will be on your conscience. Perhaps you weren't there when Quarles shot the wounded—or when he burned Evering alive. It may be that you've nothing on your conscience but protecting a friend. But *this* death is on your hands. When Brunswick hangs, it will be you who slides the hood over his head and the rope tight around his neck—"

"Stop it!" Penrith put his hands over his ears, trying to shut out Rutledge's unrelenting voice. "I am not guilty. I've never killed anyone. Harold Quarles was still alive when I left him—"

"You wouldn't have left Quarles alive. Not if he knew it was you who struck him. He was a bad enemy. A dangerous man. You had proof of that, whatever you want to deny about South Africa."

"I did. I wasn't afraid of him. I told him that I knew why he'd tried to make everyone think he'd slept with my wife—it was because I'd left the partnership. He always punishes anyone who gets in his way. And that was my punishment. I hit him when he turned away because he called me a liar. He said he'd never gone near my wife. I told him *he* was the one lying . . ."

Penrith stopped, appalled. He sank down in the nearest chair, his head in his hands.

"Oh, my God. What have I done?"

Rutledge thought at first that Penrith was horrified that he'd been tricked into confessing, then he realized that the man had stared into something only he could see, and discovered the truth.

"What is it?" Rutledge asked.

Penrith shook his head. "I can't believe— Look, I never put him in that harness. I was so angry, I couldn't have touched him. I left him there in his own blood, still breathing. It must have been someone from the house who put him in that barn, it wasn't me. I swear to you—it wasn't *me*!"

"You've lied one time too many," Rutledge said. "It doesn't serve you anymore."

"But it's the truth. He was alive, there on the grass by the gatehouse. *I didn't murder Harold Quarles.*"

"If you didn't, then you must know how Michael Brunswick feels, waiting to be tried. He told me the truth, and I didn't believe him. I accepted your word that you were in Scotland, and you gave it, knowing it was a lie."

"No, you must listen to me—all right, I struck him twice. He was walking away, laughing, and I knocked him down to his knees to stop him, and then before I quite knew what I was doing, I hit him a second time because I was so angry with him. But I could hear him breathing—I hadn't *killed* him."

"Weren't you afraid that leaving him alive was dangerous, that he'd tell the police what you'd done?"

"No—he wouldn't dare. Besides, I thought—I hoped that if no one found him right away, he might not remember what had happened."

"You hoped he would die. Davis Penrith, I am arresting you on the charge of willfully murdering your former partner, Harold Quarles."

"You can't do this. I haven't killed anyone. I was tricked—"

Rutledge shook his head. "It's finished. Will you go with me now, or must I send for constables to bring you in?"

"You don't understand. I was misled—it was Ronald Evering who told me that Quarles had slept with my wife. And I believed him, because it was the sort of thing Quarles would do. He punished his wife by having affairs with every woman in Cambury he could seduce. Why not *my* wife, to punish me? Dear God, don't you see? It must all have been a lie . . . ."

23

It was Inspector Padgett's nature to gloat. As Rutledge sat in the man's office and reported the arrest of Davis Penrith and the evidence that supported it, Padgett smiled. It was nearly a sneer.

"Didn't I tell you from the start that it was someone in London? And you so certain the killer was among us here in Cambury?"

"It was the way the evidence pointed. Davis Penrith told us half truths about Scotland. He was there—but he'd driven through the night, like a bat out of hell, to make certain he was in time for the dinner his wife and he had been invited to attend."

"And her letter was equally unenlightening. Yes, one of the problems of not being on the spot, wouldn't you say?"

Rutledge, heeding the succinct advice Hamish was pouring into his ear, held on to his temper with a firm grip.

"Penrith swears he was tricked. That he'd deliberately left London early in order to discuss a business matter with Ronald Evering, and instead it turned out to be a trap. I'm on my way to the Scilly Isles to look into it."

"Never been there. Never had a reason to go, and never expect to. I'm not the best of sailors. Where was Penrith all the while on that Saturday evening?"

"He'd intended to go directly to the house to confront Quarles, but just as he neared the gates, Quarles was getting into the motorcar driven by Mr. Nelson, who was joining Quarles and Mr. Greer at dinner. They sat talking, and so Penrith didn't stop. He went as far as the next village, waited a decent interval, then drove back. The motorcar was gone, and so was Quarles. He turned in at the main drive, in front of the gates, and waited again, for some time, in fact, not sure what to do. On the chance that Quarles might have taken his visitor into Cambury to dine, Penrith walked into Cambury to look for Nelson's motorcar. By now, Penrith was impatient and worried about his timetable. But he found the vehicle by Greer's house and hung about out of sight, angry and frustrated. He didn't want to return to Hallowfields, he'd have to explain why his business couldn't wait until morning. Then Quarles obliged him by leaving the dinner early. Penrith stopped him, they had words, but Quarles was in no mood to entertain Penrith's suspicions. He walked on home, and Penrith had no choice but to follow—the High Street was hardly the place to discuss his wife's fidelity. He caught up to Quarles again on the road, and again Quarles gave him short shrift. Penrith thought Quarles was taunting him, and as they went past the gatehouse at the lane turning into the Home Farm, he was so angry he picked up one of those white stones and struck Quarles from behind. Penrith only remembers two blows, and he says Quarles was alive when he got the wind up and ran for his motorcar. He flatly denies carrying the body to the tithe barn."

"I thought you said you had a full confession."

"We do. As far as it goes. The question becomes, is Penrith still lying—this time about the apparatus in the tithe barn—or is he finally telling the truth? He doesn't strike me as a man of courage. But if he didn't move the body—who did?"

"Mrs. Quarles."

"How did she know it was lying there? I don't see her taking nightly strolls around the grounds and stumbling over her husband's corpse in the course of one of them."

"Jones? Or even Brunswick for that matter."

"When you consider the point, it's rather difficult to beard Quarles in his den—it's a house full of servants and potential witnesses. Waiting for him to come to you, outside the gates, can be hit or miss. It was sheer luck that Penrith saw him with Nelson, but jealousy that made him persist. Brunswick guessed that Quarles was somewhere about when he saw Penrith come out of Minton Street. He wasn't likely to follow the two of them. The question now is, who did?"

"Brunswick. Who else?"

"Brunswick had no reason to believe Penrith was about to kill Quarles. And that's true of Jones. But someone was expecting it. And that's the man I intend to call on when I leave here. He's the one who told Penrith that his wife was having an affair, and Penrith must have left him in a fury. Evering might have followed, to see what would happen. Why else would he tell Penrith such a thing? True or not, it led to Quarles's death."

Padgett said, "You don't give up easily, do you?"

"It's a matter of justice, you see. Even justice for an ogre."

Rutledge left soon after and drove on to Cornwall, spending the night just across the Tamar, and arriving at his destination in time to meet the mail boat on its return from the first crossing of the day.

The sea was calm, the skies clear. Rutledge had an opportunity to speak to the master as he stood at the wheel.

The man remembered bringing Penrith.

"He was in something of a state when I met him on the quay, ready to return to the mainland. He thought the fog bank on the horizon was going to swallow us and lead to catastrophe on one those skerries out there."

"Did Evering leave the island that same morning?"

"If you're asking if I picked him up on the next run, no. Nor the next day, for that matter."

"Does he have a boat of his own?"

"He does. And he's handled it in these waters all his life."

"Where would he leave it, on the mainland?"

"Wherever he chose to put in. There are a dozen coves, not to mention fishing ports, where he could tie up."

"What about a vehicle, once he did?"

"He keeps his motorcar on the Cornish mainland. It's no use to him on St. Anne's."

Rutledge nodded and changed the subject. They came alongside the quay at St. Anne's, and Rutledge helped the master tie up. There was no mail for Evering this trip, and Rutledge walked up the hill with his mind on what he was about to say. But before walking through the arbor gates, Rutledge took a brief tour around the small island, following the road until it became a lane and then a path.

The Evering family graves were tucked in a fold in the hillside, protected from the prevailing winds, and covered with flat stone slabs rather than the more conventional stones. When the winter gales washed across the island, they were less likely to erode.

He moved slowly among them, looking at the dates—going back to the seventeen hundreds, weathered but still legible—and took note of one in particular. A small memorial chapel stood just beyond the graves, and inside he found pews, an altar, and a memorial window set in the thick wall high above it. It showed a young soldier in khaki, standing tall and unafraid against the backdrop of the veldt, his rifle across one knee, his gaze on the horizon. The commissioning date on the brass plaque below it was 1903.

Leaving the chapel, Rutledge followed the path down a hillside toward a tiny cove. Here was Evering's sailboat and a strip of sand beach protected from the wind. The sun touched the emerald green water as it ebbed, and it was shallow enough to see the bottom. There was almost a subtropical climate in

these sheltered slopes. Rutledge could easily understand why flowers bloomed here before they did on
the mainland. These islands were Britain's most west-
ward outpost, and as he looked out at the cluster of St.
Anne's neighboring isles, he found himself wondering what lay submerged between here and Cornwall.
The south coast was full of tales about vanished lands,
swallowed up by the sea.

There were half a dozen small cottages on the island
as well as the main house, tucked beneath another fold
in the land, and he could see the wash blowing on lines
in the back gardens. Staff? Or the families who worked
on the estate? From the sea these cottages would be
invisible, the ancient protection of island dwellers
the world over from the depredations of pirates and
raiders. But neither could they see the Evering house
from here or the cove or even the docking of the mail
boat. Evering could be sure there were no witnesses
to his comings and goings.

Satisfied, Rutledge walked back to the house and
lifted the knocker on the door.

The middle-aged maid again answered his summons and left him to wait in the parlor for Evering to
join him.

"You might be interested to hear," Rutledge said,
as soon as Evering walked into the room, "that it

was Davis Penrith who killed his partner, Harold Quarles."

"I am interested. That was an odd pairing if ever I saw one." He gestured to a chair. "I can't imagine that you came all the way out here to tell me that."

"Penrith told me that on his most recent visit here, you reluctantly informed him that Quarles was having an affair with Penrith's wife."

"Did I? I hardly think so. I don't travel in the same circles. If there has been gossip, I would be the last person to hear it."

"Or the first person to make it up."

Evering laughed easily. "Why should I care enough about these two men to make up anything?"

"Because they let your brother burn alive when they could have saved him. Because—according to Penrith—it was even possible that Quarles had engineered his death. I don't know why. But having spent four years in the trenches, I find myself wondering why the two most inexperienced soldiers in that company survived when no one else did. Unless they were hiding and Evering threatened to have them court-martialed for cowardice. Apparently the army went so far as to make certain Penrith's rifle had been fired."

"I'm afraid I don't know what you're talking about. I don't know how my brother died."

"I believe you do. Someone brought his body home. It's there, among the family graves."

"The stone was set over an empty grave, to please my grieving mother. You'll find no bones beneath it."

"We can order an exhumation to find out. But it would be simpler to wire South Africa and ask the authorities if your brother still lies where he was buried at the time of his death. There will be a paper trail we can follow. Signatures . . ."

"Yes, all right, I was in South Africa for a time, and I made the arrangements for my mother's sake. It was not an experience I care to remember. But I learned nothing from the military authorities there. Possibly to spare my feelings."

"You knew when you first went to James, Quarles and Penrith exactly who these two men were. And they were well aware that you knew. I think that's why they allowed you to invest in Cumberline. To teach you a lesson."

He sighed. "That well may be. On their part. I couldn't say."

"I think you deliberately told Penrith lies about his wife and Harold Quarles, knowing that would be the one thing that would set them at each other's throats. I think you didn't really care which one killed the other. It was revenge you were after."

"This is a very unlikely story. Not one you can prove, certainly."

"It's my belief that you followed Penrith to Hallowfields, and watched him kill Quarles. And then it was you who put Quarles's body into the rig in the tithe barn. I don't know how you learned that it was there. But you've been planning your revenge for some time. You might have heard the story of the Christmas pageant from anyone. It would be interesting to take you back to Cambury and see how many people there recognize you as an occasional visitor."

"It would be rather stupid of me to visit Cambury, don't you think? Strangers stand out in small villages, people are curious about them. No, if I went to the mainland, it was only to hear news that never reaches us here on St. Anne's. But save yourself the trouble. You can ask the master of the mail boat. I didn't leave the island."

"You have your own boat. Your staff would know whether you were here or on the mainland."

"While you're here, you must ask them."

Which meant, Rutledge was certain, that they would lie for him. Or were paid well to do so.

"It's going to be very difficult, I agree. But I know the truth now. You'll be summoned to give evidence at Penrith's trial. Will you call him a liar, under oath?

Will you deny ever telling him about his wife and Quarles?"

Evering walked to the cabinet that stood between the windows. Opening the glass doors, he reached in to align the small figure of a man seated in a chair, his yellow waistcoat tight across his belly, one hand raised, as if in salute. "I have nothing to fear. I'll gladly give testimony. Under oath. It's far more likely that Penrith knew about that contraption you speak of. Not I." He closed the cabinet door and this time turned the key in the lock.

Evering, unlike Penrith, was not likely to break.

Rutledge said, "Does it bother your conscience that Quarles was murdered and Penrith will hang? And that you are very likely responsible?"

"I hardly know them. I won't lose sleep over their fates. I'd like to offer you tea, again, Mr. Rutledge, but I think perhaps you'd prefer to await the mail boat down at the quay. It is, as you can see, one of our best days. The water in fact is beautiful. Admiring it will pass the time. There are a number of interesting birds on the islands. You might spot one of them."

Rutledge picked up his coat and his hat. "Thank you for your time." He walked past Evering to the door, and there he stopped. "Quarles has a sister, you know. And he has a son. Penrith has a family as well. You are the last of your line. You may have found a way to destroy your brother's killers, but revenge is a two-edged sword. Survivors are sometimes determined—as you well know—and somehow may find a way to finish what you began."

Evering said, "I have no interest in vendettas. Or vengeance. I can tell you that my mother was of a different temperament and would have stood there below the gallows to watch Penrith die. There are many kinds of justice, Mr. Rutledge. As a policeman you are concerned with only one. Do speak to Mariah on your way out. She'll confirm—in writing if need be—that I never left St. Anne's."

Rutledge did speak to the maid. She gave her name as Mariah Pendennis. And she told him, without hesitation or any change of expression, that it was true, Mr. Evering had been on St. Anne's for a fortnight or more, as was his custom this time of year.

"The man's guilty," Rutledge told Hamish as he leaned against a bollard, waiting for the mail boat. "As surely as if he took that stone and killed Quarles himself."

"But ye canna' prove it. Guilty or no'."

Overhead the gulls swooped and soared, curious to see if this stranger intended to offer them scraps or not. Their cries echoed against the hillside behind Rutledge.

He turned and looked back toward the house he'd just left. He could feel Evering's eyes on him, watching to be certain he left with the boat when it came in.

Where had Evering learned such cunning? And why had it taken so long to wreak havoc among his enemies? He'd been young, yes, when his brother died, but nearly twenty years had passed since tragic news had reached the anxious household at the top of the hill.

Hamish said sourly, "He waited for a way that didna' compromise him."

Rutledge watched the mail boat pull around the headland, the bow cleaving the waves and throwing up a white V as it moved toward the quay.

It was a long twenty-eight miles across to Cornwall. Rutledge had time to think, and at the end of the journey, he was no closer to a solution.

But as he turned his motorcar east, he suddenly realized that the answer had been staring him in the face since the beginning, but because it was so simple, it had gone undetected.

24

Inspector Padgett was startled to find Rutledge waiting for him in his office when he returned from a late tea with his family.

"I thought I'd seen the last of you."

"Yes, well, sometimes wishes are granted and sometimes not. I went to see this man Evering. I think he set in motion the train of events that led to the murder of Harold Quarles, but he knows very well that it can't be proven. He's as guilty as Penrith, in my view. More, perhaps, for using a weak man as his tool, and finding the right fear to provoke him. But that's beside the point."

"You know as well as I do that policemen often have suspicions they aren't able to prove. You'll have to live with this one."

"Possibly."

"A bit of news at this end. Mrs. Quarles came to Cambury in person to apologize to Betty Richards. She also brought a bank draft for the sum that Quarles left the woman in his will. I don't think Betty quite knew what to make of it all. Miss O'Hara tells me that she sat in her room and cried for an hour afterward. Tears, according to Miss O'Hara, of relief rather than grief. I don't know that she cared for her brother as much as she cared for the money he left her."

"She was frightened about the future."

"It's secure enough now."

"Which brings me back to something we never resolved. Not with Brunswick and not with Penrith. How the body of Harold Quarles was moved from the scene of his murder to the tithe barn, to be strung up in that cage. I was convinced that Evering must have done it. To humiliate the man in death. But the more I considered the matter, the more impossible it seemed. I know Penrith left his motorcar in the drive, where it wasn't visible from the house, but what did Evering do with his? We found no tracks to explain what happened—and that's a long way to carry a dead man."

"I've told you my opinion—Mrs. Quarles borrowed Charles Archer's wheeled chair."

"Yes, but what brought her, in the middle of the night, down to the gatehouse just minutes after her husband was murdered?"

"She heard something. The barking dog, remember?"

"She'd have sent one of the staff."

Padgett said, smiling broadly, "You can't have it both ways."

"But I can. The only vehicle that had driven down the tithe barn lane was yours. Whether you heard that dog barking and came in to investigate, or something else caught your eye, you found Quarles dead, and it was your need to make him a laughingstock that gave you the idea of putting him up in the cage. You drove him there, a piece of cloth or chamois around his head, and because you knew where the apparatus was and how it worked, you could strap him in very quickly. A stranger would have had to learn how the buckles and braces worked. Then you went in to Cambury, alerted your men, sent for me, and waited until I got there to remove Quarles, so that someone else was in charge of the inquiry. You've already admitted that much. But it explains why we never found tracks to indicate who else had been there in the lane and driven or dragged Quarles to the barn."

"You can't prove it," Padgett said, his face grim. "Whatever you suspect, you can't prove it."

"That's true. Because you've had time to remove any bloodstains from your motorcar and burn that rag. That's why you left your motorcar with Constable Jenkins, because your evidence was in the boot."

"I did no such thing—"

"But you did. The tracks were yours, and only yours, until your constables got there. And then the doctor came after I arrived. I shall have to tell the Chief Constable, Padgett. You tampered with the scene of a crime, with the intent to confound the police. And you did just that."

"I'll deny it."

"I think you will. But he's had other reports against you. This will probably be the last straw."

"I'm a policeman. I had a right to be in that lane. I had the right to decide if this murder was beyond the abilities of my men."

"And you spent most of your time trying to derail my investigation."

"I was no wiser than you when it came to finding out who killed Quarles."

"Didn't it occur to you that the killer might still be somewhere there, out of sight? Or that Quarles might still have been alive—barely—when you got to him? Why didn't you shout for help or blow your horn? But that's easier to explain. You hadn't seen Penrith's motorcar as it left, so you must have believed that someone from Hallowfields had murdered Quarles. It was safer to let him die and bring down Mrs. Quarles with him."

"I did nothing of the sort—O'Neil himself said the second blow was fatal, that there *was* no help for it. He was unconscious and dying as soon as it was struck." Padgett's voice was intent, his gaze never leaving Rutledge's face.

"You couldn't have known that at the time, could you?"

Padgett swore. "You've been after my head since I was rude to Mrs. Quarles on our first visit. Well, she's a piece of work, I can tell you that, and neither wanted nor needed our sympathy."

"It was you who let slip to someone the fact that Quarles had been trussed up like the Christmas angel. It didn't serve your purpose to keep that quiet. The sooner he became a subject of ridicule, the happier you were."

"You can't prove any of this."

"You also saw to it that I suspected Michael Brunswick, because you believed him guilty of his wife's death. It was you, manipulating the truth behind the scenes, just as Evering had done. And because you were a policeman, your word was trusted."

Rutledge stood up, preparing to leave.

"Where are you going?"

"To the Chief Constable. It's my duty, Padgett. What you did was unconscionable."

Padgett shouted after him as he went down the passage, "You were a damned poor choice for Scotland Yard to send me. Talking to yourself when no one is looking. I'll bring you down with me, see if I don't."

His voice followed Rutledge out the door and to his motorcar.

"A poor enemy," Hamish warned him.

"He'd have killed Quarles himself, if he'd dared. I rather think what he did do gave him even more pleasure than he realized in the feverishness of the moment. Quarles has become a nine-day's wonder."

Rutledge drove to Miss O'Hara's house and knocked at the door. It was Betty Richards who answered and led him to the parlor. "I didn't go to the funeral," she told him, before announcing him. "I wasn't asked. But it's just as well. I never wanted to see that village again. I made a bad marriage to escape it. We went into service together, and that was worse. He drank himself to death, finally, leaving me not a penny, and when I was turned out, it was Harold who rescued me and brought me to Hallowfields, though I wasn't to tell a living soul I was his sister. I paid for my freedom, and now I have money of my own. I still have nowhere to turn. I don't know how to live, except at someone else's beck and call."

"You must find a home of your own, and learn to be your own mistress."

"Yes, I must, mustn't I?" she said doubtfully, then announced him to Miss O'Hara.

"You keep turning up, like a bad penny. What's this visit in aid of now?"

"Tidying away loose ends."

"That doesn't sound to me like an invitation to dinner."

Rutledge smiled. "Another time. I have other calls I must make. I hear Mrs. Quarles has made restitution."

"Yes, that was the oddest thing. I was never so shocked as I was when I found her at my door. It's Betty who worries me. I told her I would keep her on here, until she can decide what she wants to do with herself. But she's been so browbeaten all her life, she doesn't seem to have tuppence worth of backbone. It's really quite sad. I shall miss you, Ian, when you've gone back to London. Perhaps I can arrange a murder or two to bring you here again."

"Yes, do that." He said good-bye and left, while Hamish rumbled in the back of his head, telling him to be careful.

After calling on the Chief Constable at his house in Bath, Rutledge turned back toward London.

He had some explaining to do when he got there. Chief Superintendent Bowles was not pleased about his absence.

"Why couldn't this inquiry have been wrapped up sooner?"

"Because there was misinformation from the start. And there were people to whom it was advantageous to muddy the waters."

"This man Padgett. What possessed him? A policeman!"

"Pride."

"And what about Evering. What are we to do with him?"

"There's not much we can do. He didn't touch Harold Quarles. He in no way encouraged Davis Penrith to kill the man. He simply told him a lie."

Bowles said, "A lie can be as deadly as the truth. See to your desk. There's more than enough work on it to keep you busy awhile. I don't hold with this running about. Leave it to the lawyers now."

Dismissed, Rutledge went to his office and sat down in his chair, turning it to look out at the spring shower washing the London air clean, his mind far away from the papers in front of him. All he could see was a hot dry morning in the bush and a train burning while a man screamed.

Four days later, he was dispatched to Cornwall. A body had come ashore off Land's End, and in the dead woman's pocket was a waterlogged letter. They could make out Rutledge's name, and Scotland Yard. Much of the rest was indecipherable.

He left London as soon as he could and reached Penzance late in the evening. A young constable at the police station greeted him and said, "I'm to take you directly to Inspector Dunne. He lives in that small farmhouse you passed on your way in."

It was no longer a working farm, where the inspector lived. But the gray stone house, built in the distant past, its slate roof heavy on the beams, had a charm that was very obvious. The outbuildings had for the most part been cleared away, save for the barn and the large medieval dovecote. As they pulled into the yard, Rutledge could hear doves fluttering and calling, unsettled by the brightness of his headlamps.

Dunne was a middle-aged man graying at the temples. He had waited up for Rutledge, but he'd already replaced his boots with slippers, and shuffled ahead of them as he led Rutledge to the room where he worked when at home.

"You don't often find a victim of drowning with Scotland Yard's address in her pocket. We thought you might want to have a look."

"I appreciate that. No idea who she was?"

"None. That's what we're hoping you can tell us."

Rutledge had an odd feeling that it was Mariah Pendennis, who was the only person who could swear that Evering wasn't in his house on the night that Quarles was murdered. His spirits rose. There might yet be a way to catch Evering.

Even as he thought about it, he had to accept the reality of winds and tides. It would be nearly impossible if she'd drowned off St. Anne's for her to be found off Land's End.

Hamish said, "He would ha' taken her out to sea. Else she might wash up in the Isles."

Dunne was telling Rutledge the circumstances of finding the body. "Fishermen spied her on the rocks. That's where a good many drowning victims turn up. Know anyone living in this part of Cornwall? Dealt with a crime in our fair Duchy, have you?"

"Only one, and that was some time ago. Nearly a year. And farther north, above Tintagel."

"Not my patch, thank the Lord. Want to have a look at her tonight? Or wait until the morning. I'd be glad to put you up. The house is empty at the moment. My wife's gone to Exeter, a christening."

Rutledge accepted his invitation, and the next morning, Dunne took him to see the body of the drowned woman.

Her face had suffered from the waves tumbling her against the rocks, but shocked as he was, Rutledge had no difficulty identifying her. What he couldn't grasp was why Betty Richards should have drowned herself off Cornwall.

A sad end, he thought, moved by pity. He reached out, gently touching the cold, sheet-clad shoulder nearest him.

Rutledge said to Dunne, "You were right to summon me. Her name is Betty Richards. She was the sister of someone who was killed in Somerset recently. I'd like to see the letter. It may be important."

They brought him the stiff, almost illegible pages, and he tried to read them, using a glass that someone found for him. Even so, even magnified, the ink had run to such an extent that Rutledge could decipher only one word in three. Something about money, and her duty, and at the end, her gratitude for what he'd done for her.

But it hadn't been enough.

She'd tried to kill herself before, and this time she'd succeeded.

Why here?

She couldn't have known. He'd told no one but Padgett—

He turned to Inspector Dunne. "I must find a telephone. It's urgent."

Dunne took him across to the hotel, and there, in a cramped room, Rutledge put in a call to The Unicorn.

He recognized Hunter's quiet voice as the man answered. Rutledge identified himself and said, "Can you find Miss O'Hara, and bring her to the telephone. It's pressing business."

"It will take some time. Will you call back in a quarter of an hour?"

Rutledge agreed and hung up the receiver.

Inspector Dunne said, "Mind telling me what this is about?"

"I'm not sure." He looked at his watch. "Can someone hold the mail boat to the Scilly Isles? We should be on it, but first I've got to wait for my call to go through."

"The Scilly Isles? She wouldn't have come from there. Trust me, I know the currents in this part of the world."

"Nevertheless—"

Dunne sent a constable peddling to hold the boat. Rutledge paced Reception, mentally counting the minutes. Where was Miss O'Hara? Had anything happened to her?

He swore under his breath. The hands on the tall case clock beside the stairs moved like treacle, their tick as loud as his heartbeats, and his patience was running out.

Hamish was there, thundering in his mind, telling him what he already suspected, calling him a fool, reminding him that he had thought it was finished, and reiterating a handful of words until they seemed to engulf him.

"Is this no' what ye wanted to happen? Is it no' what would balance the scales?"

"Murder never balances the scales." He almost spoke aloud, and turned away to keep Dunne from reading the fear in his face.

Ten minutes still to go. Five—

And then it was time. Rutledge put in the call and waited for Hunter to answer. On the fourth ring he did, saying, "Rutledge? Are you there? I have Miss O'Hara with me—"

Thank God, she was safe . . .

And then Miss O'Hara's voice, strained and tired. "What is it? Where are you calling from? What's happened?"

"It's Betty Richards. She's killed herself."

"Oh, no. Oh, God, keep her." There was a brief silence. Then she said, "She left two days ago, in the night. There was a message—"

He could hear her fumbling with a sheet of paper, and then Hunter's voice in the background. "Here, let me."

And Miss O'Hara, again.

Dear Miss,

You've been awful kind to me, but there's something I must do. It's about my brother. I don't know what to do with all this money, so I might as well use it for my own self. What's left, will you see that it goes to young Marcus?

"Why didn't you call me?" he demanded when she ended her reading.

"I thought—she'd said something about her brother. I thought she might have decided after all that she wanted to see his grave. That's all that made sense to me."

Because she didn't know what Padgett had known . . .

"Did Betty leave the house the day before she went off?"

"I sent her to market for me. She wasn't gone very long. But she seemed upset when she came back—silent and distressed. When I asked her what had happened, she said, 'Someone just walked over my grave.'"

Rutledge swore then, with feeling.

Padgett had taken it upon himself to tell Betty Richards that the law couldn't touch the man behind her brother's death. Rutledge would have given any odds that Padgett had intentionally done so, just as he'd let the gossips have the information about the way they'd found Quarles in the tithe barn, and half a dozen other bits of troublemaking.

It was the only explanation for Betty Richards being here in Cornwall. Nobody else knew—*no one*—

"Where's Inspector Padgett now? Do you know?"

He could hear Miss O'Hara speaking to Hunter, then she was on the line again.

"The Chief Constable sent for him. I don't think he's come back."

"It doesn't matter. The damage is done."

"I thought—" Her voice down the line was very disturbed. "It's my fault, I should have—she never gave me any reason to suspect that she was going somewhere to die. I knew the money overwhelmed her. It sounded as if she didn't want it after all."

"There was nothing you could do. It was out of your hands. Someone wanted to hurt her, and he succeeded. Thank you. I must go—"

"Someone? Padgett? I always thought him an unparalleled idiot. I didn't know he was also a cruel bastard."

She put up the receiver as he turned to Dunne. "We need to be on that boat to St. Anne's."

The two men ran to the harbor, where the mail boat was bobbing on the turning tide. The master had the ropes off before their feet hit the deck.

Rutledge said to him, "Did you take a visitor to St. Anne's in the last several days? An unremarkable woman wearing a black dress and a black coat?"

"Yes, I did, as it happened. She wasn't there long—she was waiting for me at the quay when I swung back round to St. Anne's, to see if she was going back then or later. She said the people she'd come to see weren't at home."

"Thank God!" Rutledge felt a wave of relief wash over him. If she had killed herself, it was because she hadn't succeeded.

But Hamish said, "Ye canna' be sure it's suicide. Yon Evering might ha' killed her, to be rid of her."

"There's the letter in her pocket . . ."

He watched as the distant isles grew larger almost incrementally until the smudge divided itself into many parts, and then the individual isles were visible, spread out before him on the sea.

"I've never been out here," Dunne said. "There's hardly any crime. A constable looks in from time to time, as a matter of course, but it's not really our patch. Pretty, aren't they, like the ruins of the ancient kingdom of Lyonesse. There are stories along many parts of the English coast about church bells ringing out to sea, where there's nothing to be seen. Even as far as Essex, I think."

But Rutledge was urging the boat forward, forcing himself to sit still and wait.

At last they reached the small harbor and touched the quay as the master brought the boat in close.

"Wait here," Dunne ordered him as he leaped on the quay after Rutledge.

The two men took the track leading up to the road at a forced pace, and finally Dunne said, "Here, slow down. I'm half out of breath."

Rutledge waited for him to catch him up, and then turned toward the house.

"That's the Evering place?"

"Yes. See, the road's just ahead. We cross that, and follow the shell path beyond the arbor." Rutledge could hear his own heart beating. The sound was loud in the stillness.

"Peaceful, isn't it?" Dunne said as he turned back to look at the panorama behind him. "And that view—

you'd never tire of it. Beats the farm, I'm afraid. And I thought nothing could."

Rutledge was ahead of him, moving fast through the open arbor gate without seeing it, his mind already walking through Evering's front door. By the time Dunne had caught up with him, Rutledge had lifted the knocker and let it fall.

He realized he was holding his breath as he waited.

No one came to answer his summons.

"He's taken the boat out. He went after her. The housekeeper, Mariah Pendennis, must have family in the village. We'll try there." He led the way again, and as they passed the small burial ground of the Everings, he said to Dunne, "That's the stone for the son killed in the Boer War."

"Burned to death, did you say? Horrid way to die. Ah, I spy a rooftop. That must be the village."

But Rutledge's gaze had gone to the small cove. He could just see the mouth of it from here. Another fifty feet—and there was Evering's boat, swinging idly on its anchor.

"You go on to the village, and ask for the woman who works for Evering. Mariah Pendennis. I'm going back to the house."

"What if she's not there?"

"Bring back a responsible man. We'll need him."

Dunne nodded and set off without another word. Rutledge thought, *He's a good man.*

He turned back, past the burial ground and the chapel, down the road to the path to the house. The last hundred yards he was trotting, though he knew it must be too late.

This time as he went through the open gate he stopped to look at it.

The lovely piece that had formed the top of it was missing. The swans with curved necks.

He didn't bother to knock again. He tried the door, and it was off the latch. For an instant, he hesitated on the threshold, dreading what he knew now must be here.

He walked into the parlor, and it was empty. The dining room too echoed to his footsteps, the bare boards creaking with age as he crossed to the window and looked out.

The study was next, a handsome room with photographs of the various islands hung between the windows, the shelves across the way filled with a variety of mechanical toys. Rutledge barely glanced at them. Evering lay in front of the desk, crumpled awkwardly, the handle of a kitchen knife protruding from his chest. And in his hands, as if shoved there as an afterthought, were the swans from the gate, bloody now.

Rutledge knelt to feel the man's pulse, but there was no doubt he was dead. He had been for some time.

Hamish said, "When she came, he didna' think she was sae angry. A plain woman in a plain bonnet, ye ken. He must ha' thought she was no match for him. And the knife in the folds of her skirt."

It could have happened that way. Rutledge thought it very likely had.

He went on to search for the servants' quarters, and there he found Mariah Pendennis, dead as well, this time the knife in her back as she prepared the tea things. Sugar and tea had spilled on the work table and down her apron, and a cup was smashed on the stone floor beside her, another overturned on the table. The kettle on the hob had boiled dry, blackened now above the cold hearth.

Rutledge went through the rest of the rooms, but Mariah Pendennis had been the unlucky one, unwittingly answering the door to a murderess. He couldn't find any other servants in the house.

Ronald Evering must have lost more money to the Cumberline fiasco than he could afford. Still, one man didn't require a houseful of servants. Mariah had been sufficient for his needs, with perhaps someone to help with meals and the heavier cleaning chores, and someone to take his wash and bring it back again. His needs were few, and he had got by.

Rutledge could hear Dunne, calling to him from the foyer. He came down the stairs and said, "There are two dead here. Evering and the woman who took care of him."

The man standing behind Dunne sharply drew in a breath.

Dunne said, "I wouldn't have thought—" He left the sentence unfinished.

"She managed it because they didn't suspect her. Evering had no way of knowing who she was or why she was here. A poor woman, harmless." He led the way to the study.

"What's that in his hands?" Dunne asked, crouching down for a closer look.

"It's from the gate outside," the man with him said. "Whatever is it doing *here*?"

The closest she could come to the angel in the tithe barn. Aloud, he said, "A gesture of some sort?"

"What are these?" Dunne gestured to the collection of toys behind Rutledge. "Odd things to have in a study. My grandson has one like that." He gestured to a small golden bird on an enameled box. "He's allowed to play with it of a Sunday, with his grandmother watching."

"Mr. Evering was that fond of all manner of mechanical things," the man from the village answered him. "When he got a new one, he was like a child, playing with it by the hour. Where's Mariah, then?"

Rutledge directed them to the kitchen. He stood where he was, looking down on Evering.

It had come full circle, what this man had set in motion with a few lies. Now he was dead, and Betty Richards with him. She would be buried beside the brother who never acknowledged her. And if Mrs. Quarles read the brief account in a newspaper of a drowning in Cornwall, she might guess why . . .

There were no more Everings. The cycle would end here, in this house overlooking the sea.

But there was Padgett still to be dealt with.

"Ye can no mair take him in than ye could this one," Hamish told Rutledge. "Their hands are bloody, but ye canna' prove it."

"He sent that poor woman here to confront Evering, as surely as if he brought her to the door."

Hamish said, "If she wasna' her brother's blood, she wouldna' ha' come here. She would ha' stayed with yon Irish lass until she was settled in her own mind what to do with hersel'."

The seeds of these murders had been sown in the way Betty Richards had gone to the bakery and done as much damage as possible with her bare hands. And the seeds of her death were sown when in despair she threw herself into the pond at the Home Farm.

"I don't think she was avenging her brother," Rutledge said slowly. "I think it was avenging the life she was most comfortable with, that died with him."

Hamish said grimly, "It's too bad she didna' include yon inspector in her vengeance."

The Scots, who for centuries had raised blood feuds to a fine art, were not as shocked by them as the more civilized English.

"He'll bring himself down. He won't need a Betty Richards for that."

Back in London, Rutledge went to see Davis Penrith in prison, where he was awaiting trial. Fighting against the sense of the walls closing in on him, Rutledge told the man what had become of Evering.

"I can't say I'm heartbroken," Penrith told him. "The law couldn't touch him. And I'm to hang because of him."

"Hardly that. You needn't have acted on his information."

"Yes," he said bitterly. "It always comes down to that, doesn't it? A choice. The fact is, no one ever chooses well in the throes of jealousy and anger."

"Why did Quarles burn Lieutenant Evering alive? It's the one piece of the puzzle I've not uncovered."

"I won't burden my wife and children with that. I didn't kill the man. I just didn't report what I suspected. I gave Quarles the benefit of the doubt. I wasn't even there when it was done. I didn't see his hands until months later, when they were healing. Whatever it was that drove him, he paid for it in pain and suffering. Let there be an end to it." In spite of his denials, he looked away, as if ashamed.

"Something happened on that train."

"And whatever it was died with the men on it. Now Quarles is gone. I will be soon."

It was all that Penrith could be brought to say.

Leaving the prison, walking out through the gates and into the bright air, Rutledge found himself in a mood that he couldn't shake. Hamish was railing at him, dragging up the war, unrelenting in his fury. It was a symptom of Rutledge's own emotional desolation. His head seemed to be close to bursting with the sound of that soft Scots voice, and memories that rose to the surface unbidden, as clear as if he were in France again, and seeing what he had hoped never to see then or now.

He drove aimlessly for a time, only half aware of what he was doing, until he found himself in Chelsea.

In the next street was the house where Meredith Channing lived.

Rutledge went there, got out of the motorcar, and walked to the door.

Standing in front of it, his hand raised to the brass knocker, he thought, *I should go and find Frances.*

But she would ask too many questions. And the blackness coming down wouldn't wait.

The door opened, and he heard Meredith Channing say, "Why, Ian, what—" She stopped. "Come in. What's wrong? How can I help?"

"Will you drive with me? Anywhere. Kew. Windsor Great Park. Richmond. I don't care. Just—sit there and say nothing. I don't want to be alone just now."

"Let me fetch my coat."

She was gone less than a minute, but he had already decided he'd made a mistake in coming here. He was turning away when she took his arm and said, "I'm here. Shall I drive?"

He couldn't have said afterward where they had gone or for how long. When the black clouds of despair began, very slowly, to recede, Rutledge found he was embarrassed and turned his head to look at the passing scene, wondering what he could say that could possibly explain what he had done in coming to this woman, of all people.

She seemed to sense a difference in the silence that filled the motorcar, and she took the first step for him. "I should very much like a cup of tea."

The panacea for everything the English had to face. Grateful to her, he said, "Yes. Not a bad idea."

It was one of the worst spells he'd had in a very long time. He wasn't sure whether it was the claustrophobia that had surrounded him in Penrith's narrow cell, or the blow on the head when his motorcar had missed the bend in the road. But when did Hamish need an excuse? It was always Rutledge himself who looked for one. Who tried to pretend there had to be a reason for madness.

There was a tearoom in the next village, and they stopped.

Rutledge found he was hungry and ordered a plate of sandwiches as well as their tea.

Taking off her coat and settling it on the third chair at their table, Meredith Channing said, "Elise told me you'd stopped in for one night, on your way to somewhere else in Somerset."

"Yes, they put me up."

"Her father was looking for you. Elise didn't know at the time. He missed you at your hotel."

Rutledge frowned. "When was this?"

"I don't know. Apparently no one answered the telephone, and so there was no opportunity to leave a message."

"I'll make a point of getting in touch."

She changed the subject, talking about the weather, pouring the tea when it came, offering nothing more demanding than quiet conversation, never expecting him to say more than he felt like saying. It was a kindness.

When they left the tearoom, he found the courage to say, "I must apologize for what happened today. Sometimes—" He broke off and shook his head, unable to explain. To her, to anyone.

She smiled. "I'm glad I was there. Would you like to drive now?"

He took the wheel, and in another half hour they were back in Chelsea. He had no memory of how he'd got there earlier. Or how, for that matter, he had negotiated the streets of London without hitting something or someone. It was a frightening thought.

When he had seen her to her door, he looked at his watch and decided he just might catch Caldwell at his office. The war had receded, it would be all right.

Caldwell was preparing to leave for the day when Rutledge was shown in. He said, "You look worn out. Is it another case?"

"I suspect you are a better judge of the answer to that. I understand you tried to reach me in Somerset. Was this to do with the Cumberline venture?"

"I was curious about this man Evering. I have a few contacts, here and there. It took some time but I found out more than I felt comfortable knowing. I wasn't aware that Evering had a brother, nor that both Penrith and Quarles fought off the Boers in an action where the elder Evering was killed. I had no idea either Penrith or Quarles had been in the army, much less South Africa. It was quite a surprise. I couldn't be sure you'd discovered any of this, that's why I called Somerset. I felt rather foolish after telling you that you could safely ignore this man Evering!"

"I was able to piece together some of the story," Rutledge replied carefully. "Sometimes the past has a long reach. Ronald Evering is dead. He was killed by Harold Quarles's sister, who then took her own life."

"Dear God. I saw that you'd taken up Penrith for Quarles's murder. I would never have expected him to be a killer. It seemed so contrary to his nature. He was always in Quarles's shadow. Ever since the war, apparently."

"With the right goad, even people like Penrith can kill," Rutledge answered neutrally.

"There's more to this business of Quarles and Penrith. Since my telephone call to you, I was told something by a friend, in strictest confidence. I trust you'll treat it as such. There was a fair sum of money going up the line the day the Boer attacked. I'm not privy to why it was on the train, just that it was. It was burned when the carriages caught fire after the attack. There was some question in the doctors' minds whether—judging from the nature of his wounds—Quarles was trying to save the money or Lieutenant Evering. The Army kept an eye on him, but after Quarles got back to London, he was poor as a church mouse. And so after a time, the Army lost interest in him. A man of that sort, they reckoned, would have spent every penny in months, if not weeks, on whatever whims took his fancy. Instead he worked hard in the firm that hired him, rose through their ranks on his own ability, and led an honest life."

It explained why Penrith wouldn't talk—he had been given a share of that money. It explained why Lieutenant Evering had to die—he would have told everyone if Quarles had taken the money. It explained why the carriages had to be burned—otherwise the Army would have searched for the missing currency. And still they had been suspicious. But Quarles had outwaited them, clever man that he was.

It had all begun with greed. With money that could be had for the taking, if one had no qualms about committing murder.

Rutledge said, "Thank you for telling me. It will go no further."

"Just as well," Caldwell said. "It will only hurt the survivors. But I thought it might be useful to you."

Pray God, Rutledge thought, *Michael Brunswick never learns the truth. Or if he does, never acts on it. Or the killing will go on.*

And Marcus Quarles might prove to have more of his father and his aunt in him than his mother ever imagined . . .